High Praise for Steven Wilson and
Between the Hunters and the Hunted

"*Between the Hunters and the Hunted* is a
tremendously exciting read. The characters
were well drawn; the action riveting. I
couldn't put the book down."

—Alan Topol, author of *Conspiracy*

"A gripping, superbly told story of war at
sea. A masterful blending of fact and fiction
that thrusts the reader into the center
of white-hot action and the heart of
momentous events, which, had they
been real, would have changed the course
of history."

—Peter Sasgen, author of *War Plan Red*

ALSO BY STEVEN WILSON

Voyage of the Gray Wolves

Between the Hunters and the Hunted

ARMADA

A NOVEL

STEVEN WILSON

PINNACLE BOOKS
Kensington Publishing Corp.
www.kensingtonbooks.com

PINNACLE BOOKS are published by

Kensington Publishing Corp.
850 Third Avenue
New York, NY 10022

All Kensington titles, imprints, and distributed lines are available at special quantity discounts for bulk purchases for sales
promotions, premiums, fund-raising, educational, or institu-
tional use. Special book excerpts or customized printings can
also be created to fit specific needs. For details, write or phone
the office of the Kensington special sales manager: Kensington
Publishing Corp., 850 Third Avenue, New York, NY 10022,
attn: Special Sales Department; phone 1-800-221-2647.

This book is a work of fiction. Names, characters, businesses,
organizations, places, events, and incidents either are the prod-
uct of the author's imagination or are used fictitiously. Any resemblance to actual persons, living or dead, events, or locales
is entirely coincidental.

ISBN-13: 978-0-7860-1822-2
ISBN-10: 0-7860-1822-4

First printing: May 2007

10 9 8 7 6 5 4 3 2 1

Printed in the United States of America

For so appears this fleet majestical,
Holding due course for Harfleur. Follow, follow;
Grapple your minds to sternage of this navy,
And leave your England . . .
—William Shakespeare, *Henry V*

The destinies of two great empires . . . seem to be tied
up in some goddamned things called LSTs.
—Winston Churchill

Chapter 1

Something was wrong. Cole was aboard PT-155, standing to one side of the tiny bridge with the microphone in his hand, but it was much too light and yet he couldn't quite make out the other PTs. Something was wrong.

Then he knew—they were out in daylight. They never went out in daylight. A thick veil of fog smothered everything so that at first it looked dark. That was all right, the darkness was all right. But it was a false night. He could see the other boats, to port and starboard, but they were vague, ghostlike shapes that floated silently over the flat sea. He looked aft in confusion and could just make out DeLong with the 40-millimeter, its long snout trained over the stern. He was comforted by DeLong's presence.

"Some soup, huh, Skipper?" It was Harry Lowe. He was at the wheel, his easy smile just as much a comfort as the presence of Eckstam, Murray, or

Tommy Rich, or any of the other crew members of Cole's boat. Except that Harry Lowe was dead.

Cole stood, stunned—watching his handsome executive officer pass the wheel lightly through his fingertips, scanning the compass, glancing out into the fog. But they were out in daylight—they never went out in daylight.

You go out at night because that's when the enemy convoys sailed, trying to pass unnoticed. Cole knew that—Lowe knew that—why were they out in daylight? Had somebody made a mistake? Cole's mind stopped on that one word, *mistake*. It was a mistake.

"Some soup, huh, Skipper?" Lowe said again, but this time, when Cole looked at him, half his head was missing.

Cole stifled a scream, but when Lowe turned to him this time, he was fine.

"What's going on, Harry?" Cole asked. He didn't *hear* himself speak. It was as if he had imagined the words.

"Orders, Skipper," Lowe said. Again that smile on a face so handsome most of the guys had said, at one time or another: "Mr. Lowe, you oughtta be in pictures."

"Orders?" Cole said, confused. He didn't remember the orders. They go out at night—hunt for freighters, barges, and E-boats—because that's when *they* go out. Maybe run up against MAS boats if they were lucky. F-lighters if they weren't. F-lighters were thick skinned and the most heavily armed enemy boats.

"We've got something off the starboard quarter, Skipper," Lowe said, and looked at Cole expectantly. Cole didn't reply—he was trying to think this situation out. Everything about it was wrong, and underlying that awareness was the sharp stench of fear. After a moment Lowe reminded Cole gently: "Better tell the other boats."

Cole knew to do that. He should have done it immediately. He had the microphone in his hand and he always took station on the starboard side of the bridge so that when he got the word from radar he could pass it on to the other boats. He looked at the microphone as if it were some mysterious device. He pushed the TALK button, held it close to his mouth, and said: "Cole, to all boats. Starboard quarter." He realized that he didn't have the distance and speed and suddenly grew frightened because in this fog—just like at night when there are no stars and no moon and you might as well be swimming in ink—the enemy could be on you in no time.

Cole turned to Lowe, Harry Lowe with the Clark Gable mustache on William Powell features with a Robert Taylor smile, and was about to ask him speed and distance, because he was suddenly very afraid. But now everything was in slow motion, and his words hung in his throat. He felt as if he were drifting with no way to control what he was doing.

He had to warn Lowe. He remembered now. It wasn't in daylight, in a thick fog. It was at night, and it was very cold. And then he had the speed and distance, but it didn't make any difference. He had to tell Lowe but he couldn't; he could feel his body moving like a plump, tethered balloon, but he had no voice.

Lowe was smiling at him again and Cole grew

angry, wanting to scream at Harry Lowe to pay attention to what he was doing, to call off the attack because it was a trap. He heard himself screaming, but his words were sucked into the silence of his dream, and he felt rage and impotence. Call off the attack! He was cursing Harry Lowe now, something he had never done when Harry was alive; but Harry wasn't listening, he was just maneuvering the boat into position, sailing inexorably toward his own death.

Now Cole was sitting in the tiny shack that they used for the ready room at the base, trying to explain to a very sympathetic but tired debriefing officer what had happened and why Harry Lowe's blood and brains were all over him. Cole leaned forward in his chair—he didn't have enough strength to hold himself upright—and told the debriefing officer, who kept yawning, what had happened.

"Why'd you go out in daylight?" the debriefing officer asked, sliding his hand over his mouth to cover a yawn.

Cole tried to straighten up to answer, but he thought if he stayed hunched over like this, he could hold himself together. He didn't tell the debriefing officer that he was afraid that his body would fly apart like Harry Lowe's head. Cole realized that the officer had asked him a question. "We didn't," Cole said, trying to make the man understand. "We went out at dusk, like we always do. We ran into the convoy at oh-two-forty-eight."

A tiny yawn was forced into submission by a shrug. "Yes. But why did you go out in daylight?" he asked again. And then he looked at Cole with a mixture of sympathy and pity and said: "Was it your fault?"

"My fault?" Cole thought, and realized that he could save himself by just waking up—knowing now that it was a dream and he didn't have to put himself through this. Everything was very familiar now, and the confusion that Cole had felt earlier in the dream was replaced by dread. He knew where the dream was taking him. "No," he said. "You see, the E-boats and F-lighters were hiding behind the slower vessels. In the convoy. We didn't pick them up until it was too late."

An excuse.

The debriefing officer was writing something down, and Cole knew that what he just said was an excuse. *It was my fault. I should have known better. I should have made sure.*

Cole could tell now that he was close to waking up, how, he wasn't sure, but something told him that he would wake up soon. It wasn't much comfort.

He was on the bridge of PT-155 again, but this time they were in the middle of a battle. Red and green tracers were sawing through the air and someone had fired star shells into the fog in a vain attempt to illuminate friend and foe. They were on the step now, racing ahead at full speed, with the boat shaking from the recoil of the guns, her hull trembling out of fright or excitement.

Cole knew what was going to come next. He'd seen it when he was awake and a thousand times in his dreams, but he couldn't stop it. The memory of it, the sight of it, was always present. Harry Lowe, rich, good-looking, decent—"That Mr. Lowe is a helluva guy," the crew said . . .

Cole's eyes shot open. He saw the patient blades

of the overhead fan turning slowly, pushing a touch of air throughout his room. He rubbed his face roughly, felt the tears mixed with the sweat, swung his legs out of bed, and dropped his feet to the floor. Sometimes the tears kept coming even after he woke up. He stifled his sobs with the ball of his fist, trying to choke back the sounds and the taste of guilt.

He sat on the edge of his bed, knowing that none of the other officers were up yet, thinking that maybe he could get dressed and make his way to the base galley for coffee. But he decided against it. There was always some guy over there who wanted to talk about something or other, and Cole just wanted to be left alone.

Guilt had become his companion. It was in him at all times; sometimes he could hardly feel the weight of it, but he could always feel its presence. It snapped at him when he had nearly forgotten that it was there. Cruel reminders of his faults, responsibilities, mistakes—sometimes embellished or distorted—guilt taking a perverse pleasure in coating reality with imaginary failures. It didn't make any difference—he accepted them all.

Jordan Cole took a deep breath, wiping the corners of his eyes with the heel of one hand, and stretched the stiffness out of his back. Harry Lowe.

He leaned forward, resting his elbows on his knees, and lapsed into an inventory of duties out of habit. All of the boats needed engine overhauls. The few remaining boats, his guilt reminded him, but in a surprisingly gentle manner as if to show Cole that guilt was not without compassion.

His eyes fell on a gray, battered metal ammunition box. In its previous life it had held .30-caliber ammunition, according to the stenciled legend on its side. Now Cole used it for another purpose. Pictures from home, his will, mementoes of friendships, and a stack of letters bundled by a thick rubber band.

Sometimes Cole would slide a letter out and read it, remembering Rebecca. There weren't many letters—eight in fact—but there were so few because Cole wrote nothing in return, and Rebecca did what Cole wanted her to do. She stopped writing. One tiny victory for Jordan Cole.

He sat on the edge of the bed for several minutes, his mind frozen into inaction by fatigue. The best way to stop thinking, Cole thought one day. Insomnia. Lack of sleep turned the brain to mush; pretty soon you don't have enough energy to form a single coherent thought.

He stood, fished around the room for his clothes, and got dressed. He glanced at his watch; oh-two-oh-five, and shook his head in disgust. Two fucking hours—he'd slept for less than two hours. He'd decided that maybe he'd go over to the galley and pick up some coffee and head to the duty shed, find a quiet corner, and settle in, listening to the radio chatter.

Cole had the door open when he turned and glanced at the ammo box. He hadn't read her letters in a while. He'd thought about her, first with regret and then with anger at what she'd done, and finally with a longing so intense that he could barely stand it. Well, he thought, it's over anyway. Things happen, there's nothing you can do about it.

Guilt reemerged, refreshed and ready to accompany Cole. Lowe's face flashed before his eyes—guilt taunting him again. And in a whisper so faint that it could have been the distant rustle of leaves, guilt told him: "There was plenty you could have done about it."

Chapter 2

The English Channel, Spring 1944

Seaman 1st Class Foster watched a tiny blip dart across the SG radar screen under the slow pass of the strobe. "Hey, Mr. Lewis? Take a look at this."

Lieutenant (j.g.) Lewis shook his head in disgust as he moved through the crowded Combat-Information-Center to the radar station. Foster should have made petty officer, but his mouth and holier-than-thou attitude had kept him at seaman 1st. Maybe he had the prerequisite ten hours of training, but that had been on the old SC radar and the SG was far more complex than the SC. Lewis never let on that he still didn't completely understand the intricacies of the SG. Not to the captain or the exec, and certainly not to the enlisted men. And never, never to the chiefs. They could make a young, inexperienced officer's life a living hell aboard a destroyer escort. Better to act like you knew what you were doing even if you didn't, especially in the CIC. They sure didn't teach you that at the Reserve Midshipman's School.

The tiny room, pulsating with life, was stuffed with speakers, situation tables for surface and air activities, and plotting boards with the names, call signs, and other data of the ships in the convoy. The bulkheads and overhead were alive with cables, wires, and conduits—the nerves that carried the information in and out. It was a clearinghouse for information that came in from radio, radar, sonar, and from the lookouts positioned at various stations on the *Southern.* It was dark in the CIC; the only light allowed was the eerie red glow of the emergency lamps. To the uninitiated the cramped room was a confusing maze of instruments half hidden in the gloom. The five or six men who manned CIC were ghostly images who moved silently in the tiny space, caring for the instruments. The fragile electronic gear needed constant tending; rangefinders, radars, transmitters, identification gear, direction finders, and receivers, everything sensitive to saltwater, salt air, and the pounding that the ship endured while under way. The only other movement was that of the strobe arm that flicked across the pale green face of surface and air radar screens.

"Foster, how many times have I asked you not to say 'Hey, Mr. Lewis'?"

"Yeah, but, sir, something screwy just happened."

"You see, that's what I mean," Lewis said. He'd tried since he came aboard to bring a sense of dignity to the USS *Jeremiah B. Southern,* but the captain and the other officers had ignored his efforts. The crew followed suit, behaving in a lackadaisical manner, completely lacking in professionalism. Lewis studied the screen. It was blank except for the column of steady ships in the convoy. "I don't see anything." He was tired and anxious for his relief. They had been steaming Condition II, half the guns manned and the men working four on and four off because they were nearing E-boat Alley. It was a state of readiness ordered by the captain. To Lewis it was a waste of time and another example of Captain MacKay's inability to grasp the obvious: the Nazis were on the ropes, anybody could see that. And the invasion would be a cakewalk. Lewis had seen the buildup in the ports, the long columns of infantry marching along the narrow British roads, and the flights of bombers that thundered overhead on their way to Germany.

Now the captain was worried about a bunch of torpedo boats in the goddamned English Channel. Where the hell was his relief? Lewis thought again. He suddenly realized that Foster was talking.

"Yes, sir, but it was there a minute ago. Just on the edge of the scope."

Lewis's eyes traveled furtively over the screen. "Whatever was there is not there now. You know we've got a couple of AOGs just aft of us." He felt salty using the official acronym for tankers that carried aviation fuel, oil, and gas. He hoped it made up for his youth and inexperience.

"Jeez, Mr. Lewis, even I can tell the difference between a gasoline tanker and something that shouldn't have been there. Besides. That last target was to port."

Lewis was unconvinced. He looked over the array of intimidating gauges and dials covering the console to either side of the screen, his mind racing over the operating instructions about the SG that he had tried to commit to memory. But his mind wasn't fast enough and the dials warned him to leave them alone. "Maybe you just imagined it," he finally said, ending the mystery.

"Yes, sir," Foster said grimly. He felt Lewis leave his side and cursed the officer silently. That guy was an embarrassment to the ship and to the uniform. Nothing but a chicken-shit attitude. . . . Foster leaned back in his chair and motioned to Chesty Marx at the Plotting Board. Marx looked at him quizzically as Foster mouthed the word *Chief*.

Foster saw Marx nudge Chief Petty Officer James and gestured toward Foster.

James walked over to the surface radar station. "What is it, Foster?"

"I picked up a skunk, right at the edge of the screen. It was gone in a flash. I mean sixty or seventy knots."

"Switch to max-range," James said, reaching for the bridge phone.

Foster did as he was told. The screen flickered briefly and settled into the new range setting. With the greater distance the resolution became distorted and smaller images were hard to pick out. Even larger targets at maximum range had a distinctly fuzzy appearance under the sweep of the patient strobe that swung loyally around the screen once every three seconds.

"There it is," Foster said excitedly, but the words

were barely out before Chief James had the bridge telephone off its cradle and up to his mouth.

Seaman 2nd Class Greer, Bridge Talker for the Mid-Watch, stood back against the bulkhead of the open bridge. He'd run afoul of Captain MacKay two or three times by getting in the captain's way when MacKay paced from port to starboard wing on the cramped bridge. Greer had learned his lesson; give the Old Man room to roam. The seaman 2nd class wore the outsized helmet that concealed bulky earphones. A speaking horn rested on his chest, suspended about his neck by canvas straps. The stiff collar of his bulky kapok lifejacket made keeping the earphones and horn where they should have been difficult.

"Bridge, aye," Greer said into the horn. He listened for a moment and then reported to Captain MacKay on the open bridge. "CIC reports surface target."

MacKay turned, his features lost in the darkness except for the dim glow of the gyro. "Where away?" MacKay said.

"One-three-seven degrees heading oh-two-three degrees at twenty-five thousand yards. Speed," Greer hesitated but decided to report it anyway. Those guys were supposed to know what they were talking about. "Speed, six-oh knots."

MacKay glanced at Jake DeArmas, his executive officer. "General Quarters," MacKay ordered Greer. "Who's in CIC?" he asked DeArmas quickly.

"Lewis."

"He's too young. Get down there." MacKay turned to Greer. "Acknowledge that report. Tell CIC to contact the convoy. Unidentified target running to port at approximately twenty-five thousand yards. . . ."

Greer slid his hand under his helmet and clamped the earphone against his ear. He looked up at MacKay, doing a remarkable job of containing his excitement. "Sir, CIC reports multiple targets approaching from the southwest. Same distance. Speed increased to seven-oh knots."

"Yes?" Hardy said hovering over the brass speaking tubes. The night was clear and very cold, and he had just finished his third cup of tea. Now he had to piss.

"Bridge, W/T *Southern* reports multiple targets approaching at high speed from the southwest. They've gone to Action Stations, sir."

"Well, then, why should we be any different?" Hardy grumbled. He turned to the yeoman stationed at the Tannoy Box. "Action Stations."

"Right, sir," the yeoman said. He switched on the speaking system and said, in a very matter-of-fact tone: "Do you hear there? Do you hear there? Action Stations. Action Stations."

Hardy flipped back the cover on the speaking tube to the Engine Room. "Engine Room? Bridge here. How's that engine?" Number Two engine had been giving HMS *Firedancer* fits for the last two weeks. Hardy had ordered the boilers lit off for Number Two but on standby only. The engine would not be engaged unless absolutely necessary.

"Bridge, Engine Room."

It was Courtney, a gnomelike little officer who preferred to spend all of his time with his beloved engines. Hardy suspected that if he could, Courtney would remain in the noisy, hot confines of the engine room and never venture on deck unless ordered.

"Well, Courtney? What about it? I've need of Number Two."

Courtney had been working for days trying to isolate the problem. He had reported to Hardy, layering technical difficulty upon technical difficulty until Hardy, as well versed as any Royal Navy captain on the machinery that drove his ship, had capitulated.

"Goddamn it, Courtney," Hardy had said. "Just fix the bloody thing." Courtney just rubbed his knuckles contentedly into the palm of his hand as if his complicated report had been a successful stratagem to bewilder the captain into leaving him alone, then returned to the depths of his engine room.

"It's no good, Captain," Courtney's muffled voice came through the voice tube, accompanied by the distant roar of the machinery. The steady thump of the pistons was like a heartbeat, a rhythm that reminded Hardy that the ancient destroyer still had life in her. "It's the engine shaft bearing. If we engage the engine she'll seize, and then we'll really be up against it."

Hardy glanced to see his Number One, Edwin Land, appear on the bridge, just slipping into his duffel. Spring or not it got cold in the Channel at night. "I have some Germans out there, Courtney," Hardy said irritably.

"Yes, sir, but if the shaft seizes there goes the engine. And you'll be down a sight longer anyway except then she's in the yards for a good bit of time." Courtney's warning was obvious—the damage to the engine might be so severe that she'd require repair work in the yards. They turned ships around quickly enough, Hardy knew, repair crews working day and night, but they did so on a priority basis and he was certain that no priority would be attached to an overaged destroyer. She would be laid up for weeks or months and his crew would be stripped of critical ratings and replaced with clumsy landsmen direct from Portsmouth. The thought caused Hardy to shiver—*Firedancer* in the hands of clods.

"Well, then," Hardy growled, conceding defeat for the moment. "Stand by. You can do that, can't you?"

"Standing by," was Courtney's reply, delivered much too calmly to suit Hardy.

They were escorting eight ships—two gasoline tankers and six freighters, *Southern* in the lead and *Firedancer* in the rear, down to Portsmouth at a steady if boring pace of 8 knots. *Firedancer* could manage that speed all right and she could be coaxed up to 15 knots without protest, but, with one engine out, she would resist anything beyond that. A part of the fight would be maneuver, and another part speed, but Hardy was denied that part so that the fight would be tipped in the enemy's advantage.

* * *

MacKay felt a shudder run through *Southern*'s deck. His mind calculated the impossible. Run aground? Out here? What the hell was going on? His second officer had joined him on the open bridge of the destroyer escort and they exchanged glances. Suddenly he realized what it was.

"Flares," he ordered. A torpedo had brushed the ship's bottom. A torpedo whose depth had been set too deep, probably to puncture the hull of a lumbering merchantman. *Southern* had been given a gift by the miscalculation of an enemy torpedo man. "Signal to the convoy, 'Under attack by E-boats to port. Remain in position.' " He didn't want the merchant ships scattering. They could just as easily run *Southern* down in the darkness or end up being silhouetted by their own flares. If that happened they would make a lovely target for the E-boats.

"Sir," Greer said. "CIC reports vessels approaching bearing one-three-six degrees. Speed seven-oh knots. Distance . . ."

The first shell hit *Southern*'s hull below 51 Mount just as the second series of flares burst in the darkness, filling the sky with an eerie green glow. It was a signal to start the battle. Tracers ripped through the night, red from the Americans' guns, green from the Germans', angry fingers searching under the pale light of the flares for a target.

Southern's forward 5-inch gun barked, and the brilliant flash of its discharge nearly blinded the men on the open bridge. The 40-millimeters joined the fight, pumping dozens of shells at the speeding enemy boats under the feeble light of the dying flares. The long gray barrels of the twin 40-mm mounts recoiled in sequence, the shock of the discharge taken up by the heavy recoil springs that then threw the barrels back into place, ready for another round. They spoke with determination, one round every half-second screaming into the darkness, their fiery birth contained by the funnel-shaped flash depressors on the muzzles of the guns. But the targets glimpsed only as fleeting shapes were hidden by the night.

Three more shells hit the *Southern*, one so close to the bridge that it knocked MacKay and the others to the deck.

"What the hell was that?" MacKay shouted in exasperation as he pulled himself to his feet. "Damage report." That couldn't be an E-boat. Not with firepower like that. They mounted 40-millimeter and 20-millimeter but their main weapon was their torpedo. But this was a hell of a lot bigger than a 40-millimeter. What was the *Southern* fighting?

Hardy watched the flare float slowly toward the surface of the Channel. So far the attack was directed at the head of the column, but it might be a feint to draw the escorts away from their stations. *Firedancer* could not respond for that reason and because she could not move fast enough. Number One stood next to him peering through his binoculars.

"Well?" Hardy said, fuming at his inaction. "What do you see?" His blood was up and he paced the deck like a lion that sensed nearby prey.

"E-boats," Land said, catching nothing more than a glimpse of the enemy vessels as they flashed under the soft light of the flares. "Fast boats. Very fast."

"Wireless/Telegrapher?" Hardy called into a voice tube. "Make to *Southern*: 'Shall I come up?' Send it in plain language." He moved to windshield, and then to the port side of the bridge, and finally back to the tubes.

He's going to explode, Land thought ridiculously, but the frustration that Hardy felt was clear to Land. It was all very simple; the battle had been joined and Hardy was not a part of it.

Hardy turned suddenly and practically leaped at the voice tubes. "W/T? Did you send the message by pigeon? What . . ."

"Bridge, W/T. Message from *Southern*. 'Take station midway up the column, port. Enemy E-boats and other vessels. . . .' That's it, sir. End of message."

"Right," Hardy said. "Right. Helmsman, port 15. Land, you will inform Guns that we expect to engage the enemy shortly. Everything to port is fair game so he needn't be shy about shooting." Hardy turned to the voice tubes as if they held the key to his victory. "Engine Room. Hardy here."

"Engine Room. Courtney," came the muffled reply.

Hardy leaned close to the tube and gripped the mount in determination. "Now see here, Courtney. I'll have no more nonsense about engines and yard work. We're going in now, and I must have every ounce of power out of Number Two."

"So long as you know that she's likely to seize at any moment," Courtney said. "Aye, sir. You give the order and I'll engage the engine."

"Very well," Hardy said with satisfaction, reassured that he controlled every aspect of his ship, as any good captain should. Engines, indeed. All *Firedancer* needed was a reason and she could overcome anything. Grand old girl. "Up fifty on both engines," Hardy ordered, increasing the revolutions per minute of the screws.

"Sir," Greer said. "Damage Control reports hits on the torpedo deck above Repair II. Aft tubes severely damaged. The mast carried away the antennas." Greer fought to keep his voice calm; he was the Talker and it was his job to repeat what he had been told to report, and to pass on the captain's orders. But he was scared, especially when a shell had ripped away the big 36-inch signal searchlight on the bridge wing. *Southern* was only 306 feet long, the smallest vessel in the convoy except for that Limey destroyer aft, and the tankers, but it seemed as if the Krauts had planned to put a shell in every foot of the destroyer escort. The worst hit had been near the waterline forward, although no one had been killed or wounded, flooding the forward 5-inch magazine. Other hits had killed sailors: hits in the chief's quarters, Repair I, the port 20-mm mount—all six men there died, the sonar shack atop the pilot house—mostly hits topside, but dead sailors nevertheless.

It was Greer's second battle—the first one had been against U-boats and German planes. Afterward he remembered the noise, things crashing and exploding and men shouting as if they could defeat the enemy with their voices alone. It was not that, he knew, because he was shouting as well. He was on the mid-40 mount then. He was shouting out of fear and anger and because his blood was pumping so quickly through his veins that he thought his heart would explode. Now, it was different.

It was odd. Everything seemed to have slowed down, Greer thought. He saw the signalman at the Aldis lamp, the chief bo'sun of the watch, and the other officers and men on the crowded bridge move about as if they were completely indifferent to the fury that enveloped them.

Greer was aware of noises, muffled sounds or fragments of whole sounds that crept into his brain. He heard the whir of the electric motors of the 51 Mount as it drove the turret into position and laid the gun on target. He heard the orders and responses of the men in the pilothouse—the voices of the helmsman, engine order man, the quartermaster—and that bo'sun's mate who loved to play poker with washers. Maybe he wasn't really hearing them speak—maybe he just thought he was.

Everything was slow. Movements, sounds—everything he saw or heard dipped in molasses and spread before with a broad knife.

The AOG exploded.

She was the USS *Connery* and she was smaller than the *Southern*, and she was aft and to starboard the prescribed distance, but when she blew up it was like she was alongside the destroyer escort.

The AOG erupted into a huge fireball, mocking the ridiculous light of the tiny flares, illuminating every ship as if it were daylight, for a half-mile

around. But the triumph of the explosion was
short-lived and night swiftly moved in to reclaim its
dominance, leaving only the boiling fire consuming the ship as a remnant of the blast.

Hardy was beating the inoffensive speaking tube
with his fist as *Firedancer*'s speed dropped to just
under 10 knots.

"Five seconds? Five bloody seconds you give me?
I haven't gone twenty feet, you insufferable me-
chanical boob," Hardy shouted into the tube.

"I gave you no guarantees, sir," Courtney replied,
his tone bordering on vindication—just a hair's
breadth from "I told you so." "Only that at some
time or other the engine would surely seize. That
time was almost immediately after you asked for
increased revolutions."

"Christ in heaven," Hardy shouted into the sky.
He shook his clenched fists at nothing in particular and turned to Land. "Take her to starboard of
that tanker," he said, calming. "We'll look for survivors. Keep her as much out of the light as you
can, Number One. I don't fancy giving those bastards another target."

"Right, sir," Land said. He gave the necessary orders and joined Hardy as the captain scanned the
darkness through binoculars.

"Gone," Hardy said, peering into the darkness.

"Nothing on radar. Nothing in sight. They've
gone back to their lair," Land confirmed.

Hardy settled the binoculars on his chest by
their leather strap and pursed his lips in thought.

"E-boats and others, *Southern* said. I wonder, Number One, what others?"

"There was something out there, sir. Those were six-inch guns, anyway," Land commented. He knew the sound of guns and the sharp crack that the shell makes speeding through the air, and he could tell by the impact what size the shell was.

"Now, has Jerry gone and figured a way to mount a cruiser's guns on their E-boats?" Hardy said incredulously. But a note of concern crept into his words because he had heard the report of the guns as well and from experience he knew them to be 6-inch cannon. But not on E-boats. They were formidable little vessels all right, but they were too small to handle any gun that big. Then, what had been out there? "How I hate not knowing things," Hardy said into the darkness.

Chapter 3

Korvettenkapitan Peter Waldvogel staggered to the side of S-boat 317 and vomited into the oily water of the dank S-boat pen. He stopped retching long enough to pull a handkerchief from his tunic with a trembling hand and wipe his ashen face. Then he vomited again.

The deep-throated rumble of the boat's three 2,500-horsepower Daimler-Benz engines echoed off the concrete walls and ceiling of the pen as she slid easily toward her berth. Two other boats were already nestled against the quay, already tied off by the crew.

Waldvogel heard Reubold shouting orders, something about lines and fenders, but he didn't care. He was weak from emotion and vomiting, and the god-awful pounding that the boat had taken as it sped across the water before raising up on her foils. He had never been so frightened in his life as when they sighted the convoy—that moment before the attack he thought he would die of fright.

And then when they went in: madness, sheer pandemonium. Endless explosions tearing the darkness to bits and the boat weaving crazily across the water—full daylight with the brilliant flash of cannons, alternating with night. Kettledrums, Waldvogel thought, trying to find something comparable to describe the sound. But there were no words to describe it. How Reubold functioned was beyond any sane man's comprehension.

Waldvogel wiped his face again, grateful that his stomach had finally calmed. *Best not to mention sane men and Reubold in the same sentence.*

"I told you not to come."

Waldvogel turned, still holding on to the lifelines for support.

"You wouldn't listen," Fregattenkapitan Reubold said, flashing a crooked smile.

"I wanted to see . . ." Waldvogel managed in a weak voice, but his stomach began to churn.

"You wanted to see what it was like," Reubold said in a knowing manner, finishing the sentence for him. "Yes, I know. You Silver Stripes always talk about going into action just one time, and then you have plenty of stories to tell after a fine meal and drinks in a comfortable restaurant far from any danger."

Waldvogel clenched his jaws tightly, willing himself not to vomit again. When the wave of sickness passed, he shook his head. "No. I wanted to see how the Trinity functioned."

"Yes," Reubold said, waving to the divers stationed

on the quay. "Well, they killed a gunner who stood too close to the breech despite the training and my warnings, and it's well that we had so many fat targets. Your boat is fast enough, Korvettenkapitan, but it's practically impossible to aim your guns. We have proved one thing: we are not ready for the real war."

Both men were silent as the stretcher bearing the dead gunner was handed up to four sailors on the quay. One of the gunner's lifeless arms dangled from beneath the blanket covering his body. Waldvogel shivered as he saw the wedding band gleam under the dull work lights scattered along the quay. Did I do that? he wondered. A torrent of accusations ran through his mind. *Perhaps I should have trained them better? Maybe they weren't fully prepared. Didn't they read the manuals? I conducted classes; surely they made notes and listened to me?* He remembered the young faces set in bored resignation as he droned on about this new type of gun.

"Check the struts and wings," Reubold's voice broke into his thoughts. He was speaking to the divers. "I'll sound the hull but I want you to go over those mounts like you're looking for gold. They took a beating before we got up and I was hard on them in the fight." He glanced at Waldvogel for confirmation.

"Yes," the korvettenkapitan said. "Yes. Look for fractures. Please, be very careful. It's very delicate, you see . . ."

Reubold jerked his head, releasing the divers before Waldvogel finished his instructions to them. They moved to the access ladder, pulling the cables for their cumbersome underwater lights.

"Don't worry about your precious wings," Reubold said, dismissing Waldvogel's concerns. He unzipped his overalls and pulled out a cigarette case. "They'll search every inch of them for defects." He lit his cigarette and then examined the gold lighter. "Goering gave this to me," he said in remembrance. "Flags, medals, a sea of uniforms; everyone was there." Reubold slipped the lighter into a pocket and drew deeply on the cigarette. He watched as the lights glowed like miniature floating suns under the surface of the black water. There was something absolutely peaceful and innocent in the ballet of the golden orbs gliding silently back and forth.

Reubold shrugged, dismissing his own thoughts. "Now, each morning before his morning toilet, the Fat Man asks: 'Is that shit Reubold dead yet?'"

Waldvogel straightened, feeling secure enough to stand without gripping the lifeline. Such a strange man. Such a strange man. Each day he learned just a bit more about Reubold, certainly not from the man himself but from observation. He had heard him described as a fallen romantic, a tragic figure, and a scoundrel. He had heard from one man that the famous fregattenkapitan was a hollow shell—drained of life. Waldvogel was more confused than ever about the man he hoped would prove the worth of his boats and guns. But Waldvogel was deeply concerned as well—Reubold's instability might be the undoing of his hard work. The fregattenkapitan was his last chance.

Reubold tossed the cigarette into the water. "We were lucky. We got a tanker and managed to hit other ships as well. But the men need more training, and you, dear Waldvogel, must find a way for us to aim those guns of yours without killing more gunners."

Waldvogel winced at the mention of the dead man. It did not bother Reubold to be cruel—at times he seemed to relish it.

"It was his own fault," Reubold said coldly, taking some of the burden for the man's death from Waldvogel. "He forgot what he was doing and where he was. You do that once in this business and you'll never do it again. Take them back into the classroom and take Junghans with you. I'm sure the oberbootsmannmaat can keep their attention focused on the lesson."

Waldvogel nodded. The men feared Junghans, but they respected him as well.

The fregattenkapitan threw his arms over his head, stretching. He yawned and rubbed his eyes. "I must go and do military things now."

Such a strange man. One moment lighthearted, the next grim and unrelenting. Sometimes he was distant, as if his mind had been called back to another place and time, but then he became gentle and open, speaking of art and music. At such times Waldvogel could almost feel the torment that lay within Fregattenkapitan Richard Reubold. But then a veil would descend and darkness would fill the man's eyes.

"Find me a way to aim your guns, Waldvogel," Reubold said as he moved forward. "Our dear admiral sees little use for S-boats and no use for your devices. They aren't big enough, you see, our little fast boats. No battleships or cruisers in," he gestured to the confines of the dark pen, illuminated only by the harsh glare of the work lights, "this cave. Dresser has no faith in our fast boats." He gave a short laugh. "I doubt that he has much faith in me, either."

"They haven't proved themselves yet," Waldvogel said over the din of the gantry moving into place overhead. "It isn't fair. I haven't had time to properly demonstrate what the boats and the guns are capable of. You see that, don't you? You realize their potential, don't you? We've talked."

"Talked, yes," Reubold said. He did a poor job of hiding his pity for the scientist. "Talked here and in Paris," he glanced out the huge open maw of the pen to the brightness of the sky and the sparkling waters of Cherbourg Harbor, "and out there when you weren't vomiting. As far as time goes, you've had enough, I'm sure Dresser would say. Out there, on the other side of the Channel, our enemies await." The half-grin again, but this time Reubold's eyes were filled with concern. "Time the Allies will not give you, nor will our dear admiral, so what doesn't work on your remarkable boats must be corrected, now."

Jordan Cole watched the Aldis lamp flash in the distance as Bill Ewing on the 168 boat reported in. The sun had just broken the horizon behind Ewing's PT boat so that the flashing lamp was difficult to read.

"He hasn't seen anything at all, Skipper," Randy DeLong said, standing next to the signaling searchlight on the starboard side of the small bridge. The

signalman handling the light flashed END OF MES-
SAGE and then switched off the light. He waited for
additional orders.

The two PT boats had searched the choppy Channel waters for a downed Hurricane pilot for most
of the night. The French coastline was clearly visible on the horizon, even in the glare of the rising
sun. The sky was barren of clouds. They were two
80-foot boats far from base, within sight of German-
occupied territory.

"Okay," Lieutenant Cole said to his executive officer. "That means we go in." He nodded at the
signalman. "Tell them to keep station off our starboard beam, Barney." He leaned over the voice
tube to the chart house jutting from the instrument panel. "Bob? We're going in. Pull out your
charts and I'll be right there." He turned to Ensign
DeLong. "Take over, Randy," he said, moving away
from the wheel located on the portside of the bridge.
DeLong took the wheel, advanced the three throttles, and checked the flux gate compass and pioneer compass on his left.

The two boats had been easing toward the French
coast at just over 10 knots. Now that Cole had
made the decision, the speed was increased to 30
knots. DeLong felt the apprehension of every man
on board. As he gripped the wheel and looked over
the rising bow, he saw the gunners on the 37-mm
mount double-checking the gun. The seaman on
the 20-mm gun was doing the same. He heard the
brush of the twin-50s on the track as the gunners
scanned the sky.

They'd been doing this sort of thing for a while.

First in the Mediterranean and now in the English
Channel. There'd been twelve boats in 142(2)
Squadron a year ago—now there were six.

DeLong scanned the compass and then the sea
ahead. The skipper stood near the torpedo direc-
tor stand, training his binoculars on the horizon as
the boats sped through the gray-green waters, trailing a frothy, white wake behind them.

Cole had been withdrawn since they'd been ordered to England. He'd barely spoken since they
had loaded the boats on the backs of two grimy
tankers and begun the voyage, safely embedded in
the interior of a large convoy. The PT boats didn't
look right, hauled out of the water and braced and
tied down on the decks of the ponderous ships—
helpless if the Germans attacked. The boats' crews
were nervous during the trip, concerned about
the welfare of the boats and unused to the maze of
passageways and bulkheads of the tankers. So they
stayed on deck, near their boats, playing cards or
sleeping, or checking equipment, and Cole was
always present—his quiet, commanding manner
enough to reassure the crews that everything was
okay. But DeLong knew that it wasn't okay with the
skipper. He was edgy and lost his temper more
than normal. It could have been the loss of the
other boats. That hit everyone hard. It had been a
SNAFU all right; somebody had forgotten to tell
them about the E-boats and F-lighters. Somebody
at ONI had failed to pass on the information, or
didn't cross a T or dot an I, or something. Nobody
knows how these things happen, they just do. It
was a mistake. A SNAFU; a lot of good guys dead.

"Going below, Randy," Cole said, disappearing down the tiny hatchway to the Chart House.

"Okay, Skipper," DeLong replied. He drew a deep breath, pulling in the scent of the ocean. It was peaceful out here. He felt the thump of the boat's bow breaking into the Channel waves, heard the muffled roar of the Packard engines, and turned his head slightly to let the salty breeze flow down into the collar of his jacket. One of these days he'd have his own boat. He'd miss the men and the skipper of course—there wasn't a better crew than the guys of the 155 boat. And there probably wasn't a better squadron commander than Jordan Cole. But DeLong wanted his own boat.

He put that thought aside, however, as the French coast began to grow on the horizon, and with it the increased knowledge that the enemy would be waiting for them.

Admiral McNamar shook his head. "I'll say one thing for you, Mike. You're persistent."

"It's about the *Southern*, sir," Michael Edland said. "May I join you?"

McNamar motioned to the chair across the table. He'd been enjoying lunch when he'd spotted the lieutenant-commander entering the dining room and making a beeline for his table.

"You know it's hard to find a decent chicken dinner over here," McNamar said, stabbing at the remains of a tiny pullet. "The first thing I'm going to do when I get home is get a good chicken dinner with mashed potatoes and gravy."

"Yes, sir," Edland said.

McNamar laid his fork next to his plate, placed his elbows on the table, and folded his fingers together. He focused his attention on the sandy-haired man with the deep scar running from his right ear to his nose. "Okay," he said. "Let's hear it."

"After I read the action report of *Southern*'s encounter with the E-boats, I contacted her XO. He and I knew each other before the war."

"You fellows in ONI have quite a network, don't you?" McNamar said drily.

"It doesn't hurt that I'm on your staff, sir," Edland countered. "The XO confirmed the points in the report that were in dispute."

"E-boats traveling at sixty knots or more and mounted with six-inch guns? You're damned right they were in dispute."

"Yes, sir. The fire was generally wild. Torpedoes did most of the damage."

"Their aim was off. What of it? They sank a tanker and shot up some of our ships. I'll give the little bastards high marks for that."

"Yes, sir," Edland continued patiently. "The tanker was torpedoed. Obviously a conventional E-boat weapon. But the hits on the *Southern* were not the results of a conventional weapon. The rounds appear to have burned through the hull and superstructure of the destroyer escort."

"Burned? What do you mean, burned? Look, Mike, ordnance is not your bailiwick, right? You're an intelligence officer, the Office of Naval Intelligence. The blackened area around a hit and the fact that the round is traveling at a high rate of speed is likely to give the impression, and rightly so, of a 'burned' area."

"Of course, sir," Edland agreed calmly. "But the metal was fused. Melted and fused at the point of impact—like it was done with a torch, the XO said."

McNamar sat back in his chair in resignation and signaled to a waiter. "Take this away," he instructed the man, "and bring me a martini, neat." After the table was cleared, the admiral eyed Edland.

"With your permission, sir," Edland said. "I'd like to pursue this."

"In plain language, Mike."

"I want your authorization to capture prisoners. Perhaps an E-boat."

"Oh, is that all?" McNamar said as the waiter arrived with his drink. "You know, the British have been trying to do that for the past five years."

"Yes, sir. I'm aware of that. I've been researching the subject."

" 'Researching?' Yeah, you're an intellectual, aren't you? Archaeologist or something?"

"Anthropologist. Specializing in the Far East," Edland said, watching McNamar carefully. The admiral was not the sort of man to reveal what he was really thinking, so Edland wasn't certain if McNamar would accept his idea. They'd known each other for ten months, since he had been assigned to McNamar's staff, and Edland had been impressed by the admiral's pragmatic intelligence. McNamar was a clear, concise thinker who seldom ventured into the abstract. That was why he depended on Edland, to form concepts into realities.

"How do you plan on doing this?" McNamar said.

"There's a PT boat squadron at Portland," Edland said cautiously. "We know that the E-boats are operating out of Cherbourg, Boulogne, and Le Havre."

"So you want to snatch one of the Cherbourg boats." The statement was obvious. Cherbourg was closest to Portland, half the distance of Le Havre— a straight run across the Channel. "Well, you got guts. I was on a PT boat once and by God I'll never do it again. Those guys are insane, which means the E-boat crews are probably just as bad. I'd bet they're both just one step short of being pirates." He sipped his drink and made a face. Edland saw him mulling over the idea. "You're not bigoted, Mike, but you're damned close. You know something about the invasion."

"Everyone knows something, sir," Edland said. No, he wasn't bigoted; he was not declared important because his knowledge of some aspects of the invasion was deemed critical. Bigots bore the responsibility of carrying vital information, of maybe knowing how and where—but not when, only SHAEF knew that—the invasion was to take place. Bigots carried an additional responsibility: don't get captured. If the Germans captured a bigot, they could force him to talk. It wasn't like the movies where the handsome American outsmarted a comic German interrogator. There was a good chance the bigot would talk under torture, and they had information that could doom the invasion, or at least cost the lives of several thousand men.

"Yeah," McNamar agreed, unimpressed. "Everybody knows something. And some of it may actually be true. But why take the chance, Mike? You know that I can veto this harebrained scheme of yours from the get-go. Or maybe I'll just beach you and you pick someone to send."

"Yes, sir," Edland admitted. "You can do that."

McNamar's eyebrows arched as he realized that his bluff had been called. Edland was the type of man who could agree you into coming around to his way of thinking.

"There may be something to what you're saying," McNamar said, considering what Edland was proposing. "But—"

"Pardon me, sir. But if the Germans do have a new weapon, it's better to find out about it now than to be surprised later on. During the invasion."

"Yeah," McNamar said skeptically.

"Yes, sir," Edland said. He had his arguments all carefully arranged if McNamar denied him his PT boats. He planned his negotiations well in advance, playing the roles of both participants in his mind until he had exhausted point and counterpoint. From this intellectual encounter came his strategy. He expected McNamar to be skeptical at first; he also expected the admiral to accept his proposition.

"Okay, Mike," McNamar said. "You've got your mission. I'll cut the orders today and you'll be on your boat in no time, puking your guts out."

"Thank you, sir."

"Just one thing, Mike," McNamar said. "Those E-boat crews have been fighting their war for a long time. They're very, very good at what they do, and the ones that have lasted this long are the best of them. Their boats are twenty feet larger than PT boats and they're made of steel, not wood like our little cockleshells."

"I'll be careful, sir."

"Yeah," McNamar said, signaling for another drink. His eyes traveled over the starched white tablecloth before he turned them on Edland. He liked this boy, man really, but everyone seemed so young. Young men dying in war, what a waste. "You just be careful not to get yourself killed. Good staff are hard to come by. I sure don't want to waste my time training another guy to put up with me."

Chapter 4

The English Channel

PT boat 155 had slowed down to 10 knots, the mufflers closed and the exhaust pumped into the sea at her fantail. The sea burbled and burped along the stern of the boat as the gases mixed with water. The boat ran almost silently at this speed, but 10 knots was as fast as she could go with closed mufflers. Any faster and the powerful exhaust from the three Packard engines would blow the mufflers off.

Ewing's 168 boat was about a mile off the starboard quarter of 155 as the two Elco boats neared the French coastline. Cole scanned the shore, still a good mile off, through binoculars.

"I've got a good view of the beach," he said, the 7x50 Bausch and Lomb binoculars training steadily along the shore. "Looks like an abandoned shack, nothing on the bluffs overlooking the beach. There's a derelict freighter just offshore. She's been there for a while." He lowered the binoculars and added thoughtfully: "I don't see any Krauts. I don't see anyone at all." He grabbed the windscreen of the PT boat for support as an errant wave slapped the boat's hull roughly, pushing her to port.

"Skipper?" Torpedoman 1st Class Tommy Rich called from the bow where he had been standing lookout. "There's something floating at that freighter's stern." The rusting hulk was bow in to the beach and listing heavily to port. The shore had a firm grip on the old ship, the breaking sea battering her stern.

"I got it too, Skipper," said Eckstam at the forward 20-mm gun. Cole watched as he adjusted his binoculars. Eckstam turned to Cole with a smile. "It's our boy, Skipper. Sitting pretty as you please in his life raft."

"About five hundred yards off the beach," DeLong said, still manning the wheel.

"Yeah," Cole said. He scanned the beach and bluffs again. "Okay. Let Ewing know that we're going in. Tell him to wait here and cover us. The charts say twenty fathoms rising to five."

"No telling what's built up around her stern," DeLong said, studying the motionless wreck.

"Yeah," Cole replied, rubbing the stubble on his chin. "Tommy? You and Murray lay back to the life raft on the Day Cabin. Get it ready to go over the side if we can't get the boat close enough to get that guy. Pass the word as you go aft. Tell everybody to keep their eyes open and their fingers off the triggers until I say. Eckstam, don't let that pilot out of your sight." He slid the binoculars into their pouch underneath the windscreen. "Randy," he said to DeLong, "I want you to take us in at forty. Split the difference between the hulk and that point of land off to the right. Two hundreds yards out from the hulk, cut to the left and drop her down to twenty. We'll use the wreck to shield us from the shore in case the Krauts have any guns on the bluff."

"Think that'll fool them?" DeLong asked.

"No," Cole said. "But it might confuse them long enough for us to buy a little time. Eckstam? Still got that pilot in sight?"

"Yeah, Skipper, but he ain't moving. You'd think the guy would be waving or something. Jesus, I hope he ain't dead."

"We'll find out soon enough," Cole said. He nodded at Delong. "Okay, Randy. Give her the gas."

DeLong picked the microphone and said: "Leo, we're going in. Open the mufflers."

The response crackled through the speaker mounted on the instrument panel. "Right, Mr. De-Long."

Randy DeLong watched as the engine enunciator signaled ALL SPEED. Slipping his fingers through the throttle mounts, he pushed them forward steadily.

The 80-foot PT boat's bow rose abruptly as the screws bit deeply into the water. The 1,550-horsepower Packard V-12 engines roared to life, driving the 60-ton craft through the waves. As she increased speed her wake swelled to twice her 20-foot beam and a rooster tail of boiling water jetted almost as high as the barrel of the 40-mm gun on her stern. The 155 boat raced forward at 40 knots and it would take only minutes to close the distance to the wreck and the Hurricane pilot. She drew five and a half feet but this close to shore that might be too much. It was a gamble, Delong knew—that the charts were right, and Cole was right, and they could get in close enough to the pilot without running aground. If they did run aground, the 168 boat could come in and give them a tow. If they didn't rip the bottom out of the 155 boat. And if the bluffs weren't covered in German guns.

DeLong hoped that Cole was right. He kept an eye on the three tachometers. Their needles rose steadily, piling rpm on top of rpm. Below the tachometers were the three gauges that read the engine manifold pressure. Both sets told DeLong that the Packards, well past time for rebuilding, were running smoothly.

Cole glanced astern at the low Day Room. Seaman 2nd Class Murray gave him a thumbs-up. He and Tommy Rich were ready with the life raft. "Eckstam," Cole shouted above the engines and the waves pounding against the hull, "what do you see?"

"No movement, Skipper. Nothing on shore, either. Looks like nobody's home."

Cole saw the flashes near the crest of the bluffs. He barely had time to shout, "Randy," when the shells from the shore batteries exploded a hundred yards ahead and to the left of the speeding boat.

DeLong spun the wheel and the 155 boat twisted quickly to starboard and back to port again. He let the boat run in one direction for another hundred yards before turning her again to starboard. The

agile craft whipped over the ocean as her three
rudders cut into the water. Cold spray splashed
over her sides, soaking the deck and everyone on
it as DeLong tried to throw off the enemy gunner's
aim. The wreck might have been a haven for the
downed pilot, but DeLong knew that the gunners
had probably been using it as a range marker for
some time, setting their shell fuses based on an
imaginary checkerboard laid out on the ocean's
surface. Now the 155 boat sped across the board;
each space precisely marked and each component
of range and deflection carefully computed by the
gunners.

Cole clapped his hand on DeLong's shoulder
and shouted: "On the next turn take her in on a
forty-five." He turned aft and cupped his hands
around his mouth. "Tommy, pass the word to the
forty-millimeter to fire at those flashes when we
turn in."

Rich waved his understanding and made his way
aft to the long-barreled 40-millimeter cannon.

Cole watched as Ewing on the 168 boat moved
in closer to the beach. He would provide covering
fire with his 40-millimeter and 37-millimeter guns
when he got close enough, but those German shore
batteries were probably securely emplaced; there
was a good chance that they'd be irritated by the
return fire from the little boats, but not injured.
"Eckstam, is that guy moving at all?"

"No, sir," the sailor called back. "Jeez, I hope
that guy ain't dead."

"Is this trip really necessary?" DeLong said as he
spun the wheel. Three more rounds from the shore
battery landed in the ocean ahead of the boat, but

much closer. DeLong steered directly into the boiling water where the shells had landed and then spun the wheel hard to port. "Here we go, Skipper."

They were committed now, coming in hard astern of the grounded freighter.

Behind them the 40-millimeter began its steady firing, each report a dull thud as it pumped shells at the bluffs overlooking the beach. Cole tracked the hits through his binoculars, wiping the lenses of salt spray as DeLong maneuvered the boat in a wild attempt to dodge the shore battery fire. The enemy guns were well hidden and the chances of actually hitting them were practically nonexistent. It was more than Cole had a right to expect, but he'd seen stranger things happen in war. He swung the binoculars to the wreck and the downed Hurricane pilot. The life raft rose and fell with the waves, bumping against the exposed rudder of the derelict freighter. The pilot was slumped over the edge of the raft, one arm trailing in the water.

"Hell," Cole muttered, "that guy does look dead." It didn't matter; they had to go in anyway. "Put me right alongside that raft, Randy." He turned and made his way out of the cockpit, around the starboard twin .50-caliber machine-gun turret and back to the Day Room Canopy. "Belay that raft, Murray. Secure it and come forward. Rich, grab a boat hook and meet me at the forward hatch."

"Okay, Skipper," Rich said.

Cole quickly moved forward, stopping only long enough to shout his intentions to DeLong. "Get us next to him and we'll pull him in with a boat hook.

The minute he's in, I'll give you a signal and you haul ass out of there."

When Cole got to the bow, he knelt at the Sampson Post and watched the stranded freighter grow. The enemy fire intensified as smaller caliber guns found the range and glowing green tracer rounds reached for the 155 boat. Right for my nose, Cole thought. He'd always felt that way. One night in the Mediterranean they'd run into a long silent convoy escorted by MAS boats and E-boats; things turned ugly very quickly. Later one seaman had said that he could practically read the *Saturday Evening Post* by the light of the tracers. Maybe, Cole had said, all I know is that every one of those little bastards was aimed straight at my nose.

Now dozens of waterspouts danced across the water; each spout the result of a falling shell—every shell aimed at the 155 boat. The eruptions were getting closer—the gunners had found the range.

As Rich joined him, holding tightly to the long boat hook, DeLong swung the boat to starboard and then quickly to port, and back to starboard again, trying to throw off the shore battery. But Cole realized that the PT boat's goal was obvious to the German gunners, even if they couldn't see the bright yellow life raft nudging the freighter's stern. Shells began striking around and then on the freighter, as if the enemy was happy to confirm Cole's fear. A large-caliber shell exploded on the ship's superstructure, sending large pieces of rusted metal careening into the air.

"Give me that boat hook," Cole said to Rich.

"Skipper, you shouldn't . . ."

"Give me the boat hook. My arms are longer than yours. You just hold on to my belt so I don't fall in."

Cole laid flat on the deck, half of his long body laying over the gunnel, the slightly raised toe rail digging into his stomach. He carefully fed the boat hook through his hands. The boat hook was exactly that—a hook fastened on the end of a pole that was used to secure the dock when they pulled in, pick flotsam out of the water, or draw in life rafts filled with downed aviators. Now Cole may be using the useful instrument to secure the life raft of a dead aviator.

"Here we go," Cole said as the boat slowed, using the freighter as a shield from the guns. It worked partially—now the air was filled with the crazy bell-like tones of the small rounds peppering the metal hull and superstructure of the ship. The larger guns added percussion to the concerto— huge explosions that shook the pitiful vessel.

"Hey," Rich said behind Cole. "That guy's moving."

The pilot straightened slightly and glanced over his shoulder as if the rescue were some sort of secret. The explosions rocking the freighter dispelled that notion.

"Grab the boat hook," Cole shouted.

The pilot threw his left arm over awkwardly and took hold. He nodded his readiness.

Cole quickly pulled the boat hook back through his hands, drawing the life raft and obviously injured pilot in. "Rich, drop the cargo net. He needs help." The pilot grimaced with each jerking motion of the raft through the water. His right arm hung uselessly in the water.

Cole glanced over his shoulder to see Murray join Rich. The rolled net, secured to the toe rail, hit the water with a splash. Rich was over the side in an instant and climbed down the net. Cole reached out with his left leg and felt the slight raised forepeak hatch behind him. Using it as leverage, he twisted his entire body to swing the raft aft to the net. He felt his muscles strain in protest and his shoulders burn fiercely as he tried to guide the raft, feed the boat hook, and twist his body at the same time.

Rich, his legs below the knees in water and his left hand gripping one of the footholds of the net, stretched out and grabbed the tiny lifeline that ran the circumference of the raft.

Cole heard the pilot say something in relief; the language wasn't familiar but the sentiment was.

Cole released the boat hook from the raft, stood clumsily, and joined Murray and Rich, who were just hauling the pilot aboard. He turned and whipped his index finger in tight circles at DeLong; it was the universal signal to take her out. "Eckstam," Cole said, tossing the boat hook to the gunner. "Secure that."

The other two seamen had propped the pilot against the Charthouse Deadlite. Rich unscrewed a canteen lid and gave the shaking pilot carefully measured sips.

"Buddy," Murray said in his slow Southern drawl. "We all thought you was dead."

"I pretend dead," the pilot whispered in heavily

accented English. "Pretend." He turned to Cole, obviously the ranking member of the crew that had rescued him. "Flight Lieutenant Stanislav Bortnowski, Number two-oh-eight Squadron, City of Gdansk. Thank you."

"Jordan Cole, U.S. Navy," Cole said with a smile. "You're welcome. Polish?"

The pilot nodded, turning his eyes to Rich hopefully. The seaman looked to Cole for permission, and Cole nodded. It was dangerous to give someone who'd been at sea for any length of time too much water. It was especially dangerous if you didn't know the extent of the person's injuries. The pilot took more water gratefully and answered.

"Yes. Formerly of the Third Cavalry Brigade. Now I fly airplanes."

Cole heard the soft burp of the smoke generator aft followed by the hiss of the titanium tetrachloride as it emptied into the air, forming a thick white cloud. They were running at top speed now with DeLong's competent hands on the wheel, and the white smoke billowing over the fantail would mask their escape.

"Your arm," Cole said.

"Broken, I'm sure," Bortnowski said. "But I'm alive. It's a small price to pay for one's life."

Cole nodded and stood. "Bring the stretcher forward and lash our guest down," he ordered Rich. "I'd hate to lose him over the side."

"Okay, Skipper. I'll look him over and get him squared away."

Cole made his way back to the cockpit but stood away from DeLong. He knew that the ensign understood that he didn't want to be approached, didn't want to speak to anyone when he did this. Something that the pilot had said troubled Cole; some words had brought back memories of the Mediterranean. It sounded so much like what Harry Lowe would have said: "It's a small price to pay for one's life." Harry Lowe, handsome, erudite, good-natured; only son of a wealthy man. A decent man. Cole's friend. Dead because of Cole's mistake.

Chapter 5

Portsmouth, England

Captain George Hardy entered Schiffer's Artist Supply Store reluctantly. He'd been the center of an ongoing debate as he walked down Gosport Street—a hotly pursued squabble between Captain George Hardy, RN, and George Hardy, bachelor. A bachelor, he had once confided to a friend, because he "would not be silly enough to have any woman who was silly enough to have me." But that strongly held belief had been under siege for some time, and the whole subject had been distressing to Hardy.

He closed the door quietly behind him, irritated at the tinny sound of the charming little bell suspended above the door. The bloody thing tinkled merrily every time the door opened, Hardy recalled, announcing customers as they entered.

He quickly slipped down a narrow aisle, safely

hidden among tall shelves stacked with tubes of oil paint, rolls of canvas, endless bottles sprouting clusters of drawing pencils, and a thousand other things that professional or budding artists might require. He stopped briefly, taking time to gather himself, and carefully studied a colony of small articulated wooden models, frozen in a variety of poses. He'd never got the hang of the human figure and was absolutely horrid at the human face. "Give me the inanimate," he told Land one clear day as they shared a watch on *Firedancer*'s crowded bridge. "Nothing moves. I can take as bloody well long as I want. None of this nonsense of people twitching or growing tired."

But Hardy was not being entirely truthful. He admired those artists who could capture the human spirit reflected in the geography of an individual face. Every element of the soul, under the skillful touch of a talented artist, was reflected in a portrait in any medium. Sometimes it was the shape of the features—eyes, nose, cheekbones. Sometimes in the arrangement of them all. Mostly in the eyes, though—brooding, haunted, bright, intelligent, longing. A person's soul reflected in their eyes, Hardy had heard once but had dismissed it forthwith. Later, when he had seen what war did to men, he considered them the truest words that he had ever heard spoken. It gave him a newfound appreciation for the portraitist. None of that abstract nonsense, Hardy sniffed. Silly children's drawings of eyes suspended on a person's forehead and triangular heads; bloody insult to artists everywhere.

"Why, it's Captain Hardy," Topper Schiffer said,

behind him. "Thought I heard the bell. Bea and I were just in the back."

Hardy turned and smiled at the little proprietor. His thinning white hair was combed carefully across his round skull in an attempt to hide his baldness. He looked like a happy cherub.

"I must get a bigger bell," he said to Hardy, his bright blue eyes reflecting genuine happiness at seeing the captain again. "Can't half hear that one most of the time."

"Yes," Hardy said, slightly pleased that the little bell's days were numbered.

"Come for a few things, then?" Schiffer said, smiling. "Let me pop back and tell Bea you're here. She'll be pleased to see you."

Hardy started to protest, but the man was gone in a flash. He scratched his chin roughly out of frustration and followed Schiffer. He suddenly felt overwhelmed by the stacks of goods that had once protected him but now towered over him, leaving no room to maneuver, no room to come about if need be. He stationed himself at the relatively open area in front of the low wooden counter. Behind a flowered curtain that was still drifting from Schiffer's passage he could hear Beatrice Schiffer's soft voice. His heart started a little and he wondered what to do with his hands. He finally decided to lay them casually on the counter. A fleeting image of the stiff wooden artist models crossed his mind and he quickly withdrew his hands and let them fall to his side.

The curtains parted and Beatrice Schiffer appeared, followed by her brother.

"Why it *is* Captain Hardy," she said in a voice just over a whisper. Her eyes were as blue as her brother's and the siblings were nearly the same height, a good head shorter than Hardy. Her dark brown hair, flecked with gray, was carefully arranged so that it came just to her shoulders. Hardy always felt that was most sensible in a woman; keep your hair short and under control, no outlandish hairdos that require constant maintenance. Sensible.

He swallowed before replying. "How do you do, Miss Schiffer?"

"Years he's been coming here," Schiffer said to Beatrice, "and it's still Miss Schiffer."

"Topper, please," she said.

"You see, Captain Hardy," Schiffer said. "Topper. And she's Bea. Short for Beatrice, you see. Bea since she was a girl and Topper from the clocks."

Hardy was perplexed. "Clocks?"

"Tower clocks. Me job was to clean and repair them before the war. Then me legs gave out on me. Too many steps, you see. Get to the tops of the towers in no time. Wring a few pigeons' necks on the way."

"Topper, must you?" Beatrice reprimanded her brother mildly.

"Well, it's true, Bea and many's the time you've heard me complain about those filthy birds," he said. Then he turned to Hardy. "Pigeon dung gums up a clock's works faster than anything. Can't tell you the times I've had to shovel—"

"Tea? Captain Hardy?" Beatrice interrupted her brother.

"That's right," Schiffer said. "We've just brought

the kettle to a boil in the back. Come join us for a spot."

"No. Thank you," Hardy said. "I've come for a few things." He had written down a list of supplies that he needed but couldn't bring himself to reach for it. That would hasten the end of the visit.

"Now, Captain Hardy," Beatrice said. "You're a busy man I'm sure, but certainly a cup of tea wouldn't demand too much of your time?"

"Best mind Bea, Captain Hardy," Schiffer said. "I did when I went into this business. Didn't know charcoal from chilblains but Bea made it all work out."

Hardy saw the hope in Beatrice's eyes, and for a moment he even thought that his continued presence was the object of that hope. But that would be too much to expect. Still it was only tea.

"Yes," he said. "Tea it is."

Chapter 6

Rommel was distracted. He paced the room appearing to listen carefully to Admiral Thomas K. Dresser, Commander-in-Chief of the Kriegsmarine Gruppe West. Dresser's report of S-boats and R-boats and Channel activity droned on and on, covering every detail of his command's activity over the past week. But Rommel was aware of the rationale behind Dresser's endless self-serving account of all that the Kriegsmarine had done; it was Goering.

Hermann Goering was a harbinger of disaster. He would rush to the Fuehrer's side and begin a hurried litany of the calamities that the other services had brought upon themselves because of their own ineptitude. But not the Luftwaffe; oh, certainly not the valiant Luftwaffe that could not keep American and British bombers from destroying the

beautiful cities of the Fatherland, or from deci-
mating the forces being rushed along French
roads to strengthen the Atlantic Wall. No, Reichsfuehrer Hermann Goering would never report the
failures of his own command; he would wax eloquently on the triumphs of the Luftwaffe. And the
Fuehrer listened, and the Fuehrer fumed, and he
ranted about the imbecilic commanders whose idiotic decisions cost the very resources that he, the
Fuehrer, struggled endlessly to provide. And Goering, his face wreathed in sympathy for the Fuehrer's
untiring devotion to the welfare of the nation,
watched Hitler storm about, and smiled secretly.

That was why Dresser spoke as he did. Because
somewhere, in this mass of officers gathered around
the long table in the large dining room of this vast
hotel that had been turned into Wehrmacht Headquarters, there were several ambitious men, jackals
really, who passed on to Goering distorted accounts
of what was being reported. Best state that the impossible was being done to prevent the improba-
ble—to keep the Allies away from the coast of
France. No, no. To crush them. To color the waters
of the English Channel with their blood so that
the English and the Americans would never again
dare think of invading the continent. Be assured
in your predictions, unwavering in your convic-
tion. And cognizant that the Fat Man's ears heard
everything.

Rommel was suddenly aware that Dresser had
stopped speaking.

Kommodore Karl Walters, Rommel's naval attaché, thanked the admiral smoothly, covering the
feldmarschall's inattention. Rommel cocked an

eyebrow in mild irritation at Walters's presumption that he was not listening. He had stopped listening long before Dresser finished his report, but that was beside the point. Walters took too many liberties. He assumed too much and certainly presumed too much, always seeming to anticipate Rommel's questions about the navy's readiness or the Allies' intentions as regards to naval strategy, and the final insult to the feldmarschall's sensibilities was that Walters was always right.

He was very smooth, Rommel had decided after the kommodore had joined his staff. Correct in action and deed—each word properly chosen and presented. Quietly, if voraciously, ambitious. Rommel saw some of himself in Walters and was disturbed by the image. As highly polished as marble, he decided, and just as cold. Be careful of his ambition, Rommel had reminded himself.

Commander of Army Group for Special Employment. Rommel. Go to France, Hitler had ordered him, and turn the Atlantic Wall into an impregnable defense. Make every port a fortress. Make certain the Allies impale themselves on the bayonets of Wehrmacht soldiers with the sands of France clutched in their dying hands. Von Rundstedt rolled his eyes at that one.

"Thank you, Admiral," Rommel said, glancing at Walters. That was a signal that the meeting was over and that the fieldmarschal wanted his naval attaché to remain. After the others had gone Rommel approached the large map of the French coast, the English Channel, and the coast of England. "Walters," he said, an indication that he was ready for the officer's comments.

"Yes, Feldmarschall," Walters said, walking from the end of the table to the huge map. "Admiral Dresser argued most effectively against using his S-boats exclusively as minelayers."

"His opinion is not my concern," Rommel said. He had no interest in Dresser's reasoning. "Mines, Walters. The first line of defense."

"Of course, Feldmarschall."

"Mines in the water, mines on land. Is that so difficult to grasp?"

"No, Feldmarschall."

Rommel turned, annoyed. Walters recognized this as a signal. The feldmarschall, never a patient man, wanted his attaché's opinion.

Walters said smoothly, "I think that the admiral's position has some merit. So too, do the S-boats."

"Toys," Rommel said. "There is no Kriegsmarine presence in the Channel. Little toy boats. Scattered up and down the coast. What good are they to me? To the defense of France?"

"They might be of some use," Walters said. "Particularly the boats at Cherbourg."

Rommel's eyes reflected irritation.

"S-boats, Feldmarschall," Walters continued, "with attachments on their hulls. They rise above the surface of the water and travel at very high speeds. Limited resistance against the hull."

"Toys," Rommel said dismissively.

"Of course, Feldmarschall," Walters fell back but advanced with diffidence. "It is only a squadron of course but the boats are fitted with a new cannon. A very powerful gun, one hundred ten millimeter. Much larger than the armament on comparable vessels."

"Walters . . ." Rommel said, growing weary of the discussion.

"Quite a revolutionary weapon, these boats," Walters pushed the matter subtly.

"I don't care," Rommel said. "One hundred million mines should be buried along the French coast. Every square mile should hold one hundred and sixty thousand mines. I demanded ten million mines a month and was told"—the fieldmarschal's patience gave way to frustration—"and I was told that I would have them. I do not have them. What I cannot have on land, I will have at sea. Revolutionary? Seaworthy? The S-boats will pepper the approaches to the beach with mines. Seed the English Channel with a vast garden of mines. That is what the S-boats will do. Dresser argued eloquently because it is expected of him. He's made it quite clear that he despises those little boats." The feldmarschall paused. "His protests were a formality. You will tell Dresser that the Commander of Army Group for Special Employment," the title was impregnated with sarcasm, "has so ordered." Rommel's tone became harsh. "And you may add that the Fuehrer wishes that the Commander be accommodated in his duty to see to the defenses of the French coast."

"Of course, Feldmarschall."

"Cannons on S-boats," Rommel said. "Wings. What good are they? Revolutionary? Untested you mean. You will see to it, Walters." The decision was final, Rommel meant; turn the S-boats into minelayers and let's have no more business about winged boats and fantastic cannons.

"Yes, Feldmarschall," Walters said. What good are they? *I don't know*, was Walters's unspoken reply to Rommel's question. Could they be better employed laying mines in the Channel? *I don't know.* Could they really be of any use against the vast armada that the Allies were assembling in English ports? What role could they possibly play? *I don't know that either,* Walters concluded as he left the conference room.

Walters was intrigued when Dresser had told him about the boats. He had first read about them in one of the daily report summaries that passed over his desk. He read each summary because he was methodical. He read this particular report a second time and then studied it after he rang for tea, and then made notes in the margin of the paper while adding cream and sugar. There was potential here—fast boats, guns, and an opportunity to place them directly in front of the invasion fleet. He glanced at the cover sheet and noticed that Dresser had advanced the report with no comment. He had either not taken the time to read the report, or had simply dismissed it.

A second cup of tea and a small pastry—he was a man of moderate habits—provided Walters with an idea. The one remaining Kriegsmarine resource was S-boats. A considerable number, in fact. Expendable if need be and most likely that need would arise. He made more notes and kept returning, although he wasn't sure why, to the idea that these new boats were very fast.

He was dismayed to find that they were in the hands of Reubold. As an officer the man was a disaster, as a human being he was a failure, but Walters supposed that Reubold held his post because of the mystique that surrounded him.

But the boats. Rommel was right; they were un-tested except for an inconclusive sortie against an enemy convoy, and they certainly could be used as minelayers—preparation for the invasion was every-thing. But could they be better utilized? Was there something that their unique qualities could provide to the defense of the French coast; some way that they could significantly impact the invasion? Were they an unspoken answer to an unknown question?

"I don't know," Walters said as his footsteps echoed off the parquet floor like a clock ticking away the seconds. There might be time to find out what these strange boats could do but that depended on the answer to a question that was known and had been debated endlessly; when and where would the Allies attack? And that question, despite the certainty with which a great many generals and admirals ar-gued, could honestly be answered: I don't know.

When Seaman 2nd Class Tyne picked Cole up at the quay, all the seaman said was: "Captain wants to see you, sir."

Cole hopped into the gray jeep with U.S. NAVY stenciled in black letters on the bumper, and set-tled in for the short ride to Captain Candelaria's office.

"What's it about?" Cole asked Tyne, who seemed to be habitually sucking on a piece of food that he had stuck between two teeth.

"Got me, sir," Tyne said, steering the jeep easily through the mass of traffic that crammed the nar-row streets of the base.

"No guesses, huh?" Cole asked, trying again.

"Not a one, sir," Tyne said, shifting into neutral and coasting to a stop at an intersection.

"You'd think a man with discretion like yours would at least rate seaman first," Cole said.

"Yeah," Seaman 2nd Class Tyne said in disgust. "That's what I thought too, sir."

Captain Candelaria, a short, squat man with a widow's peak that did nothing to increase his height, quickly read over the orders. He felt Edland, sitting across the desk, waiting with some degree of impatience as he flipped through the pages once, and then began carefully reading the instructions. Let him wait, Candelaria thought. He didn't care much for errand boys from headquarters coming down here with harebrained schemes and crazy notions about how the war needed to be run. And always in a hurry, too. Everything was a goddamned emergency for these guys.

Well, now they wanted Cole to go on some fool's errand and Candelaria would have to listen to Cole bitch and bellyache. "That guy would try the patience of Job," Candelaria muttered to one of his officers after a tense staff meeting. Cole may have been some hotshot squadron commander in the Mediterranean but he wasn't fighting the Italians out here; no sir. This was the Channel and these were the Germans and by God they were a damned sight tougher than those goddamned Wops.

"Okay, Commander," the captain said, tossing the orders aside. "So you wrangled yourself some top secret assignment and you want some of my boats."

"I'll need two PT boats from a squadron stationed at the base, yes, sir," Edland said.

"My boats," Candelaria said, "my base." Goddamned snotty-nosed, intellectual fag.

"Yes, sir," Edland said.

"Yeah," Candelaria said. "Well, maybe you can't
tell me what you're doing with my boats but I want
to know when you leave and when you get back,
and if anything happens to them, I want to know
that, too. Now, this guy, Cole. He's a pain in the
ass, so if you get any trouble from him, you let me
know. I've sat him down once or twice and gave
him a good talking-to and he knows who the boss
is around here."

"Yes, sir," Edland said.

The intercom at the captain's elbow buzzed and
a raspy voice announced: "Lieutenant Cole, sir."

Candelaria depressed the TALK button and said;
"Yeah. Send him in." To Edland he quickly added,
"You just remember what I said."

Edland stood as Cole entered.

"Cole," Candelaria said, "this is Lieutenant Commander Edland."

There was a flash of recognition between the
two men. "Yes, sir," Cole said. "The commander and
I know each other."

"Well, this is a fine time for me to find that out,"
Candelaria sputtered to Edland. "You could have
told me that you two know each other."

"Yes, sir," Edland said. He glanced at Cole. The
man had changed. He was taller than Edland remembered or maybe he appeared taller because
he was so thin—gaunt, in fact. His face was lined
and haggard looking despite the deep tan, and his

eyes had the look of a man who had seen too much for his own good. But they still burned with emotion.

"How are you, Commander?" Cole said, not bothering with the civility of a handshake.

It would have been a courtesy for Cole to extend his hand, despite their differences, but Edland recognized and accepted Cole's reason for not doing so. There was no subtlety about the man; he either liked you or he didn't and he didn't waste any energy pretending one way or the other. He would have made a poor diplomat and an inept player in the politics that were an integral part of any naval officer's advancement. "You have to get along to come along," an elderly officer had informed Edland. He knew from his contact with Cole at the beginning of the war that it was often difficult for Cole to get along with anyone.

"Fine," Edland said.

"I'm real happy for both of you," the captain said, obviously angry that Edland had not bothered to tell him that he knew Cole. "Why don't you two take it down to the conference room? I got a lot of work to do."

Cole and Edland both came to attention and saluted Candelaria. The base commander returned the salute and waved them out the door.

A goddamned fag and a goddamned troublemaker. The Krauts can have them.

When they entered the deserted conference room, Edland closed the door behind them and set his briefcase on the desk.

"Still with ONI?" Cole asked, walking to the far end of the table. He couldn't stand being close to Edland. Too many bad memories. Besides, he was wearing a tailored uniform and there weren't any bags under his eyes and he didn't move as if he hadn't slept worth a damn in a month. He was staff, and Cole, who was line, distrusted staff with a passion. And then there was the other thing.

"Yes, I am," Edland said, pulling several files from his briefcase. "Attached to Admiral McNamar's staff."

"Chairborne, huh?" Cole said, prodding Edland. His kind sat far away from danger and talked in broad theories and hyperbole. It was all very clean and pleasant where they lived, and the only time Cole saw them venture far from their comfortable perch is when they thought it necessary to explain carefully crafted opinions on strategy. He liked pushing these guys as much as he could. "You seem to relish that role."

"Just so there's no misunderstanding, why don't you remember that you're addressing a superior officer?"

"Yes, sir," Cole said, the insolence hardening.

Edland laid the files on the table and unfolded a map of the Channel. "The Germans have developed a new type of E-boat," he began. "It's operating out of Le Havre, Boulogne, or Cherbourg, we're not sure which . . ."

"That's a surprise, sir," Cole said, and then added: "The 'we're not sure' part."

Edland turned angrily. "All right, let's get this out of the way right now. You want to blame me. Go ahead and blame me. Whether or not I'm at fault is irrelevant. This isn't a thing that can be done now. This is something else, another place, another time. You're in on it whether you like it or not. I need your boats."

"Why don't you get Buckley, sir?" Cole said. He wanted nothing to do with E-boats or Edland.

"He's not available," Edland said. "And even if he were I would have chosen you."

Cole's own anger flared and he fought to control himself. "Am I supposed to feel honored by that?"

"You're supposed to follow orders, Cole," Edland said.

Cole moved around the table and advanced on Edland. "I followed your orders once, sir," he said bitterly. It was all a show and Cole knew it. Like a dog that was frightened—bark as long and as loud as you can and the fear would go away. Cole knew that Edland wasn't the cause of his friend's death, *he* was; but attacking Edland helped relieve the guilt that Cole felt. It was stupid and futile, but Cole had nothing else to fight his guilt with. It was illogical, but Cole knew that. If you don't learn to keep your mouth shut, a friend of his commented, and keep that goddamned temper under control, you're going to be the oldest lieutenant in the navy.

Edland refused to back down. "It was another place," he said quietly, "another time."

Cole glanced at the materials on the table and back to Edland. It was a truce. Tentative and hardly binding and fragile at best, but it was all that Cole's pride would allow him.

"You look worn out," Edland said.

Cole smiled, despite himself. "Maybe I ought to try another line of employment, sir." He willed himself to relax. He could feel the tension in his arms and back and he knew that his nerves were close to snapping. He fought back the panic that Edland would see the same thing. He gave Edland a look that said: "Okay, talk."

"There was an E-boat attack on an Allied convoy," Edland began, and then told Cole all that he knew.

Cole listened skeptically to Edland as he detailed what information he had about E-boats traveling at 60 knots and the 6-inch guns; but it was only a brief skepticism, lacking depth and form, and offered as if it were perfunctory. Cole was intrigued.

Edland handed the report to Cole and waited while he read it.

Maybe it was because before this madness they were both scholars, although Cole admitted that he wasn't much of one. Cole was a fighter with an imagination, a fluid mind that wrapped itself easily around unexpected turns in events. He would also not dismiss an idea out of hand because it did not fit the norm, because such a thing hadn't happened before, because people said that it was impossible, or because the concept was too farfetched for those who traveled in conventional packs to understand. Cole was certainly not conventional.

Cole's eyes traveled over the report, turning the pages, reading farther into the document. He was concentrating on the information that Edland had provided, dissecting it, examining it, making a decision. His eyes finally returned to Edland, wanting more.

"The only way to find out what we're facing is to capture some E-boat crewmen. Or one of these boats," Edland said.

"Capture?" Cole laughed. "My, aren't you the optimist."

"I know it'll be a challenge but I believe it can be done."

"Oh, do you? If we can get close enough without getting blown out of the water. They won't wait for us to sneak up on them. Maybe we can get a prisoner, but I wouldn't bet on getting a boat. They have teeth, you know."

"Their radar is not as sophisticated as ours and some boats don't carry any. We'll have an advantage because we can see them on radar before they have us in sight."

"I know all about E-boats, Commander, so don't tell me my business," Cole said. "They may not have radar but they can detect the impulses from ours, so that's nearly as good." Cole let the statement linger before he added the obvious. "But you really don't know about these new boats, do you, sir? There may be some surprises on these superboats of yours, you know."

"These boats may have better radar than most," Edland admitted. "Although I consider it unlikely. In any case, if we move quickly and disable them, I think we've got a fighting chance."

"You're right about that for sure," Cole said. "There'll be fighting all right. You know," he added, dropping the report on the table, "you could just go in and bomb the pens. No muss, no fuss, no crazy schemes. No dead sailors."

"I want one intact, now," Edland said. "Not in pieces later on. It's important for the war effort. If I can't get a boat, I want prisoners."

"Oh, hell, yes," Cole said. "The war effort. I guess I don't have much of a choice in this, sir?"

Edland shook his head.

"In that case," he said, "I'm in. Three boats."

Edland nodded his acceptance.

"We've got to catch them coming back in," Cole said. "Just before dawn. That means that we'll need to lie along the coast."

"Off Cap de la Hague," Edland said. "There's a cove just east of Auderville. High cliffs, no beach."

"I wasn't figuring on putting myself in their laps. I'd like a little more room to maneuver. Besides, I don't know the coast that well."

"I do," Edland said.

Cole smiled in remembrance, but there was no warmth to it. "Yeah. Right," he said. "Summers in France, wasn't it, sir? Your dad's place?"

"Grandfather's. I used to play along those cliffs. You can't see the cove unless you're right on the edge. It's a straight drop. Enough water for a PT boat. Or three if that's what you want."

"That's what I'll need. They usually come out in twos or threes but we may get lucky enough to nab a tail-end Charlie. When?"

"As soon as possible."

"Day after tomorrow," Cole said. "I've got to get my boats serviced. I want to make sure that they're in tip-top shape before I get that close to the Krauts. I'll shove off at nineteen hundred. That okay with you, sir?" He didn't leave time for an argument.

Edland said: "I'm coming along."

"Oh, now wait a minute," Cole said.

"I'll be on board your boat, Cole, and that's an order. Besides," Edland said, "just think how much fun you'll have ordering me around. That's how it works, isn't it? On board his own vessel the captain is supreme?"

"Look, I gave you what you wanted. We go out, get your boat, if we don't get our asses shot off, and that's that. Nobody said anything about supercargo on this little trip, and I sure as hell don't want somebody along who's going to be second-guessing everything I do. This isn't a pleasure cruise, Commander."

"I'm going. You can lead the mission or you can stay here and your exec can lead the mission, but I'm going. I know the coast and the E-boats. I'm going. You're the captain. Once we get under way, I'll follow your orders."

Cole considered the situation. He didn't have much of a choice. If Edland could requisition boats for a mission, then he had the clout to tag along. You can't fight city hall, Cole had told his crews when they complained about having to carry out ridiculous orders. Gripe all you want to, but do as you're ordered. "Yes, sir," he said. "I'll take the boats out and you're going. But, you'll have to do exactly what I say, when I tell you. If you do anything that puts my boats and my men in jeopardy you and I will have a reckoning."

"You know that you just threatened a superior officer, don't you, Cole?"

"Sure do," Cole said. "I hoped you noticed it as well."

Chapter 7

Commander Dickie Moore sat quietly behind Admiral Sir Bertram Ramsey and made detailed notes on the rather drawn-out meeting. Minutes of what was said, and by whom, and what was decided would be supplied, along with mountains of supporting documentation, through the traditional administrative mechanism. But Moore, even before being tasked by Ramsay, made notes of those subjects that concerned the actions required by the Royal Navy. "A condensed account, if you will, sir," Moore said dryly, handing Sir Bertram his version of what had transpired in an earlier meeting.

Now, in the well of a former classroom surrounded by narrow benches rising in tiers, with a gallery supported by thick, black columns, packed with officers of all ranks, the discussion turned to the Channel. *La Manche*, Dickie recalled, "the sleeve" the French called it, a long narrow body of water that kept the Germans from invading England, had kept the French from invading England, and might, and everyone was most concerned with this point, might keep the Allies from invading France.

Narrowest at the Straits of Dover, it offered endless possibilities for defense and disaster, victory and catastrophe, or the continuation of the war for many more years if Hitler's Atlantic Wall was as stout as most believed.

But the land wasn't Dickie's concern, or the Royal Navy's purview except as it was to be observed from the water. It was the sea that held Dickie's interest, although most sailors would snort derisively at the notion that this tiny strip of water had any sealike qualities. It fact, it had its own standards: wild currents, crosswinds, shoals and deeps, and the violent reputation enjoyed by shallow water when in the grips of a nor'easter. Add to this, on either side of it were hundreds of thousands of men poised to kill one another.

Dickie watched Admiral McNamar enter the well, surrounded by a bevy of staff officers, toting easels and maps, preparing to address the assembled multitude. He had stopped briefly to chat with Admiral Sir Andrew Cunningham, First Sea Lord, sitting just to the right of Churchill. Dickie liked McNamar. Like most Americans he was outgoing and good-natured but capable of getting "down to business" as an American staff officer informed Dickie. "Down to business," Dickie had mused in delight after they had parted. "What a wonderful expression."

McNamar's booming voice, amplified by the microphone situated in the center of the well, broke into Dickie's thoughts. The Royal Navy officer wrote quickly, his Waterford pen fairly dancing across the notebook in shorthand of his own creation, nearly indecipherable to anyone who attempted to read it.

More talk about the invasion fleet, and routes, and the need for ships, all ships but especially the LSTs—Landing Ship Tanks—a British idea but an American creation pounded out of steel throughout the inland ports of the United States. There were barely enough of those odd, boxlike, flat-bottomed craft that looked more like floating warehouses than ships. But they held promise for the invasion; loaded to the gunnels they could snub their high squat bows onto the French beaches, open their huge clamshell doors like great beasts come to feed, and spew out tanks, jeeps, trucks, men, cannon, and the thousands of tons of supplies necessary for the armies who would need to have replaced that which lay immobile beneath the guns of the German defenders. Logistics, young staff officers insisted, really wins wars. And England has become a giant commissariat of all that was required for victory.

But from here to there was water—the English Channel—and what Dickie knew as his pen glided across the page was that the invasion involved a vast, complex choreography of big ships, lesser ships, boats, and landing craft. It also involved schedules more intricate than those that ensured that trains arrive and depart in all of the terminals in all of the United Kingdom. Two thousand or more ships, each assigned a position that must be maintained at a certain place at a certain time, moving in several fleets in carefully plotted lanes that must be cleared of enemy mines, to arrive at designated points at the specified moment. An extraordinary ballet of destruction performed across a narrow stage. Any disruption of that complex array as it steamed slowly toward its objective would hamper the invasion—perhaps cripple it so that the invasion of France would be the greatest debacle of the war.

Dickie had, until the moment that he heard McNamar mention the problem, concentrated on capturing what was being said, his eyes following the jerky motions of the pen nib across the paper. That was until McNamar mentioned the problem.

"The problem is E-boats," McNamar said. "Flotillas at Le Havre, Brest, Guernsey, and Cherbourg. A total of perhaps sixty boats distributed among those points, safely hidden from conventional bombing, in E-boat pens." Except for the Channel Islands of course, no pens needed there. It was a delicate situation; the Channel Islands were British territory occupied by the Germans. The occupation forces were, on orders from Hitler, who still held the insane notion that Britain and Germany might come to terms, on their best behavior. Because of the real possibility that British bombs might kill British subjects, the islands, situated closer to France than to Britain, were off-limits to attack.

"Can't we get at them?" Montgomery asked, making it sound as if one only need send a terrier down the rat hole after the rat.

"If I may," Air Chief Marshall Leigh-Mallory said to McNamar. "We can indeed, Field Marshal. What is required are Tall Boy bombs, placed rather precisely next to the pens."

"Next to them?" Montgomery said. "I should think that it would be more appropriate to drop them directly on Jerry's head."

Leigh-Mallory allowed the audience a mild chuckle before continuing. "Not in this case, Field Marshal. These so-called earthquake bombs are most effective when they undermine the structure of the pens. They are quite large and very effective."

"You haven't been all that successful with U-boat pens," Churchill growled. "Isn't your optimism a bit misplaced?"

"No, Prime Minister," Leigh-Mallory replied. "We didn't have these bombs when the U-boats were a threat. Now that the American and Royal Navies have effectively countered the U-boats, it has become almost superfluous to attack U-boat pens with these bombs. They are expensive and in limited quantity. Best to save them for special targets."

"Have it your way, Air Chief Marshal," Churchill said, waving his objection aside with a cigar. "But I won't have them used against the Occupied Channel Islands." He nodded to the American admiral, whether to continue or to emphasize his edict, Dickie wasn't sure.

"There is no other viable threat at sea to the invasion except E-boats," McNamar continued. "We've had some reports of miniature submarines, but those have yet to materialize. The E-boats do pose a serious danger to the invasion fleet and should not be discounted just because they have remained relatively inactive over the past few months. I think that the Air Chief Marshal is correct; crush them in their pens before they have a chance to be employed. There is one other thing; one of my staff has discovered what he believes to be an improved E-boat. Very fast and very powerful. He's talked me into letting him have a closer look."

A wave of laughs filled the room and someone commented, shaking his head at the impertinence of young men: "Brave man. Brave man."

"That remains to be seen," McNamar said.

"Air Chief Marshal," General Dwight Eisenhower said. "Will you attend to the E-boat pens, please?" Ike, Dickie thought. Ever the diplomat; nearly always cordial, until someone crossed him, then the famous smile disappeared and the equally famous temper exploded.

"Delighted, sir," Mallory said. "I'll draw up the response and have it to you immediately."

Dickie fell back to writing, the question of E-boats seemingly addressed. The mention of PT boats brought Jordan Cole to mind. Cole had called him when he returned to England and the two had shared dinner and drinks in a tidy pub in Southampton. It had been two years since they had seen one another, and most of the time was spent catching up on what both had been doing. Dickie commented on Cole's deep tan and lamented the fact that he seldom saw the sun, even when it shone. "Too busy," Dickie had commented as he cut into a thick slice of lamb. "Far too busy." The pub was crowded with diners, enjoying the warmth of each other's company in the gentle din of a place where, for at least several hours, there was no war.

Dickie could see that Cole thoroughly appreciated being among people whose only concerns were a good laugh and bright conversation. As it was since they had known each other, Cole listened and Dickie talked; Cole laughed at Dickie's amorous adventures that always seemed to end in a tragic farce, and Dickie feigned hurt at Cole's lack of sympathy for his romantic pain.

What was not said during the meal was most important, Dickie recalled. What Cole did not ask and what was not mentioned by Dickie because the subject was too sensitive, although Dickie felt that it lay just below the surface, was Rebecca Blair.

There was little that Dickie could tell Cole that would not hurt him. She was miserable in that big house of hers, married to a man who was physically crippled by the war, but what was much more pathetic, emotionally crippled as well by the selfish manner in which he chose to live life. It was obvious that Gregory Blair rarely considered his wife's needs or her feelings. He seemed intent on bedding every woman he met, and in doing so in such a callous and inconsiderate way that Rebecca knew of his escapades. She tended to Gregory, cared for him in the manner that a good nurse does for a patient. She was, after all, a nurse, and he was a partial invalid, but the care that she provided stopped short of investing any love in a man and a marriage that had long since dissolved.

Dickie knew with certainty that she still loved Cole and that Cole loved her but the fact that she had chosen to stay with her husband meant that, to Cole, she no longer existed. It was how he, Dickie knew as well, dealt with the pain and long-

ing that ate away at him. To deny Rebecca's existence, Dickie knew that Cole reasoned, was to alleviate
the suffering. How strange, Dickie thought, it was
always the seemingly strong, cold-hearted blokes
who grieved most after love failed them.

Chapter 8

Peter Waldvogel knocked and heard the muffled command to enter. He had been summoned to Fregattenkapitan Reubold's office and he was nervous about the meeting. He had been working diligently on the sighting mechanism and gyro stabilizing platforms of the S-boat's forward cannons—the Trinity it was called—but the delicate instruments failed to perform the moment that the boats hit rough water. There was simply no way to aim the 110-millimeter guns effectively. S-boats were poor gun platforms for anything larger than rapid-firing 4cm guns, which spewed a steady stream of rounds at the target. Effective enough against small ships and aircraft, the 4cm, and the even less effective MG C/38 2cm "doorknocker," did not have the force to pierce enemy steel.

The Trinity guns with their hollow-shaped charges

had the power to hole the hulls of enemy vessels, the shells burning their way into the interior of the ship before they exploded. Waldvogel had proved it. He had proved it during static tests before excited cadets and officers at the *Marineschule* in Murwick. He had proved it to a second tier of Kriegsmarine officers at Le Havre, but there the response had been nothing more than mild interest. He had proved it at Le Havre after a frustrating seven months lost to scheduling, canceling, and rescheduling trials because the senior officers who needed to be present found themselves far too busy to commit to a time and place.

These officers saw the same three short-barreled guns arranged in a triangular formation on a stationary mount. There was nothing graceful about the guns. They were stubby with outsized breech mechanisms, and projecting from the rear of each was a long cone. Everyone had examined the curious weapons—the cadets with wonder, the officers with interest, and the senior officers with disdain. Especially after the gun was fired, filling the air with a blue haze of gaseous discharge.

"It does not recoil," Waldvogel explained patiently. "There is no shock to the gun, or mount." He saw that he was losing his audience of high-ranking officers as they signaled for staff cars to carry them away.

Finally one kommodore glanced at him with a look of pity reserved for an idiot and said: "They have torpedoes, Waldvogel. What do they need with stovepipes?"

Waldvogel closed the door behind him to find Reubold lounging on his cot. All of the S-boat offi-

cers and men had quarters in the Cherbourg sub-
urbs, at Urville, and in a museum that had once
been a villa, at Tour La Ville. But not Reubold.
Generally outgoing and open with his crews, the
fregattenkapitan insisted on staying in his single
room that served as living quarters and office, in
an ancient building on the naval base.

"A self-imposed exile," he once told Waldvogel.

Fregattenkapitan Richard Reubold, back propped
against the wall, rested on one elbow with the
other draped across an upraised knee. There was a
decadent air about his languid pose.

"In England," Reubold said in welcome, "you
would be called a boffin."

"Boffin?"

"It is their pet name for scientist. Fellows whose
minds work on a higher plane."

Waldvogel noticed a slight smile etched across
the officer's face.

" 'Chaps,' " Reubold continued, "who never quite
fit in the real world."

Waldvogel noticed a half-empty bottle of calvados, a local apple brandy, on the desk. That would
explain Reubold's odd behavior. Perhaps he had
drunken himself. . . .

"No," Reubold said, sliding into a sitting position. Both feet were planted firmly on the floor,
but his body had fallen back against the wall. "It's
not the brandy if that's what you're wondering."

Waldvogel shook his head. "No. I . . ."

"I received a directive from Dresser this morning," Reubold said. "The army wants to turn us all
into minelayers. Yes, that's right," he said in response
to the stricken look on Waldvogel's face. "Minelayers.

Nothing official yet. No lightning bolt from the high command. Just a note preparing us for the fall of the axe."

"But they can't."

Now it was Reubold's turn to look shocked. "You *are* a boffin, aren't you? Gods can do as they wish, my naive friend. It is a shame," he said, unfolding his body from the bed to stand, "that we never got to experience the true potential of your remarkable boats and wonderful guns. Although it is quite evident that your hydrofoils make the boats go very fast. A little clumsy up on those long legs. Not agile, if you understand." He said those things as if they were acceptable traits, but his manner changed as he continued. "Your guns"— he emphasized the words with arched eyebrows— "are erratic. Perhaps dangerous to the enemy one day, but particularly dangerous to our men now. Our gunners especially."

Waldvogel's words poured out in explanation. "The guns expel poisonous gases through the breechblock. The funnels are meant to direct the blast away. I told them . . ." He stopped, trying to arrange his thoughts. "Many times. I told them. . . ."

"Yes, yes," Reubold ended the explanation. "I attended the classes and read the manuals. You were careful to explain everything." He changed the subject. "You know that we will have to remove the boat's sea legs—the foils. If she couldn't fire torpedoes from that height, she can't drop mines with her hull that far out of the water, either. So all six boats will be held in port, returned to their original configuration. The Trinities will be removed and the original twenty millimeters installed in the gun wells." A humorous thought struck him. "We are moving backward."

"Fregattenkapitan Reubold, can't you talk to Admiral Dresser? Perhaps if you explain that we have very nearly resolved the problems." He began to tick off a list of difficulties they had overcome. "The steering. The rudders and struts. The mounts and traverse mechanism for the guns." His mind worked rapidly to build a case for the defense while Reubold listened without comment. "The men's training. The gun well. Oh, yes." He suddenly remembered. "Overheating. The engines no longer overheat the way that they used to. We've corrected that. I've worked so hard to perfect these boats. They are very fine weapons. Every day I think; 'How can I make them better?' I think: 'If I do this or do that, we can solve the problems.' Perhaps if you go and tell them, they will listen to you. You are highly decorated. A hero of the Fatherland. A Knight's Cross! There, you see. They will listen to you. They must listen to you."

Reubold looked into the pleading eyes and shook his head slowly. "Not me," he said, walking to the desk. "They won't listen to me. Goering has made sure of that. I am not welcome in Berlin. Nor are my opinions. And what would I tell them? That the bow rides too high out of the water because of the foils so that we can't shoot your lovely guns forward. We must shoot them to port or starboard and sometimes we actually hit what we aim at. Should I tell them that we must constantly inspect the hull around the foil struts because, although they make the boats as fleet as stags, they have a tendency to snap off."

"That was in the beginning," Waldvogel reminded him. "The hull and struts have been reinforced. They haven't been given a chance. I thought that you supported them? That your interest was genuine?"

"Don't you understand?" Reubold said. "The Reich applauds failure. They embrace it like a long-lost relative. Success breeds suspicion and foments enemies. To fail is to be shunned, to fall off the stage, and exit the absurd play with its cast of remarkable idiots and madmen. Be joyous, Waldvogel. Don't despair, we have been granted the special privilege of invisibility. We exist, and yet do not exist."

"But don't you see . . ." The korvettenkapitan struggled to find an argument that would reverse this terrible injustice. "You must find a way," Waldvogel said. "They will not listen to me. You must be the one that carries this message. You're a brave man. I am nothing of the sort. But you are brave. Honored. Everyone has said this of you."

"Yes," Reubold said quickly. After a moment of silence when his shoulders appeared to sag and dullness swept over his eyes, he added: "Yes, it is well known that I am a brave man," and this time the words were edged in humiliation but carried inevitability. "Were I brave, I would kill myself outright. As it is," he moved to the desk and opened the top drawer, "I have chosen to kill myself one needle at a time.

Waldvogel looked into the drawer. In one corner, lying on a blue velvet cloth, was a syringe and several small vials.

"Morphine," Reubold answered Waldvogel's questioning glance. "At first for the pain of a broken body. Later, because it helped me to escape the world of excess that I created. Now, because life has gone mad and I have a covenant with the devil. My life in exchange for eternal peace. After the life that I've lived, I deserve that much."

When Waldvogel spoke his voice was steady, confident, as if the truth of what he said was undeniable. "Your life is not yours to take, only to give."

Reubold slid the drawer shut. "I have given so much of me, Waldvogel, that there is nothing left. I am as you see me now, a man who once was. Dresser appears anxious to appease the great General Rommel. Who am I to defy the gods? I follow orders without hesitation because . . ." He let the sentence hang. "Make preparations for dismantling the hydrofoils and removing the cannon. Your wonderful boats will soon become trawlers."

"I thought that they meant as much to you, Fregattenkapitan, as they do me," Waldvogel said.

"But of course they do, Korvettenkapitan Waldvogel," Reubold said. There was no compassion in his words. "But as with all things in the Reich, only so long as is expedient."

The two Mosquito PR Mk XVI, painted the standard PR blue, flew side by side, sweeping the area 35,000 feet below. In their bellies, where bombs would have been carried had they been B models, were two F24 Split Vertical cameras peering from two separate ports. Farther along the fuselage, just aft of the wings, were two F52 Split Vertical cameras and an F24 Oblique camera.

Accompanying these two photographic reconnaissance planes was another Mosquito aircraft,
but of a different sort. It was an Mk FB VI, and pro-
truding from its blunt nose were four .303 caliber
machine guns, and directly beneath them, almost
hidden in the round body of the aircraft, were
four 20-millimeter Hispano cannons. It was the FB
VI's duty to ensure that the two unarmed Mosquitoes could go about their job, undisturbed by enemy
aircraft.

The PRs were stationed at Benson and had been
since early in the war, but the FB came from a Pathfinder base at Walker and was flown by a Polish
crew: Pilot-Sergeant Casimir Gierek and Navigator/
Radar Operator Jozef Jagello of the No. 105 Squadron. They had escaped to England soon after the
fall of Poland and had two things in common. First,
they hated the Germans with every once of their
strength and lived for the day when they could return to their homeland. Second, they hated the Rus-
sians with every ounce of their strength and lived for
the day that they could return to their homeland.
Other than that, they were complete opposites.

Gierek squirmed, trying to get comfortable atop
the parachute that fit into the hollow box that was
his seat, below his buttocks. He stretched his left
leg along the thigh rest just underneath the compass attached to the instrument panel and glanced
from the oil and fuel pressure gauges to the left
and right manifold pressure gauge. He had yet to
master the art of becoming comfortable in the tiny
cockpit of the two-man aircraft.

Jagello, on the other hand, seemed entirely at
home in the confines of the Mosquito. He seldom

spoke, hardly moved, and, once settled into his seat
situated to the right and slightly behind Gierek's,
was content to consult his charts, read the compass, make navigational computations, and watch
the soft green face of the radar screen in front of
him.

They had, before they flew off to rendezvous with
the two photographic reconnaissance unit Mosquitoes, gone over the details of the mission with their
squadron commander. After he was satisfied that
they knew exactly where and when they were to accomplish their mission, they walked to the aero-
drome and talked with the Welsh RAF sergeant who
led their ground crew. "Erks," the British called
them, Gierek discovered one night at a squadron
get-together, but no one was sure why. The sergeant's
name was Williams, and Gierek was convinced that
his booming voice and slow delivery were somehow
based on the misconception that the language difficulties that sometimes arose between the two na-
tionalities could be overcome with words delivered
patiently, and at a great volume.

Both Poles finally accepted Williams and his ec-
centricities, especially after they saw the great care
that he lavished on their aircraft. They were not
entirely sure about Williams's eternal companion,
the Black Prince.

"Mascot," Williams shouted at them in explanation, and then began some ridiculous sign language
that was apparently intended to clarify the presence of a large black dog, whose fur was coated
with oil from the hangar floor.

"He looks like a bear," Gierek commented, eyeing the beast with some suspicion but to Williams's

untutored ears it sounded like: "Eee luks lik ah beer." Gierek's English was substantially less refined than Jagello's.

"Yes," Williams agreed loudly, as if the two were thirty yards away, and then bent down and roughly stroked the solemn dog whose eyes were hidden behind a thick mass of greasy fur. "Good dog. Bloody good luck." The Black Prince responded by ponderously shaking his large head in slow awkward motions, his wide ears flopping ludicrously in the air.

What Jagello and Gierek came to understand is that the English mechanics viewed the Black Prince as a good-luck token and so, too, eventually, did the Polish members of No. 105 Squadron. To catch sight of the Prince before you took off on a sortie was necessary for a successful return. It worked nearly all of the time, enough so that the consensus was that the Black Prince was indeed, lucky.

The one member of the squadron who felt otherwise was Gierek, who thought the animal nothing more than a pest. There existed a silent conflict between the two, Gierek unwilling to give credence to either the dog's ability to bring luck, or comment on the fact that he alone despised the animal.

The Black Prince seemingly ignored the pilot's distaste for him and chose, on a regular basis, to collapse in a heap of filthy black fur in front of the plane's left wheel. Gierek had named the aircraft *Kele* after his hometown in the foothills of the Carpathian Mountains, and Williams and the others were used to the Polish pilot storming into the hangar immediately before each mission, pointing in anger at *Kele* and sputtering a single word: "dawk."

Williams would then dispatch one of the men in a lorry out to the hardstand, carefully lift the apparently unconscious dog, and place him in the bed of the truck.

This, to Gierek, was a far too common occurrence. To Jagello it was just one more item to be checked off the preflight list.

"Cherbourg," Jagello said, nodding below them. The reconnaissance aircraft would drop down to 30,000 feet and begin mapping the area with their cameras while the Fighter-Bomber stayed well above them, searching the skies for German fighters. Flak was almost incidental, the enemy having learned that it was better to save their ammunition for large bomber raids than to reveal their positions trying to shoot down aircraft that were virtually out of range anyway.

"E-boat pens," Gierek said, scanning the sky. "Our German friends are going to have many visitors, soon." *Kele* had led bombing raids on harbor facilities, U-boat pens, rail yards, and enemy fortifications. They were Pathfinders, leading the bombers into the target—marking the way. But always it was the same, the satisfaction that they were helping to kill Germans with each mission, and each mission brought them closer to the day when they could return home. "Anything?"

"Clear," Jagello said watching the radar. "Everything is clear."

"I wonder if they'll let us lead the raid. We've flown over Cherbourg enough to be able to walk the streets with our eyes closed. Will they, do you think?"

"I don't know," Jagello said.

"I shall speak with Papa," Gierek said, referring to their squadron commander. "Papa is very influential with the Wing Commander."

"Perhaps."

"Will it take place just before the invasion?"

"What?" Jagello said.

"The raid? On the E-boat pens? It's getting so that they bombed the same targets a dozen times over. There will be nothing left when they land. They're running out of targets. Don't you think?"

"No."

" 'No?' " Gierek said in surprise. "What do you mean 'no'?"

"The E-boat pens," Jagello said. "They haven't been bombed. When they are, it will be a very big raid. I think that it will stir a bees' nest when we return."

"Oh," Gierek said, satisfied with the answer. "Then we shall accompany them. More dead Germans."

"Anymore," Jagello said in one of the rare times that he ventured an opinion, "it is not so much the dead Germans that I am concerned with. It is the safe return of two Polish airmen."

"That is nothing to worry about," Gierek said grimly. "Don't you remember that we are blessed with the lucky dog?"

Chapter 9

"Edland?" DeLong said to Cole, puzzled.

"Lieutenant Commander," Cole said as he followed DeLong to the cockpit of the 155 boat. "ONI. We'll take the one sixty-eight and Dean's boat with us. Make sure everybody's topped off, and for God's sake have them check the torpedoes."

The PT boat's torpedoes ran on 180-proof ethyl alcohol. Enterprising crewmen often mixed a potent cocktail of half a cup of grapefruit juice with half a cup of alcohol to create kick-a-poo joy juice. The navy countered by adding pink coloring to the alcohol and passing the word that it was poison. The sailors countered by passing the alcohol through a chammy cloth or a loaf of bread with both ends cut off to filter the supposedly poisonous torpedo fuel. It was a standoff between the navy and the thirsty sailors. Now Cole ordered the alcohol levels in the torpedoes checked before each mission so he wasn't embarrassed by the torpedoes running out of fuel short of their intended target and dropping impotently to the seabed.

"Wasn't he the guy . . . ?" DeLong said.

"Yeah," Cole said quickly. "Get Dean and Ewing, and their execs, and have them meet us aboard the one fifty-five boat at fourteen thirty hours. Have duplicate charts ready. I'll will lay out the mission then and we'll get under way by nineteen hundred hours. Tell both of them that this trip is going to be tricky and I don't want any screwups."

"It couldn't be any worse than picking up that Polish pilot," DeLong said.

"Oh, yes it could."

Dean and Cy Moontz were the last to squeeze around the table into the crowded Day Room of the 155 boat.

"Jeez, Moose," Ensign Johnson of the 168 boat said, "haven't you stopped growing yet?"

Moose Moontz, former linebacker at the University of Illinois, snorted in response.

"Okay," Cole said. "Listen up, gentlemen. This is a tricky mission; here's the low-down."

The other officers in Day Room grew silent as Cole began the briefing. "The Germans have a new type of E-boat," he said. "Faster and more heavily armed than conventional boats. This mission is to capture some prisoners who will tell us something about the new boat. We need to know what we're up against—what the invasion fleet is up against—before the big event. That's the plan at least. I have a single copy of the report of our first encounter with the E-boat. You can pass it around, but it's not to leave this boat. Basically the plan is for us to lay just off the French coast at a point marked on the charts provided to you. Our location should put us near the most obvious path of any E-boats returning from patrols at either the Bill of Portsmouth or Lyme Bay."

"Skipper," Moose said, looking up from the chart. "You mean lay off the coast and get a look-see at them boats?"

"No," Cole said. "I mean capture some prisoners. That means an engagement. Maybe," he added, watching the reactions on the men's faces, "even one of the boats."

The men in the room exchanged shocked glances. They'd been fighting E-boats for a while. They had a healthy respect for them and, with that, respect for their capabilities. Capturing prisoners in the past had simply been luck. This was different.

"Excuse me, Skipper," Ewing said. "But those things are more than a handful in a running gunfight."

"Yeah," Moose said. "Usually, they're gunning and we're running."

The men laughed nervously.

"Knock it off," Cole said. This wasn't going to be easy, and every man at the table knew that there was a good chance of one or some of them being killed. He hated Edland and this ridiculous mission. He was putting his men in danger—for nothing. "We'll need to disable it," Cole continued, "board and secure it, and return it to port for examination. It doesn't do us any good to sink it. That's if we're lucky. If not, we'll just scoop some Krauts out of the water and haul ass for home."

"It's a lot safer that way," DeLong commented.

"Apparently our safety is not an issue," Cole said. "The successful capture of that boat is. Go over your charts, check your boats, and pass the word to your crews. We cast off at nineteen hundred hours. I don't want any screwups. You'll get your frequencies and call signs before we shove off. Lay off your IFF broadcasts. The Krauts know them anyway. . . . Randy," Cole jerked his head at his executive officer, who followed him topside.

Cole was silent for a moment as he checked the tie-down on the radar mast. Finally, he turned to DeLong. "I want you to sit out this one."

DeLong looked at him, surprised. "Sit out? Why?"

"It's going to be tough," Cole said. "I want you to sit it out."

"When aren't they, Skipper? What's going on here? Don't you think I'm pulling my weight around here?"

"Let's not make it a federal case." Cole heard the men talking below. He just wished that DeLong would just do as he was told. It was that feeling again—helplessness. He couldn't help his men, he couldn't save Lowe. He couldn't get anyone to listen to him because they were out in the daylight and not at night, and they never went out in the daylight, and all Lowe did was smile at him.

"What the hell is going on here, Skipper?" DeLong asked.

"You want your own boat, don't you?" Cole said.

"What's that got to do with the price of apples?"

Nothing, Cole thought. He was trying to find a way to convince DeLong not to go. He saw Randy DeLong standing next to the wheel and fear gripped him as Delong turned to smile at him. "You won't get your boat if you're dead," Cole finally said in frustration, trying to mask his anxiety with humor. He forced a smile, but it froze and he knew that whatever he said would not make sense to De-Long. He was helpless again.

"I don't plan on being killed," DeLong said.

"You want me to order you to stay?" Cole said. "I could do that, you know." He could, but Cole realized that he could never bring himself to shame his friend. He was responsible for Randy DeLong, and Moose and Ewing and the others. Responsible. They all depended on him to make the right decisions, to protect them, to bring them back home, but his power to do so had been taken away, and all he could do was watch as they died.

"What's eating you, Skipper?" DeLong said softly.

Cole shook his head and pulled on the mast's lashings, testing the tension in the wire.

"I've got to go, Skipper. You know that. I couldn't live with myself if I wasn't out there with the guys." DeLong smiled. "Hell, half the time we ignore your orders anyway. You know that."

Cole knew that. They followed him because they liked and respected him and they had a job to do, but they didn't know that Cole could no longer protect them. "A favor," he tried again. "Do me this one favor."

"Don't ask me to do that, Skipper," DeLong said. "Look, I know what we're in for. I know it's going to be tough. Hell, we might not even find an E-boat.

We could end up empty-handed. Besides, we're a team, you and me. You know, like Abbott and Costello.

Cole nodded and watched a string of LCMs slide past. He was afraid, sick with fear, certain that he would never be able again to help his friends, his men. He felt abandoned and helpless, and dismay swept over him so completely that he felt like he couldn't breathe. He was afraid because, in this light, Randy DeLong looked exactly like Harry Lowe.

"Mutton," Topper Schiffer said, "is just the sort of thing to make a man glad there's a woman around."

"Yes," Hardy said, uncomfortable at the comment. Beatrice had passed the plates round to Topper, who had carved and dropped thick slices of meat on the plates, handing one to Hardy, one to Beatrice, and keeping one for himself. Hardy had enjoyed his tea with them two days before, and had agreed, reluctantly, to return for supper. He had accepted despite a little voice that warned him he was behaving foolishly and would only embarrass himself. It was that he found himself wanting in the art of making small talk—filling his part of the conversation during tea with awkward compliments on the quality of the scones baked by Beatrice. When Topper pressed him about service aboard one of His Majesty's ships, Hardy found himself a bit more at ease, but he still answered the questions stiffly, trying to decide what sort of accounts were fit for discussion with a lady present, how much Beatrice and Topper really understood

of what he said, and at the same time berating
himself for the clod and bore that he was. Beatrice, God bless her kind heart, listened closely to
all that he said, interrupting only twice to offer
more tea.

And when Hardy had finally extricated himself
from the tiny table crammed in the cluttered back-
room of the art supply store, Topper said: "Come
to supper. I won't take no for an answer, Captain
Hardy." His exuberance nearly knocked Hardy
over and the question was flung at him with no
preamble; he was unprepared and had therefore
not concocted a suitable reply offering his thanks,
but declining because of duty—responsibilities
aboard ship, or some silly, meaningless excuse.

"Of course," Hardy said, regretting the words
immediately. Doubts pummeled him without ceas-
ing as he walked back to the ship, accompanied by
sharp notions that he would certainly regret his acceptance, and the evening would prove awkward
for everyone. "Stupid. Stupid," he muttered under
his breath, denouncing himself for attempting any
social event except those connected with official
activities. Put him in his uniform, with prescribed
rules and regulations amid the flurry of the King's
Instructions, and he was entirely at ease. Everything laid out in an appropriate manner, enlisted
men and officers, with the proper ceremony observed—that was how it was to be; that was Captain
Hardy's life, his world.

But for some unaccountable reason he had ventured from the safety of his world, paid a visit to a
shop on the pretext of needing art supplies, when
his Day Cabin aboard *Firedancer* was filled with every-

thing that he could conceivably need. He had gone in and when he saw Beatrice, panic surged through his chest and he heartily damned his weakness. And now supper.

Topper ladled a huge portion of peas onto his plate beside the mutton. "Must be exciting at sea, Captain Hardy?"

"A bit," Hardy said, remembering that it was bad manners to smash your peas to a green pulp before scooping them up on your fork. Remembered that much, he thought, pleased at the tiny victory that he had wrested from the potential disaster of the evening.

"You must show us more of your work," Beatrice said shyly, her soft voice barely carrying across the table. She sat directly opposite Hardy, and he made every effort to keep his eyes from falling on hers.

"Yes, do," Topper said emphatically. "What you've brought by is splendid. Can't draw a straight line myself but Bea there knows her stuff. Don't you, Bea?"

"Oh, Topper. Please don't go on like that."

"Take the credit, Bea," Topper said. "Your work is top-notch in my book."

Hardy eyed a small carrot suspiciously, not sure if he should cut it in half or chance cramming the whole thing in his mouth at once. Drawing his knife on the innocent vegetable seemed a bit extravagant, but he worried that forcing the thing into his mouth might result in an unintended comic moment; his cheeks puffed out like an adder as he tried to crush the carrot with his teeth. He chose the knife, feeling ludicrous as he stabbed the carrot and pinned it with his fork, slicing through its body.

"So you'll do it then?" Topper said to him.

The knife stopped. "Beg pardon?"

"Bring them around, Captain. Your paintings and such. Show them off a bit."

Hardy's mouth suddenly went dry. He wavered between answering and reaching for a glass of water.

Topper suddenly slapped the table. China and silverware bounced into the air. "Can you believe it, Bea? Can you believe it, Captain Hardy? Two days I knew that you were coming, two days for me to have some sherry in the house, and have I done it? I have not."

"Topper Schiffer, you've frightened ten years from me," Beatrice said. "Pounding the table like that, and in front of Captain Hardy."

"Well, there's nothing to be done," Topper said, quickly standing and yanking the napkin from his shirt collar. "Nothing to be done but pop down to Burly's and get us a bottle."

Fear gripped Hardy. Topper would leave and he would be alone. With Beatrice.

"No, Mr. Schiffer," he said, trying to hide the alarm that he felt. "It's not necessary for you to go out."

"Topper," Beatrice instantly joined in. "I'm sure that we can make do with tea."

"Tea?" He slid his arm into a tattered coat. "Tea, Captain Hardy," he said, appalled at the notion. "And a fighting man at the table? A sailor at that. Tea won't do, Bea." He disappeared through the curtains and Hardy heard that despicable little bell tinkle happily as the door opened and closed.

A cold silence invaded the little room. Hardy glanced at the partially dissected carrot and carefully laid his knife and fork on either side of the plate. Somewhere he heard the steady tick of a clock. He glanced at Beatrice and forced a smile.

"The mutton was satisfactory, Miss Schiffer. Most satisfactory."

"Oh, do you think so?" she said brightly. "I've never quite gotten the hang of fixing it, although you'd think that it was fit for the King the way Topper goes on about it."

Hardy swallowed heavily. "Fit enough for me, Miss Schiffer," he said. He studied the room as the unseen clock grew louder, each tick an accusation—*talk, talk, talk*. "Shall I help you with the table, then?" Hardy finally blurted out.

"Oh, no. No, Captain Hardy." Beatrice jumped up and began quickly gathering dishes. "It's woman's work, you know."

Hardy stood, grateful for something to do and for the noise that broke the oppressive quiet. "Nonsense. Nonsense. I've never held with that. Work is work. Man or woman, makes no difference. The only thing a woman can do that a man can't is have . . ." He suddenly realized what he was saying and the words stuck in his throat. He was frozen solid, a cluster of silverware trapped in his hand. *My God. My God, could you have been a bigger fool? What a callous, stupid thing to say.* "I'm terribly sorry," he said, the words rushing out in embarrassment. In polite company of all things. At the dinner table, talking about women giving birth to . . . *children*.

"No, don't you give it a second thought, Captain Hardy," Beatrice said easily. She scrapped food from the plate into a small bucket. "You're quite right about that. And I find your attitude most enlightened. Most men treat childbirth as if it never happened. It's the most natural thing in the world. A wonderful event."

Relief filled his hollow body and he became eternally grateful that she did not stab him with a carving knife in outrage.

The awkwardness was broken and he stood, quietly handing her dirty dishes, filled with admiration for her gentleness. She spoke continuously as she took the dishes and placed them in the dry sink. Her voice was soothing and she moved with unhurried grace. She was at ease, not only because this was the kitchen, her domain, Hardy thought, but because she was one of those rare creatures with integrity of existence—she was imperturbable. He thought at first that she might have been as nervous as he and that talking was a way to overcome the fear that she felt, but he decided that that was not it; she was happy, and happiness expressed itself in an endless stream of words. She said something about a sister, and her sister's children, and what a lovely child their youngest, Jack, was. She spoke of Mrs. Tarkington just down the street and how her eyesight, poor dear, was beginning to fail her and how she, Beatrice, always found time to take her some food and visit with her each day.

Hardy was amazed as this compassionate creature told him about people who filled her life and from whom she derived so much pleasure. It was a family, Hardy suddenly realized, she was speaking of a family. Not just father-mother-brother-sister, but a gathering of people whose lives were linked through the kind heart of Beatrice Schiffer. Her sensitivity was boundless, her understanding of human nature and her acceptance of people and their foibles unlimited.

She stopped suddenly and turned in distress. "Oh," she said. "I have done it again. Prattle on like a schoolgirl. Beatrice Marlene Schiffer, when will you ever learn? How can I be so silly?" She fixed Hardy with a look of sincere apology. "Captain Hardy, I must ask you to forgive me."

Hardy stood, holding a half-filled gravy boat. He set it on the table. "Miss Schiffer," he began. "Don't . . ."

"Beatrice, please."

Hardy nodded, not trusting himself to use her Christian name for fear that he would stumble over it. "You mustn't concern yourself. I enjoyed very much those things that you spoke of. Ships and the sea. That's all I've ever been. Around men of course. And old *Firedancer*. They are all that I have. I had forgotten that other lives exist, that there is something beyond what I have been accustomed to. Odd, isn't it? I never considered anything that wasn't right in front of these old, tired eyes."

She watched him choose his words carefully, letting him speak at his own pace, feel his way around an unfamiliar subject.

"I must confess," he drew a deep breath and was silent for a moment. "That I made excuses to come to the store so that I might have the opportunity to speak with you." He abandoned all caution, surprising himself. "A few words from you were all that I needed to tide me over through the worst of times. I am probably the clumsiest man in the world when it comes to making myself known. It is nothing for me to do so on *Firedancer*. I know that sort of life all right. But with you. Here. Now. Well, that's a different matter, altogether." Hardy heard the front door open and the bell ring merrily.

"There," Topper announced, pushing through the curtain. "Here I come with the sherry. Got the old man out of bed I did. Told him that I had a right proper hero to supper and that the man needed something to brace him against the cold."

Beatrice and Hardy exchanged glances as Topper scurried about the kitchen, searching through cabinets for glasses, giving a blow-by-blow description of his discussion with the old man who ran the spirits shop. He stopped.

"Why, you've cleared the table," he said in astonishment. "Bea, the table's cleared."

"Yes, Topper," Beatrice said, smiling softly at Hardy.

"In front of the Captain?"

"Captain Hardy helped me, Topper."

"Helped you? Good Lord, Bea, you didn't put the man to work in the kitchen, did you?"

Beatrice turned to her brother. "He volunteered, Topper," she said calmly.

"Quite right, Mr. Schiffer," Hardy said warmly, his eyes falling on Beatrice. "It was my pleasure."

Chapter 10

Even under the low light of the arc lamps, the S-boats of Flotilla 11 looked dangerous to Kommodore Walters. The armored skullcap bridge and the wheelhouse roof painted a dark gray, contrasting with the pale gray of the vertical surfaces, sat low on the deck; its black windows soulless eyes that stared into the dim interior. The clean hull swept back from the bow's knife-edge to the sculpted cutouts for the enclosed torpedo tubes. Just aft of the bridge was a twin-mount 2cm gun with its armored shield surrounded by ammunition lockers, racks for extra barrels, and helmet boxes. Next was a large rubber dinghy and a 4cm Bofor's cannon, its long, thin barrel secured so that it pointed aft.

It was the deepened and enlarged well in the bow that held Walters's interest, or rather what sat

in the well. The Trinity guns, he had been told, recoilless cannon with stubby barrels, were an aberra-
tion on a vessel whose sleek lines denoted speed.
The guns and their mount, rising from within the
deck, were a hideous growth, begging to be cut out
and tossed overboard. That, in fact, was going to
happen. The monstrosity would be removed and a
4-barrelled 2cm Flakvierling, or 3.7cm flak gun,
would be inserted in the well.

Walters moved to the edge of the quay and
peered into the dark water that surrounded the
boat's pale hull. The hull below the waterline was
covered in a black, anti-fouling paint so that any
light that penetrated the water was immediately
sucked up by the dark surface.

"You can't see them," Reubold said behind Walters.

The kommodore turned as Reubold joined him
at the edge. The Raven, he was called for his dark
moods and fast boats. He looks ill, Walters thought,
noting the man's sunken eyes.

"There," Reubold said, pointing into the dingy
water. "If you lean over, you might see the leading
edges of the struts and supports. Be careful not to
fall in."

Walters made a show of not being interested. He
studied the roof of the pen. The large work lights
glared back at him. Electric cables ran along the pit-
ted concrete ceiling, clinging to the dull surface
like thick vines, dropped down the wall, and disappeared into the rusting, gray metal cabinets. The
large derrick that served the boats rumbled down
its glistening rails suspended from the ceiling and
stopped near the head of the pen.

Walters glanced around. "Busy place," he commented.

"It's the war," Reubold said. "It continually interferes with day-to-day activities."

"Are they as fast as they say?' Walters asked, restraining himself from looking into the water. He knew that Reubold thought him a fool and Rommel's stooge, and the act of peering into a greasy, stagnant pool of water simply reinforced that idea. There was a mutual distrust of staff and line: staff certain that the men who did the fighting were egotistical and erratic, with line firmly convinced that staff was nothing more than a brotherhood of fat, soft idiots who knew nothing of the sea or boat handling. The tension arose continually, when each thought that the other intruded in its domain, and lessened their efficiency. No matter, Walters knew; it was a common state of affairs that had to be dealt with. The kommodore viewed himself as a diplomat, and his mission was to investigate the resources of the Kriegsmarines in defense of the Atlantic Wall. Even if they were volatile men such as Reubold.

" 'They' say so much. It's very difficult to keep up with what is actually said."

"Forty knots," Walters said, baiting Reubold.

"Forty knots," the fregattenkapitan scoffed. "You people . . . sixty knots and more if the sea is right. We can keep that speed for thirty minutes at a time."

"Why just thirty?"

"Her wings won't take any more than that."

"Wings?"

"Hydrofoils," Reubold said. "Waldvogel's wings,

we call them. The fellow that invented them and
that mighty weapon on the bow."

Walters watched as several men worked around
the triple-gun mount, inserting chains and strapped
through the supports. There was nothing threatening about the guns. They did not look deadly—they
were just machines, awkwardly industrial. They were
not graceful. They were functional and ugly.

"Off they come," Reubold said, following the kommodore's gaze. "Orders, you know. Perhaps your orders."

"No, not mine," Walters said, unfazed by the accusation. "What is their range?"

"Just over seventy-nine hundred meters, maximum load. Standard load, half that." Reubold lit a
cigarette and regarded Walters. "Why are you here,
Kommodore? Why travel all the way from Paris
with Allied fighters snapping at your heels, just to
ask a few questions? Dresser has already issued orders to dismantle the boats."

"He was a bit premature," Walters said, walking
away from Reubold. He needed a moment to
think and the fregattenkapitan's negativity inter-
fered with his thinking. But Reubold followed, apparently unwilling to let go.

"You mean that you've come to give us a reprieve?" Reubold asked, the question nearly a statement, wreathed in sarcasm. "How kind of you. You
must be very close to the fieldmarschal. Tell me,
does he know that we exist down here? Does he
have confidence in us? We are such a little force—
nothing to be reckoned with. It is so difficult for
we who fight to understand the complexities of

command." Reubold examined the silent vessels. "No matter. They aren't ready for war yet—not real war. Not yet."

They stopped at the bow, Walters studying the strange guns. Reubold was a defeatist but the kommodore laid that thought aside. One day he would say too much and the SS would come and take him away. The guns caught his attention again. "Can they be fired at top speed?" He turned, wanting to be more precise with the question. "They can't be very accurate if you are moving through the water at that speed. Have you overcome that?"

"You mean can we actually hit anything?" Reubold said, "Hit, yes. Aim, no. Still if one puts enough rounds in the air, one is bound to hit what one is aiming at. Eventually. Kommodore? Why won't you answer my question? Why are you here?"

"To learn," Walters said, lost in thought.

"Yes," Reubold said, "but *why* are you here?"

"The fieldmarschal has determined that the most effective use of these boats is in laying mines across potential invasion corridors," Walters said. "I agree. From what you've told me, and from what I already know, it is highly unlikely that these S-boats, as intriguing as they are, have any likelihood of inflicting significant damage on the invasion fleet."

"We have certainly raised hell with enemy convoys in the Channel."

Walters continued to study the guns. "Everything is the invasion, Reubold," he announced. "Preparation is all. The fieldmarschal has decreed that the enemy must be stopped at the beaches. Sea mines are a very important part of that strategy. They can potentially disrupt an invasion fleet, influence the enemy's tactics . . ."

"We're lucky," Reubold mused, "if the enemy possesses no minesweepers."

"What?" Walters asked, the connection lost.

"Nothing," Reubold answered.

Overhead the gantry burst into life, the diesels driving the crossbeam along the tracks toward the boat. Thick steel cables with hooks, pulleys, and straps swung rhythmically with the movement. An oberbootsmann shouted instructions, sending half a dozen matrose onto the S-boat's deck to secure the straps around the gun.

"After they pull her stinger," Reubold commented, "we'll take her out of the water, remove the foils and mounts, replace the shafts, and she'll be a good little girl again."

The gantry stopped with a loud clank, the sound echoing off the concrete walls and ceiling.

"Time-consuming, no doubt," Walters said. "Removing the guns."

The steel cables played out, dropping the hooks and straps toward the gun.

"Something that requires particular care, I should imagine," Walters said. Reubold cocked his head in question.

"A very complex task," the kommodore said, looking at Reubold. There was a message behind the words.

Reubold cupped his hands around his mouth and shouted: "Hold." He turned back to Walters. "You're playing a dangerous game, Kommodore," he said coldly. "I'm not sure that I care to play."

"Games are for children, Fregattenkapitan. Perhaps," he added, "your strange vessels are destined to play another role. My only interest is defending the Fatherland from her enemies."

Reubold considered the kommodore's reply. He answered with a smile. "I might be one of those enemies."

"Are you, Fregattenkapitan?" Walters said.

Reubold's smile grew broader, but he did not answer.

"Well," Walters said as the straps swung back and forth. "I must return to Paris and select the field-marschal's wine. I'm very pleased to see that the work is progressing at a very deliberate pace so that there is no danger of damage to the boats."

"Admiral Dresser may find the lack of progress confusing," Reubold said.

"Yes," Walters said, "so might the fieldmarschal should he learn of it. But they are both busy men. I'm sure such details would go unnoticed for a time." His eyes swept the long, low, ominous shape of the S-boat. "Before I entered the Kriegsmarine, my father held out the hope that I would choose the ministry. Are you familiar with the works of Charles Fletcher Leckie?"

"No. Who is he?"

"He was an American clergyman and teacher. He died in 1927. I actually attended one of his lectures in England. He said: 'It is a world of startling possibilities.' Don't you agree, Fregattenkapitan?"

Reubold eyed the kommodore with a new appreciation. "It is a world of surprises."

"Yes," Walters said. "Truly. Shall we combine the

two then, and say that it would be to our benefit to investigate any possibility to surprise our enemies? Good day, Fregattenkapitan Reubold."

The fregattenkapitan pulled a cigarette from his case, lit it, and gave the strange visit by Walters a great deal of thought. What he had learned while immersed in the hierarchy of Nazi high command was that everyone wanted something. Certainly they all wanted to win the war, but success was decided by personal gain, not victory for the Fatherland. He kept that observation to himself, of course. The heady talk that floated around glittering receptions and opulent dinners as counterpoint to Brahms or Wagner was guaranteed to advance one's position. In a world where so little was certain—this was.

Walters had come to set a plan in motion, but Reubold had no idea what the plan entailed. Was it necessary that I know? he asked himself. *Is it so important at this late date in the war that I suddenly become privy to what others have in store for me?* Reubold's answer was blunt: *You've never cared before—why now?*

They had run most of the night, relying on radar to see into the blackness, in unspoken relief that dark clouds covered the moon and stars so that their broad wakes were nearly hidden.

DeLong took the wheel of 155 almost immediately as Cole moved to the farthest reaches of the tiny bridge, melting into the structure, a man finding sanctuary in solitude. It was as if, DeLong thought after glancing at the silent form, Cole had willed himself far away from the living, that he had built a prison and quietly closed the cell door.

DeLong switched on the hooded light over the pioneer compass to get his bearings, then quickly turned it off. Even the tiniest of lights on the flat plain of the English Channel was enough to alert a vigilant enemy.

Edland, as silent as Cole, stood behind DeLong, his arm wrapped casually in the intricate framework of the radar mast. He's a cool one, DeLong thought long after they had cleared the harbor and full night wrapped itself around the tiny vessels. All business. But he was the one who had told Cole, over a year ago—a century before—that the target was escorted by only a few MAS boats. No E-boats, he had said confidently in the steamy confines of the operations shack at Bastia.

"No E-boats," Edland had said in response to Moose's question.

"Good," Moose had said, voicing everyone's opinions. "I hate those guys."

"We'll go in on the step," Cole had said, rubbing the end of a pencil over his bottom lip in thought. His eyes traveled over the chart, lingered on the enemy convoy's supposed path, and narrowed in concentration. DeLong watched the Skipper and saw the questions forming in the man's brain. On the step—flank speed, hard-chinned hull out of the water, bow up, hungrily looking for the enemy— the only way that Cole operated.

"You guys are sure about this, huh?" Cole had finally said.

"We're sure," Edland returned quickly. His confidence eased their concerns.

"Sure as shootin'," Tommy Turner had confirmed to himself. Harry Lowe laughed and smiled broadly at Turner. It was fun to make Harry laugh, to drop a curse in the middle of a perfectly innocent sentence and catch Harry off guard. Harry didn't smoke or drink, and the only curse words he knew were mild—hell or damn—and even then, when he said them they really didn't sound like cussing. "Hell, man," DeLong had said after they'd known each other for a while, "you're not for real." He was good-natured, and the pictures of his wife showed an exquisite blonde flanked by a couple of kids. Harry and Cole were close—Harry the leavening to Cole's sometimes harsh moods—Harry there to bring reason to Cole's occasional outbursts. Harry the guy Cole went to when his own unidentified emotions had him wrapped so tightly that anything, *everything*, anyone did was wrong.

Harry Lowe, the guy who turned to Cole when the E-boats that weren't supposed to be there slid out from behind the enemy transports with a strange, stricken smile that said: I'm going to die.

Harry Lowe's matinee-idol good looks and his Clark Gable mustache disappeared in a flash of red as a 20mm shell blew his skull into a thousand pieces, covering the bridge, Cole, and DeLong with an obscene spray of flesh, blood, and brains.

"How far out, Barney?" Cole said into the microphone. DeLong was no longer in Bastia.

"Just about ten miles, Skip." Barney was navigating from the auxiliary compass and had the advantage of the radar set tucked into the starboard corner of the chart room. He also had a light when he needed it to consult the charts that led them to Edland's inlet.

"Can you make out Bill and Dean?" Cole asked DeLong.

"One sixty-eight is just abeam of us, to port," Edland said from the darkness. "Dean is off our starboard quarter. Both about eight hundred yards out."

"Good eyes," DeLong whistled softly in appreciation.

"I've been watching them for some time," Edland said, moving closer. "I'm sure that your radar man will confirm their position."

"Throttle back to twenty," Cole said, ignoring Edland. "Bill and Dean should pick up the speed change on radar. When we're five miles out, drop to ten and we'll ease her in. I'll put Rich in the bow with a lead line."

"That won't be necessary," Edland said. "It's deep water all the way to the cliff face."

"Keep an eye on everything, will you, Randy?" Cole said. "Commander, let's take a walk."

Edland followed Cole aft to a midway point of the Day Room canopy.

"This is about as private as we get on a PT boat," Cole said, his voice low and his features obscured in the darkness. "I'll forget all the niceties that come with rank and tell you if you ever again interfere in me running this boat, I'll give you another scar to add to that one."

"All I said . . ."

"I don't give a fuck what your reason is and I sure don't give a fuck about any of your opinions."

"I thought we agreed . . ."

"We agreed that you may run the show but I run the fucking boats. That's what we agreed on. You want an E-boat. I want to get out of this mess without getting my ass shot off, or piling the boats on some uncharted shoal, because when we're high and dry fifty feet from a bunch of Krauts, a simple 'Gee, I'm sorry as hell' won't mean a fucking thing."

The figure facing Cole in the darkness was silent for a moment. The PT boat pitched gently in the calm sea, the deep rumble of the engines vibrating throughout the deck planking. The passing water hissed playfully against the hull.

"Okay, Lieutenant," Edland said in a measured tone. "You've made your point. You're the captain."

"Yeah," Cole said, turning.

"It wasn't my fault," Edland said.

Cole stopped.

"It wasn't my fault. Your boats and your men."

Cole didn't bother to face Edland when he said: "No, it wasn't. It was mine for believing you."

Chapter 11

Matrose Willy Hellwig had been aboard S-204
for nearly a year. He was the youngest member of
the crew of twenty-eight, a loader on the forward
MG C/38 2cm Oerlikon gun, and not well liked by
the other members of the crew. Especially Leutnant Meurer. No, Bootsmannmaat Janzen despised
him even more than Meurer. Meurer simply held
Hellwig in disdain.

It wasn't Hellwig's fault. He was only nineteen
and he was not very comfortable around the doorknocker, and when it went off, the loud, constant
bang startled him so that he nearly forgot to feed
the shells into the hopper atop the gun. Then Janzen would curse Hellwig's stupidity, his mother's
idiocy for giving birth to such a dolt, his village—
he was from Cloppenburg, and the rest of the crew

found that somehow very amusing—and finally the Kriegsmarine for allowing itself to come to such a sorry state that it had to settle for imbeciles like Matrose Willy Hellwig.

So the end of each patrol brought a sense of tense relief to Hellwig as well as the first sliver of dawn that announced that it was time to seek the shelter of the S-boat pens in Cherbourg, where S-204 was safe from the Allied bees and Hellwig was safe from the boxing that Janzen gave his ears.

What a war.

They had seen nothing all night; the wind had been calm and the sea so mild that even the canvas dodgers that kept the sea from slipping over the low freeboard were dry. There was no Victory Pennant bearing the tonnage of destroyed enemy ships to fly just below the *Reichskriegflagge*—the State War Flag—but that suited Hellwig. That meant that his ears were safe from the stinging blows of Janzen or the constant ringing that he endured after the guns had ceased firing.

They had been on a *Lauertatik*, simply loitering around possible enemy convoy routes in hopes of sighting a target, with another Schnellboot—S-209— but sometime in the night S-209 had gone off on some unidentified mission and left S-204 alone. This intensified Hellwig's anxiety, but he kept his concerns to himself. Better to suffer in silence than give that brute Janzen an opportunity to slap him.

It had been a nightmare for Hellwig since leaving the *Schnellbootsschuleflotille* at Swinemunde. The training had been sparse and the instructors belligerent and Hellwig had been certain that he would be killed almost immediately when he got to the front. He had hoped that things would be much better at Cherbourg and S-Boot Flotilla 5. To his great surprise he hadn't been killed, but the abuse that he had suffered, this time at the hands of his comrades, had been worse than at Swinemunde. He realized that he had merely exchanged one level of hell for another.

What a war.

Liebs, the gun captain, ducked into the gun well and lit a cigarette, reemerging amid a cloud of smoke.

"Almost home, Willy," he said, relaxing as he enjoyed the minor luxury.

Hellwig coughed into the back of his hand, trying to avoid the smoke. He didn't like cigarettes and he was certain that the men surreptitiously blew smoke in his direction to torment him.

"Did you see that fat barmaid at the café?" Liebs said, leaning back against the rim of the well.

The men sometimes went to a tiny café in Urville. The food was horrible and the meals overpriced, and the waitresses treated their customers as if they were vermin.

"No," Hellwig said. He found the men's constant preoccupation with sex disgusting. He was secretly delighted when the French whores gave one of the men the clap. Serves them right.

"Big tits," Liebs said, holding his hands out from his chest in appreciation.

"No, I didn't see her," Hellwig said again, hoping his abrupt tone would send a message to Liebs.

"Why don't you two pay attention to your gun?" Janzen said, appearing next to the well. He unwrapped the straps from around binocular frames and put the lens to his eyes, studying something in the distance.

"We were talking about my gun," Lieb said, winking broadly at Hellwig. "Didn't you see that French cunt . . . ?" Hellwig saw Lieb stop talking and focus on Janzen. The bootsmann had stopped sweeping the distance ahead and locked on to something. A feeling of dread swept over Hellwig. Not here, not now. They were too close to home. Surely this was a mistake. Janzen was just playing with him. Just tormenting Hellwig like he always did.

Janzen held up his hand extending three fingers. It was a signal meant for Meurer in the bridge.

"What is it?" Lieb asked, moving to his position on the doorknocker.

Janzen said nothing. Hellwig looked aft, over the low edge of the gun well, for some signal of what was happening. What he saw shocked him. Gun crews were manning their guns. Wait. Something was wrong. They were almost home. He was just an assistant loader. Janh was the loader but he was ill and had been taken off the boat. Now he was the only one to load the gun. It wasn't fair. He needed help. There should be someone to help him.

Jansen's eyes never left the binoculars. "Get ready," he said calmly to Lieb and Hellwig.

Oh, no, no. Not now. They were home. This was a mistake, Hellwig thought, moving quickly to the ready ammunition boxes against the bulkhead. He saw Lieb push his shoulders into the padded mounts of the doorknocker and glance at him as if to say: "Ammunition." Hellwig hefted a shell pack in his arms, the weight of the explosives one more confirmation that something horrible was happening. He noticed that Janzen was gone and he suddenly missed the rough man's presence. If he had stayed next to the well everything would have been all right. Now it was just Lieb. The gunner retracted the chamber handle, feeding the first round into the breech.

"Probably some Frenchy out fishing or something," he muttered, adjusting the shoulder mounts. "Fucking Frenchies lost the war but they behave as if we did. These are restricted waters. But here they come. Stupid bastards." He threw Hellwig a harsh look. "Ready?"

Hellwig nodded, gripping the shell pack tightly to his chest. He felt the vibration in the deck increase and he knew Meurer was speeding up. His anticipation grew sharply at each meter consumed by the boat, collectively advancing the situation to an inevitable conclusion: he would die.

"See anything?" Lieb said.

Hellwig leaned over the edge of the well. Nothing. The blackness of the bluffs of the French coast and the sharp brightness of a newborn sun. The sky was pretty, he thought, orange and red but just above that a pale blue. He lost himself in the colors for just an instant but then remembered where he was when fear washed over him again.

"No. Nothing," Hellwig said, moving to the side of the gun. It wasn't fair. Janh should be here. *I can't do this myself.*

"I wish the hell that Janh was here," Lieb said.

Hellwig was relieved that Liebs agreed with him and thought for an instant that the gun captain would tell Meurer that they must not fight because there was only one man to load the gun. There was only Hellwig. But Meurer would not listen. He didn't care about them—he barely said anything when Janh was carried off the boat in agony. Appendicitis, they said. Meurer would give them no one else. Now Hellwig had to feed the gun by himself. It wasn't fair.

S-204 veered sharply to the right, throwing Hellwig against the bulkhead. The sea exploded to port. He heard the order to fire—he thought he did but he couldn't be sure because he was trying to make his way back to his station. He almost lost the shell pack, but he regained his footing in time to see Lieb train the gun to starboard and depress the trigger.

The world turned to fire and smoke as Hellwig swung under the barrel and fed a shell pack into the magazine. He quickly pulled another from the ready ammunition box as red tracers flashed overhead. He slid the pack into the magazine and pulled another from the box. He could hear Lieb cursing in gasps in between the flat bark of the gun. Explosions surrounded them as Hellwig continued to feed the gun. He exhausted one ammunition box and quickly moved to another—one eye on what he was doing and one on the position of the gun. He had to stay just to the side of the breech, near the hopper, so that he could drop shells into the magazine. But he had to keep an eye on the movement of the gun as Lieb swung it wildly along the horizon. Hellwig suddenly remembered that Janzen had held up three fingers. They were outnumbered three to one.

He flipped the lid open on another box, and at that moment he heard a crash aft. He saw the skullcap blackened and covered in flames, and his bladder emptied.

He turned quickly, shaking so violently that he could barely feed the shell pack into the magazine. He was going to die. This time he would. He knew it. He felt it.

Lieb screamed profanities at the unseen enemy as the doorknocker pumped shell after shell into the darkness.

Hellwig heard the roar of the engines of S-204, but he heard the rumble of other engines as well. The enemy. British or Americans. They were going to kill him. He would die. He prayed frantically, asking God that he be killed quickly, that he not be horribly mutilated and take hours or even days to die.

A blast surrounded Hellwig, and the noise was gone, replaced by a dull rumble and even that seemed muted somehow. He found himself on the deck, lying awkwardly over an ammunition box. He pulled himself to his feet. He saw Lieb shouting angrily at him, but the gunner's voice had been taken from him and all that remained in Hellwig's world was the rumble.

He wants shells, Hellwig finally realized. He staggered to an ammunition box and threw back the lid. The world exploded and as Hellwig sailed through the air he thought that somehow he was responsible because he opened the ammunition box.

He hit the water awkwardly and lost his breath. It was black and cold and he felt himself bob to the surface. His life vest saved him. He tried to avoid wearing it in the beginning, explaining to Janzen that he couldn't handle the shells because the life vest got in his way.

The bootsmannmaat called him an idiot and said that one day he'd thank God for that life vest. Was Janzen dead? Was Lieb dead?

He heard a deep roar and a huge shape slid alongside him. He was saved. S-204 had come to rescue him. Relief filled completely and he thought with joy that they really did like him: Janzen, Meurer, Lieb, and the others. They weren't going to abandon him. He would write his mother and tell her that these men weren't such a bad lot after all and maybe after the war they would all get together and his mother could fix them a fine meal.

Then a wave spun him around to show him the flaming wreck of S-204, a hundred meters away. The sight of the burning hulk drifting on the Channel waves numbed him.

He felt something hook into his life vest and he heard voices—loud men talking with words that made no sense to him but did confirm the fact that the English or Americans had him and he would be tortured.

They were going to kill him, Hellwig thought. The British were animals and the Americans were worse.

A rope dropped in front of his eyes and he instinctively grasped it, ignoring the fleeting thought that told him to try to swim away to die near his friends. The call of life was too strong and Hellwig decided that those men on S-204 weren't really his friends and that they treated him horribly and he would be ashamed to have his mother meet them.

Hellwig took the rope and held on tightly, while reaching hands gripped his life vest and turned him around. He dare not look up as he felt himself pulled from the water and dragged onto the deck of an enemy craft.

He saw a knife blade flash, but before he could cry out in horror the life vest straps were cut away and a man with a healthy growth of beard examined him. A doctor, Hellwig thought, but he was rough looking and his hands were not gentle.

He looked up tentatively and saw two men standing over him. Officers, he knew immediately, then he knew that they were American officers by their uniforms. Several other men stood around him, sailors he thought, all grim looking.

One officer was tall, very thin, and Hellwig felt as if his eyes were piercing his soul. The other was shorter, and when he turned his head to talk with the sailor who examined him Hellwig saw the scar. A gangster. One of the Jew Roosevelt's gangsters. He'd read about them. His mother had written to him about the American gangsters. He began to tremble more but not from the cold.

One of the sailors pushed through the group, holding a cup. The aroma enveloped him. Coffee. Real coffee, not ersatz. Hellwig always drank tea when he could find it; he thought coffee was too vulgar, but the scent that was coming from the cup in the enemy sailor's hands called to him.

Hellwig took the coffee cup, wrapping his fingers gratefully around its warm surface. His eyes

darted from Tall American to Scarface to the other
sailors surrounding him. He felt their eyes examining him as the boat dashed across the water,
throwing plumes of white foam high into the air.

Scarface was talking to Tall American now. His
voice was very measured and calm but his words
might just as well been thrown over the side. Tall
American ignored everything that Scarface said,
Hellwig could tell that easily enough because Tall
American's eyes never left him. They were dark,
hate-filled eyes, impatient and cold. He had first
thought that Tall American was someone who
could help him; despite his rough appearance he
looked civilized, kind. Perhaps he would protect
him from Scarface. Now, he wasn't sure.

Hellwig couldn't understand the language, but
he knew that Scarface was making a case of sorts,
of what and for what, Hellwig didn't know. His
fright had subsided somewhat, and he kept his
focus on sipping the steaming coffee. He had survived, he alive, and he was going to a prisoner
of war camp where he would never have to fight
again. A sudden thought occurred to him: what if
there was torture? What if Roosevelt's gangsters
hanged him as a criminal? Strangely, the idea carried no weight, and he marveled at the idea that
perhaps he was brave—that he had defeated death.
Then he realized he was alive and that was the
paramount thought that occupied him. Briefly the
images of Janzen, Lieb, and the others flashed before his eyes, but he paid no attention to them—
dead perhaps or on one of the other boats, captives
like himself. And if they were dead there was some
sort of God-delivered justice for their smoking,

drinking, and whoring, and for an instant Hellwig considered death an adequate retribution for the beatings that Janzen had given him.

Scarface turned to him, either satisfied that his words to Tall American had accomplished what he had in mind, or simply because the words had been useless.

"How are you? Are you feeling better?" Scarface asked. His German was clumsy and the accent made the words sound stilted and awkward.

"Yes," Hellwig said. He tried to appear calm although his hands still shook uncontrollably. He noticed Tall American's eyes narrow.

"You'll be taken back to England. A prisoner of war camp. You understand?"

"Yes," Hellwig said, his eyes unconsciously drawn to the long scar on the man's face. He remembered one American movie. Cars raced down deserted city streets and from the darkness, a horrible thunder of a dozen machine guns.

"You won't be harmed," Scarface continued. Tall American stood silently behind the other American, swaying slightly with the motion of the boat. It was then that Hellwig noticed the holster and pistol on the man's hip. Tall American followed Hellwig's eyes, glanced down at his hip, looked at Hellwig, and smiled. The eyes taunted him and the smile said, *"You understand that I will use this, don't you?"*

"I have some questions," Scarface said. His voice was soft and low and his eyes bore sincerity. It might be a trick, Hellwig cautioned himself. He may appear to be friendly and then the torturing will begin, but the thought drifted away. He felt strangely superior, as if selected by God to survive, to be plucked from the dismal life aboard S-204, and despite the absolute terror of the last few minutes, granted salvation by the Almighty because he was deserving. The idea filled him with strength and the arrogance of those who defeated death even if the victory were won by pure happenstance.

"You come from Cherbourg? Yes?"

Name, rank, and identification number. That was all that you're to tell the enemy if captured, Hellwig had been told, over and over. Above that, say nothing, the instructors had ordered him at *Swinemunde*. Nothing. Hellwig shrugged, concentrating on the coffee. It was much better than anything he had tasted before but he wished it were tea.

Tall American said something and Scarface tossed a curt reply over his shoulder. They did not like each other, Hellwig saw that well enough, but a disquieting thought snuck into his mind: can Scarface protect me?

"You will protect me?" Hellwig whispered to Scarface. He let his eyes dart in the direction of Tall American so that the meaning would not be lost.

"Don't worry," Scarface said. "But you must answer my questions. Do you understand me? You must answer all questions that I put to you—truthfully."

Hellwig felt the coffee cup slip from his hands as Tall American eased the pistol from his holster. Scarface saw the shock on Hellwig's face and looked over his shoulder. He stood and put himself between Hellwig and the Tall American, blocking the German sailor's view of what was going on. Hellwig could hear if he could not see. He heard the unmistakable sound of a round being chambered in the big pistol and Scarface's soft voice berating Tall American, and finally Tall American's short, harsh replies.

Hellwig realized that everything before had been a lie. He was not superior and death had not been cheated; it was simply playing a cruel game with him, and he would die after all, and God had not granted him salvation. God had abandoned him, and the others were probably alive and would live for many years, and that he was the only one who would die. The thoughts rushed at him, mocking him for being a fool and for thinking that he was safe and would never suffer again.

Tall American pushed Scarface to one side, and suddenly the huge muzzle of the pistol filled Hellwig's vision. A tiny cry escaped his throat as the hammer clicked back.

Scarface was still arguing with Tall American, but Tall American wasn't listening. His eyes were focused on Hellwig, and a single word screamed out at Hellwig from his mind: murder.

Scarface was talking rapidly at Tall American but the words had no effect, so finally he turned to Hellwig and said: "You have to answer my questions or he'll kill you. Do you understand?"

Hellwig gave a clipped nod, but he wasn't sure if he had responded to Scarface's question because he was trembling again. "Yes," he said, His mouth was so parched with fear that it was difficult to talk.

"You're from Cherbourg?"

"Yes."

"What squadron?"

"Squad . . . ?"

"Flotilla," Scarface corrected himself quickly.

"The Fifth. Cherbourg, yes. The Fifth." The muzzle of the gun never wavered and Tall American's eyes pinned him to the deck of the rocking boat. Scarface barked an order over his shoulder, but the other American slowly shook his head. He's going to kill me, Hellwig thought, and he felt weak, all of the remaining strength flowing from his body.

"The special boats. The S-boats."

Scarface's insistent voice brought him around.

"Yes," Hellwig confirmed, puzzled. Special?

"The fast S-boats," Scarface said. "They're faster than yours. They carry big guns. Large guns. What do you know about them?"

"I . . ." Hellwig began and then he remembered. He had seen them once from a distance, across Cherbourg Harbor. "You mean the flying boats?" he said.

"What do you mean? That they fly? That they actually fly?"

"No, no," Hellwig said. "We call them that. They fly across the water. They have wings, you see. They come down, from the bottom of the hull. We weren't allowed to get close to them."

"What do they look like? Can you draw them? Can you make a drawing of them?"

Scarface was speaking quickly in his awkward German, and Hellwig had an almost uncontrollable urge to laugh at the absurdity of everything, but he bit the inside of his cheek to stifle it. He knew that if he did, Tall American would pull the trigger and nothing that Scarface said or did could bring him back from the dead. He nodded.

Scarface straightened quickly and called out. He took the Tall American by the elbow and led him a few paces aft. They talked briefly while Hellwig tried to interpret their tone. The other sailors examined him, some indifferently, some with pity in their eyes. Another appeared and handed Hellwig some paper and a pencil. He handed Scarface a chart of some kind. The sailor, a thin, small man, called Hellwig "buddy," but he said it kindly. Buddy.

Hellwig took the pencil and paper and began sketching what he remembered of the flying boats— Reubold's flotilla. He drew the hull of an S-boat and then from amidships a long set of legs and moving the pencil aft, a shorter set.

Tall American snatched the drawing from Hellwig and studied it, while others gathered around him. Scarface laid the chart on the deck next to Hellwig, water soaking into the paper.

"This is Cherbourg," Scarface said. "Where are your pens?"

Hellwig pointed to a spot near the Seine Mole. "Here," he said.

"The special boats? Where are they?"

Hellwig looked at Scarface and shrugged. "I don't know. Someplace up here," he pointed. "Or here. They kept us away."

Scarface thought a moment and folded the chart, handing it to a sailor behind him. "The guns. What kind of guns are they?"

"I don't know," Hellwig said. "They kept us away and no one ever spoke about them. We went out with them on only one mission." He decided to mention nothing about sinking ships. Or about the arrogance of Reubold's men.

"What is the number of the special flotilla? Who is their commanding officer?"

"The Eleventh. Reubold. Fregattenkapitan. Please. That's all that I know," Hellwig said. He was beginning to tremble again and he picked up the cup and handed to the man who called him buddy, hoping to get more of the delicious liquid. He wanted to go someplace, anyplace but the sea, and he wanted dry clothes, and to crawl into a bed and sleep. He was very tired and he felt that he could lie down on the pitching deck and fall asleep with no difficulty. His eyes were very heavy when he remembered something. He debated telling Scarface because he didn't think it was important, nothing more than sailor's talk, but he thought that if he were helpful they would give him dry clothes and a place to sleep.

"Please," he said as Scarface rose. "One more thing. Sea Eagles. That's what they called the boats. *Zee Adlers.*"

Scarface looked down at him and nodded. Hellwig wasn't sure if the information was worth a bed or even another blanket. He caught the attention of the man who had given him the paper, holding his middle finger and index finger out expectantly in the universal sign for a cigarette. "Buddy," he said, hoping that the word would draw the American's sympathy.

The American smiled, lit a cigarette, and slid it between Hellwig's two fingers. He nodded gratefully, placed the cigarette between his lips, and drew deeply. God in heaven, Lieb was right. There was nothing better.

Cole followed Edland into the Day Room. "Get what you wanted?"

Edland spun on him. "I didn't get the boat."

"They didn't want to be got," Cole said.

"You were supposed to capture the E-boat. Not blow it out of the water."

"Oh, now, Commander. Let's be kind here," Cole said. "This is war. Things don't always go as planned in war. You know that, don't you? There was a lot of lead flying around out there. Maybe somebody was smoking near the paint locker. Besides, you got Fuehrer Junior."

"How the hell did you last this long, Cole? We had a chance. We could have captured that boat."

"I lasted this long," Cole said, "despite guys like you. Some guys weren't so lucky. But you got something, so the mission wasn't a total loss. What are those things you're after, Commander? Flying boats? Atomic death rays? Sea Eagles? Yeah, I know enough German to get by and I saw the drawing. Boats with wings. What will they think of next?"

Edland's eyes narrowed in understanding. "You would have shot that boy."

"Just as sure as you're standing there, Commander."

"For what purpose. Has killing made you that insensitive to humanity?"

"You may not have realized this in your ivory tower, Commander," Cole said. "But you can't have a war without killing somebody. It's what comes of war, except generally we do it with spectacle. Yeah, I would have killed him because he's the enemy, even if he is a sad sack. Had the situation been reversed, I would have been the one dead. So do me a big favor; don't lecture me on the morality of war and killing, and don't pull that intellectual kindred spirit crap on me. I gave up the classroom a long time ago. You want to dwell on the philosophy of war? Stay in London, sleep on clean sheets, and go to fancy restaurants, where you can hobnob with your fellow wizards and think deep thoughts. Translation: stay the fuck away from me because one day I might just lose my temper and you'll see firsthand just how much thought that I give to killing." Cole reached up and slid back the Day Room hatch.

"Lieutenant!" Edland said. Cole looked over his shoulder. "I do what I do to keep American boys from being killed."

"Gee, Commander," Cole said, disappearing through the hatch. "I'd say you're doing a piss-poor job of it."

He made his way as Rich was throwing a blanket over the prisoner's shoulder and helping him to his feet. He wanted to get away from everyone, to find a place on this tiny boat where he could wall himself up. He was trembling uncontrollably and he didn't want anyone to see him. He knew if he reached the bridge and took up his familiar station he would be safe. He could have gone below to his cabin, but he hated the claustrophobic feel of the place and seldom set foot in the closet-like space.

Cole's nerves were so tightly strung that he could

feel them drawing up within his body, threatening to pull his arms and legs into some grotesque shape.

It had been a quick fight, a clean fight, with the inexperience of the enemy boat apparent the moment that they had joined. Cole had ordered all three boats in at the same time so that their combined power would overwhelm the E-boat. In the sharp conflict, nearly drowning in the pandemonium and confusion, Cole had to fight the urge to look at DeLong. He knew that if he did, DeLong would die.

His mind screamed at him to look as the boats battled one another, the thick waves of the Channel crashing over the bow or against the hull as 155 chased the E-boat. The starboard twin .50-caliber machine guns banged away at the enemy boat, and each time they fired, Cole felt himself jump. He's okay, he's okay, Cole kept telling himself, but he could not bring himself to look.

When the E-boat burst into flames and sank low in the water, he heard DeLong shout in triumph. Cole's body began to shake in relief. He fought back the vomit stinging his throat as they picked up the German and Edland questioned him.

Now, as he stood on the bridge, the sharp taste of bile in his mouth, he clung tightly to the spray shield, willing his body to be still.

All the time he could hear DeLong singing some little silly song about fishies and a dam. He wanted to shout "Shut up!" but he kept silent. After an hour or so he felt normal. He hoped no one had seen him lose control, especially DeLong, and he finally relaxed. He forced himself to look toward the left.

DeLong was at the wheel, scanning the horizon. He noticed Cole looking at him and rewarded him with a broad grin.

"Hell of a day at sea, wasn't it, Skipper?"

Cole smiled weakly in response. *How much more of this can I handle?*

Chapter 12

Dickie Moore lit Rebecca's cigarette in the relative quiet of the tearoom. The place was nearly deserted; a strange state of affairs when there always seemed to be thousands of people swarming to or from trains. But it was almost four o'clock in the morning and most people had fallen asleep on the long wooden benches in the waiting areas or sat close over tiny tables, trying to ease their fatigue with cup after cup of strong tea.

Rebecca nodded her thanks but stayed Dickie's hand. "A new lighter, Dickie?"

"A present," he said, his eyes alight with playful conspiracy. "From a very dear friend."

"A lady," Rebecca said, smiling.

"Well, I bloody well wouldn't accept such a gift from a man," he said, slipping the lighter in his tunic. "Dear father would have been the first to suggest that I was a nancy, but I was pleased to prove him wrong. I think that creates a dilemma for the old boy. His only son likes girls, but his only son likes girls far better than he likes anything else, so he achieves little in life. Ironic, isn't it?"

"You should never say such things about yourself," Rebecca said, mild reproach in her pale blue eyes. "You give yourself far too little credit."

"Ah," Dickie said, "but far more than my creditors do." A waitress swept by, filling their teacups. Dickie waited until she was out of earshot before he said: "So you're off to the country?" He thought that this was the best way to broach the subject of Rebecca leaving her husband. He might have started with something such as: "So you've finally come to your senses," but that would have been too blunt. She was his friend and he had sense enough to realize that she had been a long time making this painful decision.

"Yes," Rebecca said, "back to Farley Park for a while. Both Mother and Father are pleased at the thought of me moving home."

"And," Dickie began, half in spite and half in jest. "Oh, I can never recall that chap's name."

"It's Gregory, Dickie," Rebecca said, shaking her head at her friend. He would never be more than a delightfully mischievous boy. "You know very well what his name is."

"I forgot. I truly did," Dickie replied, tossing in just enough sincerity to fool no one. "Is it permanent? I mean that you're not going back to him—are you?"

"No. I shan't be going back. There's no reason to continue with the marriage, really. He has settled on a life that doesn't include me." She looked at her teacup in resignation.

"Makes him a fool, doesn't it? A perfectly lovely creature such as yourself. A philandering husband, war hero or not. He must be blind, is all that I can say." Dickie looked around as if he suddenly realized where he was. "And why, oh, why did you insist upon this ungodly hour to depart London?"

Rebecca laughed. "I thought that you belonged to the night, Dickie?"

"Night, yes. But, dear girl, this is early morning, and at this time of day I am usually tucked in and doing"—he smiled—"doing whatever good little boys should be doing at this hour."

"It was the only connection that I could make, Dickie, and you are a lamb for coming to see me off."

"Some of my lady friends might consider me more a wolf in sheep's clothing."

The shrill wail of a train whistle broke the expanse of the huge train shed, while several engines lay next to their platforms, chugging softly.

Dickie shook off the silence that had descended over them with a subject that had been bothering him since she arrived. He had seen her walk into the tearoom, stop, and search over the few patrons and scattered tables until her eyes finally rested on him. It seemed an ordeal for her. "You're not looking well, Rebecca."

"What a perfectly dreadful thing to say," she responded playfully.

"We must not be humorous about this," Dickie said. He was serious and he wanted Rebecca to understand that he was concerned. "You look all done in. Although, I shouldn't wonder considering Gregory's nocturnal habits. And your job cannot have helped. Sixteen-hour days at the hospital, I mean, really, dear. Didn't you ever consider your own well-being?"

"There was never any time for that, Dickie," Rebecca explained. "I was needed there. People needed me. That's what kept me going through all of this nonsense with Gregory. There was so much to do. There still is. I hated to leave; I feel as if, in a way, I'm abandoning the hospital."

"Well you're not going back," Dickie said. "Not to the hospital and not to that randy husband of yours. You've come to your senses and you're getting away, and from the looks of the circles under your eyes, not too soon."

"I'm tired, dear," Rebecca said. "That's all there is to it. And I hate not being active. When I was a child I spent nearly a year in bed with fever, and I vowed that I would never give in to that nonsense again. So you mustn't worry about me. Don't give it another thought. When I'm well again I shall return to nursing. It is, after all, my life. I am devoted to caring for others." She lifted the lid of a creamer and peered into the tiny pitcher. Satisfied that there was enough left, she replaced the lid and poured some of the contents into her tea. The white liquid turned into a brown swirl, and she spooned it into oblivion. "Have you heard from, Jordan?" It was a casual question but Dickie could tell that it had been carefully prepared and timed.

"I have," he said brightly. "Last week, in fact."

"How is he?" she asked, seemingly preoccupied with her tea.

"Well," he lied. He thought it a bit amusing that she pretended not to care, but then he remembered that Jordan was not the only one who suffered when she sent him away. "Quite well indeed. You know those American chaps. Overpaid, oversexed, and over here. He's on PT boats; like our Motor Torpedo Boats. He was in the Mediterranean. Did I tell you that?"

"No."

"No. Well, there he was and when things cooled a bit there, he was shipped back to England."

"Is he well?" she asked hopefully. "Really?"

Dickie reached across the table and patted her hand in reassurance. "Of course he is. Never better." He realized that the charade was failing and smiled at Rebecca. "Why am I such a bloody poor liar? One would think that with all of my experience that I should be a positive expert at it. No, he isn't well. He is terribly thin, and he looks very worn."

"Is he . . . ?" Rebecca rested her chin in the palm of her hand. "Is he happy?"

"Happy? Jordan? We are talking about the same chap, aren't we? Closed off, I'm afraid." He knew what she was asking. Had Cole withdrawn from everyone? Bloody fool; more than willing to face the Germans, but let anyone get close to him and he becomes as stoic as a gargoyle.

Rebecca looked sad. "Because of me."

"No," Dickie said. "Because he was confused and hurt, and turned away from everything. He is a remarkably bright young man, my dear, and perfectly capable of making decisions on his own. If he decides to be a horse's arse, you must let him."

Rebecca laughed. "Dickie, you mustn't be so un-kind. He is your friend."

"Of course he's my friend and a damned fine man, but if friends aren't allowed to be honest with one another, who is?" He shrugged. "He's a strange case, our Jordan. A good man."

"It could not have been different. You can see that, can't you, Dickie? I couldn't leave my hus-band, despite my feelings for Jordan. I had to give my marriage a chance. I'd seen what became of my parents and I thought . . ." She left the sentence unfinished.

"I know that, Rebecca. And perhaps Jordan knows it as well, but he can't admit it to himself. It is easier for him to be angry. He understands that emotion. He can deal with anger. He simply doesn't know how to deal with loss or hurt. He's a bull in a china shop—stumbling around, banging into things; clumsy as an ox." He cocked an eyebrow. "Is one permitted to mix metaphors when one de-nounces one's friends?"

A trace of a smile crossed Rebecca's face. She hesitated for a moment before speaking, her voice pleading for understanding for herself and Cole. "He's a good man, isn't he?"

"He is," Dickie said gently. "You're a good woman. I'd give my left arm to end this distance between you. It appears that you two are floating within sight, but never within touch, of one another." He glanced at his wristwatch. "What time is your train?"

"Four-twenty," she said. "What time . . . ?"

"We've got another fifteen minutes, dear." She didn't appear to be in a hurry, Dickie thought, lin-gering over her tea and conversation as if she were loath to end it. There was a distance about Rebecca lately, some part of her that she held back so that if it were not said, it could not be true. She had always been a gentle woman, Dickie knew. When he had been wounded in a bombing raid she was the nurse who cared for him. A tender soul, but troubled—little china animals all neatly arrayed along narrow shelves where the slightest bump could send them all to the floor and destruction. Then she had met Jordan, and he, it turned out, was just as fragile as she. She was hiding something from him now; Dickie sensed that much during the short time they had been together. Perhaps, whatever it was, she was hiding it from herself as well. Something to do with the marriage or that dreadful husband.

"Gregory is to have the house," she said, as if reading Dickie's mind. "It doesn't mean much to me in any case. It will do him good to have something permanent in his life, I suspect."

"You're too good to the blighter," Dickie said.

"No," Rebecca said. "It's only right. I'll go home and rest up and when I come back to London, I'll look for a flat."

"They're hard to come by, my love."

She stirred her tea and slipped into a reverie. "It's funny, Dickie. When I go home, I gain strength. Farley Park has that effect on me. The gardens, the fields, the deep forest near the river. I draw comfort from the place. Do you find that odd?"

"Odd? No. Everyone has a secret hiding place I suppose."

"What's yours?"

"Mine?" he said, searching through his memory.

He decided to keep that to himself. "Why the boudoir of any willing young lady."

Rebecca laughed deeply, tears coming to her eyes. "I should have known better than to ask." A moment passed, and she grew reflective. "I wonder if you would do something for me, Dickie?"

"Anything, love."

"Would you tell Jordan that I should very much like to see him? As soon as he can get away. It is important and I'm much afraid that I should not be able to get away from Farley Park. At least for some time. Would you do that?"

"Of course. But you know," he tried to find a way to say what he had to in a way that would cause the least pain. "He might not want to see you. He can be such a blighter at times."

"I know."

"He's very stubborn and he's been hurt."

"I know he has been, Dickie. I shall never forgive myself for that. But I want him to come, for both of us. It's important that we speak. Things should not go unsaid." She glanced at the clock on the wall over the long bank of grimy windows facing the platforms. "I really must be going." She stood and gathered her things. Dickie stood and put two pounds on the table.

"I'm feeling extravagant," he said to no one in particular.

They pushed their chairs under the table and Rebecca slid her arm under his.

"You promised me, Dickie. Make him come to Farley Park, won't you?"

He patted her hand. "I promised and I shall," he said, leading her to the door. He knew it would be

difficult. Cole was a decent man, and there was no
doubt in Dickie's mind that the American still
cared deeply for Rebecca Blair. It was evident that
Rebecca knew that as well, but what she didn't
know was that Cole had changed. Three years of
war and separation had combined to harden that
man. It would not be easy to get Jordan Cole to
Farley Park.

The swirling sands along the beach at Yport,
picked up by the stiff winds that came across the
gray waters of the Channel, peppered the group of
Wehrmacht and Kriegsmarine officers. Long ranks
of angry waves raced over the shallows and as-
saulted the men erecting bundles of Belgian gates
in the knee-deep water. Beyond them, in deeper
water, their snouts thrust above the surface begging for air, were hundreds of other obstacles and
beyond them were wooden posts topped by anti-
tank mines. All of these were designed to stop the
landing craft that Rommel knew would come by
the hundreds. Behind the group of officers who
pulled their heads down below the collars of their
great coats to keep the sand out, and turned their
backs on the wind, were the pillboxes and anti-
tank obstacles. They were linked by snaking trenches
that blossomed with machine-gun nests, mortar
positions, and firing steps. Thousands of TODT
workers—forced labor—swarmed over the fortifications at a pace that drove Rommel mad. "You
could lash them, but if you did they grew sullen,"
he explained in frustration to his staff. "You could
withhold their food, but this only made them re-

sentful. You could shoot them, but then you would have even fewer men than you needed and would have to press more German troops into construction service."

"You alternately threaten and reward the TODT workers, praising their work and handing out extra food when goals are met. Still, we must raid garrison troops and watch as officers and men string barbed wire and plant mines."

"In the end, it's not enough," Rommel said, turning into the wind to face the two dozen officers at his heels. "There should be a thousand more obstacles there." He pointed down to the beach, his voice rising above the surf. "And there. There, as well. And more mines, gentlemen. Many, many, many mines." He began walking again, and the group, with Walters hanging back, followed him dutifully. "Deepen the trenches and build up the firing steps. When the enemy comes in, they will attempt to blast our defenses with cannon fire, from there." He pointed to the Channel with his marshal's baton. "They must not get beyond the water's edge. Is that understood? Stop them here!" His voice became strident and he kicked a clump of sand into the air. The wind snatched it up, scattering the grains into the air. "Here. On the beach. Everything depends upon us denying the enemy time to employ their material wealth. I have seen it, gentlemen. It does not matter that our soldiers are better and our tanks far superior to theirs. They will bury us under a mountain of materiel once they have secured a beachhead. But we will deny them that. Yes?"

Several members of the group looked around for someone to speak first. Rommel finally answered his own question. "Yes. Deny them the beaches." He looked around and saw Walters. "Go back to the bunker," he told the others. "I will join you."

Rommel's naval attaché stepped forward, knowing that the fieldmarschal wanted a word with him. When the others were far down the beach, Rommel moved closer to Walters so that he would not have to shout above the wind.

Rommel's gaze was drawn to the sea. He tapped his marshal's baton against his shoulder, gazing into the distance. Finally, he came back to the kommodore. "Preparation, Walters," he said, stroking the stiff collar of his greatcoat with the silver knob of his baton. "Dresser contacted me. Naturally, he was upset. Quite disturbed that work was not progressing on his boats. The new boats at Cherbourg. By my orders, he said, work had ceased."

"Clearly a misunderstanding, Feldmarschall," Walters said.

"Clearly," Rommel said sharply. "For I can think of no reason that my instructions to Dresser were ignored and his orders to his men brought no response. I gave no such orders. Can you explain, Walters?"

The naval attaché's attention was momentarily drawn to the sky. Far overhead the sun glinted off an enemy reconnaissance plane. They were a daily occurrence, lone aircraft, or aircraft in twos or threes flying safely above anti-aircraft and fighter protection, busily recording the preparations that were being made to strengthen the Atlantic Wall.

Because of their overflights, there would be no surprise for the Allied troops. They were the distant eyes of the enemy.

"I can, Feldmarschall," Walters said. "If you would grant me a few moments of your time. The Allied invasion of North Africa was a clumsy affair. But they learned much from their mistakes and were able to land on Sicily without the general confusion that marred the first invasion."

"I need no schooling in enemy tactics," Rommel said bitterly. "Continue."

He had not arbitrarily dismissed Walters. It was a small victory from a man who was well known not to grant them easily. But Rommel could be mercurial and Walters knew that his reasoning had to be flawless. And quickly delivered. "Generally, their invasion fleet was constructed so." Walters picked up a piece of driftwood and drew a few marks in the sand. The wind nibbled at the edge of the lines. "Transports," a series of quick Xs; "bombardment vessels," a group of crude Os; "and escort," smaller Xs. "They will come across the Channel in lanes, each fleet assigned its place and time of travel."

"Each fleet will have more than enough guns to protect it, Walters," Rommel said, his tone pointing out the obvious. "The Kriegsmarine has no battleships, and the Luftwaffe has no aircraft, and that is why I have requested sea mines be so thickly scattered in the Channel that one can walk from Cherbourg to Portsmouth without getting one's feet wet." His voice rose and the words became sharper. "It is why that I requested of Admiral Dresser that he set his S-boats to seeding the Channel and why I was particularly disturbed to learn that you took it upon yourself to countermand my order. And for this action, you have a reason, I suppose?"

Walters answered with the fieldmarschal's own words. "To stop the enemy at the beaches, Feldmarschall."

Rommel's temper exploded. "I fail to see how your little boats can achieve that. I do not appreciate officers undertaking projects that run counter to my expectations, Walters, particularly those officers in whom I have placed a great deal of trust. This is something that one of the Fuehrer's lackeys would have done, but to have a member of my own staff do it is incomprehensible. I have not the time for such foolishness." He wiped away the sand-diagram with the sole of his boot. "We will speak no more of this. You will do as I ordered and you will never again interfere with my commands. Understood?"

"Yes, Feldmarschall," Walters said.

Rommel drove the baton firmly into his palm, watching as a patch of fog obscured the waves in the distance. The shouts of men dragging an anti-tank gun into position could be heard from just over one of the sea grass–studded dunes, and black figures waded into the surf, carrying Teller mines to the first line of obstacles. "The Fuehrer," Rommel said in passing, "is consulting mystics and astrologers about where the Allies will land. Strategy is determined by charlatans. Von Rundstedt refuses to talk to our great leader. The only thing separating us from the greatest battle in history is a thin strip of water," he reached down and picked up a handful of sand, letting it drift through his gray leather gloves, "a patch of earth." He turned, studying the pillboxes and fortifications. "And what little we have been able to erect in the short time allotted us. The fate of the Fatherland, Walters." The last of the sand slipped between his fingers.

"Feldmarschall, what if we can disrupt the invasion fleets before they reach the beaches?"

Rommel looked at Walters.

"If this can be done," Walters continued, "it might prevent them from coordinating some important element of the invasion. Fire support, some part of the landing. Any confusion introduced into the array of ships that make up the fleet would throw off the timetable established by the enemy."

"They will have contingency plans," Rommel said.

"Yes, Feldmarschall," Walters said. But once the fleets are committed they cannot easily be turned. The very size of the enemy fleet could be its own undoing."

Rommel lapsed into thoughtful silence. There was no indication that he accepted Walters's theory. After a moment he spoke, his mood one of interest mixed with skepticism. "The S-boats. Those pitiful little things. What can they do?"

"Shock troops, sir," Walters said.

Rommel glanced at him and shook his head, dismissing the notion. He walked off, leaving Walters standing near the scattered remnants of his master plan. Imagination, Walters thought. *One of the greatest military minds of the century has suddenly lost all imagination. There is potential here—with these few boats. I will not dismiss them so easily.* He smiled at his own determination. Normally one would not run counter to a high-ranking officer. It was a practice that ended careers. But neither does one advance without taking at least a few chances. It would not be an unconsidered risk on Walters's part; he had given the idea a great deal of thought. In the end what he saw was not the success or failure of Reubold's boats or even the result of the enemy invasion. What he saw was Berlin and his rightful place alongside the powerful.

Chapter 13

Over Le Havre

Pilot-Sergeant Gierek sang quietly, his eyes alternately scanning the fluorescent dials of the instrument panel and the darkness ahead.

"Hej, gorale, nie bijcie sie.
Ma goralka dwa warkocze podzielicie."

He stopped long enough to find the bright blue engine exhaust of the other Pathfinder Mosquito far ahead, and just slightly about the course that his aircraft had been flying. "You like the song?" he asked Jagello. "You like it? It's a mountain song. It's about a girl with two pigtails. *Goralski Taniec.* We used to sing it. I've forgotten the words so I use my own."

Jagello held up his hand for silence, while he copied down the message coming in on the wireless. He held the paper under the soft glow of the compass lamp. There were three letters written across it—PPD. The Pathfinders were going in.

Gierek nodded, increased power, and climbed to 34,000 feet. They weren't after U-boat pens; they were after E-boat pens, but the drill was the same. Link on to the three transmitting stations along the east coast of England, calculate the pulses with the onboard detector, consult the chart, and estimate the position. Gee was what it was called, and it was the first step in setting out for the intended target. That was when Cat and Mouse took over; Cat the tracker station that emitted a 1.5 meter radar signal, which was then reradiated by the Cat plane, usually a Mosquito, and Mouse measured the Mosquito's ground speed and altitude, plotting its exact distance from the target. All very neatly done, until you got over the target. You always went over at night, and thank God for the Telecommunications Research Establishment at Malvern that produced the wonderful electronic eyes that saw through the darkness, because it was sheer suicide to go over in daylight.

The Americans did. Daylight precision bombing, they explained, was certainly the way to go. Their massively armed bombers flying in close echelons, protected by squadrons of fighters, provided all the protection they needed to complete the missions with acceptable losses. Besides, they pointed out, trying to strengthen their position after so many dead young Americans became acceptable, their fabulous Norden bombsight was designed for daylight use.

After a visit to an American base and a heated discussion between Gierek and another pilot, he and Jagello returned to Lasham. Over a cup of tea, Gierek filled in the other pilots about the crazy Americans and their daylight raids, and finally after he had mined his exasperation to the limit, turned to Jagello and said: "They're crazy. The Americans. Aren't they crazy?"

Every head turned to Jagello, who looked thoughtful for a moment before announcing: "I need more tea."

The dense black clouds parted, and Gierek made out the dim form of bombers in the rearview mirror. The big planes, far behind them, were framed in the trembling reflection, each only a rough silhouette etched against the black sky by a frail moon. He did not like Lancasters. They were superb bombers and the men who flew them swore by them, but Gierek preferred the speed and maneuverability of the little Mosquito. He had trained on Lancasters, but he felt too conspicuous in the big plane as it lumbered through fields of flak, and when an opportunity came to sign up for the Polish Pathfinder Squadron, the City of Krakow, he took it.

This was the first time that he had met Jagello, and at first the two didn't hit it off—Jagello was quiet, Gierek was talkative. But they were both highly competent, and they soon settled into a routine of professionalism that kept them returning to the base at Walker after each mission. Others in the squadron were not so lucky.

Jagello held up a message: IT. The first flight of Pathfinders were dropping the special target indicators now, clusters of colorful flares—pink, green, red, yellow—that guided the bombers to the tar-

get. Still not precise enough, still far too general
for dropping bombs on targets with 14-foot-thick
concrete roofs. The illumination flares would be
next, Gierek knew—brilliant white stars that drifted
to earth under black parachutes so that their brightness did not blind the bomber crews. Their signal
would come next and then Jagello would slap Gierek
on the leg twice: get ready.

Flashes of light began in the distance, not flares
or the few stars that managed to pierce the overcast, but flak. Anti-aircraft—very accurate, perva-
sive, frightening. There was no defense against
that, not the daylight sun or the inky blackness of
night. You could dodge fighters, or shoot them
down, or settle into darkness and run from cloud
to cloud where they couldn't see you. But flak was
different. Talented men far below, men who calculated speed, distance, wind, humidity, temperature,
and who methodically lobbed shells into the sky.

The Mosquito shook violently as it passed through
a flak ridge.

"Come back to me, my lover," Gierek sang.

Three shells exploded close by the aircraft, bouncing Gierek in his seat. He tightened his harness
and glanced at Jagello. The man was made of iron.

"Why did you ever leave . . ."

There was a huge explosion somewhere behind
them and Gierek glanced in the mirror as one of
the lumbering Lancasters, flames boiling from its
midsection, slowed and veered to the left. Its fiery
death lit up the night and its slow descent lacked
drama; as if tired of flying on, the huge aircraft
had simply decided to lie down and go to sleep.
He could not see the whole incident in the mirror,

and that was best because if he could, his eyes would be drawn to the death of the Lancaster and the sight of flaming bundles, men and parachutes on fire, hurling themselves into the sky.

Jagello slapped Gierek's leg. The Mosquito's bomb bay doors opened with a soft rumble and the sound of whistling air piercing the interior of the craft.

"Can't you see these teardrops . . . ?"

"Release," Jagello said. The Mosquito bucked as the packets of flares dropped away.

Another explosion tore the sky, far ahead. Gierek hurriedly crossed himself. Release. Far behind, the Lancasters—those that survived—had just dropped their huge bombs, six-ton monsters filled with Torpex, MC deep penetration bombs. Tall Boys. They would fall at supersonic speed and when they struck the earth, they would bury themselves before exploding. These bombs were not meant to hit the target; they were meant to land next to the target, and the resulting blast would shake a structure until it collapsed. Earthquake bombs.

Flak detonated around the Mosquito, and Gierek gripped the wheel firmly and wedged his feet into the rudder pedals. He'd been in flak barrages before that had tossed the Mosquito high in the air, and once the aircraft had been thrown violently sideways, and it had taken all of his strength to regain control.

"Don't you know I grieve?" The Mosquito jumped and Gierek heard shrapnel strike the aircraft. He noticed a large round hole through the Perspex windshield and wondered briefly where in the aircraft was the object that had made that hole.

"Don't you know I grieve?" he repeated, each word coming with an exhaled breath as he quickly checked the instrument panel, searching the dials for telltale signs that manifold pressure was dropping, or the radiator temperature was spiking.

"And so I know do you," he said, gingerly applying pressure to the stick, feeling the response through his fingers that told him that there was still the right amount of tension on the cables. The explosions were constant flashes destroying his night vision, angry stars of fire and smoke that lived only an instant before disappearing; the never-ending thud of shrapnel striking wood ribs and canvas skin. Balsa-plywood sandwich, a beaming mechanic had told him proudly, running his hand along the smooth underbelly of the aircraft.

Wooden aircraft. Like the first war.

A blast shook the aircraft and Gierek kicked left rudder to bring it back on course. He shouldn't have been mean to the dog. The filthy thing is always in the way, he argued. Bad luck, bad luck, he countered. Every mission I must have him moved, why my plane? Why me? He began humming *Goralski Taniec.* The flak was subsiding but occasional clusters filled the night. He dropped a few lyrics into the humming; *"Oh, why did you leave me?"* as he studied the instruments.

"Gierek?" Jagello said, the first word that he had spoken in over an hour.

"Yes?" Gierek said.

"Is that the only song that you know?"

* * *

Reubold sat on the case of 2cm ammunition in the pen, waiting for the last of the men to gather around him. He longed for a cigarette. His hands were trembling and the last shot of morphine had long since drifted away, leaving the dull ache that gripped his body at a dozen points. It was his legs especially; they cramped when he remained motionless, and the pain was so unrelenting that he wanted to cry out. They actually felt as if they were twisted and misshapen, and he knew that if he looked down he would see gnarled limbs, withered and distorted. When he did look down, of course, his legs were perfectly normal, long and elegant. He wanted to scream liars, liars, and beat them senseless with his fists.

A man beating his own legs, Reubold decided; now that would be a sight.

Waldvogel joined him, the little man's overalls covered in grease. He and a couple of armament artificers had been trying to decrease the drag on the guns so that they trained smoothly. He was surprised when the work to remove the guns and foils had stopped. Reubold had told the men nothing except to stand down; an explanation would come later. At least he hoped an explanation would come later. Silver Stripes like Walters had a way of changing their minds so that orders were as fleeting as the morning dew. Let the first mild light of reconsideration strike a perfectly sensible order and it disappeared. This was different, however, and Reubold was surprised to receive a telephone call from Walters confirming what he didn't say on his visit to the pens. The boats will remain as they are. For the moment. That was another thing; Silver Stripes, naval officers who hovered around bases, were reluctant to be specific about anything so that should it return to them they could very easily turn it away at the door like a long-lost relative with doubtful antecedents.

"I'm glad that you could take time away from your whoring and drinking," Reubold said, the words echoing against the concrete walls of the pen. There was hearty laughter in return. Most of the men had been with Reubold for a while and they respected him. "We've been given a true reprieve," he continued. "That's like a fallen woman calling herself virtuous again, but I am satisfied with that." The laughter was louder this time. Reubold thought of the vials in his room as his legs slowly twisted into knots. "The high command apparently has need of us. For what and when, I am not certain. They did not bother to inform me of that. They did inquire about Waldvogel's wonderful guns and what they did. I said my gunners are blind and the guns are shit." There was sustained laughter and Reubold rubbed his leg roughly. He grew serious, his eyes sweeping his crews. "We have a chance, comrades. I don't know what high command wants of us, but we have a chance to show them what we can do. These are fast boats." He glanced at the S-boats comfortably nestled alongside the quay. "We have got to practice firing, running at full speed, and hitting our targets. Those big gas bags of Waldvogel's"—more laughter, but subdued because the men knew that this was serious business—"can do some damage when they hit. We've all seen the results. But they're the devil to aim at high speed, as steady as the boats are. And we want to be fast to confuse the enemy and because we stick out like a floating island on Waldvogel's foils. Fast and accurate, those are the watchwords. Fast and accurate. I want to report to the Silver Stripes that we can thread the eye of a needle at three thousand meters. That means that we have to improve. That means more practice."

Reubold surveyed the gathering. They shared a look of intense concentration mixed with defiance. Good. They understood what needed to be done. They knew that they could hold nothing back, that if they failed. . . . He decided to give the pot one more stir.

"There is something else. Something I'm sure you'll be pleased to hear. The army, you know those fellows that keep marching to and fro?" Laughter and a few catcalls. "The army says that if we can't make our boats work they're going to take them away and use them as minelayers." There was an explosion of profanity and insults. Reubold silenced the group by raising his hand. "Feldmarschall Rommel wants more boats to sprinkle mines in the Channel to scare the Americans and English away." He paused, letting the men's anger simmer. "Let him find the boats someplace else," Reubold said calmly. "These are warships, not trawlers. Let us show them that Flotilla Eleven has the fastest, most dangerous boats on La Manche. Work hard, gentlemen. Work well. Those Silver Stripes will see what these boats are capable of." He nodded to an oberbootsmannmaat, who shouted: "Dismissed."

Reubold stepped off the box gingerly, his legs

crying out in resistance. The speech had drained him and his hands ached to hold the needle. Waldvogel was suddenly at his side.

"I've been working on the gun traversing mechanism. It's much smoother. Much more fluid," Waldvogel said hopefully.

"Can you *hit* anything?" Reubold asked, deciding to sit a moment before returning to his rooms. He was very tired and sick of promises.

"Yes. Certainly."

Reubold nodded. "Good. That is very good. They don't give us medals for misses, you know." He stroked his legs, wanted desperately to hammer them into compliance. "We'll go out in two hours, then. We'll take your boat out and check the marvelous new traversing mechanism."

"Yes," Waldvogel said. "Yes. That will do nicely."

"Waldvogel," Reubold said, easing his legs straight out in front of him. "Walters made it very plain to me. Rommel wants our boats. Dresser doesn't care about them. For some reason, and he hasn't told me what, Walters wants us to be successful. In his very words; fast and accurate. If we can't prove that to him," he struggled to his feet. "We join the army."

The slide flashed on the large screen in the darkened confines of the briefing room, and Dickie Moore began to speak.

"PRU Squadron 542 chaps brought these back after the raid on Le Havre. They went right to PIU for mark-up." The Photo Reconnaissance Units were the eyes of the Royal Air Force, their cameras pinpointing targets or bombing results. Photo Interpretive Units examined photographs to determine if targets were selected or if bomber command had succeeded.

The long wooden dowel centered on a circle drawn on the photograph. "Here is the E-boat pen." The dowel swept the length of a thick dock. "This is called Mole Centrale." Dickie tapped an area above it, partially obscured by a tuft of clouds. "This rectangle in the Basin Theophile is a floating dock. Obviously much too large for E-boats and intended, I'm sure, for the larger ships of the Kriegsmarine in those heady days before the bottom fell out."

"Might we dispense with the editorial comments, Lieutenant?" Admiral Sir Bertram Home Ramsey said from the darkness.

"As you like, sir," Dickie said, nonplussed.

"What ship is that?" an officer asked. "The one capsized at the top of the photo?"

"The *Paris*," Dickie said cheerfully, as if he had had a hand in sinking her. "No danger of her coming back to life."

"Bomb damage?" Ramsey chided, moving the briefing along.

"Right, sir. Here is an impact crater. Here." Dickie searched the enlarged photograph. "And here."

"Damage to the pens?" Admiral McNamar asked.

"Minor, I'm afraid, sir," Dickie said apologetically. "Everything around it has taken quite a beating, but unless there is evidence of some damage within the pens, it looks as if it'll require another go."

McNamar sat back in his chair and shot Edland a disappointed look.

"Another go it shall have to be," Ramsey said. "Regardless of the losses."

"Four out of ten Lancasters, sir," Dickie said. "And one of the Pathfinders."

Ramsey passed Dickie a cross look for reminding him. "Regardless of the losses. Turn that thing off."

The room plunged into darkness as the slide disappeared. Lights suddenly flooded the interior. The men rose, stretching. They'd been meeting for the better part of two hours and most of them were stiff with fatigue. They would take a break and come back to the briefing room for another round of meetings.

McNamar hunched his shoulders and twisted, trying to drive circulation back into his muscles. "So you didn't find what you were looking for?"

"No, sir," Edland said to the sound of chairs being scooted out of the way and the flurry of rustling papers. "Prisoner interrogation gave us very little."

"I told Ramsey that the immediate threat on D-1 and D-Day was the E-boat. He agreed and that's why the RAF went in." McNamar nodded toward the blank screen. "Now it looks as if they have to go back, the poor bastards." A British air marshal stopped by and led McNamar aside, obviously intent on keeping their conversation private.

"You're the PT boat chap?"

It was the Royal Navy officer who had done the briefing—Moore.

"I beg your pardon?"

"PT boats? Aren't you the fellow who went out looking for an E-boat? Didn't find one, but jolly good show just the same."

"Oh, we found one," Edland said, remembering the blazing mass bobbing up and down in the water. "We just didn't get to keep it."

"Still, quite an adventure. Quite the problem, Adolf's little boats. It'll take some doing to catch them in their lair. It'll take the lives of a lot of good chaps as well."

"That's true," Edland said, hoping that he could return to McNamar soon. He had an idea, something that had been nagging at him since he questioned the scared German sailor onboard the 155 boat. A wild, unformed thought that hung on a conversation that he had had many years before. A friend of a friend, he thought. Some academic who never saw the light of day because they were trapped in a self-made cage of theories, computations, and models. Then Edland heard Cole's name. He turned to Moore, startled.

"Jordan Cole," Dickie said. "He's in PT boats, too. Tall chap. Thin. Do you know him?"

"Yes," Edland said, wondering what else he could say about Jordan Cole. He decided to leave it at that.

"Splendid," Dickie said. "Absolutely splendid. Known Jordan since forty-one. Great friend. Great friend, indeed. I wonder, would you mind telling him that you and I met and we must talk? Would you do that?"

"I'd be happy to."

"Splendid. Perhaps I'll run into him first but one never knows these days, does one? We really should talk. Catch up on old times and such. Still, with the war being the war it might be a while. So you'll tell him that we chatted and I asked after him? Won't you?"

"I'll tell him."

"My. My, my. Fancy meeting a friend of Jordan's."

Edland saw McNamar motion toward him. "Excuse me, will you?"

"Certainly," Dickie said. "You won't forget, will you? Tell Jordan?"

"I won't," Edland said, and made his way to McNamar.

"The Royal Air Force is about to turn up the heat," McNamar said. "The consensus is that if we can't smash them up in the pens then we'll catch what's left of them at sea. It'll be a couple of days before anything happens; no Tall Boys."

"Somebody should get a close look at one of those new E-boats," Edland mused.

"That's not our concern, Mike. Why the interest?"

"Just curiosity, that's all, sir."

"Well, your curiosity is depriving me of one of my most valuable staff when I need him most, so knock it off. You want to solve a mystery, do it on your own time. Put in for some leave."

"Would you grant it, sir?" Edland smiled.

"In the middle of a war? Not on your life. Come on, we're going to start again."

"Will you excuse me, sir? I'll read over the minutes and catch up."

"Yeah, okay, but get with me later on. We've got a lot of work to do."

"Yes, sir," Edland said.

When Edland was outside, he decided to take a walk to clear his head. He fought the urge to jam his hands into his pockets, a habit of his, because it wasn't military. He'd been told this by an elderly captain, rather forcefully, and conditioned himself never to do it again, clasping his hands behind his back instead. But his head drifted down so that he studied the cracked sidewalk in front of him, another civilian mannerism, because, as far as he knew, there was no military code against walking with one's head down. He was dissecting memories, following bread crumbs, his father had called it when his father could be bothered to speak. "Intelligent men are often preoccupied," his mother explained, using one of several excuses that she kept nearby to account for his father's coldness. One day Edland, who had reached the age when such things are said, replied at the dinner table: "Yes, mother. Or perhaps he's just an arrogant, insensitive bastard who cares for no one but himself." That certainly gave the meal a unique flavor.

McCreay? McCary? Edland's mind traveled down a twisted path from Columbia to Stanford and finally settled on MIT. It had to be MIT, Edland told himself. But MIT? Why was I . . . Potter! Probably the most undisciplined individual in academia, a short, round, brilliant man whose personal life was always in tatters. "I wear pants with oilcloth pockets," Potter had once confided to Edland, "so that I may steal soup." Potter was one of those men who declared intelligence a burden but whose creativity and genius was a joy to watch unfold.

It was Potter, and it was MIT, and the man's name was McGill.

Edland bumped into a bowler-wearing individual with a trim mustache and umbrella. "I say, old chap," the man said, lifting an eyebrow. "You walk on your portion of the sidewalk and I shall walk on mine."

Edland mumbled an apology and hurried on, looking for a cab. He had to get back to headquarters. He had to send a cable to McGill at MIT. Several years ago Potter had taken him to a long, dank building that held a massive water tank, because McGill's secretary had captured Potter's interest. While Potter smiled and spoke with great charm to the secretary whose only attribute Edland could see was a massive bosom, Edland watched McGill hoist a strange miniature ship from the water. Outriggers, Edland thought, having seen devices such as that used to stabilize long, narrow craft in the Pacific. But the explanation troubled him the moment he said it; he knew that it wasn't correct but before he had time to investigate further, the secretary had dismissed Potter and so there was no reason to stay.

Outriggers, he remembered as he flagged a cab down. But not outriggers. Wings on boats. Flying boats. Sea Eagles.

Chapter 14

In the Baie de la Seine

There were six boats in the 11th Flotilla. Schnell boats, fast boats, in other words, or E-boats the British called them—simply enemy boats. Four of the six boats mounted Trinities, one boat remained in the pens in the process of having the guns installed, and one boat, S-317, had its well enlarged but carried nothing forward; no teeth, the crew told one another. It was on S-317 that Reubold stationed himself during the trials with the nervous Waldvogel at his side. They were just off a sandbar, far out into the bay, and the object of their test was a grand old bark that had strayed off course during a storm many years ago and died in the shallows. She was an unnamed wreck, her destination long forgotten. And everything topside had been swept away by winter storms except for the stubby remains of five masts that had once held fields of glistening canvas, bleached white by the sun. Now, embarrassed by her condition, she lay low in the shallow water so that no one could see what had become of her.

Reubold fired a flare and handed the gun to a matrose, receiving a set of binoculars in return.

"Now, let us see if your hard work has meant anything," he said.

Reubold and Waldvogel watched as an S-boat rapidly increased speed and then began to rise slowly out of the water on its foils. The wake was minimal as the boat moved ahead, becoming more difficult to track in the growing darkness as it roared across the choppy waves of the bay. Deep in the water the boats churned up a wide swath of phosphorescence—once up on their legs nothing marked their passage except three, slim, shimmering trails.

Waldvogel saw the S-boat swing slowly into position, its Trinity training round at the target. The boats could not turn sharply on their hydrofoils but had to make careful course adjustments as they flew through the water. It was the speed that he and the others counted on to elude the enemy gunners; speed and the power of the three 110-millimeter guns mounted in the bow.

"Coming in now, sir," Leutnant Kunkel reported to Reubold.

The fregattenkapitan said nothing, concentrating on the gray blur in the distance. There was a sharp puff of smoke behind the guns, followed by another and a third, and then the sound of the low boom reached them. Three distant columns of water appeared beyond the wreck and Reubold ordered: "What was their distance to target? Find out. Send Mueller in."

A sailor shot a green flare into the air, the harsh wind snatching at the smoky trail as it soared overhead.

"Three thousand five hundred meters," an officer reported to Reubold.

"Maximum range," Waldvogel said. "Maximum range. It's unlikely that they would have hit anything at maximum range." He was willing Reubold to accept the explanation, but the fregattenkapitan chose to ignore him.

"Have Mueller go in at twenty-five hundred," Reubold said to Kunkel, who disappeared down the narrow hatch into the radio room.

Waldvogel watched through his binoculars as Mueller's boat veered slightly to the starboard, making a long crescent through the water, and then turned hard to port. He was a thousand meters closer than the first boat.

When Mueller's boat was nearly parallel with the wreck it was suddenly enveloped in a large plume of dirty brown smoke that dissipated almost as quickly as it appeared. A flat boom echoed across the water as Reubold dropped his binoculars and shook his head.

"He's showing off. Firing a salvo." He looked at the others situated on the skullcap of S-317. "Well, did anyone see anything? Did he hit the wreck?"

An oberbootsmann near the starboard aerial lead-in called back: "All misses, sir. Far to the right."

Reubold turned to Waldvogel. "Now what? Moor them next to the wreck and let them fire?"

"Perhaps the sea makes it difficult," Waldvogel said.

"Yes," Reubold snapped. "Perhaps the sea makes it impossible to hit the target. Perhaps we should wait until it is calm. Perhaps we'll contact the Americans and British and say: 'Please, sir. Will you run your convoys only when the sea is as smooth as glass?'" He turned in disgust to the leutnant. "Send in Fritz at 40 knots. Have him fire in sequence at one thousand meters. No salvos. Send to Mueller that I want that shit to check his mount when he gets back. There's no telling what kind of damage he's done by showing off." He nestled the binoculars into his eyes and heard the soft pop of the flare gun behind him. "Korvettenkapitan, we have not done well tonight. We have practiced loading and firing your guns until we can do it in our sleep, but we still can't hit the target. What do you want me to tell high command?"

"I don't know," Waldvogel said. "I don't know what to say."

"Nor I," Reubold said as the next boat roared in toward the target. "I'm sure that the Silver Stripes won't be at a loss for words."

"Going in now," Kunkel said, excitement ringing in his voice.

Reubold located the S-boat. She was running flat out. He knew that Fritz would throttle down when he was near one thousand meters. He could practically feel Waldvogel's anticipation as the sound of the boat's engines rolled across the water. *He has every right to be concerned*, Reubold thought. *There will be no second chance if we fail this time.* He felt a twinge of regret. Such lovely machines, so sleek and fast and ominous in repose. How he loved fast things—cars, airplanes, boats; speed in any form was intoxicating. Machines that gobbled up distance and time were worthy of being honored. Products of men certainly, but the whole greater than the sum of the parts; those fast machines transcended design, parts, labor; calling on only the very best men to guide them.

"First gun," Kunkel shouted.

Brown smoke billowed out of the rear of the gun mount.

It had been seaplanes at first. Long, sleek, monoplanes, the pontoons an extension of the craft—an eagle's talons. Reubold raced them around gaily painted pylons festooned with flags, down broad watery avenues bound on either side by ships and boats of all sizes. Everything was a blur; every color smudged as his aircraft neared four hundred miles an hour. The only shapes that were distinct were the other planes and the pylons.

"Second gun. Fregattenkapitan, he's fired the second gun."

The first crash in a seaplane; the oil cap worked loose and smashed into the cockpit. Six inches to the right and it would have taken off his head. Oil covered the windshield, his goggles, filled his mouth, and he pulled back the stick, trying for altitude. Put some distance between yourself and the ground so that you have time to think. The engine sputtered; you throw off the goggles and spit the oil out of your mouth, looking desperately through a clear spot in the windshield for a place to land. The engine seizes, catches fire, the plane begins to yaw, and you realize that you haven't enough air speed left to control it. The sea races up at you. Darkness.

"There goes number three."

Reubold watched the shell splash into the water well beyond the target. He tossed his binoculars to an oberbootsmann.

"Again," he called to Kunkel. "Send them around again."

"Fregattenkapitan," the leutnant said, looking into the sky nervously. "It is not safe to stay out here too long. The bees."

"Yes, yes," Reubold snapped. "The enemy owns the skies despite what the Fat Man says. Well, do you see any bees? No? Neither do I. Have them line up again, leutnant, and we'll see just how much of a difference Waldvogel's tinkering has made." He turned on the korvettenkapitan. "Is it the sights, Waldvogel? Or the *treibladung*? Are they using *Ub A1s* or *Ub B*? Come on, you're the expert. These are your guns. Of course we can't hit a damn thing, but that's of little concern, isn't it?"

"Mueller coming around, sir," Kunkel said.

Reubold jerked the glasses from a bootmann-maat's hand and focused first on the S-boat, and then on the target. Waldvogel moved close to him and spoke in a whisper.

"It does no one any good to become cross," he offered. "I know that you're disappointed, as am I. I've racked my brain trying to find a way to sight the guns, trying to compensate for the movement of the boats."

Reubold said nothing, his attention on the boat flying across the water.

"If I could give my life for the Fatherland to ensure these guns functioned as I hoped," Waldvogel said, "I would certainly do so. I know that you think little of me. I frighten easily and I become seasick whenever we leave the bay. I'm not a good sailor."

"I don't care about any of that," Reubold said tersely, his eyes still at the binoculars. But he did. Something in the weak little man repelled Reubold—his manner, his sensitivity, the deference that he offered to everything and everyone around him. Weakness, Reubold finally decided; here was a weak man who made ineffective weapons and fast boats that rose out of the water on spindly legs. When Reubold did allow himself to think he realized that he found fault with Waldvogel because he envied him. Here was a man who possessed quiet passion, an inexplicable, unassailable drive to succeed. He did so despite self-doubts that threatened to devour him. He was like a coward who had decided to become a high-wire walker. His legs trembled so badly that the wire jerked uncontrollably beneath him and yet he continued to place one foot in front of the other, never losing sight of the platform at the other end of the wire. Reubold quickly crushed the idea that he was the lesser of the two men—the thought was far too disturbing. "Give me boats that run fast and guns that shoot straight," Reubold said coldly. "You can do that much, can't you? If you can't these things are of no consequence and they are certainly not ready for war."

"Firing." It was Kunkel again. He glanced from

the sky to the other on the S-boat. His mind was on
enemy planes. They could see in the darkness with
their radar.

"I know that," Reubold muttered crossly. His
shoulders sagged. "Misses. All of them. We can't
even hit a stationary target."

"Here comes Mueller again," an oberbootsmann
said.

"Come on," Reubold urged, his voice becoming
strained. "Come on, you delicious pervert." Reubold
saw a quick succession of clouds from the muzzle
flare and heard the dull reports of the cannon fire
as they echoed across the water. Just a moment
later three ghostlike shapes erupted out of the
water, well beyond the hulk.

The men gathered along the deck and skullcap
of the S-boat and lowered their glasses in disappointment, none daring to speak.

"Sir," Funker Lerch called to the bridge. "We've
picked up several aircraft about ninety kilometers
out."

Reubold turned to Kunkel. "Send Fritz in. Tell
him to take his time."

A shocked look crossed the leutnant's face. "Sir,
funker said . . ."

"Do as I order!" Reubold shouted.

The leutnant's "Yes, sir," was barely audible.

"Man the guns," Reubold said to the oberbootsmannmaat. There was a scurry of feet on the deck
as the men raced to their battle stations. The barrels of the 4cm and 2cm rose skyward in anticipation.

Reubold swung around the armored bridge,
tossed his binoculars to a matrose, and dropped

through the bridge hatch into the radio room. "Get out," he said to the surprised funker on duty. As the man was making his way up the hatch, Reubold took a moment to calm himself. He unsnapped his duty bag, pulled out a syringe and vial, filled the syringe partially with water, then with morphine, rolled up his sleeve, and turned to see Waldvogel.

"The men deserve better than that," the korvettenkapitan said.

"Yes," Reubold said, injecting himself. "They do." He closed his eyes, preparing for the familiar, comforting euphoria. It would be a moment, he knew. The warmth would spread throughout his limbs and his heart would beat with a renewed strength. There would be no doubts, his body would not ache, and his regrets would be subdued. All this from a pinprick.

He brushed passed Waldvogel and went back on deck. "Fritz?" he said.

"No hits," the leutnant said, shaking his head.

"All right," he said. He saw the radioman standing uncertainly near the canvas dodger. "Go on," Reubold said playfully. "Get below. Go on. Let's not have the bees catch us out here."

"Shall we line up for another run, sir?" the leutnant said.

"No," Reubold said. "We're going in. Let the others know."

"Fregattenkapitan," Waldvogel said, joining him. "Please. Let us continue with the tests." He pulled a handful of crumpled papers from his tunic. "You see? I've been making notes. Here." He flipped through the stack. "You see? Notes on the *schubkur-*

belverschluss. I thought that I might modify the breech. For the loader's benefit. Here," he pulled out a crumpled paper covered with calculations. "It must have something to do with the *zielfernohr*. Don't you agree? Surely you can see that?"

Reubold's body swayed with the motion of the boat.

"They don't work," he said finally, watching the hope in Waldvogel's eyes drain away. There was no pleasure or pain in his voice. "Your guns don't work. And without them your hydrofoils are useless. We will go back and I will make my report."

"But I'll find a way," Waldvogel pleaded. "There's always a way, Fregattenkapitan."

"This is nonsense, Waldvogel," Reubold said, wishing the little man would simply accept his defeat. "Just because you desire it, does not mean it will be achieved." He turned to the leutnant, dismissing Waldvogel from his mind. "Radio base. Tell them we're coming home."

The emergency lights glowed a dull red in the rich darkness of the S-boat pen. No other light was tolerated except the small work lamps the crews used on deck. The Allied bombers owned the day and night and, like hawks dropping on their quarry, would swoop down if the tiniest sliver of light showed in the darkness. They had returned from the bay and the disappointing trials nearly three hours before—the boats sitting in silence, the men, exhausted, nearly as quiet.

The red glow subdued everything—movement, talk over the low hum of machinery. The air was heavy with humidity; the weight of it slowed a man's responses and his interest in anything except the most mundane things. Add sweat to humidity and strength melted away. A man felt filthy all of the time, a matrose once remarked as the men labored over replacing a gun barrel. Clothing clung to a man's skin because of the dampness of the pens. The concrete walls of the pens were cool and clammy, and wet to the touch.

Reubold's crew sat on the deck, just forward of the skullcap, loading ammunition belts. They did so silently at first because they were tired and hot, and the dank interior of the pen irritated them. After a time their good spirits revived and they began to insult each other good-naturedly, embellishing stories about one another so that laughter accompanied the boring but necessary task. Waldvogel sat near the gun well that held the Trinity guns, not because he wanted to be a part of the conversation—he would not go where he was not invited—but because he thought that if he was close to the guns, he might be inspired.

The crew ignored him. He was not one of them. He wasn't even a seagoing officer. He wasn't a Silver Stripe either, so the men weren't quite sure what function he performed, and everyone must perform some function to be accepted in their world. So they tolerated him, but with coolness reserved for things they didn't understand and that they were highly suspicious of. They knew boats, engines, and guns; and they knew the enemy, especially the British, but they were beginning to know the Americans. They accepted things only if they were familiar with them, and could understand their rationale for existence. Nothing else was of consequence.

"Go get another box of shells," a bootsmann ordered a matrose.

"And don't drop it," another matrose said. The men laughed at the weak joke.

"You suppose he dreams of those things?" the bootsmann said, jerking his head toward Waldvogel.

An oberbootsmann shook his head and unbuttoned the collar on his shirt. Any breeze that came off the harbor was captured by the maul of the pen and denied entrance. "He's a strange one," he observed.

The matrose returned, lugging the box. He set it on the deck with a thump.

"Easy," an oberbootsmannmaat said. "Those things explode."

"Like our commander," the bootsmann tossed the opinion over the case.

The men gave a low laugh and began sliding the shells in the belt.

"Did you hear him take the leutnant's head off today?" a young matrose said, glancing around to see how the older men received his comment. They were quick to put anyone in their place that spoke out of turn.

"Everyone heard that," the bootsmann said, to the matrose's relief. It was the first step toward acceptance by the other men. He was becoming one of them.

"He isn't what he used to be," someone said.

The oberbootsmannmaat snorted. "He's got only himself to blame for that. Mind you, he's a fine fighter but he's one of those men who always manage to shit where they eat."

"What do you mean?" the young matrose said.

"You don't know the true story of our commander?" another man said.

The matrose shook his head.

"Goering wants him dead," the oberbootsmann-maat said. "If the Fat Man wasn't so close to being finished himself, he would have gotten his wish."

"Why?"

"Reubold was a pilot," the bootsmann said, apparently comfortable enough with his seniority to join in the oberbootsmannmaat's story. "Shot down a hundred Ivans."

"I heard two hundred," said an old matrose who liked to drink too much to keep his rank.

"All right," a bootsmannmaat conceded. "Two hundred." He finished a belt and reached for another. "Goering called him back to Berlin to award him the Knight's Cross or something at a big dinner. Reubold drank everything in sight and then turned and threw up in Goering's lap."

The men laughed while the young matrose looked shocked.

"Not that Goering minds having a man's head in his lap," the bootsmannmaat said. "But he doesn't want the fellow to throw up."

The low wail of air-raid sirens stopped the laughter. The men looked up, as if they could see through the 14 feet of concrete overhead.

"Well," the oberbootsmannmaat said. "This isn't such a bad place to be after all. Is it?"

"Watch the bastards blow up our billet again," the old matrose said. "I hate the British."

Searchlights cut on in the darkness, thin gleaming trails that swept the dark sky. Anti-aircraft guns began to boom, splitting the night like lightning.

"Goering hates him for that?" the young matrose asked.

"Nobody takes the Fat Man too seriously any more. Especially the Fuehrer." The oberbootsmannmaat's head swung toward the entrance of the pen when lesser caliber guns began to stitch the darkness with tracers. He glanced at Waldvogel. The little man was intent on the bright flashes outside the pen entrance. A child, the oberbootsmannmaat thought. *They send us children and idiots who like to watch pretty things in the sky. Go out there, child. See how pretty those lights really are.* He returned to the conversation. "That just gave people one more reason to make fun of the Fat Man."

"So Reubold is here," the bootsmannmaat said. "At least until he gets killed. Maybe . . ."

The oberbootsmannmaat interrupted him. "Where'd that fellow go?"

The bootsmannmaat looked around. "What fellow?"

"The fregattenkapitan," the oberbootsmannmaat said. "He was standing right there."

"You don't think he's gone to report us to Reubold, do you?"

The oberbootsmannmaat stood. "Turn out that light," he ordered. Someone switched off the work light, leaving just the red emergency lighting. The oberbootsmannmaat's eyes swept the pen. "He was just here. I hope he didn't try to leave. The bombing's picking up."

Anti-aircraft guns boomed constantly as the

bombers neared the harbor. Once in a while a
bomber would fall to earth in a fiery streak. But
there would be more bombers, and they would
come every night until everything was destroyed.

"There he is," the young matrose shouted, pointing.

Waldvogel was walking as if in a daze toward the
giant maw of the pen. The oberbootsmannmaat
jumped onto the dock and, followed by several of
the other men, ran after Waldvogel. "Korvettenkapitan! Stop. Don't go any farther."

The worst place to be during a raid was the entrance to the pen. It was the only place that enemy
bombs could get you. The insides of the walls at
the entrance were deeply scarred by bomb fragments, and the leading edges of the pen roof were
chipped and split. And yet Waldvogel walked on,
oblivious to the shouts of the men who raced after
him or the deadly rain of bombs headed toward
the pen. He saw only one thing: the graceful trails
of green tracers as they searched for enemy planes.
They arced into the night, the slim glowing trails
curved by distance and gravity. His eyes flicked
from tracer band to tracer band, his mind working
quickly, absorbing and calculating everything that
he saw. He vaguely heard the shouts of the men
behind him, but they were a minor distraction and
he ignored them.

Waldvogel's mind flew over the possibilities as
he watched the spectacular demonstration in the
night sky over Cherbourg. It was all for his benefit,
and he accepted it without question because it
gave him the answer that he needed.

Now he knew what could be done. Now he knew

how to solve the problem that had threatened to destroy everything. Now he could tell Reubold.

A Tallboy dropped from a Lancaster struck the water and buried itself in the harbor mud a short distance away. As Waldvogel approached the entrance, it exploded.

Chapter 15

London, England

Edland had sublet a small apartment; it was not
luxurious by any standards, but he seldom indulged
himself in luxuries. He had learned to get by
with very little. His expeditions to China, rather, accompanying his father on *his* expeditions to China,
had convinced him that most things were unnecessary and were encumbrances to everyday living.
"You don't need that," was his father's common re-
frain as he packed for the trips, or the few times
that the Great Man came to visit him. "Clutter,
clutter," his father sniffed, surveying what Edland
always considered rooms remarkably free of anything except the basics. For the first few times Edland was irritated, and even angered. But then he
began to ignore his father's opinion and even toss
in a remark about having new furniture delivered,

or something guaranteed to prick the Great Man's remarkably thin hide.

Edland would not admit it to himself, and would certainly never share the thought with his famous father, that his father was right. So he conditioned himself to live with little. He divested himself of memories, tokens, souvenirs, and the hundreds of other things that reflect a man's experiences. His life, like his apartment, was barren of such sentimentality.

A persistent knock at the door brought Edland out of a satisfying sleep, filled with dreams of the vast Gobi: endless caravans of plodding camels, and the high, mysterious mountains of Tibet that look to have been created by God simply to shoulder the ominous clouds that crowded the sky.

He made his way out of the bedroom, checked to see that the blackout curtains were in place, and switched on a small lamp atop his scarred desk. Opening the door in mid-knock, he found a young naval officer waiting in the dimly lit hall.

"Lieutenant Commander Michael Edland?" the officer asked.

"Yes," Edland said, wondering what time it was. His body told him that it had to be very late and he had been nearing deep sleep when the knock awoke him.

"Can I see your ONI I.D., sir?"

Edland nodded, retrieved the card from his wallet on the desk, and handed it to the officer. The young man scanned the card, glanced at Edland, and handed it back.

"Thank you, sir," he said. "This arrived for you

about an hour ago." He handed Edland a sealed gray envelope stamped USN SECRET, saluted, and left.

Edland closed the door slowly, locked it, and carefully tore off the flap of the envelope. That was quick, he thought, and then took the time to calculate when he had sent the cable, what time it was in the States, and how quickly McGill would respond to his series of questions. If McGill understood what Edland was asking him. He moved to the chair near his desk, adjusted the lamp to give himself more light, unfolded the three sheets of paper, and smoothed them across his knee.

Edland began to read the reply.

"Are you a madman?" Reubold shouted at Waldvogel in the cavernous pen, his voice bouncing off the hard concrete walls.

The medical officer gave Reubold a look of reprimand and continued wrapping a bandage around Waldvogel's head. A tiny stream of blood stained the pure white cloth.

"How many times have I told you to stay well inside the pen during a bombing raid? Didn't you hear me order the men to do so? You must have heard that; I said it often enough."

"Please, Fregattenkapitan," Waldvogel said, grimacing. "Please don't chastise me so loudly. My head hurts terribly."

"You could be dead," Reubold said, the volume of his voice rising. "Dead you don't help me. Dead you're no good to me."

"I was under the impression that you were through with me and my boats," Waldvogel ventured.

"Do not tax my patience," Reubold said. "This is no time for silly words. Look at that." He pointed to a large crack in the concrete ceiling. A powdery dust continued to sift from the jagged edges of the crack, covering the surface of the black water. "That was a bomb that landed a hundred meters from here. The shock wave sent a wave into the pen that almost swamped the boats."

"That must have been what knocked me down," Waldvogel mused in appreciation. "It must have been a very large bomb."

"Yes," Reubold said. "It would appear so." He turned to the group of officers and men watching the exchange. "All right. All right. You have things to do. Get out." The officers and noncommissioned officers hastily shepherded the men back to the boats. "How is he?" Reubold asked the medical officer.

The officer took a strip of tape from a medical officer and sealed the edge of the bandage in a fold. "I think he has a concussion. He could have cracked his skull. I don't know."

"You don't know?"

The medical officer straightened and gestured to the steward to gather his belongings. "I didn't bring an X-ray machine," he said as if Reubold was slow-witted. "And I can't adequately examine him in this cave. My advice is to get him to the hospital and have someone there look him over. Until then, lower your voice, and don't be such an ass."

Reubold helped Waldvogel to his feet as the medical officer and orderly left. The korvettenkapitan examined his drenched clothing.

"I am a mess," he said. "I think the uniform is ruined. They are so hard to come by."

"What were you doing?" Reubold said.

"What?"

"What were you doing? Where were you going? The men said you walked to the maw as if you were drunk. Were you trying to kill yourself? If that's the case, just wait. The British would gladly do that for you."

Waldvogel rubbed his head tenderly. "No, no. Nothing like that." He looked toward the entrance to the pen. The night was black and calm, except for the dim light of the faraway fires set by falling bombs. He began to shiver. Reubold removed his leather jacket and covered Waldvogel's shoulders.

"Thank you," Waldvogel said. He studied the entrance, trying to remember what had drawn him near the edge, what had almost gotten him killed. He tasted grit in his mouth and looked at the crack in the ceiling. "Such a bomb," he said in admiration.

"Yes," Reubold said. "I'll write the RAF and congratulate them. Let's get away from here."

"Yes," the korvettenkapitan said, trying to sort through his memory. "The guns," he said, when the thought came back to him in a flood of images. "The anti-aircraft guns. How simple it was. What a dunce."

"What?"

"The guns," Waldvogel said excitedly. His hands came up and began to piece the scene together for Reubold. "I watched them for a time before I real-

ized that they held the answer. I did not realize it
before. The searchlights, I thought at first. I watched
them sweep the sky," his hand pantomimed the
movement of a searchlight. "And I thought, yes.
That will certainly work. And then I thought, how
ridiculous. They would present the perfect target
for the enemy."

"What are you talking about?" Reubold said, losing his patience.

"The boats, Fregattenkapitan. I did not understand. They have such little movement when on
the foils. They are not like other craft, bouncing
over the waves, being battered by the sea."

"Yes," Reubold said. "They are fast. But we still
cannot aim what we shoot at. What of it?"

"Precisely," Waldvogel said. This time it was his
turn to become excited, and his hands became little fists as the full memory of what he had discovered before the explosion came back to him. "The
slightest movement, the very least movement at
the gun barrel, is translated into many times that
by even a minor intrusion."

"So?"

"The variation is multiplied by the distance to
the target. The gunners have no time to compensate for the slightest movement, even if they are
aware of it."

Reubold remained silent, listening. Waldvogel,
heartened by the fregattenkapitan's attention, continued.

"The gunners need a simple device to lay the
Trinity exactly on target. I've wasted my time with
gyroscopes and complicated sighting devices, and

even blamed the gunners for their inability to hit the targets."

"Imagine their frustration and what they thought of you," Reubold said. "Continue."

"I saw the tracers fill the sky," Waldvogel said, almost breathless with revelation. "Long, thin lines of light. And then, I realized—we will use tracers. We will sight by the line of tracers as they strike the target. When we see the fall of the shell, we fire the Trinity. The target is illuminated by the 2cm shells striking it."

"How does that help?" Reubold said, trying to keep the disappointment out of his voice. He could not take the boats out again simply to fail. He had felt Waldvogel's possibility and for an instant had accepted the man's excitement as his own—willing the idea's success. But he dare not promote an idea that he felt would have little chance of success. He could not stand the defeat. "If we use the mid-ship's doorknocker we have their distance from the Trinity's to contend with. Not a great distance in meters but enough to throw off anyone's aim. It is also lower than the Trinity. Remember that when we rise on your hydrofoils our bow is up. I am not a gunner, but if a slight movement presents a problem than surely height and position impact on the situation as well."

"Yes," Waldvogel said, undaunted.

"Well then, how can you think that this is a solution? We are exactly where we were before, Waldvogel: half-formed ideas and idiotic notions." Reubold's anger was fueled by the idea that nothing would ever come of the boats and their guns. Sea Eagles the men called them. They might soon be eagles without talons.

"No. No," Waldvogel said hastily. "I did not explain myself properly. Forgive me, please. Next to them. Atop them perhaps. If we attach a 2cm in place on the mount, the trajectory will be exactly the same."

"The same," Reubold said, his mind forming a picture. A quad arrangement. It would be cramped in the gun well. It was a tight fit with the Trinity alone. The placement of the doorknocker would not be the problem; there was more than enough room on the mount. But the gun crew would now be forced to man both the Trinity and the doorknocker. Could it be done? The 2cm ate up ammunition at an exorbitant rate—it required constant attention from its loaders. Could it be done? He noticed Waldvogel looking at him expectantly.

"Fregattenkapitan?"

"You shit," Reubold said. "Just when I thought that I was through with your boats and guns."

"What do you think?"

"I think that it will require a great deal of training. I think also that I shall have to approach my superiors and convince them that we have at last found the key to this filthy mystery. We have, haven't we, Korvettenkapitan? We have found the key at last?"

Waldvogel smiled weakly. "I hope so."

That poor shit isn't even convinced, Reubold thought. *How am I going to take this idea to the Silver Stripes?* But he saw the possibility and it was amazingly simple. Use the 2cm's tracer strikes on the target to aim the Trinity. Reubold's eyes lowered in concentration. Where was the weakness? Every solution had a weakness; where was Waldvogel's? Was there one? Have the gun trainer or layer fire the doorknocker—the other fires the Trinity. The doorknocker eats up ammunition. The Trinity loader and assistant loader will have to feed both guns. Difficult, but it could be done. Especially if the rate of fire was reduced. There would be no need for a constant barrage—just a few shots to locate the target. Everything would have to happen instantaneously. Seconds, Reubold thought. *Strike, sight, fire. Seconds.*

Where was the weakness? Reubold challenged himself. What would cause this plan to fail, like all the others before it?

A cloud of concrete dust descending from the huge crack in the ceiling caught his attention. It settled slowly, covering the calm waters with a gritty film. What would have happened, Reubold reasoned, if it had landed directly on the S-boat pen? It would have destroyed the boat anchorage, or trapped the S-boats inside.

Move the boats, he suggested to himself.

"Fregattenkapitan?" Waldvogel said. "May I be excused? I should like to lie down."

"Yes," Reubold said. "First, go to the hospital and have them examine you. If you die before this problem is solved I'll be very distressed."

Waldvogel nodded, offering a sickly smile, and left Reubold pondering his options. Move the boats. Where? They are nocturnal animals—the night hides them from the Allies. In the bright light of the sun they could be too easily found and destroyed. He walked closer to the entrance, examining the concrete walls and ceiling. Tiny fissures feathered out from the main crack but they appeared stable. Best to take our chances here, Reubold thought. I'll order the boats out before the next raid, he concluded. Maybe that will save them.

Save them from the enemy, yes, his mind countered, but who will save them from the Silver Stripes and the army? He turned to see the hunched figure of Waldvogel disappear among the crews tending the boats.

Perhaps you are the better man, Reubold thought. *I hope that you are. I hope that your ideas bear fruit.*

Chapter 16

The U.S. Navy Base at Portsmouth

Cole hung up the telephone, thanked the duty officer, and made his way back to his quarters. He had spent five minutes talking to Dickie Moore and he was drained.

"But you must go and see her," Dickie had said, his insistence irritating Cole.

"No," Cole had said. "I can't."

"Oh, now, Jordan. Let's not be silly about this. I know perfectly well that you can go and see her. She lives not two hours' drive from you, and don't forget I know exactly where you are. Simply hop in a jeep—there must be dozens of those things lying around there—and pop in. Do her a world of good."

"Dickie," Cole had said, "how is it you have time to stick your nose in my business? Aren't you doing important things elsewhere?" Every conversation had a certain cryptic quality to it. The lines were monitored and if someone made the mistake of mentioning a place, or ship, or anything else that might be construed as giving aid and comfort to the enemy, he'd be on a fast boat back to the States, if not charged with some offense. So everyone used caution and the telephone conversations were sometimes reduced to a series of silly guessing games. They reminded Cole of the child's puzzle—connect the dots.

"Important? Don't be silly. I have a remarkable talent for avoiding anything of consequence. Unless there's a beautiful young lady involved. I see that as my true service to the Empire. Now you must go. As a friend."

When he was called to the Duty Hut for a telephone call and signed his name in the log, he thought at first it might be Rebecca Blair calling. His mind raced with the possibilities of the role that he would play—cold, arrogant, disinterested, abrupt—emotions that he could, lately, call up without effort. But it was Dickie and the one emotion that he hadn't counted on came as a surprise to him—disappointment. He really wanted to hear Rebecca's voice.

"She's left that filthy husband of hers," Dickie continued. "High time I say. Bloody bastard. Almost makes one wish that he'd bought it in . . ." Dickie caught himself, "wherever the filthy pig was."

"I'm glad she left him," Cole had said. He turned away from the duty officer's desk so the man couldn't eavesdrop on the conversation. The officer took the hint and headed for a coffee urn on the other side of the room.

"Then you must go and see her. The poor thing. She looks positively worn out."

The conversation went on like that for several minutes until the duty officer returned, and, to Cole's relief, mouthed the words: "I'm sorry, sir." He had to get off the telephone. He said good-bye to Dickie, walked the short distance to his quarters, and found the gray .30-caliber ammunition box that held all of his important papers. He snapped it open, rifled through the contents, and found the envelope he wanted. He set the box on the floor by his cot, opened the letter, and began to read.

My Dear Jordan:

I hardly know how to begin. When you left I felt as if my world had collapsed. Gregory was most insistent about knowing who you were and why I was so upset. I made some miserable excuses about the whole thing; telling him that I hadn't gotten over the shock of his wounds. I could not tell him, of course, that I had sent away the man I loved, and still think of nearly every day. Your face, your smell, your touch stays with me. There was a chap at the hospital, an American civilian who sounded so much like you that I nearly burst into tears. He was one of your journalists. I wanted very much to ask him about you, as if every American over here knows every other American. I felt incredibly stupid and so out of sorts that I could barely do my job. I went into the stairwell and had a good cry. It was some time before I could pull myself back together.

I am concerned about your well-being, my darling, because of the war but also because I know

*that I hurt you terribly and I know that you hold
things deep within you, close to your heart. You are
a kind man, Jordan; a good man and sensitive as
well. I fear that I have hurt you so deeply that you
will always hate me and I hope that I am wrong.*

*This horrible war has taken so much from so
many and it has taken you away from me by playing a cruelest joke of all—giving us both hope. I
think how horrible that I must be that in many
ways I wish that the news of Gregory's death had
been true. I am horrible, aren't I? Now Gregory
dashes about, trying to prove that he is the best of
men, and I cannot stop thinking of you.*

*Perhaps this war will conspire to bring us to-
gether again, my darling, as sure as it drove us
apart. Until that time, please don't think ill of me
and remember, always, that you shall always be in
my heart.*

Please write. I cannot bear not hearing from you.
                              Rebecca

Cole had memorized most of it and as his eyes
lingered on her signature, he realized that he
should go see her; perhaps there was a chance that
they could be together. He lay on the bed, folded
his arms across his chest, and watched the overhead fan turn slowly.

It had happened so quickly, falling in love with
Rebecca. Days really. A flash of passion—love so intense that he felt it in every part of his body. Nothing
like that had ever happened to him before. The war,
Rebecca said, it does that to people. Maybe, Cole
thought, or maybe some people just have to be together, despite everything else.

He folded the letter carefully and slid it into the envelope. Two hours away, Dickie said; just jump in a jeep and go to her. Cole realized how easy it would be and the thought gave him hope.

Then he remembered the pain that he felt at leaving her, the betrayal because of her choice of a disgusting cripple over him. Not just a physical cripple, but a cruel, hateful man who treated her like a servant. Cole had gone far away: first to the States for training, then to the Mediterranean for service. Miles away—years away. *A man changes*, he told himself, and he felt a coldness enter his heart. *You deaden your emotions*, he convinced himself, *you don't let anything in; not love, friendship, affection of any kind, and then if it's denied you, you're still in one piece.*

Go to her. The thought was unbidden and came as a surprise to Cole. He pushed it away. He reached over without looking and dropped the letter in the box. Out in the hallway of the Officers' Quarters he heard muffled voices followed by a laugh. He closed his eyes.

Bury yourself in work. Lose yourself in the war.

More laughter. Other voices. Something about a bottle. Cole reached up and snapped off the bedside light. The noises died down as his mind detailed the work assignments for boat maintenance. Smother the memories until none remained. He was tired and he felt sleep coming easily and with it a sense of satisfaction. Nothing to it, he told himself. Just train yourself to be cold and uncaring so that nothing can get in, and nothing will get out.

Nothing to it.

Deep within he knew that he had chosen to be-

come a coward and decided as well that he would
not consider her at all. A tiny voice in his mind
said this was nonsense of course and just because
he said it was true—that he could survive without
pain by denying the memories and holding the
feeling at a distance—did not make it so. Too
much of her remained: her voice, her searching
eyes, the hurt that he caused by simply being close
to her when he knew that he should not have
been. It was, as she told him the truth when he
went away for the last time and something that he
knew to be inescapable even if he denied its existence; it could not always be as he wanted.

He had long before come to realize that he was
selfish, pursuing things because he wanted to pos-
sess them, and once they were within his grasp—he
dared not think too long on this because it reinforced the notion that he was as bad as Gregory—
he became tired of them.

Maybe, Cole thought, unwilling to accept that notion. A child she called him, not in derision but in
explanation. She might as well have said: you are
learning about the true nature of love. Maybe, Cole
thought again but the thought was bitter, tied to
the twin emotions of regret and betrayal—so often
false sensations, but they would do for a man too
afraid to embrace the idea that sometimes people
didn't get what they wanted.

He knew that the feelings swirling inside would
not answer a single question. They were—just there.

Fatigue that swept over him came from things
that had happened before: events that he had
been unable to control. A love lost, men dead or
wounded. Love lost, he thought, disgusted with him-

self. How melodramatic. Where are the violins and tears or . . . but it didn't work. He could not destroy the sorrow with humiliation.

He sunk into deep thought for several minutes, memories flashing through his mind so that each was an accusation. Each a reminder of how he had failed. He could not help Rebecca; he could not save Harry Lowe. The night that he lost six boats— he forced the memories, bringing his will to bear so that the images that haunted him were shattered.

He felt his strength returning, a solid wall of willpower convincing him that he did not have to succumb to any of it. He was strong, unassailable.

It was a perfectly attainable state of mind, Cole assured himself. But then he posed the question: *Then why am I so miserable?*

Gierek and Jagello stood among a group of Pathfinder pilots and navigators in the briefing hut, listening as the Photo Reconnaissance Interpreter pointed out their deficiencies with the help of a long wooden dowel and a batch of photographs scattered on a slanted table. It was Cherbourg in miniature and the PRI man talked in a strange combination of optimism and chastisement—the way one would talk to an errant child from whom one expected so much more.

"You see, chaps," said the PRI man with the bushy mustache. "Here is where we had hits before the last raid. Right here. See?" He was accompanied by a bored corporal whose job it was to keep the eight-by-ten photographs in place on the plywood table. "You see, here are the hits. Here. Here." The dowel flicked across the image. "Here. And we think here." He looked at the crowded briefing hut as if he were perfectly willing to admit that the chaps at PRI were fallible as well. Jagello crossed his arms over his chest and Gierek rolled his eyes.

"You Polish fellows are doing splendidly and I must say Bomber Command is top-notch. Jolly good, I say."

"Jolly good," Gierek muttered. Jagello remained unmoving.

"You can see from the hit records," PRI slapped the wall to emphasize the strikes. "Our Tall Boys hit damned close to those bloody pens."

"Jolly good," Gierek repeated.

"But our latest photos show that the pens are still fully functional. Indeed, they seem to have remained unscathed. I'm afraid that we haven't quite got the hang of it yet. We're still just a dash away from the target."

One of the Polish airmen next to Jagello leaned in and asked for a translation of the English word *dash*. Jagello obliged him.

"We didn't hurt it," he said in Polish.

The other man nodded in appreciation and wrote the word down in a notebook. He had been a schoolteacher and he liked to improve his English vocabulary.

"Now you see, chaps," PRI said. "We must do better next time. I'm sure that you can. You Polish fellows are doing a splendid job."

Squadron Commander Gabszewwicz, 205's commander, stepped forward and said something to

PRI. The English officer, not quite finished with his presentation, was taken aback. He tried to recover with a quick: "Well, there you have it." He tucked the dowel under his arm like a swagger stick and called out: "That's it, Taylor. Wrap it up, will you?"

"Leave the photos," Gabszewwicz said and waited patiently while PRI and his corporal left the Briefing Room. Somebody turned on the overhead lights. The place was a riot of photographs and maps pinned on walls and scattered across wooden tables. There was a desk against one wall next to a window with a small plaque on it that read DUTY OFFICER. The surface of the desk was orderly, a remarkable contrast to the rest of the Briefing Room.

Gabszewwicz surveyed the crowded room before speaking. His voice was clear, and the men could tell by his tone that the news was not good.

"There are no more Tall Boys," he said. "At least not for us. Not for Cherbourg. Maybe the other ports, they haven't told me. That means the Lancasters will have to go in with conventional loads. We have to be very sure where we put our markers."

The men in the hut stirred a bit. They might as well be dropping rocks on those bunkers for all the damage that conventional bombs did against the 14-foot-thick roofs.

"I know that you want to know what we're doing and how much damage that we're causing the enemy," Gabszewwicz said. "Especially now." It was the invasion. That was all anyone ever talked about. Everything was preparation for invading France. "Those pens are tough. We haven't quite done the trick yet."

"You mean the British haven't, don't you, Papa?" Lintz said. He was new to the squadron and arrogant, and he tried to bully his way into the confidence of the older men.

Gabszewwicz's eyes never left the photographs on the table, but Gierek knew that Lintz had made a mistake. The squadron commander never talked about American, British, or Polish aircraft and aircrews—he always said, "Our men." It was an unspoken understanding among the men of the City of Krakow Squadron. Every airman was a brother, and every brother was involved in a deadly pursuit. Besides, Gierek knew, Lintz hadn't earned the right to call Gabszewwicz "Papa."

Gabszewwicz waited long enough before speaking to show Lintz that he was displeased, and then he began the briefing again. "The target area is the *Normandie* Quay." The quay was especially built before the war to dock the liners *Normandie* and *Queen Mary*. It jutted into the harbor like a small peninsula. "The oil pumping stations have been destroyed," Gabszewwicz said, "but the pens aren't damaged." He looked at the group of men surrounding him. "Some of us go back soon. It can't be helped."

"I hope it's us," Gierek said to Jagello. "I don't like sitting around. It's a pile of shit." He liked American slang. It was very descriptive and made perfect sense. English slang was silly and confusing. "Erks." That made no sense—there was no reason to call the ground crew that serviced his Mosquito "erks." "Jolly good" was another English phrase that Gierek found irritating—it was laced with patently false optimism. The Americans and their slang—so much better. "Go jump in the lake." "Take a hike." "Get lost." Gierek once wondered if the lake was allegorical or was there a particular lake that the Americans had in mind?

"Some men from the City of Warsaw squadron may be joining us," Gabszewwicz said. "Number 316. That's not certain yet."

The men in the room brightened. It was always a special treat to have other Poles flying with them. They'd heard of No. 316. They were based in Northolt and had earned a reputation as a fierce bunch of airmen, wildly driving their Spitfire Vs into Luftwaffe formations, tearing at the enemy fighters like devils. It was a good sign, a good omen to have their countrymen join them on these missions. Especially these missions.

The Germans were prepared for their raids. The equation was simple; the Poles had to light the target—Germans knew that the Poles had to light the target. The Germans knew that the Poles and British attacked at night and the Americans attacked during the day. It was routine, an immutable schedule. The train arrives at the terminal at such-and-such a time and departs the terminal at such-and-such a time.

Gabszewwicz continued to brief the men and Gierek listened, but as he listened he thought of the Ariel motorcycle that lay in parts near the hanger that housed his Mosquito. He bought it three months ago from a pilot officer who went up one day and never came back. He'd seen his first motorcycle when he was flying Harvards—AT-6s the Americans called them—and he fell in love with the speed and freedom that the tiny machine promised.

He'd paid the pilot officer ten pounds for the motorcycle even though it was in a hundred pieces, and he'd refused the help of the erks to make it whole again. Jagello, upon seeing the mass of grimy parts stacked haphazardly against the corrugated steel wall, raised one eyebrow and walked off.

But the motorcycle was Gierek's and he was determined to put it back together. It was the challenge to create something for himself—a quest for personal satisfaction derived not from killing or destroying, but from making whole something that was not.

"Gierek," Gabszewwicz said. "It's you and Jagello in the lead again. There are reports of German night fighters operating out of Cherbourg. Don't let them come up on you. Lintz and Helix as well. Take off is at nineteen hundred. Assembly is nine-thirty hours off Brighton. Pick up your charts with the assembly point, course, and position." The men made notes on the small pads they carried in the pockets of their flying togs, copying information off the large chalkboard that had been rolled in behind Gabszewwicz.

"Any questions?" the squadron commander asked. He surveyed the group, waiting. Gabszewwicz was very thorough, a calm, competent commander who seldom smiled or showed any emotion. Some said this was because of what had happened to the family he had left behind in Poland. No one was quite sure what the story was, but all of the men had left someone behind, and the memories of those whom they had abandoned to the Germans haunted them.

"Gierek?" Gabszewwicz said, catching the pilot's attention. "You're senior man."

The implication was clear: lead. Lintz and Helig were new to the squadron and had been on just three missions before. Never at night, and never over Cherbourg. Lead.

As the meeting broke up, Gierek motioned to Lintz and Helig. The two pilots and their navigators joined him.

"Come to my quarters in an hour," Gierek said. "I want to go over the mission."

"Gabszewwicz told us everything that we should know," Lintz said. "I haven't eaten in hours. I'm famished."

"You can go and kill yourself out of stupidity if you wish," Gierek said. He was surprised at just how calmly he spoke. Lintz's words had enraged him and normally he would have exploded at the young pilot's arrogance. But he realized as he spoke that he had far more control over his emotions than he expected. "I won't have you endangering the bombers, Helig, or me. You'll come to my quarters in an hour or I'll go to Gabszewwicz and request that you be transferred. He will do that because he doesn't want fools in his squadron."

Lintz looked as if he had been slapped, but the anger quickly drained away. He nodded and he and the others left.

Gierek pulled a pack of cigarettes from his pocket, thought better of it, and put them away. "Why did Papa do that to me? Why did he make

me the boss?" he asked Jagello. Gabszewwicz was
Papa to the veteran pilots; they respected him immensely.

"He knows that you are lucky," Jagello said,
handing Gierek a lit cigarette. The pilot took it
gratefully before he realized what his navigator
had said.

"Lucky?"

"Before every mission the Black Prince lays in
front of our plane. And we've always come back.
Or . . ."

Gierek eyed his suspiciously. "Or what?"

"Papa's a sadist," Jagello said, walking off.

Edland waited until the officers settled themselves in the large classroom at St. Paul's School.
He had briefed high-ranking officers before—general, admirals, air marshals—even the prime minister, although he was never certain if Churchill
was awake during his presentation. This was something different; he was about to explain something
that made little sense to him.

"Good afternoon, gentlemen," Edland said. He
noted McNamar in the front row. It was the admiral's idea for him to brief the officers after Edland
went to him and said: "I've uncovered something
interesting." McNamar had listened patiently as
Edland explained what he had found, and finally
said: "Well, that makes you an expert on the subject. You'd better let them know." Them—the few
men who controlled the destiny of nations and the
lives of millions.

"Expert?" Edland had replied, surprised at Mc-

Namar's proposal. "Sir, what I told you is what little I know. There's a lot more that I don't know."

"That's the definition of an expert, isn't it?" McNamar said, unmoved. "Someone who knows just a little more than the next guy?"

Edland stood at the podium on the raised platform, wishing that he had a few slides at least, or something to help him illustrate what he was about to reveal.

"The Germans have apparently developed a new type of E-boat. A hydrofoil craft that is capable of extreme speeds."

"Extreme?" a British vice-admiral asked.

"Upwards of sixty knots to eighty knots. Perhaps much faster than that," Edland confirmed. "We have determined that the unofficial designation for these E-boats is Sea Eagles, and they are operating out of Cherbourg, although it is equally possible that there are others based at Le Havre and Boulogne."

"How did you come by this intelligence, young man?"

Edland found the source of the question in the darkness. It was Churchill.

"From an enemy seaman, sir," Edland said, wishing that the prime minister had stayed at Downing Street. Churchill had a habit of biting into a subject and of not letting go until the thing bled to death, or someone was able to convince him to move on. "And from an encounter between the E-boats and a Channel convoy."

"Sea Eagles, you say?" Churchill said.

Edland saw McNamar wince out of the corner of his eye. Dramatic phrases and extreme rhetoric often led Churchill on flights of fancy. Sometimes to disastrous results. The Allies were virtually bogged down in the 'soft underbelly of Europe,' facing stiff German resistance in the mountains of Italy.

"Yes, sir. We don't know their true designation but there is at least one flotilla. Allow me to give you some background," Edland said quickly, before Churchill was off again. "The Germans began experimenting with hydrofoils in the 1930s. By the late thirties there were at least six boats, small vessels of no more than five tons, that were built at the Sachsenberg Yards. Top speed, no more than forty knots. Sometime between 1940 and the present, development of these craft was accelerated, although we don't know the particulars. We suspect, or at least the gentleman that I cabled for information, Dr. C. T. McGill of the Massachusetts Institute of Technology, suggests that conventional E-boats were somehow fitted out as hydrofoils."

"What exactly is a hydrofoil?" McNamar prompted Edland.

"Well, sir," Edland said. "For lack of a better explanation it is a wing, or set of wings, that extends from a boat's hull, designed to lift the boat nearly out of the water at a certain speed."

"Good lord, man," someone said. "You're not talking about flying boats, are you?"

The image of the frightened German sailor, shivering on the PT boat deck, flashed before Edland's eyes.

"No, sir," he said. "The stern and certainly the rudder and screws remain in the water. Most of the hull, suspended on these wings, is out of the water.

Less resistance, more stability. All in all an extremely fast boat."

"Very interesting," Admiral Ramsey said. "What does it mean?"

Edland paused and looked at McNamar for guidance. The admiral shrugged.

"We don't know, sir," Edland said. He saw some of the men exchange glances and comments. He felt that they thought this was a waste of time. A few experimental boats dashing about the Channel. Too little, too late. "There is something else," Edland said, and the buzz in the room stopped. "These E-boats, or perhaps some of those that accompany them, carry very powerful guns. Something equal in power to a six- or eight-inch naval cannon." The room grew silent. "The captain of a destroyer escort involved in the Channel convoy fight reported as such, as well as the fact that the rounds seemed to burn their way into his ship's hull."

"Has anyone actually seen these fantastic boats?" a British captain asked. Edland recognized him as an officer who forever found fault with every report submitted. "This destroyer escort, chap, for instance? Do we have anything but your observations and, forgive me for saying so, your guess?"

"No, sir," Edland said. "It was a night engagement. No one saw anything of consequence. At least nothing they could describe."

"Commander Edland," Churchill rumbled. "I thank you for the report. I know the others and I find this information most enlightening and it certainly bears looking into. But you must remember that Bomber Command is raiding those very E-boat facilities that you mentioned, and the latest news is quite good indeed. We have a great many things to consider in our remarkable endeavor, and I should not want you to think that your information is being discounted. It is, indeed, not. At this very moment the highest priority must be given to our own craft. What are they again, Admiral McNamar?"

"LSTs," McNamar said. "Landing Ship Tanks."

"Yes," Churchill said. "Thank you, Admiral. These are the very craft that will nestle up to the beaches and disgorge men and materials. I am sure that your E-boats are worthy of attention, but I am equally sure that Bomber Command will dispose of those particular vipers and their nests in short order. We must concentrate on our own needs—these LSTs being foremost."

"Yes, sir," Edland said. He swept the room looking for interested faces. There were none. His words had been absorbed, stored, and would soon be forgotten. "Thank you, gentlemen." He stepped off the platform and took a seat next to McNamar. He and his information had been dismissed. McNamar turned to him.

"Mike, don't be discouraged. These fellows have bigger fish to fry. Churchill, Ike, and the others have a genuine concern. The key to the invasion is the LST. The entire invasion force has a reserve of exactly five LSTs. The only way to get substantial quantities of men and materials on the beach rapidly enough to support the first waves are the LSTs. For the past month that's been the number-one problem. I told Ramsey and the others more times than I care to count that E-boats are the only

viable German naval threat left. They believe more
escorts and more bombing raids will take care of
them. Frankly, I think they're right. If you want to
get their attention, you're going to have to give
them more than what somebody at MIT thinks about
what's happening three thousand miles away."

"It's all I've got, sir."

McNamar sat back in his chair. "Get more, Mike.
Nobody's convinced, including me. We don't have
any time to waste on improbabilities."

Edland watched as an RAF officer adjusted the
microphone at the podium. Improbabilities. He
felt himself becoming angry. Why couldn't McNamar come right out and say it? The focus was on
the invasion. No one thought that these boats con-
stituted a threat. And besides, anything moving in
the English Channel that wasn't Allied was going
to be destroyed. Anything on land determined to
be a viable target, including E-boat pens, would
be hammered into dust. The Allied might would
crush the enemy. *Finis.*

Edland didn't know why but he felt a profound
sense of loss. Maybe it was the E-boats that he hadn't
seen and would almost certainly not have a chance
to capture. He didn't know. All he had seen was
death and destruction, and the waste horrified
him. Couldn't he claim one positive thing out of
this mess? Even if it was a boat that flew on wings.
One thing, just one idea, or piece of machinery, or
one concept that he could claim as saved for some
purpose after the war. Even if it was a boat that
flew on wings.

Chapter 17

In the Baie de la Seine

It was nearly dark and there were ghosts about. Mysterious shapes slid through the water, the roar of their engines rumbling off the flat sea. Occasionally a signal light would flash quickly, a brief message that told Reubold that the other two S-boats were in position. It was a drill only, but there was still danger. The danger came from above; Allied fighter-bombers who dropped out of the darkness because their radar was superior to anything that the Germans had. It meant that they could see from far away, and what they could see were tiny blips darting across the blackness like water bugs on a pond. Then they would swoop out of the night sky, and strafe and bomb them until the S-boats were flaming wrecks on the black water; or if they were lucky, they escaped. It was that knowledge, Reubold knew, that ate away at morale. The enemy's planes are faster and more numerous. Their bombs are far more powerful. They have men and materiel in abundance and they will surely come. It was easy to see that the men were affected by the obvious inequities. There was an almost indiscernible pall of inevitability in the pens, and aboard the S-boats. The Trinities were more than a weapon, they were vindication. The test was more than a trial, it was salvation.

Walters was standing next to Reubold in the skullcap of S-788 wondering what would come of this night's work.

"We have the solution," Korvettenkapitan Waldvogel had assured him when Walters had showed up unexpectedly.

"We think we have the solution," Reubold, his dark eyes troubled by more than the uncertainties of the drill, had corrected Waldvogel.

"Then," Walters had said, "we shall see." The plan that he had confided to Rommel, unsuccessfully as it turned out, was based upon what these new boats could do; how they could perform against the mass of escort vessels that the Allies were sure to shield their invasion fleet with. He had added that he had wrangled a reprieve from the field-marschal with the promise that these boats could very well bring confusion to the enemy at precisely the right moment—when they neared the French coast. Reubold had believed him, which was fortunate because Walters's plans rested on balancing success with secrecy, sweetly leavened with subterfuge. Never an easy thing to do when so many ambitious men hungrily sought opportunities to advance themselves over the failures of other ambitious men.

Reubold, on board S-788, had led two other boats into the bay, straight to a grounded hulk that the fregattenkapitan knew well. Waldvogel was not with them. His wound had been giving him a great deal of pain and despite his insistence that he be allowed to go along—"It's critical that I go, Fregattenkapitan. I know the boats and the guns"—Reubold sent him back to the hospital. Walters wondered if the fregattenkapitan was concerned with the odd little man's health, or if he wished to reap the glory of a successful test without sharing it.

Reubold throttled back S-788 until she barely made headway and turned to Walters.

"Did Rommel or Dresser send you?" the fregattenkapitan asked, his features barely visible by the faint light of the compass.

"Does it matter?" Walters said. He saw Reubold nod his agreement in the darkness and waited while the fregattenkapitan issued orders to begin the test.

"We've mounted a doorknocker," Reubold said, "a two-centimeter gun, on the Trinity. Now we have a quad mount. A bit unstable, but necessary. We are going to fire the Trinities along the same path as the doorknocker, sighting with its tracer round. Theoretically," Walters saw Reubold smile at the word, "the gunners will fire the Trinity the moment we see the doorknocker tracers hit the target. The guns are on the same axis; it should be simply a matter of sight and shoot."

"Ingenious," Walters said.

"Only if it works," Reubold said. "There is another matter. We will be lighting up the night with our tracers and guns. If the bees show up, we may find it necessary to flee." He pressed his throat mike, clicked the talk button twice, and said: "Fritz in now."

Walters heard the roar of the engines increase, but the sound echoing off the water made it impossible to tell from which direction the noise came. He saw a pinpoint of light in the darkness and realized that it was the S-boat, speeding across the water. The phosphorescence of the thin wake shimmered in the rays of a moon partially hidden by clouds. He could tell the boat was moving very fast—incredibly fast—and he felt his excitement building. He may have seen the S-boat, the darkness may be tricking him; but he thought that he saw it up on its wings, gliding over the sea as if it were flying. He knew that the crew of the S-boat could see the target; at least, he hoped that they could see the target, and he wondered what it must be like to be aboard something so fast that from a distance just the sight of it took his breath away.

Walters saw the flash of the doorknocker and then the fiery trails of the green slice through the air and then there was a brilliant flash and a boom. The noise startled him, but before he had time to react, there was a larger explosion followed by a low rumble.

He glanced at Reubold and saw incredulity in the man's eyes. Had something gone wrong? Had there been some sort of terrible accident?

"Fregattenkapitan?" a leutnant appeared at the

hatchway to the radio room. "Fritz reports, 'Direct hit. All guns.'"

Reubold looked at the young officer in disbelief and simply uttered: "Mueller."

"It can't be that easy," Walters said. "Surely, they can't have hit the target that quickly?"

Reubold didn't bother to answer Walters's question. "Tietjen?" he called after the leutnant. "Have Mueller fire one barrel at a time. No salvos. You understand?"

"Fritz let go everything he had," Reubold commented. "That may have been just one hit on the target. There's no way to tell. I want to see how the hits register."

"He reported . . ." Walters began hopefully.

"He could be mistaken," Reubold interrupted. "We tried this before with salvos and hit nothing. We shall see if this idea of Waldvogel's works."

Walters remained silent. The fregattenkapitan was right to be skeptical. One boat proved nothing. It might have been an accident. Perhaps one shell hit and Fritz, in his excitement, saw them all hit. The sound of the other boat's engines broke into his thoughts.

There was a deep throaty roar, somehow coarser than the sound of the first boat, but he found it immediately by locating the telltale wisps of white water playing off its foils. It seemed even faster than the first, and the familiar sense of excitement swept over him. The sound of the engines and the sight of the wake curling back off the hydrofoils made him realize that here was primitive power.

Green tracers raced into the darkness, and he saw several bounce erratically into the air, rico-

cheting off the wreck. There was a flash of light,
and an instant later a corresponding flash in the
darkness, far away. More green tracers—another
flash from the boat as the second gun fired and another explosion in the darkness. The wreck began
to glow and suddenly it was engulfed in flames.
Walters saw the S-boat. It had the look of a deadly
predator, up on its long wings, hurtling through
the light of the burning wreck—a black phantom
against flames. Green tracers again and a white
flash, followed by a low crack and an explosion on
the wreck that sent pieces of its flaming carcass spi-
raling into the night sky.

Walters turned to Reubold, ready to ask him
something. He wasn't quite sure what, because he
was stunned by the demonstration, but stopped
when he saw the look on the fregattenkapitan's
face.

It was a look of pure concentration, of possibilities and ideas so tumbled together that the man
had to use every bit of his willpower to separate
them. Reubold had a hold of the potential of the
boats, a potential handed to him so completely by
the demonstration tonight that nothing else existed. The first man who discovered fire, Walters
thought, must have had that very look: wonder
mixed with fortune, sweetened by opportunities.

Reubold looked at Walters. "Now, Kommodore
Walters," Reubold said, "we are ready for war."

Hardy walked along the quay, wearing one glove,
the other glove trapped in his right hand. Beatrice
Schiffer was beside him, asking a question when

she thought it pertinent, generally remaining silent because she could tell that Hardy was nervous and that he did not respond well to what he called "a lot of chatter." She had smiled when he first informed her of this predilection but agreed that there was nothing wrong with silence, although a few words at just the right moment had been perfectly all right. She watched as Hardy thought this over and in kind of a half-growl, half-grunt, reasoning that a few words appropriately delivered were acceptable.

They walked along the quay with the weak early morning sun lost in a sky of fog and clouds, not an unusual thing around Portsmouth.

Beatrice had grown up in the coastal town, caring for both her parents when they became too ill to fend for themselves. And after they died, for Topper when he came back from the Great War, silencing the demons that tormented him with memories of what he had seen in the trenches. Beatrice awoke to her brother's strangled sobs in the middle of the night, and was at first unsure of how to comfort him. She had settled on simply talking with him and fixing tea, and they sat, he silent and trembling, she calm and assured. She kept him busy doing things around the house until Topper began to understand that the horror was behind him. It was a bad time for her as well; she was never certain if the poor dear man would kill himself just to find solace. Her tenderness pulled him through and after several years he cast about for something that he could make his own. When he couldn't make up his mind, it was Beatrice who said out of the blue: "I've always fancied owning an art emporium." The comment was so innocent and unexpected that Topper blew a mouthful of tea across the kitchen table in laughter. Beatrice waited for Topper to calm himself before explaining, in a very rational manner, how it could be done. The more she talked, the more she convinced Topper that such a thing was possible. A few words at just the right moment.

They rented a storefront and began to fill the shelves with things that artists, or people who wanted to be artists, needed. Fortunately, there were a number of empty stores about with landlords desperately seeking tenants. Business, to begin with, was not good, and they lived frugally on Topper's pension and any odd jobs that Beatrice could scare up.

What the pair did have, and Topper explained this not only to Captain Hardy, RN, but to others as well, was Beatrice's unassailable confidence that things would work out. After a number of years, things did work out.

"She's just up here a bit," Hardy said, slapping his hand with the glove.

He was nervous, Beatrice realized, because they were going to see his ship, his *Firedancer*, but more because he would be seen with a lady at his side. Beatrice gave this a great deal of thought, as she did nearly everything of consequence, and realized what Hardy must be thinking. He was thinking that his officers and men would see him, the captain; or rather, The Captain, in the role of a human being. Beatrice knew of course that Hardy's perception of his relationship with his officers and men was certainly not more than half correct. He was far too hard on himself and could see only his faults and never his accomplishments. She realized also that he was a very sensitive man. Beatrice decided, because she was a very good judge of human nature, that the men of *Firedancer* viewed their captain as basically a decent, if erratic, soul. Not so complicated as Hardy made it out to be, but George Hardy did not understand human nature as well as she.

Theirs had been an acquaintance that had blossomed through understanding. It was a sturdy, uncomplicated relationship. Not the sort of thing you read about in magazines or saw at the theater, but a gradual thing that proceeded as easily as a leaf floats down a creek, bobbing over the eddies and glancing off the bank because nature made it so.

Beatrice was relaxed with Hardy and Hardy was at ease with Beatrice. There was a lot to be said for two people being comfortable in each other's presence. Perhaps the blazing flames of romantic love didn't blaze as brightly as those at the cinema, but that was make-believe and had only to last for an hour and a half at most. What Beatrice knew and Hardy might come to suspect, although he was not the sort of fellow to identify it, was that theirs was a carefully tended fire that burned with reason and understanding. Beatrice smiled inwardly, feeling the warmth of Hardy's presence.

"She's had a few changes," Hardy said, waving the glove before striking. "We took out A-turret and put some new treats for Jerry there. Can't tell you what of course." The glove struck his open palm. "We've done convoys. Done them to death. Some escort duty." Slap. "Got us up to Coastal

Forces now." Slap. " 'Costly Farces,' some of the chaps call them. MTBs and the like." He noticed some confusion on her face. "Motor Torpedo Boats. We operate with them, northbound and southbound convoys. Give the American chaps a hand as needed." Harder slap with a bit of irritation in his voice. "Can't wait to get out of it. Get out of this pond, back out to sea. It may be the English Channel but this is one Englishman who wants nothing to do with it."

"I should imagine it's very thrilling at sea," Beatrice said.

"Thrilling?" Hardy said. Beatrice could tell that the idea seemed incredible to him, but then he gave the notion some thought. "Thrilling, yes." He warmed up to it. "Yes, you're right. Thrilling it is. Well said, old girl."

Beatrice smiled, turning her head so that Hardy could not see her face. It was the first time that he had felt relaxed enough in her presence to use a term of endearment. Some women might have been offended by the phrase; some women who clung to their youth with all of the resolve of a drowning man clinging to a rope. But Beatrice saw those two words for what they were: the first sign that Hardy forgot that it was necessary to cloak himself in formality.

"Yes," Hardy continued. "Storms in the North Atlantic are thrilling enough, I can tell you that. By God, Bea, once or twice I thought the old girl would go topsy-turvy. Frightened me—as close to being frightened to death that anyone can be." The glove remained motionless in his hand and the words came easily. "Land, my Number One;

damned fine fellow. Oh, excuse me." He had caught the mild profanity but in his excitement to talk about the sea, let it slip again. "Damned fine fellow to be sure—we rode seventy-two hours on the bridge during one storm. Took two of us, mind you. Old *Firedancer* creaked and groaned her way up one wave and down another. Threatened to broach a half-dozen times, but we wouldn't let her. Swept away everything topside that wasn't secured." He stopped, laughing at himself in embarrassment. "Sailors' stories. Shouldn't have gone on like that. Bored you silly."

"No," Beatrice said, smiling. "Not at all, George." His name came out of its own volition, and now she was surprised to feel her face redden, self-conscious at the slip. She glanced to see if Hardy was aware that she had called him by his Christian name, but if he was, he was doing a superb job of hiding it. She quickly tossed out a question, anxious to mask her discomfort. "Will you try for another ship? That is, would you like to command something a bit larger?" She winced at the stupidity of the question, realizing that she had probably offended him, or his beloved *Firedancer*, and she remembered how close captains were to their ships. But he took the question in stride, as if he had never before considered it.

"Hmmm," Hardy said. "You mean such as a cruiser?"

"Yes," Beatrice said. She felt more at ease although she hadn't the least idea what a cruiser was.

"Oh, I've seen them out there," Hardy said, nodding. He was becoming reacquainted with his ambitions. "Fine lot. Heavy chaps. Fine lines, all of them.

Had my eyes on *Belfast* once. Of course, when I came out of Dartmouth, nothing would suit me but a battleship. Oh, I'd have a battle cruiser if one were offered, being young and foolish, but I thought myself cut out for a battleship. My due, you understand. That was the boy in me—all stuff and nonsense. I saw some other lads, classmates of mine, come up quickly." It was thwarted ambitions that emerged—bitter disappointments at being found wanting, the insult of others given prize commands while you stood, unnoticed, in the background. His voice lost some of the levity and he spoke with a sense of failure. "It hurt, Bea. I can tell you that. I mean, I'm no scholar and I thought Dartmouth and I would part company in a bad way more than once, but what I lack in brains I more than make up for in bravado and hard work. I'm the sort of fellow that won't be easily denied his victory."

"It must have been miserable," Beatrice said.

"Oh, yes," Hardy acknowledged, the pain evident in his eyes. "Rough go a number of times. I think that's where old *Firedancer* and I have come to form a partnership—ship and captain, I mean. We understand each other. Sounds a bit daft, I know, but it's like those old fire horses. Tired and out of sorts and barely able to make it from one side of their stall to the next, but let that fire bell sound, and twenty years comes off the old beasts. Don't stand in their way, is all I'm saying. Well, that *Firedancer* and me. Let us hear Action Stations. . . ." he stopped talking, and smiled ruefully. "Never talked that much in one go."

"Now, George," Beatrice said, deciding that she

would be brazen about the use of his first name. It was how she felt about him. "You must feel free to speak to me about anything, at any time. I like to hear you talk."

He said nothing in return, but his face flushed and Beatrice hoped that she had not embarrassed him.

"Well," he said hesitantly. The glove came up, but he simply let it fall back down. He stopped. "There she is."

Firedancer was smaller than Beatrice had expected and her hull and superstructure were liberally streaked with rust. *Knifelike* was a word that came immediately to Beatrice when she saw her, and *Firedancer* was that all right. Bows on she was thin and her stem looked as if it was capable of slicing through the water at a fantastic rate. Her guns were all neatly arranged fore and aft, and they looked formidable enough although Beatrice didn't know what they were for or even if they were powerful. She saw the truth in Hardy's remarks. *Firedancer* lay alongside the quay, peppered with scars and imperfections and looking as if she were two years past a good rest and refitting.

But then another thought struck Beatrice, as if the ship herself had interceded to correct a mistaken idea. *Firedancer* was a terrier, Beatrice now realized, all teeth and heart. She would go after anything she was set on, regardless of the size, and attack it with all the violence that she could muster.

Beatrice felt foolish at the notion of *Firedancer* as a living thing, and told herself never to mention it to Captain Hardy. Who knew how he saw his ship?

He might be offended if she likened *Firedancer* to a feisty little creature. She felt that the ship was eyeing her, however, to see if she was worthy of further attention. They came, in a moment, to a mutual understanding; ashore George Hardy would belong to Beatrice Schiffer; he could be her love always because Beatrice knew that it was love. When Hardy came aboard *Firedancer*, however—and the ship made this perfectly clear by the stoic manner in which she studied the lady at Hardy's side—Captain George Hardy, RN, and HMS *Firedancer* would be, forever, man and lover. This relationship was created through experience, occasion, trust, loss, fright, terror, death, regret, and victory. They were like a very civil wife and mistress, meeting over tea, agreeing on how the shared relationship should be with the man that they both cared for; each unwilling to give up the whole life of the man, and satisfied to live in a part of that life. It was all very polite.

Beatrice turned to Hardy, straightened his tie, and brushed an imaginary spot of lint from his dark blue uniform jacket. "George," she said, her voice soft and caring. "I shall never interfere with your duties. I know them to be what makes you the man that you are." She was on the verge of saying 'the man that I love,' but she could not bring herself to say so. Not that she didn't feel it, because she did. She did not say it because she knew that there was a rhythm to things and it was not yet the right time to tell Hardy how she felt. Now, it was not even important that he felt the same way, although she suspected that he did. She would wait for the right moment, and that moment would make itself known to her.

"But you must promise me that you shall always come back to me," Beatrice said, daring to go as far as she could. "I should be quite miserable if something happened to you."

Beatrice watched as Hardy's jaw tensed and she knew that he was struggling with his emotions. These were uncharted waters for Captain Hardy and she wanted him to come along at his own speed. "Why, old girl," he said. "There's no reason to talk like that. I've come back each and every time." He nodded at *Firedancer*. "Just look at her. She's resilient, all right. She'll bring me home. Through shot and shell as they say."

"Very well then," Beatrice said. She looked down the quay to the destroyer. In her mind she made a covenant with *Firedancer: We shall share him, you and I, but you are to return him to me.* She straightened Hardy's tie again, although the action was unnecessary. She just wanted to touch him. "We'll have many such partings," she said. "Having you come home to me is all I ever want from you. You've promised me that, George. I shan't ask any more of you."

"You mustn't trouble yourself, Bea," Hardy said. He kissed her on the forehead. "Knowing that you'll be waiting for me is all the incentive I need." He smiled at her. "Give my best to Topper, will you? Now, you must let me get aboard *Firedancer*."

"I will, dear," Beatrice said. "Go along. I shall wait here a moment."

Hardy nodded, turned, and walked along the

quay to the gangway. He received a salute from the sailor on duty, then made his way to the ship's deck, saluted the Union Jack and the officer of the deck, and looked back at Beatrice. He doffed his cap, waved it once to the tiny figure gathering with the other wives and sweethearts, and disappeared amidships.

It was a moment before Beatrice, tears streaming down her cheeks, could speak. "Godspeed, George Hardy," she said. And then she added. "God bless *Firedancer*, and all who sail on her."

Land stood back to allow Hardy access to *Firedancer*'s tiny bridge. Number One had been running static engineering tests with Courtney. They had just finished up a moment ago, in time to see Hardy part company with his lady friend. He watched as the captain tried to appear busy, nosing about the bridge as if the action guaranteed that all that transpired on the quay had done so unobserved. Finally Hardy's eyes picked out a deficiency.

"Number One? Number One, what are those Lewis gun mounts still doing there?" Hardy said. "I ordered them cut off a year ago. Why hasn't it been done?"

"I don't know, sir," Land said. Hardy had ordered no such thing.

"Don't know? Don't know? Well, by God, you'd better find out." Several of the seamen present on the bridge slid as far away as they could. "Can't leave this ship for a moment, Number One. Not a moment. And here," Hardy moved quickly to the binnacle. "Look at this. Filthy. Have it cleaned. Bloody shame if we got lost because I couldn't see through the grime covering this thing."

"Indeed it would, sir," Land said calmly, catching a yeoman's eye. The exchange was simple enough—have someone see to it. "By the way, sir," Land said. "The engines are in top form. Number Two hasn't given us a bit of problem. I think we could run her out a bit without a worry." Land waited for the explosion, but Hardy was lost in thought.

"What? Fine, fine. We'll run her out and toss Courtney over the side if the bloody thing fouls." Hardy looked around surreptitiously and nodded at Land to join him at the windscreen. "Now, see here, Number One," Hardy said. "I need a bit of discretion on your part."

"Discretion, sir?" Land asked. He couldn't resist the urge to torment Hardy.

"Yes!" Hardy said, biting the word off. He dropped his voice and said: "The truth of the matter is, I've been keeping company with a young lady."

"Indeed, sir?"

"Yes. Quite a respectable lady. We've . . ." Hardy arranged the words carefully. "We've reached a sort of understanding."

"Why, that's splendid, sir," Land said, generating what he felt was sufficient emotion to deceive Hardy into thinking the situation was a total surprise. It was not. First the men knew that Old Georgie was escorting a lady about town, and then the officers learned from the men that apparently their captain was quite smitten with Miss Schiffer; that was her name, and she owned a dry-goods store or some such establishment, with her brother Topper, a right fine fellow. Old Georgie and Miss Schiffer were seen at the cinema and once at the play, and Hardy had looked uncomfortable at both places, but he was most solicitous of Miss Schiffer. Maybe it wasn't a dry-goods store, the W/T finally conceded, but that wasn't important.

The important thing was the Captain's Lady Lottery. It started in the gunnery division, from someone at B turret everyone agreed, and swept above decks, getting down to the black gang who felt somewhat irritated that they hadn't been in on it in the beginning. The officers knew about it but declined to let the men know that they knew about it because it would appear unseemly if they were involved.

That is why they created The Hardy Steeplechase. It worked much the same as the lottery, but instead of wagering on the day that Old Georgie would pop the question, it rather pessimistically suggested that Hardy's lady would toss him after a proscribed number of jumps—each jump being a certain number of days into the relationship. The first jump was called The Hat, after the famous bowler that Hardy donned when *Firedancer* went into action. That was just one week. A sub-lieutenant and an ensign quickly chose the second jump, The Dartmouth Tumble, and Courtney down in engineering, after wrapping himself in a cloak of calm deliberation, finally chose the third jump, Their Lordships Two-Step—named after the manner in which their Lordships of the Admiralty cagily avoided giving Hardy command of a destroyer squadron. The whole romantic interlude was cal-

culated by the crew of *Firedancer* to last no more
than a month, with the jumps strategically placed,
but those who settled on early dates regretted
their lack of faith in Hardy.

Land, who had known Hardy for some time,
smiled when he was asked his opinion of the captain's domestic turn and what jump he thought
that Hardy would be bumped off. He never spoke
of it, and a simple glance from him would change
the subject in the Ward Room, but he knew something that the others did not. George Hardy was
deeply in love. He saw it when Hardy lost his train
of thought in mid-statement and regained it only
when his brow wrinkled over his own confusion.
Land saw it as Hardy stood on the bridge, his stance
strong and unyielding, but with a natural ease that
came from contentment.

George Hardy was in love.

"Yes," Hardy agreed with Land's comment. "Yes.
I think it quite splendid as well."

A yeoman of signals cleared his throat behind
them. "Beg pardon, sir," he said, holding out an envelope. "But this just came straight over from base."

Land took it without Hardy having to tell him to
do so, and dismissed the yeoman. He opened the
envelope and read the single sheet of paper. "It appears as if our running out has been advanced a
bit, sir," Land said, handing the message to Hardy.
"They've got us on escort duty again, Convoy D-4.
Some Yanks are planning a landing drill at Lyme
Bay. It's to be called Operation Sunset."

"Well, easy enough," Hardy said. "Good way to
get those engines warmed up." He read the message. "Nine LSTs," he said, "and the *Huston*, a Hunt

Class. Shouldn't be too difficult to handle, should it, Number One?"

"No, sir," Land said. "I doubt we'd see any mischief in Lyme Bay."

Chapter 18

Tour-la-Ville, Cherbourg, France

"We will go hunting," Reubold said in response to Kapitanleutnant Mueller's question. Mad Mueller, irrational, quick-tempered; he was built like a boxer: compact and resolute, his fists battered and scarred. Not all of his fights were successful, but all of them were fought with joyful enthusiasm. Kapitanleutnant Fritz, silent, thoughtful, sat next to him in the classroom of the former museum, once a château, now the headquarters of Flotilla 11. Kapitanleutnant Draheim nudged Fritz for a cigarette, and Fritz grudgingly handed one over. Fritz was notoriously tight—the other officers constantly badgered him for cigarettes, socks, anything that they knew he was loath to give out, just to see him boil silently. Draheim, "Musikmaat," was a fellow who could scare up a piano, guitar, and once a trombone; and seemed capable of playing each with remarkable skill. He liked American jazz the best, he explained to those who gathered to hear him play. It was the music of colored people, he admitted, but exciting and original. He'd seen Negroes playing in a small club in Paris, before the war, and from the moment he saw sweat glistening off their broad foreheads and heard the wild, sensational music pulsating with decadence, he was captured by it.

What's wrong with good German music? Kapitanleutnant Peters had demanded one night, in the midst of one of Draheim's impromptu concerts. Peters was an ardent Nazi and a burden to the other officers of Flotilla 11. His father was some high official in the Party, at least Peters claimed that he was, and the others reluctantly were forced to agree that someone with power shielded Peters from official sanctions. He was a competent enough boat handler and his crew seemed reasonably happy, but Peters came down with a variety of mysterious illnesses just before every patrol. Then it fell to Oberleutnant zur see Waymann, Peters's executive officer, to take S-492 out. The crew of Peters's boat said little about their commanding officer's strange malady, chalking it up to good luck instead. Waymann was calm and very serious for such a young man, and he sat in the back of the classroom at Reubold's invitation, over the objections of Peters.

"What will the others think?" Peters had pleaded with Reubold, the specter of shame standing just behind him.

"It's best that you don't know what the others think," Reubold had replied.

"That's more to my liking," Mueller said. "Eagles

hunt to live." He looked around for confirmation. "Eh, fellows?"

"Or live to hunt," Fritz said, shaking his head to Kapitanleutnant Mittendorf's silent plea for a cigarette. Mittendorf the Dwarf—short, profane, obviously a man who felt bravado made up for stature. The crew of S-756 loved him, although it was common to see Mittendorf viciously dressing down a matrose, most of whom towered over him.

"Either," Reubold said, "is sufficient to explain what we must do. You will go back to the pens, inspect your boats, double-check the foils and struts, and sight your guns. Take every measure," he said, the words hard with warning, "to ensure that the doorknockers are firmly secured to the Trinity mounts." He used his anger sparingly, but he would not hesitate to humiliate anyone whose mistakes could cost lives. The others glanced at Mueller.

"I checked those mounts out myself," Mueller said in a hurt tone.

"I'm sure that you did, Kapitanleutnant," Reubold said. "But you scored fewer hits than anyone." To the officers he repeated: "Secure those guns. We've had three tests, and other than Mueller blasting seagulls out of the sky we've had more luck than we should expect."

"What news did the Kommodore have, sir?" Draheim said.

"The Allies have invaded France and captured Paris," Mittendorf said.

"None," Reubold said over the laughter. "But I'll tell you this much: we won't be plowing the Channel sowing mines. At least not yet."

"Rommel," Mueller muttered. "Everyone kisses the army's ass. Give us a chance and we'll show the Allies something."

"We've been given the chance," Reubold said. He saw that he had everyone's attention. "We are going out, close to the English shore because the enemy does not expect us at his front door." He nodded to Herzog, his clerk, who unfolded a map and laid it across the wide table. "Waymann," Reubold said, ordering the officer closer. He noticed Peters's face turning red. He was embarrassed by his executive officer's presence. Reubold felt sadistic pleasure in the situation. "We're going out tonight," he told his officers. "Twenty-hundred hours. North-northwest." He traced the course with his fingertip. "We'll pick up boats from Flotilla 15." Guernsey boats the men knew, soft living and English women. It was play-war on the tiny islands. "Turn north-northwest," Reubold continued, and see what we can find off Weymouth." He straightened and waited for the men to digest his news.

Fritz spoke first, his voice probing and thoughtful. "That puts us off the English coast at oh-two hundred. If we run into resistance . . ."

"He means if we get lucky," Mueller said.

"No," Fritz said. "I mean if we run into resistance that could put our return just after sunrise."

That observation got everyone's attention. An S-boat on the open sea in daylight was at the mercy of enemy aircraft. And there were so many of them lately—hundreds of them.

"Yes," Reubold said. "It could. That is why I want your boats inspected and your gun mounts secure. We will go in very fast, and shoot very fast, and the

Guernsey boats will come in after us. With torpedoes. We are still being tested, gentlemen. We are
testing ourselves. Some may say that we have un-
tried weapons in untested boats," he held up his
hand to silence Peters. The errant kapitanleutnant
was always ready to inject the superiority of German weapons and fighting men into any conversation. It was worthless propaganda. "Despite what
we accomplished against the convoy. That was luck.
We aren't issued luck. We make our own by training and preparation. I'll personally inspect each
boat. If your boat isn't ready, you don't go." He resisted an impulse to look at Peters. If it were up to
Peters the fuel tanks would be filled to the top with
wax and he could claim sabotage. But Waymann
and his crew would work to see that everything was
ready. The young officer and the other kapitan-
leutnants of Flotilla 11 could not face the humiliation of being left behind because their boats
weren't ready.

If they were lucky, and Reubold smiled inwardly
at the notion that luck *was* important in war, they
would stumble on targets of consequence and return to Cherbourg in one piece. If they were lucky,
Walters would be satisfied with their performance
and tell Reubold more of what he had in mind.

"The Allies are predictable," Walters had said
after they returned from test-firing the guns and
settled into Reubold's quarters. He refused a glass
of calvados from the fregattenkapitan.

"Not always," Reubold had said, downing a glass
and shivering from the effects of the harsh brandy.

"No," Walters had said. "That's true. But they
are predictable in their absolute need to organize

everything. Everything is built upon organization. Particularly their invasions."

"Invasions require a certain amount of organization," Reubold had said, pouring himself another glass. "Everything about war does, I suppose." A strange thought occurred to him. "Are there two wars, Kommodore: one for killing and one for account ledgers? In this column," his finger ran down an imaginary book, "are the materials of war. And in this column," his finger moved again, "are the dead." He chuckled and took a drink. He was tired and hungered for morphine. The brandy dulled the urge, but that was only a temporary solution. His legs began to throb and he wondered if he really were in pain or his brain was tricking him—coaxing him to seek the blissful caress of the drug.

"I've studied them," Walters had said. "The invasions. The Allies had improved with each. Remarkably. Africa. Italy. Their resources are amazing."

Reubold had shrugged. What of it? What did this Silver Stripe want?

"Africa was large. Italy was larger. France will be the largest invasion of them all. Thousands of ships I am told."

"Should I be frightened?" Reubold had said.

"So many ships. So little room to maneuver. So little time," Walters had said.

Reubold had been reaching for the bottle of calvados, but his hand stopped. His eyes narrowed as he sought to find Walters's point. He had never really liked the Silver Stripe and certainly did not trust him because the man exuded a strong odor of greed. He wanted everything. But Reubold's interest was roused, regardless of his misgivings.

"I'll have a glass if you don't mind," Walters had said, pleased by Reubold's reaction.

Reubold poured the kommodore a glass of brandy and filled a glass for himself.

Walters held the glass out in a toast and had said: "Confusion to the enemy."

Reubold acknowledged the toast and quickly downed his drink. He filled the glass again, sensing that Walters was watching him.

"When do you go out?" the kommodore asked.

"That's up to the powers who guide us," Reubold said.

Silence crept between the two men, separating the questions that each had about the other. Walters offered Reubold a cigarette and the fregattenkapitan took it, willing to give the kommodore a tiny victory by acknowledging his generosity. "This is what the Allies do," Walters said quickly as if he had made a decision to enter a covenant. He pulled a sheet of paper from Reubold's cluttered desk, found a pencil, and began to draw a series of rectangles. He remembered his sand diagrams and Rommel's rejection. But Rommel wasn't here. "Despite their organization and their ingenuity, this never changes."

Reubold, the half-empty bottle of calvados in one hand and a nearly full glass in the other, studied the paper. Walters gestured to the drawings. "Troop transports, escorts, bombardment vessels, minesweepers."

"Very pretty," Reubold said, momentarily perplexed about which hand held the bottle and which hand held the glass. "What does it mean?"

"Let us call it the elephant," Walters said, certain that Reubold was not as drunk as he pretended. "Thick hide all around, vitals within."

Reubold looked at him. Although he did not show it, he wanted Walters to continue with his explanation.

"Cut through the hide," Walters said. "Get to the vitals."

"The hide is the problem, isn't it?"

"If you cut away at one spot," Walters said. "But why be clumsy about it? Hacking at the animal? Why not precise cuts? A surgeon's skill. A scalpel instead of an axe."

Reubold's eyes narrowed in interest.

"Cut through the hide," Walters said again, watching as Reubold began to understand. "Get to the vitals."

Hardy watched as the LSTs fell in behind *Firedancer* and shook his head. Sturdy they might be and remarkable vessels for all they were capable of, but they were ugly—nothing more than long, steel boxes with high sides and flat bottoms. They were constructed in America's inland ports, Land told Hardy, someplace along the Mississippi River with exotic names like Moline, St. Louis, and someplace he thought was called Paducah.

"Paducah," Hardy snorted, turning to Land. "Sounds like something out of the funny papers. Paducah? Are you sure?"

"Yes, sir," Land said as the seven LSTs formed up

in two columns with the odd craft taking station just astern and to the center of the set. Aft of her was HMS *Huston*, another Coastal Force refugee. The sun had finally disappeared, leaving only clusters of bright stars and an occasional drifting cloud. Hardy had ordered double-watches and put his best men on radar and W/T. Drill or not, there was always the danger that one of those behemoths behind would crawl up *Firedancer*'s ass because someone wasn't paying attention, and her damage would be just as real and her crew just as dead as if they'd been set upon by E-boats.

A yeoman brought Hardy and Land tea and the two men drank it in silence, because this was the English Channel, and even though they were just miles off the English Coast, there was always the danger of E-boats. "Vigilance," Hardy had insisted to Land. "One must always be vigilant."

The leading Lancaster disintegrated with a tremendous explosion, lighting up most of the formation. As the plane's wings tore back off her body, the whole aircraft slid into a three-plane section just below and behind it. Gierek watched in horror as the pilots of the three Lancasters fought to swing their big aircraft out of the way of their dying brother. One bomber was lucky enough; its pilot had elected to nose down and speed up. It was safe. The other two pilots had tried to roll their bombers out of the way of the disintegrating Lancaster and brushed wingtips. Gierek watched as pieces of airframe flew into the sky, and then he saw the flaming wreckage crash into the struggling bombers. There was a large explosion. The light was so bright that Gierek covered his eyes and quickly whispered a prayer.

Tracers laced the blackness as flak, bright, flaming flowers, peppered the sky around them. The Mosquito shook violently, fighting to get out of this killing field, Gierek kicking the rudders and twisting the wheel to dodge the increasing barrage.

"Two more," Jagello said, and Gierek saw the fiery remains of two Lancasters as they plummeted toward the darkness below.

It was a 267-plane raid, counting Lancasters and Mosquitoes but not counting the fighter protection given by the Mustangs and Spitfires. Gierek and Jagello had come to Cherbourg countless times with smaller raids, and once with a raid that was nearly four hundred aircraft, and things had been tough before; "dicey," one British airman had commented when they finally returned. But this was different.

It had all been some perverse game to this point—not that the other raids hadn't been dangerous, because aircraft had been shot down and men had died. No, this was different. Now it seemed that the Germans, having stored up all of their frustration and anger at having been bombed constantly, had unleashed their rage in a single instant in tonight's raid.

"Where's Lintz?" Gierek shouted and then cursed himself. Veterans never shouted into the intercom built into the oxygen mask that covered their nose and mouths.

"Down," Jagello said. The statement rang with finality. Lintz's aircraft had disappeared with no preamble, no drama; it was there and then gone. It was not a thought that stayed with Gierek long; these were the circumstances of flying over Cherbourg—one learned to accept the losses of planes and men. One learns, after many close friends do not return, to keep everyone at arm's length.

Jagello announced: "Targets on radar." He pressed his forehead into the foam rubber cushion surrounding the screen. "Circling about ten miles to the left. Night fighters."

"Vultures," Gierek said, the taste of the word like bile in his mouth. The German night fighters would circle safely out of range of the fighters and their own flak, waiting until the bombers turned and headed home. Then they would move in and pick off the cripples. Vultures. The Mosquito shook violently as a flak shell exploded just off the left wingtip. Gierek held his breath, his eyes scanning the pale luminescence of the instrument dials on the panel. They returned his gaze, their needles steady and unfazed by the nearby explosion.

"Where are they?" Gierek said, his arms fighting to grip the shuddering wheel as the plane forced itself through the turbulence.

"Still ten miles out," Jagello said.

Gierek saw a streak far in the distance, a Lancaster on fire, falling to earth. Another flight, going well beyond Cherbourg to railroad yards, or troop concentrations, bridges—going farther inland, farther from home, deeper into enemy territory. He had often wondered what he would do if the Mosquito caught fire. "Get out" was the obvious answer, but the manner of abandoning the aircraft wasn't quite so obvious. It was a tight fit in the cockpit and their parachutes were bulky, and suppose the fire got to you first? Do you launch yourself into the blackness, your very own Roman candle, streaming flames and debris as you plummet toward the ground?

Four simultaneous blasts threw the Mosquito straight up and two Lancasters immediately in front of them disappeared in a cloud of flame.

"God damn it!" Gierek shouted in fear. He fought to bring his aircraft back to its proper altitude and position.

"I'm glad your dog is on our side," Jagello said.

"What?" Gierek said, trying to calm himself as he quickly studied the gauges.

"Your dog," Jagello said. "The dog that brings you luck."

"You call this luck?" Gierek said. A string of flak bursts filled the sky to their right.

"We aren't dead," Jagello said calmly. He adjusted the radar strobe. Gierek watched as his hand twisted the knob, searching. "I don't see Helig."

"We're turning," Gierek said as he saw the red taillights and engine exhausts of the bombers ahead begin to waver and move in unison.

"Right on time," Jagello said. "Mr. Nazi remains at ten miles."

"He's not my dog," Gierek said. "I hate that dog. He's always in the way. He's filthy." He glanced to his left. "God in heaven," he said. He felt Jagello slap his thigh and cradle the quick release button in his hand. The navigator/radar operator leaned over his shoulder and looked into the night. He had never done that before. Something must have caught his eye. Gierek looked out the canopy.

Cherbourg was on fire. The areas along the dock and surrounding harbor burned furiously, all light and movement but no noise. It was a pantomime of destruction. Explosions erupted through the constant flames as ammunition or fuel dumps succumbed to the fires. No one could survive that; no human being could live through that much destruction. For a moment, Gierek almost felt sorry for the Germans below but he let the thought pass—kill Germans, go home. That was what it was all about. Kill more Germans, get home faster.

"Give thanks to your dog, Gierek," Jagello said. "We're not dead yet."

Chapter 19

Reubold walked quickly through the corridors, keeping his eyes straight ahead, clear of the view into the vast wards with endless beds that held wounded sailors. He accepted his own injuries as a part of life, his life, and had learned to deal with them as well as he could. Even if to deal with the pain of those injuries was to mask it with drugs.

He could not stand to see the suffering that others endured. It was not compassion, it was more primordial than that—it was seeing the helplessness that replaced the vitality of men. It was a hunter, terribly wounded by a beast, surrounded by his companions all thinking the same thing; it was his fault. They shared the secret joy in having, by their own skills and agility, escaped the animal's attack. They were better than the stricken hunter. But deeper than that, far within Reubold's mind, was the single thought: That could be my fate, I could be helpless. That testimony was never allowed to overcome the sense of triumph tinged with arrogance in the single thought: I have escaped harm, he has not; I am better than he. But it was there.

Waldvogel shared a room with a mummified form in an adjoining bed. The edges of the mummy's bandages around his head and neck were stained rust from seeping wounds. Tubes ran into the man bearing clear liquids. Tubes ran out of the man bearing decay. The aroma of corruption hung everywhere.

"Is this he?" a man in a white coat said to Waldvogel in breathless expectation.

Reubold saw Waldvogel propped up in bed. The man, who must have been a surgeon, was standing next to him.

"This is Fregattenkapitan Reubold, Kapitanleutnant Treinies," Waldvogel said.

Treinies advanced around the bed, preceded by a broad grin and submissive posture. "Fregattenkapitan," he said extending his hand. "How fortunate I am to meet you. The korvettenkapitan has told me so much about you and of course your exploits are well known throughout the service."

Waldvogel winced at the kapitanleutnant's cloying attitude.

"Are they?" Reubold said, taking the handshake with reluctance. He loathed such men. They hovered around the moment that he had become famous, and disappeared just as quickly when fame abandoned him.

"Indeed. Indeed, yes. We follow your missions

with great interest here. Of course, our own service to the Fatherland is not without merit."

"Of course," Reubold said, trying to withdraw his hand. It was no use. It was trapped in a vise.

Treinies moved within confidential distance. "Did you know that they brought a man in to me that I suspected was a Jew?"

"How would I know that?" Reubold said.

"Of course. Of course you would not know. But I knew. I've done a study of such matters. The large nose, the slope of the forehead."

"That sounds like Mueller," Reubold said.

"Mueller? Mueller." Treinies considered the name. "He's not a Jew, is he?"

"No," Reubold said. "A lecher. I've come to see the korvettenkapitan."

"Of course," Treinies said, wrapping one tiny hand over the other, firmly trapping Reubold for the last word. "I must be off. A pleasure, sir. Frau Treinies will be most excited to hear that we've met."

Reubold watched the surgeon leave. "The only thing guaranteed to excite Frau Treinies is her husband's absence," he said. His eyes caught the motionless form pinned to the bed by a web of tubes. He pulled a white curtain along the overhead track, covering the scene before he sat down on a chair next to Waldvogel's bed. "How are they treating you?" he asked.

"Well," Waldvogel said. "Quite well."

Reubold studied the bandage wrapped around the korvettenkapitan's head. "Does it hurt much?"

"At times more than others. I dare not move

about too much. They said my skull is cracked. I suffered a concussion."

"Yes," Reubold said. "Falling concrete will do that."

"It was good of you to come," Waldvogel said. "I know how very busy you are. I can sometimes," he turned carefully to the window over his right shoulder, "see the harbor from here."

"Be careful that you don't see too much of the air raids."

"They evacuate us," Waldvogel said. His voice became hopeful. "How are the boats?"

"We're going out tonight. Don't tell the enemy."

"Then the trials were successful."

"The trials were satisfactory against a stationary target. I'm sure the harbormaster of Cherbourg is pleased that we removed the obstruction."

"You sound unconvinced, Fregattenkapitan," Waldvogel said.

"Cautious, Waldvogel. A healthy dose of caution makes for a longer life. If a somewhat duller one." He pulled a cigarette from a silver case and offered one to Waldvogel. The korvettenkapitan declined. "We did better than I expected. Much better. The doorknocker tracers were a very simple and effective means of sighting on the target. It will take additional training to refine the operation, but we did well. The men did well. Your idea, Korvettenkapitan Waldvogel, was genius." Reubold smiled at Waldvogel's shock. "Don't worry. I won't give you a medal or kiss you on both cheeks. We have," he started to speak but was uncertain of what to say. A voice told him to be cautious and in an instant he realized that he could not make extravagant claims. There were far too many variables for him to say categorically it will be a success or a failure. So he was left with an unsatisfying "a chance of success." He watched the korvettenkapitan. The man truly was humble, an innocent in the wilderness. Waldvogel's only satisfaction came from solving problems; his reward was achievement, yet in some ways his vision was limited. Reubold thought briefly of Treinies and his pandering; the man saw only what benefited him. Then he thought of himself; he wasn't sure of what he saw anymore.

"It was very good of you to come," Waldvogel said when he found his voice.

"Yes," Reubold said, knowing that he had done nothing that could be attributed to goodness in some time. A thought struck Reubold and before he could stop it, the words were out. "Waldvogel, you trouble me."

"I? But what have I done?"

"Or rather, I trouble myself. You merely represent some qualities that annoy me." He laughed at his own reluctance to admit the truth. "How I envy you," he said. "I race about trying to outrun regrets, hoping to quell the pain that exists in my soul." He saw what Waldvogel was thinking reflected in the korvettenkapitan's eyes. "No. The morphine is another matter. Let it be. I belong to it and it to me. But you . . . you have vision, while I am content to look for the familiar. I suppose that I find some safety in the familiar. Some years ago, I would have found the thought too frightening to consider. I suppose it has come upon me without notice. There was a time in my life when I took what I won, rather than what I was given." He found it difficult to say the words: "Rather than take the castoffs. What shall we call it? I now embrace mediocrity. Yes?"

"Fregattenkapitan," Waldvogel began.

"Be quiet, Waldvogel," Reubold said, "and hear my confession. I don't expect absolution. In fact I'd throw it back in your face. What I say, I say for selfish motives. Which is how I've lived my life. Well, perhaps not quite. I say it also because you should know what you have accomplished. This from your irritating inability to leave well enough alone." He crushed the cigarette out in a tin ashtray on a table next to Waldvogel's bed and realized that it was a relief to talk to the korvettenkapitan; even if in the long run it really meant nothing. "I say these things to you for my benefit. There should be equity in life. Balance. Am I speaking of justice? You do well; you are rewarded. You do evil; you die. But such simplicity is too much to expect, I suppose. We go out in a few hours, Korvettenkapitan, to find vessels that shoot back. That will be the real test of your guns' effectiveness. I have some hope that we will again be amazed. But then, hope has taken her leave of me some time ago." He stood and smiled at Waldvogel. "So I came to say thank you, and to get well. Personally I would rather be under fire than to face that simpering fool Treinies. Get well soon, Waldvogel. The war isn't over yet and I think that the fatherland will need your remarkable mind to keep us off the Devil's Shovel."

Waldvogel said nothing as Reubold left. The soft gurgling of the tubes exchanging fluids in the patient next to his bed and the muffled voices in

the corridor were all the korvettenkapitan heard.
The fregattenkapitan's visit left him unsettled. Reubold was everything he was not—articulate, brave,
strong—a leader that other men looked up to, and
yet Reubold came to honor him, to thank him.
Throughout his entire life, he had always been invisible, inconsequential, and so he threw himself
into work until the world existed only of problems
and solutions—twin havens.

He twisted slightly to look out the window, until
the pain in his neck and head forbade any further
movement. He could see the harbor and vague
shapes of the S-boat pens under the pale gaze of a
quarter moon. Reubold would lead them out, Waldvogel knew, out into the darkness and into danger
because Reubold was a fighter. But what the fregattenkapitan had come to say to Waldvogel tonight
was that they were equal; and perhaps Waldvogel was
the better of the two. True, Reubold said it for his
own benefit, but he admitted as much and that said
something for the character of the man. But he
had come to the hospital and he had said how he
felt and he had done these things out of sincerity.

Waldvogel eased himself back against the pillows, his mind drifting from Reubold's visit to the
boats. He thought of the guns and the foils, and
realized with a start that he had completely abandoned all memory of Reubold's visit. It was all too
fleeting, he thought. Perhaps the words remain
but they fade with the memories until all that exists is a shadow of the event. *I have that*, Waldvogel
conceded.

Then he noticed the bottle of calvados sitting
on the nightstand.

* * *

The wind was coming out of the northeast at
Force 2 and the barometer hovered around 30.10.
The waves were cycloidal—the abrupt, choppy
waves that indicated that *Firedancer* was in relatively
shallow water. Of course Hardy knew this because
of the charts and the reports from radar and W/T,
but he never discounted what the sea told him regardless of machines that said you should be here
and these should be the conditions. Four bells had
just sounded in the Mid Watch and all that was visible in the darkness were the vague shapes of the
LSTs as they maneuvered into position. Hardy had
doubled the watch and put *Firedancer* on Action
Stations because he didn't like being this close to
shore. And because the captain of the *Huston*, a
disagreeable man who dismissed Hardy's concern,
sent the terse radio message: "Will stand by to assist in the drill. Do not feel it necessary to go to Action Stations just yet."

Hardy had read the message and glanced in irritation at Land, and then ordered his Number
One to sound Action Stations. By God, drill or not,
it was dark out there and Jerry loves to flash about
in the dark and get into all sorts of mischief. Hardy
knew as well that there was always danger of colli-
sion between the LSTs in the darkness or of one of
the big slab-sided ships running over one of the little shoebox-size LCMs that carried thirty or forty
men. *Firedancer* went to Action Stations and Hardy
stood on the bridge, sweeping the darkness with
his binoculars, listening to the chatter over the
loudspeaker of the TBS as the LSTs began to form
up for landing practice. Talk Between Ships was a

short-range radio network that allowed the ships to communicate without giving away their positions by having their long-distance transmissions picked up.

A sharp whistle came from the voice tubes at Hardy's elbow. Hardy cupped his hand around the brass-tubes mouth and said: "Bridge. Hardy here."

"W/T. Caine, sir. We have targets fifty miles out, red, amidships."

"Once more?"

"Targets bearing two-one-zero, distance fifty miles. Red, amidships, sir."

"How many, W/T?"

"I estimate six or eight, sir. Speed about forty knots."

"Don't lose them," Hardy said, and then turned to Land. "E-boats, Number One. Have the Yeoman of Signals make to the fleet: "E-boats approaching from the southeast. Range fifty miles." He didn't wait for Land's acknowledgment. "W/T? Hardy here. Make to fleet, straight out. E-boats approaching from the southeast. Range fifty miles." Hardy wanted to warn the convoy by both radio and Aldis lamp—no use taking a chance that someone wasn't paying attention. He turned back to Land again, keeping his excitement under control. He'd gone into action enough to understand the importance of remaining as dispassionate as possible about combat. Don't let your nerves lead you astray, he had cautioned Land several times when it seemed as if Number One had let his emotions control his thinking. Cold, calculating, unimpassioned reason, Hardy had informed his junior officers, was the only true antidote to the insanity of combat.

"Kindly inform Guns, Number One," Hardy said, "that we shall go out and engage the enemy." *Firedancer*'s gunnery officer was stationed in the cramped room that held sonar, radar, and Wireless/Telegrapher so that he could coordinate the fire of the 4.5s, 20mm, and 40mm guns, as well as the twin torpedo mounts, of *Firedancer*. He was a sensitive man named Foxworthy who was very conscious of his rapidly receding hairline.

An urgent whistle from the tubes caught Hardy's attention.

"Bridge. W/T."

"Bridge, here," Hardy said. "What is it?"

"Several of the targets have broken off from the main body and increased speed."

"Increased speed?" Hardy said. "How . . ."

"They're fanning out, sir. Sixty knots, sir. No, sir. More. Seventy knots."

"Don't be daft," Hardy said, but he knew that the report was true and the admonition came out as a weak hope that the man was wrong. He trusted his radar and sonar operators because they had proved themselves on U-boat duty in the North Atlantic.

"Sir," Land said, alarmed. "*Huston* has just signaled that she is coming up to investigate and that we are to hold our station."

"Is he mad?" Hardy exploded. "Yeoman, make to *Huston*." The yeoman of signals steadied the Aldis lamp in his hand and waited for the message. "Do not expose column. I shall take the lead. Maintain station." The shutters of the Aldis lamp clicked rapidly.

"What is the man trying to do?" Land said.

"Win medals. Charge to the sound of gunfire. That's the bloody question isn't it? If we move out we'll force the bastards to sweep around us and that will keep them off the LSTs' bows. If *Huston* maintains position, they can't come in astern of the ships." There was nothing sophisticated about the plan; the LSTs were lightly armed but they could still put up a fight. Keep the ships in column so that they could bring every gun to bear, *Firedancer* protects the head and *Huston* protects the tail. All very simple. But now *Huston* had given away the advantage by moving out of position.

Reubold's boats pulled ahead of the Guernsey boats, and as they increased their speed, their ghost-like hulls rose out of the water on wings. Leutnant Dernbauer fed Reubold the distances to the target from the S-boat's radar. It was an unreliable instrument and Reubold hated to depend on it but at this speed he was forced to. Things simply moved too quickly for a man to pick things out in the darkness.

"Twenty-five kilometers," Dernbauer called from the radio room hatch. "Nine targets in column. One appears to be moving ahead."

"Destroyers?"

Dernbauer shrugged. "I think so, Fregattenkapitan. The screen is very distorted."

Reubold shook his head is disgust. "Never mind. Signal all boats. I will lead the attack down the column, bow to stern. The Guernsey boats will attack with torpedoes after we have cleared. I will signal a second attack."

"Flares, sir," called a bootsmannmaat, detailed as a lookout.

Reubold peered over the skullcap and saw the thin, fiery line wobble into the sky and then explode in a greenish-yellow light. Three more followed the first and then streams of red tracers began to search for them. He smiled and whispered, "Amateurs," before spinning the wheel to take his S-boat to port. He would close in a lazy crescent, until his boat and the following boats of his flotilla came in parallel to the column of enemy vessels. Then the Trinities would have an unobstructed field of fire and he would see how well Waldvogel's new trick worked against targets that returned fire.

"What are those bloody fools doing?" Hardy shouted. "Yeoman, make to flotilla—cease all flares. Cease all fire." He turned to Land, burning in frustration. "They're painting a bloody pretty picture for Jerry with all of that light."

Land leaned over the voice tube in response to a whistle. "Bridge. Land."

"W/T, sir. *Huston* is moving well off to the southwest, sir. It looks as if she is going to engage the E-boats."

"My, God, Number One," Hardy said. "This is a disaster." More flares sputtered into the night sky before exploding. Steady streams of tracers cut through the darkness behind *Firedancer*, hopeless efforts to ward off the danger that was approaching. Hardy suddenly felt sick as he realized that panic had seized the flotilla, sweeping away reason. The flares silhouetted the LSTs, and the tracers pinpointed their exact location. All battles were an intense series of distorted events, and the only salvation for those engaged was to ignore confusion, subdue fear, and concentrate on the task at hand—defending yourself against the enemy. But the column collapsed.

"Bridge? W/T. Many targets parallel at . . ."

The first explosion hit *Firedancer* in the hull just at the boat deck, blowing away the captain's gig and peppering the 20mm gun tub with shrapnel, killing four men. At the same time B turret fired into the night, the explosion of her 4.5-inch gun nearly blinding the men on the open bridge. Two more shells struck *Firedancer*, demolishing her searchlight tower aft and the high angle 3-inch gun nearby. Every man on the gun crew was killed. C turret fired at the unseen targets, given range and direction by the gunnery officer trying to follow the pale green blips as they raced across the radar screen. Twenty-millimeter and 40-millimeter guns joined in, their constant barking in rhythm with muzzle flashes and red glowing tracers.

Hardy called for supply parties to check the damage aft and hung over the port wing, trying to determine what had happened. They had taken fire so rapidly that he had not had time to react. They were large rounds, he knew that, and he prayed that they had hit high on the superstructure and had not pierced the hull. He realized just as quickly that the E-boats had gone, vanishing into the night before his gunners had a chance to exact revenge. Ghosts—fleet ghosts wielding mallets.

He saw flashes and corresponding explosions in the darkness some distance aft, along the column. The LSTs were being attacked.

The roar of the S-boat engines coupled with the thunderous discharge of the Trinities made it almost impossible for Reubold to be heard.

"I said," he shouted at Leutnant Dernbauer, "tell those bastards to make every shot count. I can see the targets, so they can see the targets." The Allied vessels were cargo ships of some kind, Reubold knew. Their own flares told him that much. "Aim, God damn it! Tell them to aim."

Explosions erupted all along the Allied column: enemy guns firing erratically, Trinity shells crashing into the vessels, eruptions of flame and debris hurtling into the night. Reubold fought to keep his senses about him as the firefight became even wilder. He thought he saw another S-boat cross his bow and was about to radio a warning when the boat disappeared into the darkness. The frantic radio chatter from Flotilla 11 boats and the Guernsey boats floated up from the radio room, the voices crackling with excitement.

"The Guernsey boats are attacking, sir," Dernbauer shouted over the noise.

"Tell them to wait until we clear the column," Reubold ordered. He had the wheel and could tell from the fires consuming the enemy vessels how far he was from the enemy ships. They might as well have lit themselves up with searchlights, Reubold thought as Dernbauer disappeared into he radio room.

Dernbauer reappeared with a stricken look. "It's too late. They're going in."

"God damn it," Reubold said. "God damn it." It was chaos. S-boats roaring through the night, enemy vessels exploding; the dry rumble of the engines driving S-205 through the water so quickly that Reubold dare not look away. At this speed if the S-boat hit even a small object, it would tear off the foils and probably sink the boat. "All right. All right. One pass. Signal the others. We'll make one pass and draw off. If there's anything left after those stupid bastards have had their chance, we go back in." Dernbauer nodded his understanding as Reubold looked away from the muzzle flashes of the Trinity in the bow. It was wonderful—it was working splendidly. The doorknocker quickly stuttered, throwing green tracers at the deliciously fat targets, and then there was the hollow boom of the recoilless cannon. The gunners, dim figures working in half-light and half-dark, looked like demons tending a hideous machine. Load, aim, fire. The wind off the bow occasionally sent a rancid cloud of blue smoke back over the skullcap, discharge from the gun, burning Reubold's eyes and fouling his mouth so that he tried to spit the disgusting taste away. He cursed the gunners and the guns, but without enthusiasm. It was working. It was working, and the thought of success thrilled Reubold.

First Sergeant Humboldt Gibbs, C Company, 3rd Battalion, 403 Regiment, 29th Infantry, made his way along the deck of LST 579, shouting over the mayhem.

"All right, you silly sons of bitches. Listen up."
He stationed himself in the middle of the disorganized mob of frightened men. "Drop your helmets, pack, and rifles." The LST lurched suddenly to starboard and the cries of the terrified men increased. "God damn it!" Gibbs shouted. "Pay attention to me." Most of the men, their white eyes nearly gleaming from the fires on the nearby ships, turned to him and grew quiet. "The next guy that squeals like a pansy is gonna get my boot up his ass. Drop your helmets, packs, and rifles." He brushed his helmet off his head. It landed with a clatter on the deck as he cut away his pack. Jesus, fucking Christ. This sure wasn't the Old Army. This whole fucking exercise looked like some sort of picnic at Fire Island. The men were on deck, waiting for the LCMs to be off-loaded when the attack began. Then the torpedo struck and the ship pitched to starboard.

Gibbs had taken a second to eye the deck cranes that were to have lowered the LCMs. The ship's list made them useless now. The cranes would either twist and collapse from the unnatural angle or the LCMs would break free from their mounts and sweep dozens of men overboard.

"Get them life rings up under your arms," Gibbs shouted, pulling his up snugly into his armpits. He pulled out the inflation tube. "Inflate your life rings. Now!" He began blowing into the tube, glancing around, trying to keep one eye on his men, another on the insane action in the darkness, and at the same time straining to hear the abandon ship order over the noise of battle and the shouts of desperate men.

He felt a hand grab his shoulder.

"Gibbs? Gibbs? What the hell are you doing?" Captain Small shouted. "God damn it. You tell those men to put their helmets back on. And pick up their rifles. Jesus, you told them to cut off their packs. Have you gone crazy?"

Gibbs, who had been blowing air into the inflation tube during Small's tirade, finally stopped. "If those dumb bastards," he said, tying the rubber tube in a knot to prevent air escaping, "go over the side with their helmets on, they'll break their fucking necks, sir. I don't figure they'll have much chance to use their weapons while they're treading water, either."

A flurry of blasts erupted to the rear of the column, the bright explosions eating away the darkness. Finally all that remained were the steady glow of fire and the ghostly outline of burning ships.

"Nobody said anything about abandoning this ship," Small said, craning his neck, trying to look over Gibbs's shoulder in the direction of the bridge. "Nobody said anything about abandoning ship, Gibbs. Where's Hartsell? Have you seen Hartsell? Byron?"

They were two of the company officers and Gibbs had no idea where they were. And he frankly didn't give a shit.

"No, sir," Gibbs said. "I ain't seen them. 'S'cuse me, sir." He stepped around Small, took the inflation tube out of a soldier's trembling hands, and straightened out a kink. "It's just like your dick, sonny. If it ain't straight, it don't work. Now blow." He jammed the tube into the surprised soldier's mouth. Gibbs heard the deck loudspeakers crackle and he automatically turned to the bridge.

"Now hear this. Now hear this. Prepare to abandon ship."

" 'Bout time," Gibbs muttered. "C Company!" he shouted. "On me."

"Now wait a minute, Gibbs," Small said, placing himself directly in front of the sergeant. "You wait just one damned minute. This is my company. You don't go telling my men what to do."

"Yes, sir," Gibbs said calmly. "But you'd better get your life ring inflated, sir. 'Cause if you don't shut the fuck up and get out of my way, it won't do you a bit of good when I toss you over the side." He turned back to the men. "Check your buddies. Rings inflated," he said, pleased to see that he had at least restored some organization to the scene. "Helmets, packs, weapons on the deck."

The LST's list increased sharply and the men looked at Gibbs in alarm. He knew that they were ready to panic and he couldn't blame them. The only thing that kept him from going over the side was this pack of sad sacks clustered on the deck, ready to piss their pants.

"Now hear this. Now hear this."

"Nobody goes until I say!" Gibbs shouted so loudly he felt something in his throat tear. The navy had their way but all they did was drive the boats. These were soldiers and nobody would tell his men what to do but him.

"Abandon ship. Abandon ship."

Out of the corner of his eye, Gibbs saw men from other companies jump over the side, or clamber over the railing, but he was relieved to see his men hadn't moved. They feared First Sergeant

Gibbs more than they feared drowning. Maybe
there was hope for these guys yet.

"The first one of you sons of bitches that moves
is dead," he shouted, ignoring the pain in his throat.
Every head turned to look at him. He was pleased,
at least they had sense enough to follow orders.
"Make sure nobody's underneath you when you
jump. Get your asses away from the ship. Form up
in the water. Keep them life rings under your pits.
Any questions?" He knew that there wouldn't be
any, he knew that the men were ready to explode
with fright, but he also knew that he had to instill
one last measure of discipline in them. He knew
that a lot of them would probably die.

"All right, you dumb bastards," he said, "assemble at the rail. You heard the man. Get the hell off
this fucking boat in an orderly fashion."

Chapter 20

Lyme Bay

Cole was glad that there was a gentle breeze coming from the southeast. It blew the smoke and the stench of the dead back to the shore, away from the deck of PT-155.

His squadron had arrived just after dawn, called out by a frantic message to get down to Lyme Bay. Hospital tents were set up all along the beach, rescue craft were threading the water looking for survivors, and a few LCMs were trundling back and forth between the beach and the two damaged, but still afloat, LSTs. The other five were sunk, or sinking. Too many columns of brown smoke to count marked where the fleet had been. Ships were burning, debris was burning; it seemed that the water of the Channel, covered with the remnants of the battle, was burning.

Cole pulled a pair of binoculars from the case

under the instrument panel, adjusted the strap, held them slightly in front of his eyes so that they wouldn't distort his vision, and carefully focused on the beach.

Still shapes, bundles of silent men, were washed up on sodden rows along the shore's edge. Their wet uniforms were almost black, a sharp contrast to the pale white skin of their hands and faces. Waves continued to roll in, swinging lifeless arms and legs, tugging at bodies, urging them to get up and walk away from death. It was no use.

DeLong joined Cole and shaded his eyes with his hand, trying to cut down the glare of the sun off the water. "Hell of a mess, isn't it?" He didn't wait for an answer. "I've been listening to the radio chatter. They figure maybe a thousand, fifteen hundred dead. We don't know for sure yet. We've got five boats that are gone for sure. The other two," he shrugged. "I guess the yard birds will have to take a look at them."

"Anything else?" Cole asked, turning the binoculars toward the LSTs.

"E-boats," DeLong said. "That's all that came over the radio until somebody put the kibosh to it. I guess the higher-ups don't want us to know how bad it was."

"Little late for that," Cole said. "E-boats, huh?" It was not a question; it was a confirmation. He had studied the scene clinically: the placement of the ships, what damage he could see through the smoke, and any telltale signs that these were the same E-boats that attacked the *Southern*'s convoy. Edland's mysterious boats. He knew it was a long shot; there were still plenty of E-boats out there.

And there probably weren't many of the winged boats—the hydrofoils—that Edland was trying to find, so that the likelihood that this attack. . . . He rolled the idea over in his mind and began to pick at it. Suppose Edland had a point? Suppose that these fantastic boats existed and were running all over the Channel? Maybe this was some of their handiwork. How many were there? Maybe a dozen. Maybe two hundred. Cole looked at the bodies strung along the beach again. Suppose it was ten times that? Suppose the invasion fleet never got close enough to land the invasion force. He looked at the smoldering LSTs in the bay. Suppose the greatest invasion in history ended up being a massacre?

He had noticed ugly, black scars from hits on the superstructure of a LST. They were well placed around the bridge area and the gun tubs. Extraordinarily well placed. He had adjusted the focus of the binoculars until he could see the damage clearly. Burn marks, blackened holes, precise hits. He lowered the binoculars and stood thinking. Precise. Surgical.

"Yeah," Cole said. "A whole slew of E-boats." He shook his head. "Maybe just a handful." He turned and realized that DeLong was standing next to the hatchway that led to the radio room. Cole began thinking again. A hundred of these little bastards racing around the Channel, raising hell with the invasion fleet. It would be like Times Square with the lights out—mass confusion—ships everywhere—organization . . .

DeLong rejoined him long enough to say: "Okay, skipper. We got the word to move in and start picking up bodies." He turned to the helm, eased the throttles up, and slowly spun the wheel through his fingers to bring the boat around.

Cole looked out over the waters of the bay and beyond that, the Channel. Beyond that, far beyond the dozens of boats and ships searching for survivors, was Cherbourg. And Le Havre. And Boulogne. And within those ports, in one, or some, or all of the E-boat sanctuaries, were more of Edland's eagles. There was a chance that they would be crushed from above by the weight of thousands of tons of bombs. There was the chance that their huge, impregnable concrete pens would protect them, at least long enough for them to slip out and engage the invasion fleets. There was the chance that increased sorties by the English and American air forces would somehow catch them out in the open and destroy them. They ventured out at night, however, and even with air-to-surface radar, it was unlikely that the airplanes would destroy them. Night translates into early morning, the hours that the fleet would be crossing the Channel. It was the only way to position the fleet off the beaches by dawns. Night–early morning. E-boat darkness.

Torpedoes, he thought suddenly. The chatter was that some of the LSTs were torpedoed. Could the eagles launch torpedoes? Of course they could—they did, didn't they? Did they? Cole knew that he couldn't answer that question. If the Germans had perfected E-boats that could cruise at eighty knots and mount 6-inch guns, why couldn't they mount torpedoes on those vessels and overcome the problems presented by the foils and the

speed? Conventional E-boats had torpedoes, why
not the Sea Eagles? Cole grimaced at his use of the
name—now he was beginning to sound like Edland.
The thought galled him. He didn't like to attach any
romantic notion to anything that the enemy did.

PT-155 slowed and Cole made his way to the
bridge, stuffing the binoculars in their case. Now it
was time to pick up bodies, and he willed the emotion out of his mind. It was the only way that he
knew to prepare himself for the sight of dead
Americans. He heard the gentle thump of something striking the hull.

Tommy Rich looked back from the bow with a
sickened expression. "Jeez, Skipper. This guy ain't
got a head." Tommy had the body pinned in place
with the boat hook, while several other men tried
to slip a loop around the body's leg.

"If it doesn't bother him, Rich," Cole said, "then
it shouldn't bother you. Just get him aboard and
be careful." The dead soldier was obviously beyond caring, but Cole knew it was easy to wrench
your back when trying to lift the full weight of a
dead body—especially one that had been floating
in the water for a while.

"Man," Randy DeLong said. "This is a mess." He
gripped the wheel tightly. His own way of dealing
with the distasteful duty. "There are bodies floating all over the place."

"They could have used us a little sooner," Cole
said, watching as the crew hoisted the dead soldier
aboard and manhandled the body into position
on the deck. The first of many, he thought.

"I sure would have liked to have been here when
those bastards attacked," DeLong said grimly.

"Well, we weren't," Cole said. "But we're here now."

"Little like closing the barn door after the horses got out," DeLong agreed.

Cole said nothing but the image was as clear to him as the hundreds of lifeless forms floating on the gentle swells; barn doors swinging on large hinges, the action of closing something in, or out. There was nothing else to the thought, just a picture in his mind planted by Edland's words. Sea Eagles.

"Let me do the talking," Walters said as he and Reubold approached Feldmarschall Erwin Rommel's office. The kommodore was swollen with success. Reubold thought it oddly pathetic that he subscribed to the notion that he was the architect of the victory. He found Walters's arrogance unsettling.

"I shouldn't even be talking with the army," Reubold said. "Dresser is my immediate superior, not Rommel."

"Rommel has the Fuehrer's confidence. The Kriegsmarine does not. If we can show him what your boats are capable of, we will have achieved a major victory."

"Don't brag too much," Reubold said. "Our victories include a handful of merchant ships and a derelict."

"You must learn to be optimistic," Walters said, and smiled broadly, enjoying his role. "Rommel is an innovator. He realizes the importance and the potential of unconventional weapons. But he will ask very direct questions. Your replies must be their equal."

Reubold felt his sense of alarm deepen. Walters was speaking for Rommel as well.

The two men stopped at the tall, white double doors to Rommel's suite of offices.

"I thought that I was to let you do the talking?" Reubold said.

"Anything that is not an answer to a direct question put to you by Rommel is mine," Walters said. "Ready?"

Reubold shrugged. For what? Walters's ruse? What did the man want? What did he hope to accomplish by this audience with Rommel? Reubold smiled to himself: what did he hope to gain? It would be that of course. Yes, yes. It would be patriotism—service to the Fatherland, another way to defeat the enemy. He continued calculating and decided that some men were masters of intrigue—he was not.

"Well?"

Reubold realized that Walters was waiting on his answer. Ready for what? For Rommel to suddenly embrace both of them as saviors of the *Reich*? Reubold remembered his own arrogance many years before and he thought best to explain to Walters that such ambition often demands payment in return. Payment, when one least expected it.

"Of course, Kommodore."

Walters nodded, knocked twice to announce his presence, opened the door, and walked in.

Dresser was talking to Rommel.

"Yes, Walters," the feldmarschall said. "Come in. Close the door. The admiral and I have been talking about S-boats and mines."

Reubold felt a chill as Dresser glared at him. It was reinforced by Rommel's barely civil tone. This would not go as Walters had envisioned.

"You've come to speak about S-boats as well, haven't you? Good. We shall all speak together and lay this thing to rest. I have much larger problems to deal with. What are they called? Hydrofoils? Well? We've spoken of them before, Walters. Your storm troops. What have you to say?" Rommel demanded.

"Feldmarschall," Walters said, obviously startled by Dresser's presence. He stumbled slightly over the word and it was obvious to Reubold that the kommodore's good humor was replaced by foreboding. He tried to reclaim the moment. "I firmly believe that these vessels hold great promise."

Dresser added to Rommel. "Little more than toys."

"They are innovative," Walters said. He was hopeful once more.

Reubold watched as Rommel pondered the differences. He saw the general's impatience building quickly.

"Well?" Rommel posed to both men. "Suppose they are both? What am I to do with them?" His manner was brusque. "This is Kriegsmarine business. I've asked that all S-boats lay mines along the likely invasion routes. They can do that can't they? And patrol the sea-lanes? Am I wrong?"

"My apologies, Feldmarschall," Walters said. "I

thought that you had agreed with me. That we had reached an understanding about the boats. Perhaps I misunderstood. . . ."

"Not at all, Feldmarschall," Dresser jumped in. He was being very open, very pleasant, as if his unexpected presence here today was just a happy coincidence. There was no contradiction of purposes, nothing but a sense of cooperation. The meeting today was simply to address minor matter. He was a bureaucrat with an agenda firmly in hand. But what, Reubold wondered, was the agenda? He understood, suddenly, that Dresser was the victor and the battle had hardly been joined.

"What you have so ordered," Dresser continued to Rommel. "In fact, some time ago, is already under way. Reubold's flotilla will soon take its place alongside the other S-boats. Obviously," he added, glancing at Reubold, "I was surprised to hear that they had not as yet deployed a single mine."

"I do not have time to deal with this," Rommel said, ending the conversation. The words were sharp and dismissive. Reubold noticed that a rash covered the back of the feldmarschall's hand. He saw Rommel dig at the tiny red splotches, scratching until the skin turned an angry red. It was nerves, Reubold knew. He'd seen it in other men—a nervous tic, lighting a fresh cigarette while two burned in the ashtray, pacing—a dozen signals that the pressure of command was almost too much to bear.

The famous general certainly had that burden, and the uncertainty of both the Allied invasion and the degree of interference from Berlin. From the Fuehrer. Rommel turned on Walters, his fingers working rapidly into the back of his hand. "Walters. I have some very good news. You've been recalled to Berlin and assigned to Doenitz's staff."

"I, Feldmarschall?" Walters said, shocked.

Rommel waved at Dresser. "The Admiral was very complimentary of you and your efforts on my behalf. I shall miss your expertise and guidance, but so be it." He offered an afterward: "You've performed admirably here."

Reubold watched as Walters glowed and suddenly it became very clear. So it was all a game and the boats would quickly be forgotten. They were tokens, Walters's gambit. Their success would assure his advancement, but through a strange combination of circumstances victory did not enter into it. Walters would return to Olympus and stand among the gods, Reubold thought grimly. *Should I have expected anything less?*

"You," Rommel shot Reubold a glance. "What is your name?"

"Fregattenkapitan Reubold," Reubold said. He did not bother to come to attention. Somehow, it seemed distasteful to do so.

"What do you do?"

"I am commander of Flotilla Eleven," Reubold said.

Rommel went quickly to a large table and began sifting through maps. "Here. You. You," he called Dresser and Reubold to his side. "Come here. Look at this. Look here." He slapped a map with the palm of his hand and threw it on the floor. "Here. Look at this." Another map fluttered to the carpet. "Here. Here." Rommel slammed his fist onto the table. "The coast of France. The Atlantic Wall. Half complete. Half!" His shout filled the room while the others remained silent. Rommel gathered himself, staring at a map sprinkled with fortifications. He took a pencil out of a cup on the table and became lost in sketching out an oblong shape on the paper. "Admiral Dresser?" he said, his voice even, almost mellow. "Can I count on you to place mines here?"

Dresser leaned over Rommel's shoulder and studied the map. "Indeed, Feldmarschall."

Rommel tapped the pencil on the paper in a thoughtful rhythm. "Here, then," he said, looking at Dresser as if the outburst had never occurred. "Off these beaches?"

"Of course, Feldmarschall."

Rommel nodded. "Thank you, gentlemen," he said without looking at the men. "Walters? Have Janh come in. This irrational Channel weather is becoming irritating." A grim smile followed. "Again. My congratulations to you on your appointment."

"Of course, Feldmarschall," Walters said. Reubold noticed his appreciation was sprinkled with humility. He watched the kommodore disappear through another set of doors before Dresser motioned him into the hallway.

"Fregattenkapitan," Dresser said. "You must learn to quit chasing fame. Sometimes simply doing what is asked of you is enough. You must also learn that it is far too easy for one of your gullibility to be led astray."

"It appears that you are right, Admiral," Reubold said, wondering if Walters ever had any intention of championing his boats. A champion, Reubold thought bitterly; do I really think such men exist?

Admiral Dresser looked through the tall windows on one side of the hallway. "What a barren sky," he said at the bank of low gray clouds. "Our protector, however. The Allies can't see us through the cloud cover, can they, Reubold? They can't see us build fortifications, or move troops," he smiled at Reubold. "Or lay mines."

"No, Admiral," Reubold said. Nor can we see them, he thought, but kept the idea to himself.

"Well," Dresser said, signaling to an orderly at the far end of the long hall. "Go back to Cherbourg and make your boats ready. Let's have no more nonsense about Sea Eagles, shall we?"

"No, Admiral," Reubold said. What else could he say? He searched for an argument that might extend the life of the boats, but his mind refused to cooperate. It kept returning to that single word—*champion*—and the irony of his belief that such men existed.

"Oh, Reubold," Dresser said as the orderly appeared with his cap and gloves. "I spoke with Reichsmarschall Goering this morning. A very pleasant conversation. He asked after your health."

Reubold smiled as Dresser pulled on his gloves and straightened his cap. "The reichsmarschall," Reubold said, "has had a special interest in my well-being for some time."

"Yes, I gathered that," Dresser said, fitting the gloves around and between his fingers until they appeared to be a second skin. "Strange, however. He seemed disappointed when I replied that you were in excellent health."

"Perhaps, Admiral," Reubold said. "You will have the sad duty to report to the reichsfuehrer that I perished in battle. I'm sure that his reaction will be quite different."

Chapter 21

Edland watched as McNamar walked to the fireplace, his arms locked behind his back, digesting the report. He turned.

"That bad, huh?"

"Yes, sir," Edland confirmed. "Five sunk. Two heavily damaged. At least a thousand dead."

"But they found the bigots?" Ten men who knew a great deal about the invasion had been on the LSTs. They were reported missing and for several hours there had been a frantic search for the officers. The loss of the men and ships had been a disaster; the capture of the ten bigots would have been a catastrophe. There was a macabre sigh of relief when their bodies were hauled out of the cold water.

"Yes, sir," Edland said. He had watched as the body of the last of the men who knew so much about the invasion was dragged up on the stony beach and laid with the others.

McNamar shook his head. "Jesus. We can't keep this up."

Edland understood. The five LSTs sunk comprised the reserve of *all* of the invasion fleet's LSTs. The two that were damaged would probably not be repaired in time for the invasion. There were a few LSTs, old British ships that were quickly being overhauled, but time and the condition of the ships were factors. And those ships amounted to exactly—three.

"You'd think that we'd be able to scrounge up half a dozen LSTs from somebody, wouldn't you?" McNamar said, walking back to Edland. "MacArthur won't give them up. Nimitz can't part with any. I've shanghaied every ship in the Mediterranean I could get my hands on and the goddamned British can't get theirs ready in time. Jesus. What a fiasco."

Edland remained silent. It was logistics. Men and materiel delivered to the scene of the battle. Delivered quickly and on time. This was not the part of the war that inspired paintings, songs, or patriotic movies. There were never triumphant poems written about making sure soldiers had beans and bullets—but if they didn't . . .

"Those goddamned E-boats," McNamar said. Edland saw the worry in McNamar's face. "We can't get to them, Mike. The British have finally got enough Tall Boys and it's a damn good thing because any other bomb is just too light. They won't penetrate the concrete roof of those pens. It's like throwing spitballs. This is going to be a fucking disaster unless those E-boats are eliminated. That goes for your winged boats as well. Hell, I don't know. Maybe especially your winged boats."

"Thermopylae," Edland said, and then was instantly sorry that he said it. But the word explained everything. A small band of brave Greeks holding off an entire Persian army at a narrow pass.

McNamar looked at him in a flash of anger, but it quickly died. "You think that's what this is all about?"

"I don't know, Admiral."

"Well, isn't that what we're paying you for? To know? You're supposed to be the expert on these things, aren't you?" McNamar said, his anger rising. "Jesus Christ, Mike, this is a hell of a time for you to plead ignorance. Pretty soon we're going to have a couple of thousand ships and several hundred thousand men in a hell of a fix and we need to know everything. So don't give me that 'I don't know' crap. How fast are they? How many do the Krauts have? Where are they? You've got to give me something."

Edland nodded, carefully selecting his words. "Our first encounter with these vessels showed them to be fast, but their fire was inaccurate. Maybe because of the speed. Sixty knots. Some reports gave eighty knots. Lyme Bay was different. The hits were well grouped, very accurate. A torpedo attack was the follow-up. The whole thing took less than three hours by most accounts."

"Okay," McNamar said, calming. "Now what? You're a smart boy, what do you think?"

"I think that there are only a few of them," Edland said, trying to offer some hope. "A flotilla. Maybe two."

"But there could be more? Right?"

"Yes, sir. But I don't think there are. I think if there were more, we'd be seeing more attacks."

"Maybe the Krauts are holding them for the Sunday punch?"

Edland nodded. It was just as reasonable to suspect that they would be unleashed in swarms, enveloping the invasion fleets by the hundreds.

"Yeah," McNamar said. "They don't have to win, do they, Mike? All they have to do is fuck things up. Just foul up things so badly that Ike is forced to call the whole thing off." He let a moment pass before speaking. Edland could see that McNamar was worn out. The days were too long and the nights were too short, and if he wasn't faced with emergencies he was pounded by responsibilities. The weight of command, Edland thought. It sounded trite, and maybe someone who hadn't seen what he had seen could make it sound trite just by saying it. The newspapers. Politicians. But command was a physical thing, a block of iron that good men struggled to keep aloft so that it didn't crush them, or those they were responsible for. "I saw Ike today. This morning. All he talked about was the goddamned weather. The weather looks lousy. We might have a day or two in early June, if we're lucky. *If* Ike wants to give the word. How the hell he keeps from going nuts I'll never know. I guess reading those Westerns." He looked at Edland, regaining his composure. "Thermopylae, huh? Well, it's up to us to keep that from happening." He seemed to have noticed Edland for the first time and that the lieutenant commander had something on his mind. "Okay. Spill it."

"I'd like to try again."

McNamar gave Edland a harsh look. "Hell, no. You've done your sea duty and you're not going out again. That's not your job. You stick with me and do what you're supposed to do. I'll get ahold of Harris and Ramsey. We'll turn up the heat on those pens."

"It's important that we capture one intact, Admiral," Edland pushed. "Maybe we can learn something from it. A way to fight them."

"The way to fight them is to blow them out of the water. It may not be fancy or fair, but it'll work. Christ, Mike. You're too important to go wandering all over the Channel looking for your white whale."

Edland tried again. "They might just hold some secrets worth having."

"You're carrying your own share of secrets, Mike," McNamar said angrily. "I can't chance you falling into the wrong hands."

"That won't happen, sir," Edland said. "I'll take precautions."

McNamar understood immediately. "You know what you're saying? This is no game, Mike. If push comes to shove, you can't be captured. Is your life worth some half-assed attempt to get one of these boats?"

"Yes, sir. If we move quickly enough we might have a chance to learn their secrets. It could save a lot of lives."

"That's a hell of a way to go."

Edland, despite the subject, was amused that McNamar was unable to bring himself to say the word out loud—*suicide*. "I always carry a sidearm," Edland said. "Not as sophisticated as a cyanide tablet but just as effective."

McNamar shook his head in wonder. "You're

one cold son of a bitch, I'll give you that. You'd do it, wouldn't you, just to prove me wrong?"

Edland smiled.

"God help me for being a fool and you for being seven kinds of an idiot," McNamar said. "I can't figure you, Edland. You're no hero and I'm really not sure what you think you can accomplish." A full minute passed before he said anything, but this time he spoke as if he were a man who'd just come to his senses. "What's that old expression? 'Fool me once, shame on you. Fool me twice . . .'" He shook his head slowly. "No can do, Mike. You stay on dry land and that's an order. No more adventures for you. We clear on that?"

Edland nodded. "Yes, sir. No more adventures."

Gierek watched the sheets of rain roll across the runway in the false night of an afternoon storm. He was safe inside the hangar, smoking a cigarette, with the comforting sounds of the erks working on the Mosquitoes behind him. He was cold, despite the sheepskin jacket that he wore—the dampness sliding its fingers into his bones until he found himself trembling in its grip. He could have walked away from the entrance of the hangar, sought out the kerosene heater that the erks kept burning near the work shed, but he decided against it. He preferred to be alone, staring out across the gray field, his thoughts suspended—time at a standstill.

He flicked the cigarette into the hard rain and lost sight of it. He bowed his head and lit another and thought of Poland. Sister. Brother. He would not say their names, he vowed when he escaped across the Channel with a battered group of Poles, until he returned home. They would only be Sister and Brother.

Her hair was blond, almost white, because she spent so much time in the garden with her flowers. When Gierek came home on leave before the war he would say: "Sister, tell me what those are?" She would explain the flowers carefully. What they were and how they liked to grow and whether they were annuals or perennials. She would touch the leaves or petals with her frail fingers, caressing each as if from her touch she conveyed her regard for the sanctity of life.

Gierek would sit on the bench in the bright sunlight under a clear blue sky, ignoring the hovering schoolgirls who found his airman's uniform and his newly acquired maturity too difficult to resist. He caught sight of them out of the corner of his eye but he never lost track of what Sister was saying. Time for the girls later.

He thought of Brother and the image troubled him. The boy was too outspoken and too ready to fight, and although he had just entered his late teens, he was big and aware of his size. Brother never wavered in his opinion of people or causes, and when Gierek, himself used to expressing his opinion whether asked or not, tried to explain that sometimes moderation or caution were acceptable attributes, Brother dismissed the idea.

"You're getting old," Brother had said. Gierek was surprised at the comment because he thought of himself as young, and rather good-looking, and self-possessed. Less than five years separated him from Brother, but it might as well been a century—

the old and the new of it. Especially now that Gierek had seen so much of what war was really like—not the uniforms or the adoration of small-town girls who spun like satellites around a celestial body. But the real war—guilt, fear, rage, and loss.

Gierek heard a noise and looked down at his side. The Black Prince sat next to him, looking through a thatch of greasy fur into the storm. A pink tongue hung listlessly from a parted mouth and his panting was accompanied by soft wheezing.

Gierek stared at the disgusting creature, while the Black Prince ignored him. "Are you truly lucky?" Gierek said in Polish, keeping his voice low so that no one heard him except the animal. "So many of us go up and so few of us return each time. Are you truly lucky?"

A stream of drool dropped from the dog's mouth and created a puddle in the hard-packed dirt.

Gierek stared into the storm. "I live in a little town, dog. One day the Germans came and that was that. They shot our planes out of the sky and destroyed our army. I ran and hid. Finally I found some men to fight with but soon they were killed. Then I found others to fight with. That is all I did. Fight, hide, retreat."

The dog yawned and sunk to the earth, resting its chin over its crossed paws.

"So I come to England and fly wonderful **air**-planes. Sometimes I think that I shall never see my village"; the images of Sister and Brother interrupted his testimonial and he winced. "Sometimes I fear that my family is dead. So I concentrate on killing Germans. But I am troubled. I have flown too many times. I think that my time is nearly done."

He looked at the dog. He appeared to be asleep. "If you are truly lucky, be lucky for me. I want to live to see my village and my family again."

The wind pushed a sheet of rain into the hangar, spraying Gierek. He stepped back out of the weather, noticed that his cigarette was soaked, and threw it away in disgust. He searched through his pockets for another one when he looked down. The Black Prince was gone.

"I hope that you are truly lucky," Gierek whispered, lighting another cigarette.

Chapter 22

Farley Manor, near Petersfield, England

Cole drove up the tree-lined gravel drive, his apprehension building. He had come close to turning the jeep around and heading back to the base a dozen times but he couldn't make himself do it. His better sense, or guilt, or a combination of the two, said that he had to see Rebecca. He tried to harden his attitude toward her on the drive, creating conversations where he played both roles. He was masterful in the imaginary encounters, his harsh words slicing through her weak excuses for ending the affair, until his own decency got the better of him and he realized that he was being unfair to her.

He had tried to deny his excitement, masking it by concentrating on the odd English road signs and the challenge of driving on the wrong side of the road. When he had called Dickie Moore to ask for directions to the Manor, the Royal Navy officer had been his usual cheerful self. "About bloody time," he had said over the sound of a radio playing swing music in the background and the hum of a dozen voices. Another of Dickie's parties. "I say, Cole. Are you going to be pleasant?"

"Of course," Cole had said, cupping the phone close to his ear to hear his friend's voice.

"You see I ask," Dickie said, and then apparently afraid that he wasn't being heard over the noise in the background, "I ask because you are such a piker."

"Just give me the address," Cole had said. "You can insult me later."

He had the address and he made the short drive to Petersfield, and as he dropped the jeep down into second, he could see the impressive stone building at the apex of a curved drive. Farley Manor.

He stopped the jeep, hopped out, and scanned the sky. Still heavily overcast, so dark it almost felt like night. There was bad weather coming in all right.

He took the heavy iron doorknocker in his hand and drew a deep breath when the door opened. An aged butler looked him over with disinterested eyes.

"Sir?" the old man said.

"Lieutenant Jordan Cole," Cole said, feeling as if he had intruded on a funeral. "To see Rebecca Blair."

"She is expecting you, sir?" the butler said.

"No," Cole said. "I'm a surprise."

The butler stood back, signaling Cole that he could come into the hallway. His eyes flicked at

Cole's cap. Cole quickly removed it, not sure if he should hand it over or hold on to it. The butler didn't offer to take it and the gesture said everything; you won't be staying long. "Wait here, sir," the butler said. "I'll announce you."

Cole nodded, running his fingertips along the edge of his cap as he waited. The argument continued to rage inside but it was less intense than before. He was here; it would be silly to bolt out the door. *What if she doesn't want to see me?* He tallied up a dozen reasons, mostly imaginary, why she didn't want to see him. He berated himself for his conduct, for not writing to her, for the anger that he felt toward her, for the terrible things that he called her, and for a wild, irrational instant he was certain that she must have known how horribly he treated her in his mind. He shook his head in disgust at his own insanity and wondered why he could do everything except save the relationship.

"Lieutenant Cole?" a thin woman with auburn hair approached him. Rebecca's mother; she had to be Rebecca's mother, the resemblance was amazing. "I'm Florence Bannard. You've come to see Rebecca."

"Yes," Cole said. He felt awkward, now more than ever, an intruder. "I should have called or something."

"'Or something,' Lieutenant. Carrier pigeon, perhaps?" It might have been an attempt at a joke, but Florence delivered it with just enough coolness to belay that suspicion.

He laughed despite himself. "Okay. You're definitely Rebecca's mom. Mother."

Her demeanor remained unchanged, but Cole

supposed it was more a question of British reserve than it was her mild chastisement of him. "Ringing ahead or carrier pigeon would certainly have been the polite thing to do, but I've noticed that you Americans are an informal people." That damned British reserve—sometimes Cole found it intimidating. "But you're welcome, of course."

"I hope this isn't a bad time."

A moment passed. "Not at all. I'm sure Rebecca will be glad to see you. She's in the solarium. She spends quite a bit of her time there these days. If you follow me . . ."

"Ma'am," Cole interrupted her. "If you don't mind, I'd rather show myself to her room. I mean find my own way. I . . ." He tried to find a way to tell her that Rebecca might not be happy to see him and he didn't want an audience if that was the case. His emotions were spinning about like the waterspouts he had often watched dance over the sea.

"I shouldn't worry, Mr. Cole," Florence said, releasing him from his dilemma. "I know all about you and Rebecca. We've had a splendid time getting reacquainted recently. We talk now, mother-to-daughter, like we've never talked before. You have been a recurring subject. Just walk down the hall and turn left at the third door."

"Thank you," Cole said, relieved.

The solarium was large, with a few potted plants scattered about, and in the center of the room was a large settee with a lamp just behind it. Rebecca, a coverlet thrown over her lap, sat reading a book, framed by the soft light.

Cole's mouth went dry when he saw her. Her thick hair fell, unbound, over her shoulders. Her eyes, gliding over the pages of the book in her hand, were as gentle and kind as he remembered them. The delicate curve of her cheeks and the long slope of her neck captured his eyes and he realized with a start that he had been staring at her.

"Hi," he said. The word no more than a whisper.

When she looked up her mouth parted in surprise, and for a terrible moment Cole was afraid that she would order him to leave, but she smiled and her face suddenly filled with hope. He knew that she was glad to see him. He felt his excitement growing. "Hello," she said, surprised, her voice kind and inviting. The sound of it brought back a flood of memories for Cole.

"I guess it's been a long time," he said, moving closer to her. He'd practiced this moment a dozen times on the trip to Petersfield, but everything that he meant to say evaporated. Now he simply wanted to hold her, to kiss her, to feel her body pressed against his.

She slipped a bookmark between the pages and laid the book on a low table. "Yes. It has. Much too long." Her eyes shone with longing and he began to hope that there still might be a chance.

Cole stopped, awkwardly, and then continued walking, certain somehow that it was better if he moved about. His mind raced through the countless prepared speeches, but he could think of nothing to say. He remembered their lovemaking and how passionate she was, crying out at the moment that everything, everyone was forgotten, except their pleasure. He finally stumbled onto a pitiful: "I talked to Dickie. He said that I should come and see you. He told me where you lived."

"Dickie's been here a number of times," Rebecca said, her eyes following Cole. "It's permissible to sit, Jordan."

He felt her eyes sweep over him and he wished that they were somewhere alone. He was stunned at his desire for her and felt foolish because of it. "I've been sitting all morning. In the jeep. I mean driving up. I thought I'd stretch."

Her smile grew larger and she pulled her legs up under her. "Sit here," she nodded toward the end of the settee. "I much prefer you close to me. We've been apart so long I can't stand the thought of us being in the same room and yet still separated." Rebecca noticed his cap. "William didn't take your hat?"

"No," Cole said, sitting carefully on the settee. He felt the warmth where her legs had been and the sensation was comforting. "He probably thought you'd throw me out or something." He remembered the "or something" that Florence Bannard had pinned him with. "I met your mom."

"You've met Mother, then?" Rebecca confirmed with a trace of apprehension.

"Yeah," Cole said. "I bet you she's a pistol."

"Pistol?"

"I mean a handful. Kind of a . . ."

"Pistol," Rebecca said, catching on. "Yes, she is. She has to be to survive Father. She and he have a very special arrangement. He remains discreet with his affairs and she treats him with a high degree of disdain."

Cole watched as her hand reached out to smooth a wrinkle in the coverlet and then continued over to his hand. Her skin was smooth and warm and he noticed that she was trembling as well. She intertwined her fingers into his, squeezing his hand. Her touch brought back visions of her naked body against his and he became aroused.

"Jordan," she said. "What have you done with yourself? I've missed you terribly. I cried myself to sleep and felt miserable all of the time. I couldn't shake the thoughts of us when we were together. I have missed you so much."

"I kept rereading your letters," he said. "I behaved like a jerk. I was angry and hurt and I kept thinking 'I'll get even with her.' But all the time you were stuck in my mind."

She settled against the pillows and glanced through the row of windows bound by heavy blackout curtains. She withdrew her hand from his and began tenderly stroking his forehead, pushing his hair back. "A bit awkward, isn't it?" she said, smiling to let him know there was nothing wrong with feeling a little at odds. "I damned you a dozen times for being a child, and at the same time I damned myself for being a fool."

"You're not alone there."

She ran her fingers along his temple. "Every time that I wrote, I tried to be happy and behave as if nothing were wrong. I failed, I'm sure. Everything was wrong. You were far away and I was the cause."

"The war had something to do with it," Cole joked weakly, and then was overwhelmed with regret. "I was an idiot. I wanted you. I never wanted to lose you. I tried to understand what you were doing, but I hated you for it. And then I hated myself."

"One would think that you had learned to be a

bit easier on Jordan Cole," she said. She leaned forward and kissed his forehead, and then the bridge of his nose. Suddenly their lips met and they embraced fiercely. They kissed over and over, her tears covering his face and lips, his arms trapping her body tightly against his so that they would never be apart again. Her face was pressed firmly into his shoulder, and he could feel her body shaking as she cried uncontrollably. Finally, the sobbing lessened but she did not move. He held her, his fingers drifting over her red hair.

"Yeah," Cole said, feeling drained. He began to talk, wanting her to know everything. It was important to him that she knew where he had been and what he had done. "When the Japs bombed Pearl Harbor and all hell broke loose I managed to talk myself into PT boats. Got shipped back to Newport for training. Rhode Island. I was down in the Mediterranean. PT boats. I wanted to be as far away from England as possible. Away from you, really. Silly, isn't it? Same as before. I'm still the uncertain little boy. You'd think I'd learn by now."

"You haven't changed, Jordan," she said, her voice muffled in his shoulder. She turned and looked up at him, wiping the tears away with one hand. "Economy with words, I think it's called. You were always one to use them sparingly." She smiled. "That's not very much of an autobiography." She pulled back and examined him. "Look how thin you are. You haven't been eating, have you? I suppose that's the service, isn't it? Why haven't you been eating?"

"Not much of an appetite, I guess," he said. "I

get by on lots of coffee. We have plenty of coffee, thank God."

"I thought you would have developed a taste for tea being so long in England."

"No. Nothing replaces coffee."

She fell back against his chest, nestling her head into his shoulder. He responded by pulling her tightly into him, caressing her neck.

"Have you found someone else?" she asked, her voice catching.

"No," he said. There had been no one else. He had thrown himself into his work and dared anyone to interfere with his life, careful to keep people at bay. His walls had been certain and complete. He had made himself an island and had suffered because of it.

"How about . . ." he began.

"No," Rebecca said quickly. "No. I was sick of Gregory and sick because of him, and sick because I had sent you away. The only man I wanted was the man I told to go. No. There has never been anyone but you."

She looked up and they kissed again, a deep, long, passionate kiss that tried to erase all that had happened before, and restore the promise for their love.

"I'd give a million dollars if your mother was anyplace else," Cole said, kissing her hair.

"Oh," she groaned. "Don't torment me like that. If I start thinking about how much I want you, I shall explode. Quick, change the subject before I ravish you."

"I like the ravishing idea better."

She looked up and gave a play frown.

"Okay," he said. "Still working? Nursing?"

"For a bit. Then I took ill."

"Ill?" Cole said, startled. "I didn't . . ."

"Don't be alarmed, my dear. Simply exhaustion. The pressures of the job, I suppose. And the marriage." Her voice dropped. "And here I am. If it weren't for Dickie I should never have known what you were doing or where you were."

"He is kind of a busybody, isn't he," Cole said. "All done with what's-his-name, huh?" he added, teasing.

"You mean Gregory," Rebecca said with a ghost of a smile. She was silent for a moment, and Cole could see that the memories were painful. "He has chosen to live his life, his way. I began to understand that were I to stay, I should eventually be destroyed. So I left him and came to Farley Manor."

"I thought you and your dad," Cole started, trying to find a way to broach the subject. "I thought you two had a falling-out."

"We have," Rebecca said. "But Father is seldom here. He has a flat in London and anyway, we are quite civilized to one another when he does visit, which is rarely. Mother and I get along splendidly when she remembers that I am no longer a child. William, you've met William, runs the household, although Mother thinks she does. I want for nothing, really."

Cole nodded, not sure of where to take the conversation. He could no longer resort to the menu of phrases that he had practiced in the jeep. Some of it was conciliatory, some caustic and unforgiving, much of it bitter and angry over the pain that she had caused him. They were well past that illusion now—past the imaginary world that Cole had carefully constructed so that he held all of the answers and could play all of the roles. His scripted world offered the most protection for him; everyone was held accountable to his standards. When he allowed the truth to surface, he realized that his pain was not of her making. It was his. She had chosen to stay with Gregory because she wanted to salvage her marriage. She and Cole shared love for a brief period but she was not certain that would sustain a relationship. Cole began to realize that she was right to be concerned about their love; they had found each other during war, and war distorted everything.

"You said that I was a child," Cole said, remembering. He had never forgotten those words, and whenever he felt the pain of their separation he brought them up to counter the agony of his love for her. But now they were just words—a way to carry on a conversation.

"Yes," she said. "And I shall regret that until the day I die. I had no reason to say it."

"Oh, yes you did," Cole said in a flash of honesty. The last of the bitterness in his heart disappeared. He knew that he had been foolish to blame her. He knew that his anger had been his way of coping, of protecting himself. He also knew how much it had damaged him. "In a lot of ways I was. Maybe I still am. I only saw what I wanted. I didn't care about anything else. I've had a long time to think things over. I guess I let my emotions get in the way of things. Sometimes I'm not rational."

"Jordan," Rebecca teased him. "You are human after all, aren't you?"

"Yeah," he nodded, "unfortunately."

They both laughed and grew silent for a moment. She began to trace the outline of his jaw with her fingertips, and then slid them over his lips. He kissed them tenderly.

"I could have done things differently," he said. For the first time there might really be a chance to find her again. There had been time and distance, but before that there were the harmful words spoken out of spite. His words. His way to hurt her.

"You're being much too hard on yourself," she said. "I often forget that some people don't truly know themselves. I suppose that they don't know what troubles them and they certainly can't express that notion."

"You'd make a great shrink."

"A 'shrink'?"

"Psychologist. Psychiatrist. Some guy who putters around in peoples' minds to help them understand why they hate their mother."

"Oh, I don't hate Mother," she said with a playful smile. "I just find her immensely irritating at times. You, on the other hand . . ." She let the observation hang.

"Me? I'm just nuts," he said playfully.

"Jordan Cole," Rebecca said. "You are a . . . a pistol."

They both laughed.

"Yeah, I guess I am." They were both silent until Cole said: "Do you mind if I write? Maybe drop by every once in a while for a visit?"

Rebecca straightened and looked at him in surprise. "Jordan Cole! If you don't I shall die. I shall just die. You'd better do more than write and 'drop by every once in a while.'" She took his face in her hands and looked deeply into his eyes. "You are such a silly goose at times. I will not lose you again, do you understand? If you run away I shall come and hunt you down. You must promise to write me every day and come as often as you can."

He smiled wickedly. "Well, that part is up to you."

She kissed him passionately, running her tongue into his mouth. He responded, feeling the heat between them blossom, wanted desperately to touch her everywhere, to have her naked body against his.

When they parted he breathed: "Wow." He smiled at her and added. "I may write you twice a day if you keep that up. Maybe we can slip out and . . ."

"I'll have to stay close to the Manor for a bit," she said. She gave a small shrug. "Doctor's orders."

"Doctor? You said it was nothing."

"Nothing serious, Jordan," she said. "I'm tired, that's all. I'm afraid the last little while with Gregory and the work in the hospital have been a bit rough on me."

"You're not kidding me, are you?" Cole said. "You're okay, aren't you?"

"I'm a nurse, dear. I know when a body is simply worn out, and I am most decidedly worn out. Don't worry. Between Mother and William I shan't want for a thing. In fact, if one doesn't smother me the other will." She gave him a quick kiss. "Besides, the faster that I get rested up, the faster that we can pop into bed."

"I like that idea," he said. "Can you go for a ride or anything? I mean just to get out of the house."

"When you return we'll have dinner," she said. "If Doctor Lee permits, we can go out. If not, we set a perfectly adequate table here."

"With Mother?" Cole said.

"Let's not think about that," Rebecca said.

"Okay," Cole said. He noticed dark circles under her eyes and her smile wasn't as vibrant as he remembered. She looked tired and he was afraid that he'd stayed too long. He glanced at his watch. "Look. I've got to get back. I'm practically AWOL now. I want you to promise me that you'll take care of yourself."

Her face brightened with a smile and she offered a mock salute. "Aye, aye, Admiral Cole."

He stood and looked down at her and he felt his own smile growing. "Just my luck to fall for a girl who's a wise guy." He realized just how much a part of his world she was. He saw the same feeling in Rebecca's eyes.

"You may not have noticed, Jordan Cole, but I am most assuredly not a 'guy.' "

He took her hand in his and kissed the back of it tenderly. Then he leaned down and kissed her forehead. "Lady, I noticed that about you the first time we met."

When he left, her smile was still in his memory, and the thought of her soft skin rode with him down the gravel drive and out onto the country road. While he drove back to the base he let his mind wander over when they had met in the hospital, the few days they had had together while she struggled with the thought that her husband might still be alive and returning from North Africa. Cole had wanted Rebecca to leave him but she would

not and then when Gregory came home, terribly
burned and missing a leg, Cole realized that Rebecca would never leave Gregory. Even after it became apparent that her husband was a bastard.

The rain began to pound on the windshield of
the jeep and a stiff wind drummed at the canvas
top as Cole drove on. He had to slow down because it became difficult to see, and several times
gusts of wind threatened to push the jeep off the
road. Gradually all thought of Rebecca faded and
he struggled to control the jeep on the slick road,
trying to peer between ineffectual sweeps of the
wipers.

His mind went back to Rebecca and her posses-
sions, arrayed on a small table next to her. He recognized the intimacy of those things, and for a
moment felt that he was an intruder and should
not have seen them. He knew that he was being
silly, that what he saw was everyday evidence of a
person's life. But they were private things as well.
They were a part of her and each commented on
some fragile, simple element in her life. Her hand
mirror with a mother-of-pearl back was turned
glass side down with a tiny pillbox next to it. There
were two other books besides the one that she had
been reading, each with a tasseled bookmark that
reminded her that she should return to what lay
within the pages. Near the mirror of course was a
brush and comb, and Cole imagined her carefully
running the comb through her thick hair as she
studied the movement in the mirror. She was as
delicate as the personal items arrayed on the table,
and he thought of her carefully placing each in its
proper location so that order was maintained in

Rebecca's world. Jordan craved to understand Rebecca; he wanted to be a part of the world that he had just glimpsed. He never wanted anything as much in his life.

He was tired and longed for a good, strong cup of coffee and a cigarette. He couldn't stomach navy coffee, weak with lots of milk and sugar. He liked black coffee, strong.

Cole pulled in to the main gate at Portsmouth, stopped, and pulled out his ID. He waited until a bundled figure holding a flashlight got within arm's length before he opened the door. The wind nearly ripped it from his grasp and rain flooded the interior of the jeep.

"Jesus Christ," Cole shouted above the howl of the wind. "Hurry up, will you?"

Raindrops flashed through the beam of yellow light while the SP guard tried to read Cole's ID.

"You made it back just in time, sir," the guard said, trying to turn his back to the wind.

"What? What do you mean?"

"They're closing the base in thirty minutes. Looks like it's the real McCoy this time."

Chapter 23

Eighteen kilometers from Cherbourg, on the Caen Road

The storm increased in intensity, the wind beating at Reubold's Volkswagen as he skidded to a stop in the driving rain. The little vehicle had almost been knocked off the road a dozen times, and the only reason that Reubold had been able to make good time from Paris was because Allied planes were grounded by the weather. He thought of the situation as a minor blessing.

He thought also of his visit to Rommel's headquarters and Walters's hasty retreat. At first he was confused because he had believed that the kommodore was working with Rommel's approval—even if it was an approval that was reluctantly given. Dresser's appearance and Walters's departure compounded the confusion, but his long drive back to Cherbourg gave Reubold a chance to sort out what had happened.

He came to the conclusion that it was politics. General officers were reluctant to give up control of power, and interservice cooperation existed only as far as it benefited members of either service. Dresser would respond to Rommel's needs because Rommel had been handpicked by Hitler to create the Atlantic Wall. Or at least, pile more bricks on top of those that already lined the beaches.

And the kommodore. The kommodore perhaps saw a chance to advance his position by offering up something new to Rommel; another weapon in the vast array of weapons that the feldmarschall counted on to stop the Allies. The only problem was that Rommel wasn't interested, and that was understandable. Six tiny boats. How could they change the war? What difference would they make against the invincible armada that had been assembled in the English ports?

A great deal, Reubold decided in a flash of excitement. Walters had given him the key: confusion to the enemy. The invasion had to come at dawn, the tides demanded it, the darkness required it; and if the German defenses were most vulnerable at dawn, then the approaching vessels were as well. I will hide in the darkness, Reubold decided. All six of his boats had Naxos radar receivers and they could locate the fleet by the Allies' own radar activity. Better than the crude Biscay Cross, Reubold knew.

A single word struck him—*suicide*. It would be suicide to attack the greatest armada in the world with six S-boats, even with his boats. Not with luck. Not with skill, he decided. Move fast, come at them from different directions, wait until the last minute—the very last minute, to fire. *Then we slash an opening in the escorts, and the Guernsey S-boats go in with torpedoes.* Confusion to the enemy.

Reubold pulled over as a convoy of trucks lumbered by, throwing a heavy coating of soupy mud over his windshield. He found himself marking time with the windshield wipers by tapping the steering wheel with his finger.

But Dresser wants us stripped. And Walters has faded away. We have no savior. Where is my champion? Reubold asked himself. Goering. "Yes, of course," he said, the sound of his voice an odd addition to the darkened vehicle. "Goering is my champion. Goering is my guardian angel. My god." He thought of Walters and the kommodore's easy exit from a confrontation with Rommel to Berlin. You have no champion, Reubold thought and for an instant he realized that he missed Waldvogel. He laughed at the idea that the strange little man who puzzled him so had now become a valued friend. He wondered about the complexities of life. The last truck passed. Reubold checked his rearview mirror and pulled out onto the road.

It was near midnight when he drove across the wooden bridge and out onto the quay where the S-boat pen was located. The storm had increased its fury, thick lightning bolts splitting the sky. Reubold counted the time between the claps of thunder and the flashes of lightning and realized the full storm was less than five kilometers away.

As he threw open the car door and made a run for the pen blast door he heard another clap of thunder, sharper and closer than the others. He was relieved to see that the heavy steel door was open, a rare occurrence at night when the enemy came calling. He heard shouts and cries for help as he threw off his raincoat, then he realized that all the lights were turned on.

"What the devil do you think you're doing?" Reubold shouted as he swung down the expanded metal staircase and landed heavily on the pen floor. Sailors were racing to their boats as he grabbed an oberbootsmannmaat by the collar. "What the devil are you doing? Why are the lights on?"

"We're trying to get the boats out, sir." He turned and pointed. "Look."

Reubold pushed the man to one side and watched as a dozen men played a work lamp on the concrete ceiling of the pen. The crack that had opened up the night that Waldvogel had been injured was much bigger. A steady cloud of concrete dust poured from the fissure, but what was worse, chunks of concrete broke loose and landed with an echoing splash in the water. The ceiling was caving in. Beneath it was a damaged S-boat.

Suddenly Peters was at his side. "Mueller. That silly fool was trying to get his boat out."

"When did it happen?"

"Now. Just minutes ago."

The thunder that Reubold had heard. It wasn't thunder after all, it was the ceiling collapsing. He brushed by Peters and quickly made his way along the walkway that skirted the pen channel. His boat and Peters's had been the first in and were closest to the channel head. He had a better view of Mueller's boat. Its bow was wedged against one side of the walkway and its stern against the other. The skullcap was covered with hunks of concrete, some as large as a man's head. Mueller's crew was trying to clear the bridge to get to the men who had been injured. One of them, judging from the location of the debris that covered the bridge, had to be Mueller.

"He was going out," Peters spoke rapidly, anxious to fix the blame, "against orders. Admiral Dresser specifically ordered us to remain in the pens until your arrival."

Dresser didn't waste any time, Reubold thought.

"I told Mueller, 'You're violating orders. You just wait until the fregattenkapitan returns.' He just laughed at me."

Reubold turned to Peters. "Shut up," he said calmly and climbed aboard the S-boat. The crew had sorted out some of the wreckage, enough to get to Mueller. They worked quickly, virtually ignoring Reubold. He saw Mueller, sprawled on the deck, a large slab of concrete covering his legs. Blood seeped from the corners of his mouth as he offered Reubold a weak smile.

"Richard, come to visit me?"

"You stupid bastard," Reubold said, trying not to look at the sickly pool of blood gleaming in the light. "Don't you ever listen to orders?"

"Don't you?" His voice was a tortured whisper and his eyes were losing focus.

"We'll get you out. I promise."

"Well then, get out of the way. Let the men work." He seemed to pull strength from within, but it soon faded. "Dresser beached us, didn't he? Peters was so happy he almost danced a jig. Is that it for us then?" Mueller said. He coughed softly and red bubbles appeared between his lips.

"No."

"Don't let them take this away from us, Richard. Your little schoolmaster gave us quite a boat."

There was a loud crack overhead and Reubold instinctively sheltered Mueller's body with his own. He glanced at the ceiling over his shoulder and saw a piece of concrete fall away, landing harmlessly in the dark water near the boat's hull. He pushed himself up and brushed the concrete dust and tiny bits of debris off Mueller's forehead. There was no movement from the prostrate man. His eyes looked beyond Reubold. The fregattenkapitan stared at the dead man. The sound of men rapidly clearing the rubble from the deck brought him around. "Clear the boat," he ordered. "Now."

"Sir," one of the men said in surprise. "We haven't . . ."

"Off," Reubold said. "Now. You can't help Mueller." He saw Peters pressed against the wall, well clear of the danger. "Go get Waymann."

"Waymann?" Peters was shocked. By rights Reubold should have given him an assignment—he was the senior kapitan. "Why Waymann?"

"Do you want to take this boat out?" Reubold could almost see Peters turn pale at the question.

"No. I mean, I'll get Waymann."

Reubold stood, took off his coat, and covered Mueller. He realized that Mueller's crew hadn't moved. "Get off the goddamned boat," he shouted. "Do you want to end up like Mueller? And tell everyone to stay back until I tell them to approach."

The men were filing toward the channel head, led by Peters, when Waymann ran up.

"Yes, sir?"

Reubold felt his hands shake and realized that he had almost forgotten how long it was since he had an injection. Maybe when this was done. He looked at the silent form on the deck. Maybe he wouldn't need the blessed needle anymore.

"Sir?" Waymann waited for orders.

Reubold's eyes fell on the young officer. Here was a decent man—a good man. He had once been Waymann. Stop it, he told himself. *You sold your soul to the devil long ago.* "We're going to take Mueller's boat out, you and I. I want to tie off to Peter's boat and my boat so that we take them out with us. We'll be the only boat under power. I think the vibrations from the engines caused the cave-in." His eyes swept the ceiling. "Or maybe the damn thing just fell down. This is what we'll do; I'll get us off of the walkway and turned so that we can back out. I don't think anything big enough for us to foul us fell into the channel." There was no way to tell. There could be some debris in the dark water to catch the foils, something to trap Mueller's boat and hold it beneath the unstable concrete ceiling. "The minute I'm clear, I'll straighten her up. Make sure that the crew takes up the slack on the lines so we don't string out because I don't want to spend any more time than I have to in here. Nobody is to be on the boats that doesn't have to be."

"Yes, sir," Waymann said.

"Go," Reubold said. "Wait," he called. "Make sure Peters is on the bridge of his boat."

Nothing in Waymann's look told Reubold that he understood the real message: *No time to be ill now, Peters. Now you will be the kapitan.*

Reubold inspected the side of the S-boat. The hull had been impaled at the bow by the walkway a distance of nearly three meters. He went aft. It was just as bad there except a portion of the hull was crushed. He thought it unlikely that the rudders and screws were damaged, and he hoped that the foils were unharmed, but he wouldn't know until he started the engines. He thought that Mueller was taking her out when he was struck by a piece of concrete and as he fell, turned the wheel hard over.

Reubold's legs began to ache and he cursed the pain. *Not now. Can't you leave me alone? Just for an hour? Just once?*

Waymann returned and jumped from the walkway onto the shattered deck and made his way to the skullcap.

"Well?" Reubold said.

"All is prepared, sir," Waymann said.

"Good."

"Kapitanleutnant Peters, sir."

"Yes?" Reubold said, knowing what to expect.

"He was unavailable, sir."

"Who?"

"Kapitanleutnant Draheim, sir. He said that he would interrupt his music lessons for you."

"I'm filled with gratitude," Reubold said. "Secure a line on the bow cleat. Hand it off and go below and stand by the engines. When I call for them, start them immediately. Give them just a moment to build up oil pressure and then I'll signal for engagement. Then come topside immediately and stand by." He turned to the harbor but there was very little to see. The rain was being driven from the sky in thick sheets and the wind howled in accompaniment. It was the harbor that troubled him. It was a battlefield of waves. If it were so in the sanctuary of the harbor, Reubold thought, what must it be like in the Channel? Thank God for tiny favors; at least the Allies would be trapped in their own harbors waiting for the storm to subside.

It was a small thing to take them out in reverse. Even for one boat to tow the others was manageable. Manageable under normal circumstances. But this was hardly normal. The ceiling could give way at any moment, crushing his boat or the other two in the ridiculous parade. His boat would have steerage, some power to pass water over the rudders so that he could control its movement; the others would not. And they could not start their engines. Reubold was convinced that Mueller's engines, rumbling against the hard surface of the pen, created a vibration that weakened the fissure in the ceiling. There was always the chance it would happen again.

He watched Waymann toss the line to a seaman on the walkway. It flew through the air in a long graceful loop until it was captured and run forward. The young oberleutnant disappeared below deck and Reubold turned his attention to the instrument panel. The dials captured oil pressure, engine temperature, and revolutions per minute for the engines. Another set read the available fuel for the ready tanks. They were the eyes of the powerful engines; they told him everything he needed to know.

"Fregattenkapitan?" He heard voices echoing off the walls near the other craft. "Ready here."

Reubold cupped his hands around his mouth. "No engines," he shouted to the waiting boats. "Do you understand? No engines." The heavy vibration of the boat engines in this confined space might dislodge more concrete. Or bring the whole thing down. They'd have to trust in his skill in boat handling. He glanced at the bundle at his feet that had once been his friend. The best boat handler in Flotilla 11 would never do so again.

Reubold slipped the throat mike on his neck and hooked one earphone over his head, leaving his other ear free. If the ceiling fell he might have a chance if he heard it before it landed on him. "Waymann?"

The earphone crackled. "Engine Room."

Reubold smiled in appreciation at Waymann's formality. The young officer was cool and kept any emotion he felt firmly under control. He was destined for great things. "Start the engines."

"Yes, sir."

The engines rumbled to life and the noise startled Reubold. He'd heard it a thousand times before, and always the deep roar had done nothing more than assure him that a routine was being followed. Now the noise was louder and more ominous so that he was tempted to tell Waymann to throttle the engines back, but a quick sweep of the instrument panel told him that they were functioning at operational level. It was as if he were experiencing the unadulterated power of the engines for the first time and that, uncontrolled, they were like wild animals that could destroy him.

Behind him the storm increased and he could feel the cold spray washing through the pen opening. He shivered as it covered him, and he saw the boat's deck glisten in the water. He held up his arm so that the boats ahead could see him: get ready.

He clamped the mike against his throat. "Waymann," he said, scanning the dials until the needles inched into position. "Engage reverse." There was only one reverse speed and the process of engaging the gears through the clutch wasn't as complicated as moving forward. Once in reverse, Reubold simply controlled the speed with the throttle on the instrument panel next to the wheel.

He felt the boat shudder as the engines slipped into reverse. He slipped his fingers around the throttle controls for the three engines, his palm cupping the control arm knobs. He heard pieces of concrete strike the boat, small pieces at first. There was a loud bang forward as he increased power and swung the wheel gently to pull away from the walkway. It could have been the hull breaking free or a large chunk of concrete.

Reubold tasted concrete dust and saw a white flash off to one side, followed by a splash. He glanced at the revolutions per minute and realized the hull wasn't moving. He gripped the knobs and eased them forward. A loud grating sound filled the cavern, followed by shrieks of protest as the steel hull pulled away from the walkway. Reubold felt the boat trembling as it tried to break free of the concrete. The stern should pull away as well when the bow broke free if there was nothing to catch the foils.

Reubold throttled up and the roar increased

until it equaled the noise of the storm. It began to rain dust and chunks of concrete and the S-boat trembled so violently Reubold was certain that it was lodged on debris under the water.

He felt the boat swing free and waited for the tug beneath him that said they were fouled. But there was nothing; the boat eased backward through the water until Reubold felt a solid jerk. They had played out the line and it was taut, pulling the second S-boat.

Reubold flipped on the switch for the signal light on the bulkhead just to his left and aimed it at the ceiling. He wished he hadn't. Solid pieces of debris continued to rain down, striking the water in an almost continuous barrage. Concrete dust was so thick that when the beam from the signal light bounced off it, it created an almost opaque wall. A large piece of the ceiling broke away and struck the water with a flat crack, throwing spray in every direction.

Reubold pressed the microphone. "Waymann. Get up here."

Oberleutnant zur see Waymann was at Reubold's side in an instant.

"Keep the light on the ceiling," Reubold said. "I've got to steer the boat." He would be backing into the bay soon and the storm demanded all of his attention. He wondered what he expected Waymann to do with the light; it wouldn't stop the ceiling from falling. He decided that at least the others could see their own doom approaching.

Reubold felt the wind pummel his back and the S-boat buck as the waves clutched at it. Rain came down like tiny needles trying to pierce his clothing and burned his exposed skin. He throttled up, moving quickly out of the protection of the pen, but he was afraid that if he increased power too much he would part the line, leaving the other two S-boats to be crushed.

The wind snatched his cap away and clawed at his face.

Waymann turned to him. "Second boat's clear," he shouted. The words were nearly lost in the storm.

Reubold nodded and looked over his shoulder, looking for any vessel that had broken away in the storm and was drifting in the harbor. There was nothing but sea, rain, and gray clouds.

He eased the throttle up a bit more and could see the crew of the second S-boat waving at him and pointing aft. They want to start their engines, he thought, but he didn't respond. He would not allow it until the last boat was clear. He knew what he wanted and when he wanted it and he trusted no one else. He had gotten Mueller's boat out, and Peters, with Draheim at the wheel, and Fritz was the last one.

"They're coming out," Waymann shouted and then he remembered his place. "They're coming out," he repeated, calmly.

"Signal them to start engines, slip the cables, and proceed to Potsdam Pen," Reubold said.

The other three boats were safely secured in Potsdam Pen and it would be a tight fit for three more. Reubold had no choice. If they remained in the harbor, without protection, they wouldn't last a day. Putting all six boats in one pen was hazardous; a hit by one of those giant bombs would wipe out the entire flotilla. Reubold wiped rainwater from his face and thought, fortunes of war.

He slapped Waymann on the shoulder to get his attention and pulled him close so that the young officer could hear him. "We'll go in, Fritz leads the way. Bows out. Have them inspect the boats for damage." Waymann nodded and disappeared through the hatch to the radio room.

Reubold watched the ghostly forms set off in the rain and fell in behind, keeping enough distance so there was no danger that he would ram one of the boats.

He began to understand what had troubled him on the way back from Paris, a tiny splinter that had become embedded in his mind. It revealed itself when he was steering the S-boat out of the pen—a very unlikely place to suffer a revelation. He had discovered that he had developed a fault, unseen and unrecognized, but one that had become a part of him.

Once he had been a daredevil, an adventurer. Long ago he disdained caution and conquered his fear with bravado. The qualities of a young man. After several accidents, and the horrors of combat, and especially the specter of his own death, he had developed a weakness for living. Some might have called it a fondness for living, but Reubold's was based on fear. Fear of failing, fear of death.

It was bad in Spain, became much worse in Russia, and became intolerable when Goering bounced him from the Luftwaffe, because coupled with the fear that he felt was the realization that he had come to rely on people for attention—or worse— to prevent him from making meaningful decisions.

Or did I use them as an excuse? People of position. Powerful people. This reliance relieved him of the need to decide and even Goering's hatred of him was reliance in a very real way; there was constancy, a certainty in the reichfuehrer's loathing.

Reubold was prepared to rely on Walters when the kommodore came to him with his plans, and then he was prepared to rely on Rommel—the reichsmarschall would certainly make the correct decision. And when Dresser demanded that he do as he was ordered, Reubold was willing to rely on him. Reliance required so little of an individual.

The drugs as well. Reubold relied on the drugs because they were such a pure form of abandonment. Morphine asked nothing except the pleasure of your company. In exchange, it took away pain, doubt, regrets, and dismay.

Reubold relied on it.

Waymann joined him on the bridge, peering into the cloud of rain. They exchanged glances and then suddenly both smiled, the smile that men have when they have faced danger and found to their relief that they are in one piece.

Reubold stood aside. "Take the wheel."

Waymann shifted positions quickly and grasped the wheel.

"When this weather clears," Reubold said, "I think we should go out looking for Americans and British. What do you think?"

"I think it would be a shame not to, sir," Waymann said.

Reubold nodded, almost laughing at the young man's quiet courage. Was he Waymann's champion? he thought. *No,* he answered quickly, so startlingly clear that he thought he had spoken it out loud. Waymann was his own champion and that was as it should be. *Well then, I shall be mine. As it was in the past, so it will be now.*

Chapter 24

Portsmouth Naval Base, wayside dock

Cole touched his breast pocket for the fifth time in an hour, making sure that the letter was there. It was Rebecca's letter to him, the one that he hated but could never discard, the one that he read but after putting it away remembered with bitterness. That letter.

Now things were different. He had gone to see her and remembered standing stupidly in the doorway of the atrium wondering what to say or how to simply approach her when she had disarmed him with a smile. He was surprised at how easily forgiveness came to him after three years of hating her. He thought the word was too strong as he struggled to unravel how he felt, but at times it was hate. The emotion was only that strong because there had to be something to balance the loneliness of his love for her.

But he had seen her and they had spoken, and he remembered her gentleness and the kindness in her voice and he knew, despite the misgivings that he had before, that she loved him. When he returned to the base he found the letter in his footlocker, read it with new eyes once again, carefully folded it, and put it in his pocket. He buttoned the flap, sealing her words and the moment. Now it was time for the war.

Lieutenant Bryant, a young man with a large nose, handed out the duty assignments as the storm threatened to take the roof off the operations shack. Cole and the other boat commanders took the information but concentrated on the map on the wall. This was the first time they knew the object of the invasion: Normandy.

"Okay, gentlemen, here it is," Bryant said. "Fire support is coming out of St. Georges Channel, around the Scilly Isles to link up with task forces from Falmouth, Dartmouth, and Plymouth." He traced the route of the task forces on the map with a pencil. "Task Force U, that's your baby, comes out of Plymouth and Dartmouth and links up in Lyme Bay. You'll pick them up in Area Z." He tapped the map off the Isle of Wight. "Elements of Task Force O are coming out of Weymouth, Poole, and Portsmouth." He had apparently prepared himself for his next statement, lacing the words with gravity. "In other words, it's going to be mighty busy out there, and real crowded." He looked as if he enjoyed this moment of drama. He could afford to—he wasn't going any farther than the base.

Cole flipped through the pages of the packet.

"Where do we go, and when do you want us to be there?"

The words deprived Bryant of his importance but he recovered quickly. "Ten miles west-southwest of Task Force U. Your coordinates are on the duty sheet. Your job will be search and rescue."

"That's it?" Randy Delong said. "You're sticking us out in the boonies for search and rescue."

"Every job is important, Ensign," Bryant said. "Some ships may hit mines. Some of the flyboys may end up in the drink."

"A seagull may get sick," Moose said.

"Gentlemen, I don't make the assignments," Bryant said, peeved. Every guy in combat was a prima donna. They all wanted the plum assignments. "My job is to carry the orders to the respective commands and make sure that they understand what they're to do."

"Lieutenant," Cole said, trying to soothe Bryant. "Nobody finds fault with you. It's just that we're used to playing a more active role in things."

"Hell, yes, more active," Moose said.

Cole shot Moose a look of mild reproach. "It's the biggest show of the war and none of us want to end up on the sidelines. You know what I mean?"

"Lieutenant Cole, I know exactly what you mean and all I can tell you is what the brass tells me." He held up the sheaf of papers. "And this is what they told me. Everything that you need to know is in here." He gathered his cap from the chair back where he had hung it. "Good luck, and good hunting."

Cole watched Bryant leave before turning to the

officers of Squadron 142(2). They looked at him expectantly, as if he had the power to clear up this horrible misunderstanding. Their faces were so pitiful with disappointment that Cole laughed.

"Jeez, Skipper," DeLong said. "I'm glad that you find it funny, cause I sure don't.

"What do you want me to do, Randy?"

"I don't know. Something."

"We're locked down tighter than Dick's hat-band. Nobody leaves the base or comes on. No phone calls in either direction," Cole said. "Anyway, even if I could get through I doubt they'd make any changes in assignments now."

"Yeah but, Skip," Lieutenant Ewing said. "Don't you know somebody that knows somebody?"

"If I did," Cole said, "I wouldn't be stuck nursing you lunkheads." He understood their frustration. Rolling about in the Channel in dirty weather was bad enough, having to do so without the slightest chance of seeing action was even worse. Bryant told them they were watchdogs. Even if the enemy aircraft approached, their radar wouldn't give more than a few minutes' notice—the range was only twenty miles. Maybe they'd find a few mines floating about that they could set off with a burst or two of .50-caliber fire. Maybe they could pick up downed fliers. Cole thought of the Polish fighter pilot they'd saved and he felt ashamed. If someone weren't there to pick them up they'd die of exposure. Enough talk.

"Okay. You've got your orders." Moontz started to protest. "You've got your orders," Cole said again, but louder this time. "Pull your fish. Top off the tanks. Nobody says anything to the men. Get

me? And these things"—he held up the orders for
the men to see—"stay on your person."

The shop door burst open with a rush of wind
and rain, almost tearing the little bell from the door
jam. Topper Schiffer entered with a great show of
shaking the rain off his coat and hat. Beatrice, who
had been writing prices on little paper tags, stepped
away from the rain that hurled in after her brother.

"Topper, must you go about on this horrible
night?"

"Can't be helped, Bea," Topper said, pulling off
his rain-soaked coat and hanging it on a coatrack
near the counter. He slapped his hat on the peg
and rubbed his hands briskly.

"Ought to post small dog warnings with that
blow," he said. "In fact it's raining cats and dogs
out there. You know how I know, Bea?"

She'd heard this joke a dozen times. "No, Topper, how do you know?"

"I just stepped in a poodle," he said with an en-
thusiastic chuckle. "Been down to the pub, I have."

"That is the only thing that would take you out
in weather like this," Beatrice said, printing her
numbers carefully. She was proud of her penman-
ship and was careful to properly write numbers
and letters.

"Well, scoff if you like," Topper said, "but I've
been catching up on the war news."

The pencil stopped momentarily. "Have you?"
Beatrice feigned disinterest.

"Indeed I have. It's the big push all right. They
got everybody bottled up, ready for action. I

thought something was amiss; Stan and I were talking it over. Traffic slowed almost to a trickle and then it was gone. Stan knows a bloke who feeds the Yanks at Selsey. This bloke says that it's a regular race, Yank trucks rolling in one after another, day and night, until he's sure there can't be a cot left in Selsey. This bloke that Stan knows. So he tells Stan, something big's in the wind and he ought to keep his eyes open. Why? I don't know. I'm sure Stan doesn't know either . . ."

"Topper, please," Beatrice said, wanting to ask about the navy, but holding back for fear that she would say too much. Topper was the best brother that a girl could have, but he was a clumsy sort and likely to smother Beatrice with concern. She decided it was best to let him ramble.

"Well, Bea," Topper said. "I'm just telling you what the bloke told Stan and what Stan told me. Everybody's on the move: air force, army, and the navy, too, can't forget the navy. God bless them. So this bloke, friend of Stan's, says that the waters off Selsey Bill are packed top to bottom with ships. He said every type of ship that you could imagine. Ours and theirs. He says 'Invade! Why just put them end-to-end and walk across the Channel on them.' That's how many there were."

"Yes," Beatrice said, examining a price ticket. "That sounds as if things are about to get under way."

"Under way? Under way?" Topper said incredulously. "Why, woman, this is the greatest invasion since the Normans. Under way. And your own Captain Hardy in the middle of it."

"He's not my Captain Hardy," Beatrice said. She

had kept her true feelings about George Hardy from her brother. "He is a fine man that we both care for."

"Yes," Topper shot her a skeptical glance. "Some more than others. Now, Bea, don't you go worrying about Captain Hardy. He's an experienced seaman, all right. He's got decades in the naval service. Look, he's been all through this war, hasn't he? Well, there you have it."

"Yes, Topper," Beatrice said, surrendering. "Why don't you go in and see if the wireless has something to say?"

Topper slapped his hands together. "The BBC. That's the ticket. Come in too, Bea."

"In a minute, Topper. Let me finish this row." She continued marking, waiting until she heard Topper settled into the worn easy chair situated in front of the radio cabinet, and the scratchy sounds of static as he tried to find the channel. It would be difficult in the storm, more so because of the war. All of the wireless interference of ships, planes, and the army seemed to jumble everything up so that they were lucky if they heard much more than a bit of a program. It was a way that they spent many nights. It was comforting to realize that a bit of normalcy still existed in the midst of insanity. The fact that the calm cadence of the BBC announcers appeared in their parlor on a regular basis provided stability.

They had learned to settle into a routine: Topper methodically going through his magazines, each page requiring a majestic lick of his thumb, a gentle sweep of the page with his hand, and renewed interest in the article. Beatrice would sketch.

She found some subjects in Topper's magazines, a landscape, or an interesting face, and she would take the soft lead pencil and create images on a barren plain of paper.

The wind picked up and Beatrice thought she could hear something break loose down the street and blow away. Her eyes fell on the tag in her hand and she realized that she had marked it twice.

Her mind was on Captain Hardy. He was on *Firedancer* somewhere out there and she had no idea when she would hear from him again. There had been reports of a very bad battle just to the west but no one was quite sure what had happened, or who was involved, but there were reports of dead bodies being lined up on the beach. And this before the great invasion.

It was not knowing that was most difficult. She had tried to keep busy tending to the shop and to Topper, but she found her mind would drift fitfully back to the question of Captain Hardy's safety. It was the not knowing.

She had seen it for nearly five years. Friends, customers, relatives whose sons or husbands were someplace that no one had ever heard of fighting first the Germans, and the Italians, and then the Japanese. Then there would be that awful, hollow feeling when she realized that Mrs. Dunphree's son Alex wasn't coming home, or that the Mackenzie twins would not have a father. Or old Mrs. Roget, a short, plump white-haired lady who never traveled farther than the end of Haden Street and had no idea who the Japanese were, found out that William Paul was dead. Mr. Roget had been a brick mason with features as hard as the walls he built.

Mrs. Roget, denied the warmth of a sympathetic husband, doted on William Paul, her only child.

William Paul had enlisted with his chums and gone off to camp and from there to North Africa, or at least that was his worried mother's understanding. Beatrice often saw Mrs. Roget trundling after the postman, hounding him in her inoffensive way for a letter she knew that he surely must have been carrying from her son.

She could not read and brought William Paul's letters to Beatrice with a smile of expectation, and over tea, Beatrice would read them. They always began, "Dear Mother," and sometimes the spelling was a bit unusual, but Beatrice had no trouble reading the love in them. They were like two companions, William Paul and Mrs. Roget, holding a hidden conspiracy under the nose of the solemn Mr. Roget.

There was a mix-up one day and the letter that Mrs. Roget held in her hand was from William Paul's commanding officer. Mrs. Roget handed over the letter with some hesitation because, although she could not read the letter, she could tell that it was not William Paul's handwriting.

Beatrice took it and as she opened it the dread mounted until she wished that she were not at home when the white-haired lady called. Somewhere in the first sentence were the words "we shall all miss William Paul, very much." Beatrice tried to keep her hands from trembling as she read the letter, but that single phrase, "we shall all miss William Paul, very much," hounded her. She read what had happened and how by now Mrs. Roget had received the official notification, but the commanding officer felt it his duty to write. It was obvious that the official notification, had been delayed or overlooked altogether and a letter meant to console William Paul's mother had done just the opposite.

"We shall all miss William Paul, very much. "

Mrs. Roget looked at Beatrice in disbelief when the entire letter had been read and said: "Does that mean that William Paul won't be coming home?"

The words were so tragic, so filled with pain, that Beatrice was sure that the old woman's heart was breaking as she said them.

"Yes," was all that Beatrice could say. "I'm afraid so."

Mrs. Roget might have remained seated for another ten minutes, Beatrice wasn't sure. She folded the letter and handed it to the woman, who slipped it carefully in her coat pocket. There were no tears, only shock as if the whole thing were so monstrous that it could not possibly be true.

Mrs. Roget stood and said: "I had better go home and tell Mr. Roget."

Beatrice found herself staring out the shop windows at the driving rain. Captain Hardy was someplace, out there, and she would not even receive confirmation should anything happen because they were no more than acquaintances. She wondered of the thousands of women who waited to hear something of their loved ones. She was one of them now, not the kind-hearted lady who would provide comfort, but a woman taunted by the unknown.

Topper came into the shop. "I can't get a thing. I think they've jammed us." He moved to the window and studied the darkness. "Clearing up some.

May be clear by morning." He noticed Beatrice. "Here, now, Bea. Put that up. Time enough to do that tomorrow. Why, you look all solemn."

"No," she said, forcing a smile. "Just thinking, that's all."

Topper came over to her. "Bea, it'll all be fine. Things work out, they do." He cupped his hand under her chin. "Now, if you trust me, I'll fix you a spot of tea."

Beatrice found herself smiling. She found strength in her brother's optimism and she decided that she could do nothing but wait. She felt fear gnawing at her, and the hollow feeling that comes of being helpless. What would happen, would happen, but she knew also that Topper's plain, solid reassurance that George Hardy would return was her salvation. "Topper. You're a Rock of Gibraltar."

Chapter 25

A half-dozen crumpled sheets of paper lay near Cole's bunk. The words were there, but they hid behind years of anger, loss, and frustration. The beginning of every letter was trite and awkward, and he had ripped the paper from the tablet in disgust, wadded it up, and threw it on the floor.

What could he say to her? I'm sorry for all these years? Maybe I'm not coming back? He rolled his eyes at that one; chances were they'd end up shepherding a herd of fat cargo ships to the assembly point and then be assigned to watch for whales.

The letters all started "Dear Rebecca," but then his mind refused to function and what had followed that was a clumsy string of words. He was saved by a knock.

"Come in," he said.

Edland opened the door and glanced at the scattered balls of paper.

"Writer's block?"

Cole slipped his pen in the tablet and pushed it away. "How'd you get in here? I thought we were sealed off."

"You are," Edland said, looking over the sparsely decorated room. "But I got in."

"Yeah, well, we're a little busy now, what with the invasion coming and everything, so you won't mind if I don't invite you in for a cup of tea, will you, Commander?"

Edland shook his head and leaned against the doorjamb, folding his arms across his chest. He had an unconcerned air about him. "I'm here to ask a favor," he said.

Cole smiled in interest. "A favor. Sir. Now what makes you think that I'm in a position to grant you a favor? Sir."

"You are. Trust me. And don't load your sentences with too many sirs. It might lead a person to think that you weren't sincere."

The smile disappeared. "What's the favor, Commander?"

"I want to go out with you."

"No dice."

"It's important.

"I don't care."

"It won't take me any time to get the orders cut."

"Go ahead," Cole said. "If this weather eases up we might be gone before the orders get to us. You'll just be standing on the dock waving bye-bye, sir."

"Okay," Edland said, nodding. "I was out of line. Let's forget the orders and rank and all of that nonsense. The request for a favor still stands and I know it's a favor."

"Why?"

"The hydrofoils."

Cole laughed. "Your Sea Eagles? Again? Look, those things may exist. For all I know, there are thousands of them waiting just off the French coast right now. They've got my squadron patrolling about as far south as they can without putting us at the South Pole. Even if you go out with us, and don't get excited because you aren't, we'll be lucky to see a seagull."

"I'd still like to go."

"Okay, Commander," Cole said, standing. "Let me lay this out. My boats are worn out; my crews are worn out so if those super boats really exist, like you say, it's going to be a short fight. I don't think you want to be there."

Edland nodded again, unfolded his arms, took a moment, and finally gave Cole a look that said he hadn't changed his mind.

"You know this isn't a romp," Cole said. "Guys get killed."

"I know."

"Yeah," Cole's voice hardened. "I guess you do know."

Edland heard a commotion in the hall and stepped aside as DeLong stuck his head in. "Hey, Skipper?" He realized that Edland was standing in the doorway. "Oh, sorry, Commander."

"What is it, Randy?" Cole said.

"We got the word, Skipper. Crank 'em up."

Edland looked at Cole. Cole had never liked the man. He came from a privileged class and carried himself as if he were better than anyone. But even though Cole didn't want to admit it, there was enough similarity between the two for him to understand Edland.

"All right, Commander," he said. "Draw your gear from Randy. It'll get cold out there."

"Gear?" DeLong said, surprised.

"Get him squared away, Randy. He's going with us."

"Yeah, but, Skipper . . ."

"Hop to it. We don't want to be late for the invasion."

"Thanks, Cole," Edland said, and followed the confused DeLong.

Cole looked at the blank tablet on the desk and promised himself that whatever he had to say, he'd say it to Rebecca in person.

Gierek stood next to Jagello in the twilight, a steady rain drenching them both.

"Something's wrong," he said as the erks moved about the Mosquito. He heard the sound of the other Pathfinders, the short sputter and sharp crack as the exhaust was cleared and then the steady, low rumble of the engines warming up. He could see them aligned on the hardstand; three aircraft, their squat bodies glistening in the rain, water whipping off the wings as the prop wash of the powerful Merlin 25 engines blasted it into fine clouds of mist. The frying pan the erks called it; aircraft dispersal point in official correspondence. "It's where we warm you blokes up, ain't it?" an erk had reasoned to him. The English.

"Well?" Jagello said, straightening his parachute

harness. It would be a long flight with no room to adjust the straps in the plane.

"Something's wrong," Gierek repeated, walking around the aircraft. He checked the undercarriage, the engine nacelles, elevator trim tabs, aileron tabs, and flaps. He looked for leaks or signs of structural damage, or any hint that the aircraft might betray him far from home. He watched as the erks topped off the tanks with petrol, not just full, but full to the lip of the fuel filler spout. He was careful about his aircraft and for that reason he had come back each time, but as he inspected the craft he kept looking over his shoulder as if a ghost followed him, whispering: "All is not right."

Then it struck him.

"Where's the dog?" he said to Jagello. For the first time since Gierek had known Jagello, the other man was surprised. Jagello looked at the landing gear.

"I don't know," he said in a puzzled tone. Gierek watched as Jagello approached an erk. A gust of wind blew a heavy rain down the collar of Gierek's flying togs and he pulled it close to his neck, wondering if he was shivering from the cold or the sudden, desperate feeling that the filthy dog that had always been their good-luck charm was gone.

Jagello came back with a troubled look on his face and Gierek felt his stomach fall; Jagello was troubled by nothing.

"They don't know," he said, wincing as the rain increased. He tossed the sky a reproachful glance. "No one's seen the Black Prince." Gierek read the concern in his face; whether it was concern for the dog or for them, he couldn't tell. "We'd better get aboard," the bomb-aimer/navigator said. "It's almost time."

Gierek nodded, unlatched the crew access panel in the nose, pulled himself up, eased around the radar display and viewfinder that protruded into the cockpit, and settled in his seat. He pulled the checklist out of the narrow pocket near his left foot when Jagello climbed into his seat.

Gierek heard the access panel door slam and the sound of two raps. It was the erk's final signal; the doors closed and locked—ready for engines and warm-up. Gierek looked out the rain-scarred window as the erks worked the priming pumps for the engines, hoping for some sign of the dog.

He saw an erk give him the signal to switch on ignition, left engine first since they'd started the right engine the last time out. Gierek pressed the START button and the BOOSTER COIL button simultaneously. There was a slight sputter, the prop rotated a quarter turn, another, louder sputter, and suddenly the engine turned over with a healthy blast of blue smoke. Gierek glanced at the generator lamp as the engine eased up to 2,000 rpm. The warning light, signaling that the engine was creating enough rpms for the generator, went out. They went through the same sequence for the other engine.

Jagello, until now busy with his radar and navigation charts, pulled out the checklist for takeoff.

"Trim," he said. "Elevator."

Making the adjustment Gierek replied: "Flaps, twenty-five percent."

"Rudder?"

"Ten degrees right."

"Aileron?"

"Neutral."

"Propeller?"

"Speed controls fully forward."

"Fuel?"

"Levels. Check. Cocks to outer tanks."

"Superchargers?"

"Moderate."

Jagello slipped the checklist in its pocket as he asked the last question: "Radiator flaps?"

"Open."

"So now we invade France," Jagello said calmly.

"Yes," Gierek said as he awaited further instructions from the tower. He looked across the rain-soaked tarmac again. "Where is that dog?"

Edland was glad that DeLong had scrounged up a peacoat for him; it was cold and windy, and as the 155 boat pulled into the harbor channel leading the other five boats in Squadron 142(2), he realized that it would get much worse. He was used to cold; most people thought that the Gobi Desert was like the Sahara—mountainous dunes, unrelenting sun, scorching sand. In some areas the Gobi was something like its cousin. In some areas the Gobi was as barren as the sea. But it was a frigid place in winter, with snowbound mountains that were virtually impassible unless you knew them—and the only people who truly knew them were the Mongols.

Cole turned to him as they shared the bridge. "I hope you know what you're doing. What the hell am I thinking? I hope I know what *I'm* doing."

"You said it was going to be a milk run," Edland said. "What's the problem?"

"Bad luck just seems to follow you, Commander." He turned his attention to the PT boats forming up behind 155. It was eerie seeing the harbor almost devoid of ships. It was almost as if one minute you couldn't maneuver for all the ships crowding Portsmouth Harbor, and the next minute they were gone. It was a tangible sign of the invasion, much more so than the hundreds of ships and thousands of men in constant motion that he had grown used to seeing. That had been going on for years. This—this happened in an instant. The harbor was nearly deserted. "Ease up, Randy," Cole said. "Let them get in column."

There was a trace of red in the sky behind them, trapped under a thick mountain of gray clouds. The crimson sunlight that did manage to find its way through washed across the bottom of the clouds, leaving a faint streak of color that was beginning to die. It was more than anyone expected as the boats moved into the harbor.

They came out, long craft almost invisible in the gray waters, the thunder of eighteen Packard engines rolling over them.

"What are your orders?" Edland asked.

"Move out to rendezvous with our escort, take position to the southwest, make sure no E-boats get past us. Simple enough."

"Escort? I thought that you were the escorts?"

"We are, Commander. It's just that we're on the

ARMADA

small side so we may need some assistance," Cole said. He peered through binoculars at the boats trailing his. "Okay, Randy. Everyone's where they ought to be. Let's get going."

"Right, Skipper," DeLong said, moving the throttles up. Each boat in column increased speed correspondingly, six plywood warships, their crews removing canvas covers from machine guns and cannons, the radar reflector sweeping back and forth on top of the mast with its squat rotating power unit beneath it; slender, gray hulls slicing through the green waters that led to the Channel. Determined vessels, their decks cluttered with only those things that were necessary to fight, or to save lives. Their Mk XIII torpedoes were removed; there would not be targets for them. But there might be targets for the six .50-caliber Browning machine guns, or the two Oerlikon Mk 4 20 millimeter cannons, or the Bofor 40 millimeter cannon, or the M9 37 millimeter rapid-fire cannon on the bow.

As Cole scanned the deck, his eyes falling on his crew and the weapons that bristled from the boat, he wondered if this was the end of his war. And wondered as well, if that were such a bad thing, if the return of normalcy was something to fear. He realized with a start that it was the uncertainty of a life without war that frightened him, and he smiled at the revelation. There was, in a convoluted sense, a certainty in war. Go and do your duty. Follow your orders. The thing that had both repulsed and intrigued him about the military was the finality of structure. He remembered his grandfather, a large balding man with a deep voice and impatient nature. "A place for everything and everything in its place, Jordan," Grandfather said, his dark brown eyes peering through wire-rim glasses. Perhaps he was what his grandfather was, a rebel, a maverick; but within the logic that he was able to extract from convention.

Cole studied the boats in line behind him, each at a distance of a hundred yards. After 155 came Ewing on the 168 boat, and then Dean and Moose Moontz on the 134 boat, Taylor on the 144 boat, Grant on 140, and finally Scott on Old Reliable—the 122 boat. Its engines were the worst in the squadron and its crew the most disreputable but Scott's unassuming Virginia manner kept both of them in line.

"I can't seem to get warm here," Edland said. The comment might have been meant for Cole, or it might have been simply an observation. Cole felt the need to say something.

"I thought you used to live here. In France I mean."

"Summer," Edland said. "A few. Mostly I traveled with my father. In Asia."

Cole said nothing; he'd done his bit by adding to the conversation. He had a squadron to run.

The speaker on the instrument panel crackled.

"Skipper?" Barney said. "I've picked up a target on radar bearing three-four-oh degrees. Range twenty miles. Speed sixteen knots."

Cole grabbed the microphone and pressed the TALK button. "Okay, Barney. Keep an eye on him. That should be our escort. Switch to contact frequency and let him know who we are. I don't want anybody getting trigger-happy." He released the

TALK button and held the microphone against his chest to keep spray out of the unit. "Randy, swing to port a bit and keep your eyes open." He pressed the TALK button again. "Barney? Anything?"

"Negative, Skipper."

"You're sure that's one target and not a dozen, aren't you? I don't want any E-boats surprising me."

"Nope. Just one, Skipper. Sixteen knots. Three-four-oh."

"Okay." Cole hung the microphone under the overhang on the instrument panel and picked up the signal lamp. He began clicking out a message to Ewing on the 168 boat. He knew that Ewing would pass it on to the others.

"Hey, Skipper?"

Cole picked up the microphone. "Yeah, Barney?"

"Got a reply. She's a British destroyer. Coastal Forces. *Firedancer*."

"Who?"

"*Firedancer*, Skipper. What a screwy name, huh?"

Cole shook his head. "Yeah, it is, Barney. Send my compliments to *Firedancer*. We should have her in sight within fifteen minutes." Small world. Small world indeed, Cole thought. He remembered Hardy with his bowler hat, and Land, the imperturbable Number One, and the frightening encounter against *Sea Lion*. He wondered, he hoped that Hardy still commanded the ancient vessel.

"Something funny?" Edland asked.

"Ironic," Cole said. "I served on *Firedancer* before the United States got into the war."

"Lend Lease?"

"Happenstance."

"*Firedancer* again, Skipper," Barney reported.

"She says that she has us in sight. Captain Hardy sends his compliments and asks that we form up one mile off his starboard beam."

Cole smiled. *Hardy.*

"Reply orders received and acknowledged," he said to Barney. To DeLong he said: "Let's show *Firedancer* just how sharp we are. First Division right echelon from column, Second Division, left echelon from column at my command."

"Getting fancy, Skipper?" DeLong said with a smile. He passed the word to Barney.

"Starboard, twenty," he ordered DeLong, taking the boats out away from *Firedancer.* He wanted room to maneuver so that he could bring his squadron into position off the British destroyer's beam. And, he wanted to show off.

He looked at the sky. Night was coming quickly, hastened by the heavy overcast of dark, ominous clouds. He thought that he heard the steady drone of aircraft engines but he couldn't be sure. He knew that they were there. He knew that thousands of planes were flying, unseen, directly over his head. Bombers, fighter-bombers, fighters, transports; an armada, he thought, but the description wasn't enough. That was a word that newspapermen used to excite interest in their article, or writers wove into their accounts long after events. *Then what was it?* his mind challenged him. He didn't have a word, just a feeling. A sense that what was passing overhead was a civilization.

To hell with it.

"Take her up to forty knots, Randy," Cole said, shaking the thoughts out of his mind.

"Right, Skipper."

Cole reached past Edland, pulled the flare gun from its case, and inserted a barrel-shaped flare in the breech. "Watch your eyes," he said, knowing that the discharge would rob them of night vision. "One, two, three." He turned his head and squeezed the trigger. There was a sharp plunk, and the flare hissed high into the sky before exploding. That was the command to execute echelon from column.

Cole held the flare gun in his hand, feeling the warmth of the barrel, watching his boats move through the night. Delong throttled back and stayed on course; Ewing in the 168 boat swung to starboard, taking position 100 yards off 155 boat's quarter. Dean and the 134 boat moved to port and matched Ewing's position. It was movement in unison, choreographed—engines roaring, wakes boiling, water churned into white froth as the bows heeled over—boats peeling out of position to assume their rightful place.

Hardy watched the distance flare arch into the air and explode. He reached out for Land's binoculars and studied the boats as they crisscrossed over the sea, leaving long fluorescent trails.

"Nicely done," he said. He looked at Land. "That's Cole, is it?"

"Yes, sir."

Hardy went back to the binoculars. "Well done at that, Mr. Cole. He's learned his business, all right." After a moment he said: "When they get into position we shall maintain our present course." The men were already at Action Stations with the look-

outs doubled, so there was little that Hardy and
Firedancer could do except make themselves available as needed to the newly arrived boats. Hardy
had become agitated at being informed that *Firedancer* was needed off the landing forces' flank but
he calmed himself. She had taken a beating at
Lyme Bay and had not had a chance to settle in for
repair. He accepted the assignment as something
that was due *Firedancer*. Give her a chance to lick
her wounds, he'd explained to Land. Of course,
no repair of consequence could be expected until
she was allowed time with the yard crews. Perhaps
later.

Chapter 26

Reubold finished his cigarette as he listened to Mihsler's report. The oberleutnant had been detailed as the officer of the day for the overcrowded S-boat pen, and although he was considered a prig by the other officers, there was never any question about his competence. He was thorough, professional, and when the time called for it, decisive. He had been Mueller's executive officer. Now he was Mueller's replacement.

"Many planes," he told Reubold. "Cherbourg, certainly. The others as well." It was a deadly simplistic announcement. Every port along the French coast was about to be hammered by the enemy. Bombers, fighter-bombers, fighters; the skies over Cherbourg, Le Havre, and Boulogne would be uncontested territory. On the ground, well, there was no other way to describe it—it would be hell. Reubold had decided long ago that the explosions

364 Steven Wilson

were bad enough. They shook the earth and top-pled buildings and after enough time had passed and men's minds began to turn to jelly under the constant impact—it drove the poor souls crazy. Most hated the bombing—because it was as if a giant had swept his hand over everything. Reubold hated the fires. They came first as a stench of things burning—wood, paint, metal, a dozen inde-finable odors that drifted into the shelters. Human beings burning as well. That odor was unmistak-able; meat quickly charred by intense flames, limbs slowly roasted as the fires advanced over the wreck-age. The only difference was alive they screamed—dead they just sizzled. How cruel, Reubold thought as he considered the distinction. *What,* his mind returned, *that your sympathy is obviously unconvincing, or human beings die in such horrible circumstances?* He left the question unanswered.

Reubold flicked his spent cigarette into the oily water. "The others can take care of themselves," he said. "How long?"

"B-dienst reports that they are assembling now," Mihsler said, using the slang for wireless intelli-gence. "One hour."

Reubold looked along the covey of S-boats crowded in the pen. Two by two, like Noah's ark. Six in a pen that was designed for three, perhaps four in an emergency; never six. The last two boats were most likely to be damaged by a near hit. If they were sunk, they would block the pen and the other four would be trapped. Noah's ark just sprang a leak.

If we can't hide here, then where? Reubold thought. The open sea would be better, hide in plain sight under cover of darkness in the remnants of the passing storm and head for Alderney or Guernsey at dawn. He thought of Dresser's reaction to him moving the boats without orders. The admiral would be livid. He smiled to himself as he remembered Goering's rage when he covered the riechsmar-schal's broad lap in vomit. Goering, immaculately dressed in his splendid tailored uniform, nails mani-cured, a faint layer of makeup to cover the blem-ishes—all destroyed by a putrid mass splashed over his large soft stomach and thick thighs.

"Assemble the officers," Reubold ordered. "We're going out." He patted his breast pocket to make certain that the small, flannel-lined case with its carefully measured vials was there. He needed the morphine. It was his old friend. You don't desert old friends in time of need.

He watched as the crews made ready to move out, the oberbootsmannmaats bellowing orders to ready the boats. One after another he heard the deep rumble of the Daimler-Benz diesel engines fill the interior of the pen so that he was certain he could feel the concrete walkway shake. The gun crews unsheathed the guns, removed tampions from muzzles, and begun testing the gun laying and training mechanisms. The squat shape of the Trinity sat forlornly in the bow, waiting for atten-tion, and yet when he saw it, Reubold smiled in sat-isfaction.

"Ready, sir," Mihsler said.

Reubold looked to see his boat commanders and executive officers, standing expectantly be-fore him.

"We're going to Alderney," he said. "I want to

clear the coast and stay well clear of Cap de la Hague. Thirty knots once we form in the harbor but *schleichfahrt* when we're on the open sea." Stealth speed, not up on their foils. "Get aboard your boats. Make ready. Mihsler leads off. Draheim, you follow. Column of twos." Two by two, just like Noah's ark. He saw a nervous Peters light a cigarette and then just as quickly discard it. "Waymann," he said. "You command S-209." No niceties, no explanation. He saw relief in Peters's eyes and realized that the man thought that he was to remain behind. "Peters will go along as exec. That's all."

The others moved away quickly, a sense of satisfaction following them. Peters was demoted and forced to face his cowardice, all with a few, calm words.

"Fregattenkapitan, may I have a word?" Peters said quickly, pushing through the officers.

"No," Reubold said. "There is no time."

"But, Fregattenkapitan, surely there is a mistake."

"No," Reubold said again. "Get aboard, prepare to get under way."

Peters seemed to inflate, as if to make himself appear larger, more imposing, more dangerous. "I have to protest. Strongly. You cannot do this. I request permission to remain behind to file an official report."

Reubold looked over Peters's shoulder. "Risse?" An oberbootsmann, one of Draheim's, a big man with an oversized chin, appeared. "Escort this officer to Waymann's boat. If he resists, beat him."

Risse allowed himself a flicker of surprise followed by a barely restrained smile before he said: "Yes, sir."

Now, Reubold told himself, *let's go find someplace safe to hide.*

"The darker the night, the nearer the rain," De-Long said.

Edland looked at him.

"An old sailor's saw," DeLong said. "You know, like 'Red sky in the morning, is the sailor's warning. A red sky at night, is the sailor's delight.'"

"No," Edland said.

"The commander's not a sailor, Randy," Cole said, lowering his binoculars. "He's a paper-pusher. You sail a desk, don't you, Commander?"

Edland thought of the gentle sway of his body, sitting atop a camel, or the fierce winds of Tibet howling down the mountains. "That's right," he said. "I live for paper."

"Skipper," Barney called through the speaker. "Weather report just came in. They're saying the Beaufort's dropping from seven to six and visibility ought to pick up."

"How much?"

"Maybe four miles. Maybe seven. Course that's when the sun comes up."

"This is the Channel, Barney. We never see the sun."

Soon the low-lying clouds had denied them any kind of light from the moon and only an occasional glimpse of stars. That had been enough to see formations of aircraft heading east.

"C-47s," DeLong said, "I guess this is it."

Cole cupped his hand around his watch to catch the luminescent dial. "Oh, three-twenty-two," he said. He looked up, following Randy's gaze. "Paratroopers."

"Man, that's definitely one thing that I'd never do," DeLong said. "Jump out of an airplane."

Cole glanced at him. "Yeah. Better to be in a small wooden boat in the English Channel in shitty weather."

"*Firedancer*'s signaling," Edland noted.

Cole read the flickering light of the Aldis lamp. "'Fleet joined . . . thirty miles port. Instructed . . . reduce speed to twelve. *Firedancer*." He picked up the handheld signal lamp and responded: "Received." He turned the lamp toward the other boats and passed on the information.

"Now what?" Edland said.

"Now we wait for orders, man the radar, and hope that *Firedancer* picks up something on her unit before we do."

"What do you mean?"

"Her radar range is about sixty miles, give or take. Don't forget the unit's mounted a hell of a lot higher off the surface than ours is. Our range is twenty miles, tops. If she spots something first, we get enough warning to react." He motioned to the two seamen in the bow with a BAR and M-1. "To tell you the truth, Commander, the only thing that gives me the willies are mines. We hit one of those things and it's the end of the line."

"I hadn't thought of that."

"I have. The invasion fleets have minesweepers leading the way. They'll cut lanes through the minefields and plug those that pop to the surface. Unfortunately for us, a few might get away. Those two sharpshooters are there to plug them before we plow into them. How do those C-47s look to you now, Randy?"

"Better and better, Skipper."

"Now we play watchdog, Commander," Cole said, stretching stiffness out of his back. It was the dampness and cold that combined to creep into his joints and lock them in place. Old age, his grandfather complained, miserable old age. It'll never happen to me, Cole had thought with all the certainty of youth. I'm young, invulnerable. That arrogance had been swept away by months on the pounding deck of a little wooden boat in the cold depths of early morning. He grew accustomed to the ache in his knees, and the heavy pain in his lower back, and the sharper pain that cut across his shoulder blade. Not wounds, but injuries—the kind that he was too embarrassed to mention. Pop three or four aspirin, light a cigarette when the smoking lamp was lit, and grit your teeth. The sea was picking up some. He pulled the binoculars from the ready box and swept the darkness to port.

"Anything?" Edland asked.

Cole smiled secretly at the man's impatience. "Not a thing," he said. "Just some night and some stars. How's our heading, Randy?"

"Dead on, Skipper. Think we can do it?"

"Do what?"

"Sneak up on the bastards."

"Your guess is as good as mine. The weather was a break. They probably figured that no seaman in his right mind would venture out in this shit."

Randy chuckled as he scanned the Pioneer compass. " 'In his right mind,' " he repeated.

A rogue wave pushed PT-155 heavily to starboard, shaking the little craft. DeLong increased the throttles, his lips set firmly as he spun the wheel and fought to bring the boat back on course.

"What's the scoop, Commander?" Cole said, watching DeLong's boat-handling with appreciation. He was a natural helmsman, feeling the vibration of the 155 boat through the decking and wheel, almost capable of steering a true course with his eyes closed.

"Scoop?"

"Well, we're going to Normandy? Right?" Cole watched as Edland mulled over his response. "Commander," he said, nodding in the direction of the invasion fleet, "there are several thousand clues out there. I don't think your telling me anything is going to betray the invasion."

Edland replied: "Judging from our position, we're shielding McNamar's Task Force. U. They formed up out of Plymouth and Torquay. North of them is Task Force O. North of them is the British and Canadian Task Force."

"I guess in the task force scheme of things," DeLong said, "we're kind of near the bottom."

"Okay," Cole said to Edland's explanation. "That makes sense."

"What makes sense?" Edland asked.

"Where we are," Cole said. "What we were ordered to do. When we get the word we're to lay back along this line and sit tight."

"For how long?" Edland said.

Cole shrugged. "Until Barney passes that word to me that we're supposed to roll." Even in the darkness he could see Edland's concern. "What's the matter, Commander? You look a little green around the gills."

"I thought that we might have an opportunity . . ."

"Oh, no you don't," Cole said, shaking his head. "None of that privateer stuff. I know that you were hoping to see one of those super boats. Welcome to PT boats, Commander Edland. Those also serve who freeze their ass off in the middle of nowhere. When you decided to come along, I told you not to get your hopes up. It looks likes twelve knots is all we're going to do on this mission, so I'd sit back and relax if I were you."

"Doesn't the possibility of running into one of those boats at least excite your interest?"

"At this stage of the war, a warm bed and a hot cup of coffee are all I need to excite my interest," Cole said. "Look, Commander. Maybe you look at this thing as an intellectual exercise. I don't. I'm a long way from the classroom and the groves of academe. We come out here, do our job, and go home. You've got your orders—I've got mine. That's it. So . . ."

"My orders are nebulous," Edland said.

Cole's eyes narrowed. "Come again?"

"Strictly speaking, I wasn't ordered to come on this mission. In fact, strictly speaking, I was told, specifically, not to."

"Well, this is a fine time to tell me."

"If I'd told you before, you wouldn't have taken me along."

"Why, you lying S.O.B.," Cole said, shaking his head. After a moment he smiled. "You know, Commander, there just might be hope for you yet."

"Hey, Skipper," Barney's voice sounded scratching over the squawk box.

Cole pulled the microphone off the mount. "What's up, Barney?"

"*Firedancer* reports targets, two-one-four. Range, about fifty miles. Speed, twelve knots."

"Okay, Barney. Stand by." Cole held the microphone close to his chest in thought. He glanced at DeLong and received a puzzled look in response.

"Wrong direction," DeLong said.

Cole rubbed his jaw nervously, his mind playing over the information. Something was coming *from* the direction of the French coast, not heading toward it. "Wrong everything." He pressed the TALK button. "Barney? Did *Firedancer* send out an IFF?" Identification, Friend or Foe. It was a signal that was supposed to help Allied aircraft and ships distinguish between friendly and enemy forces, but the Germans had caught on to it quickly and used it to confuse the Allies. Now it was seldom used—better to be wary.

"Let me check, Skipper."

Cole pushed the binoculars into Edland's chest and said: "Here. Hold these." He pulled the signal lamp from its cradle, positioned himself so that the light was aimed at the other boats, and clicked it twice. It was the signal to stand by—it was a warning that something was up.

* * *

Hardy rolled his eyes in disgust when W/T passed the inquiry on to him. "Any respect that I had for Cole has now officially evaporated," he said. "Why should I give away my presence simply because I don't know who is roaming around in the darkness? IFF indeed. Why not ring bells and set off rockets? Does that make sense to you, Number One? Was I obtuse in making the target's position known?" He had heard the word used on a BBC broadcast of a quiz show and was so impressed with the sound of it that he asked Beatrice what it meant. He saw Beatrice's pencil hover over the sketchpad on the kitchen table before she answered: "I'm sure that I don't know, Captain Hardy." Obtuse. Somehow it rhymed with confuse and Hardy affixed the same meaning to both. He must have confused Cole.

"Shall I answer in the negative, sir?" Number One said.

"Negative? Of course, Number One. Did we issue an IFF? Did I order it done?"

"No, sir."

"Well. There you have it. Tell Cole that I did not, and you might add that I am not in the habit of giving away my position to any Tom, Dick, or Harry wandering about the sea."

"Indeed, sir," Land said, uncovering the voice tube and whistling up W/T for the reply to Cole. Pure Hardy. As prickly as a barnacle.

"The idea of sailing about in those little cockleshells addled the man," Hardy said, and then added, proud of his newly acquired vocabulary: "Probably obtused the poor soul."

* * *

Funker Lerch appeared at the bridge hatch. "Fregattenkapitan," he said to Reubold, "Zickelbein's decoding a message."

Reubold turned the wheel over to Kunkel. "Maintain speed and course." He slipped down the hatch and moved forward to the radio room, squeezed into a small space on the port side between the bridge and the gun well. It was difficult to move in the cramped space with the bulky life vest on, but he insisted that every man on deck wear one when they were out to sea. Those men assigned below needn't worry; they'd probably be dead before they got a chance to inflate the vest. Reubold stood to one side and behind Zickelbein. Every S-boat carried three W/T operators: one to man the wireless, one to code or encode messages, and one to run the complicated Schussel M cipher machine. He saw Zickelbein shake his head in uncertainty.

"Let's have it, Zickelbein. It's supposed to be a secret from the enemy, not from me.

"Oh," Zickelbein turned in surprise. "Sorry, sir. T-22 reports some activity in the Channel. 'Large convoy.' Le Havre passed that up to *Seekreigsleitung* and now *Seekreigsleitung* says not to worry about it. But I just received a transmission from *B-Dienst* on *Offizier M* ordering all T-boats and S-boats to stand by for instructions."

"And not twelve hours ago they told us 'nighty-night.' Where is T-22 now?"

"I don't know, sir, but they are stationed at Le Havre. I think they're with the Fifteenth *Vorposten*."

Reubold glanced at the tiny radar at Zickelbein's elbow.

"Naxos?"

"Nothing, sir," the seaman said, following Reubold's glance. He went a step further. "We haven't picked up anything. No W/T traffic at all."

Reubold's eyes narrowed. "Nothing. Come, come Zickelbein. Someone has to be saying something to someone."

"Just Marine Gruppe West, sir. They keep asking for information."

Reubold turned to Lerch. "Let me know the minute you hear anything. Other than a bunch of Silver Stripes asking questions. Let me know when somebody answers and what they say." He turned to Zickelbein. "Keep your eyes on Naxos." The 10-cm radar had been developed from a downed Allied aircraft bearing an H2S radar. It had limited range and the Allies had certainly progressed beyond its capabilities, but it's all the Kriegsmarine had. "Report anything."

Reubold quickly made his way topside and waved Kunkel back when the leutnant began to move away from the helm. It was a courtesy to step aside and offer the helm to the boat captain. "Something is going on," Reubold said. "We may have changed from *lautaktik* to *stichtaktik* without knowing it."

"I didn't know that we were on either," Kunkle said in surprise.

"Always one or the other," Reubold said. "Or the Devil's Shovel." He turned and could barely make out the ghostly gray shapes of the other boats trailing behind. The W/T operators on the boats had certainly picked up the flurry of confused messages from Marine Gruppe West and *Seekriegsleitung*, and the boat commanders were probably wonder-

ing what Reubold's orders were. Reubold was wondering the same thing. His original course had
them proceeding another 40 kilometers and turning south-southeast. Things had changed, however.
He could loiter about and chance bumping into an
Allied convoy, or picking up additional information
from Marine Gruppe West, that might, he hoped,
clear up the confusion. The one thing he could not
do was to lead the 11th Flotilla back to base; even
at this distance they could see the bright eruptions
peppering the horizon where Cherbourg was. The
Allies had come in the night again, and this time it
appeared that they meant to level Cherbourg.

Reubold picked up the small, handheld signal
lamp, switched on the power, checked the louvers,
and aimed it toward the other boats. His index finger squeezed the trigger and spelled out: KMZ.
Kriegsmarschzustand 1—Battle Stations, Code One.
A single brief flash came back from the following
boats: message received—understood.

Reubold hung the lamp on its hook. He had no
answers. He didn't know what was out there, or if
there was something out there, or even what it was.
But he and Flotilla 11 were prepared, and there was
a chance that Waldvogel's flying boats with their
plump guns might get an unexpected chance to
fight.

"Sir?" Lerch looked up at him from the hatch. He
handed Reubold a sheet torn from a message pad.
"From T-22 to Marine Gruppe West. It's all that was
sent. The transmission was terminated in mid-signal."

Reubold took the page, flipped up the cover
shielding the phosphorescent dial of the compass,
and read: *Many ships.*

Chapter 27

The sky around them was a mass of explosions that robbed the night of absolute darkness, replacing it with a thousand miniature suns. The Germans really meant to kill me this time, Gierek thought.

The Pathfinders had formed up with the Lancasters and although nobody said it, everyone knew that this was the invasion. Far above the speckled clouds that gleamed under the moon's glare, Gierek saw aircraft, many, many aircraft. They flew at different levels, fleets of them, each carefully tended by its covey of fighters. And then suddenly the aircraft were gone and all that remained were the Pathfinders, and behind them the lumbering, complacent Lancasters.

Gierek felt dread pressing hard on his chest and no songs or words came to him. Jagello listened to High Wycombe for news of the invasion, and babied Gee to make sure that when the pulsating signals intersected, he was where he should be—where they should be; over the E-boat pens of Cherbourg. Gee and Oboe, the two mischievous nymphs who lead the wooden planes to the dangerous skies above Cherbourg with pulsating chirps and whistles. At the right moment Jagello would open the bomb bay doors, push the teat on the bomb release, and a dozen Target Indicators would fall gracefully into the night until their altimeters tripped and the flares exploded.

They'd done it thirty-seven times before. Le Havre, Boulogne, Cherbourg, once down to Lorient, and then back to Cherbourg, and each time Gierek had talked or sung and Jagello kept silent.

Jagello was still silent but Gierek was frightened. It was that damned dog. It had been there every time, collapsed in front of the left tire, looking as close to dead as an animal could be without actually being dead—until the erks came to retrieve it.

Gierek saw a soft band of tracers reach high in the sky and then fall away as if to announce: we see you, we are here waiting—come. He looked overhead through the Perspex canopy and cursed the moon and the men who made them fly when the moon was fat and satisfied. He knew that the moon's rays gleamed off the aircraft despite the dull paint that coated them, and he knew that German antiaircraft gunners were waiting to trap him in the lenses of powerful binoculars.

He felt . . . what was the word . . . sorrowful? An English word that described sadness coupled with longing for something that remained unidentified. A sweet loss that beckoned like a lover from the platform of a departing train. Sorrowful. He was frightened more than he had ever been. To be scared was one thing, to feel your bowels loosen, and your mouth dry up, that was to be expected. But sorrow? He suddenly realized that his future was preordained. That was to say, *I am a dead man*.

A range of explosions filled the canopy as the German gunners found the altitude. Next would come the barrage, individual guns firing as quickly as they could; 88s, 105s, big guns with menacing barrels and around their barrel a painted stripe for each enemy aircraft downed.

The firing increased, mushrooms of flame with jutting tentacles that reached into the darkness, seeking a target, searching for Gierek. The Mosquito bounced, and sideslipped, and Gierek saw Jagello's hand motion casually to the right. The bomb-aimer/navigator's face was buried in the radar-scope and he did not want to move, so the tiny wave with the gloved hand said: You're off course.

Jagello the iron man, the solitary professional.

Suddenly they were in the flak field with explosions on all four sides. Gierek fought the wheel, his eyes on the compass. He relaxed his pressure on the rudder pedals, knowing that pilots usually overcompensated in their excitement.

This is bad, he thought. The worst he had ever seen. They must have brought more guns in and stuck them on every rooftop. Three blasts, one immediately after another, shook the aircraft so violently that Gierek thought the Mosquito's back was broken but she continued to fly, untouched. "Good, old Mossie," Gierek breathed, and he heard Jagello say: "Yes."

They flew for several minutes more, the con-

stant roar of the exploding shells so great that it
was impossible to distinguish one blast from another. The sky was bright with explosions, and the
flaming remnants of flak bursts, and slender searchlight beams that swept back and forth until they
captured an aircraft and locked on, refusing to let
go. Gierek hated searchlights. They were obsolete
and ineffective but once a plane was pinned in
their evil light, they would follow it until the aircraft disintegrated in a flash.

Jagello's hand came up, and Gierek heard the
soft murmur of the bomb bay door motors and felt
the aircraft trembling as the doors deployed.

Gierek began praying, something that he had
never done before, because although he professed
to a belief in God as a good Catholic, he had seen
too much to accept His existence. He has abandoned us, Gierek decided when men he knew,
good men, died. He prayed this time because of
the fear that rose from deep within his soul, and
the certainty that this time; this mission, would
end in his death.

The aircraft was rocked again, thrown to the left
and down, and Gierek saw Jagello signal frantically
with his hand: Stay on course. It meant nothing if
they flew all that distance to drop indicators in the
wrong place. It meant that the bombers would
dumbly follow behind and drop their bombs where
the indicators glowed brightly because they had
been trained to do so. The bombers would be out
of position and the bombs would be off target and
hundreds of aircraft and thousands of men would
be put in jeopardy because a Pathfinder had made
a mistake. There was no going back to the target if

they couldn't drop their ITs. They would travel on through the flak and emerge on the other side, and hope that the other Pathfinders did the job that they had failed at. Or they would fly deep into the angry red clouds and disappear in a flash of fire and smoke.

Gierek regained control of the aircraft and saw Jagello raise the bomb release cord, his thumb poised over the teat, and he felt his heart pound through his flying togs.

Then he saw Jagello's thumb depress the teat, and he heard the clatter of ITs falling away into the darkness, and before he realized it the bomb bay doors were closed and Jagello looked at him with all of the aplomb of a man who has just successfully tied his shoe.

And then the cockpit of the Mosquito exploded.

"Double the lookouts," Hardy said to Land. And as an afterthought he added: "And send someone to fetch my hat."

"Of course, sir," Land said, and nodded to Yeoman Bertram. He turned to Petty Officer Stillwell, who shared *Firedancer*'s bridge with them, and said in a measured tone: "Double the lookouts if you please, Petty Officer."

"Right, sir," Stillwell said. His tone was unhurried, without a trace of excitement or concern. One would almost think that there was no danger ahead and the men were slightly bored with it all. Neither was true. Survival was part luck and part precaution and since luck was never under one's control, one had to be content with precaution.

And the men were justifiably concerned. They had been at this business for a number of years and knew that as melodramatic as it seems, death always lurked close by. One could appear blasé, perhaps indifferent, and in extreme cases they might even temper their fear with gallows humor. But they all knew dead men—those whose number was up, as most of the crew believed. Fatalism was an accepted commodity aboard *Firedancer.*

Land had been Hardy's Number One long enough to appreciate his captain's peculiarities, even if he didn't understand them. He trusted Hardy, and he knew Hardy's skills aboard *Firedancer* were beyond reproach, but he was embarrassed for the man when he slipped on that worn bowler. *Charge into battle with something other than a haberdasher's nightmare, for God's sake.*

A whistle came through the voice tubes. "Bridge? W/T here."

Land leaned over the tubes as the hatbox was presented to Hardy. "Bridge."

"Target's hanging steady, sir. No change in course of speed."

Hardy was at Land's side. "What's this, Number One?"

"No change in the target's course or speed, sir. They're still well away from us."

Hardy growled in thought and looked into the sky. Visibility had remained unchanged; scattered to moderate clouds, a flash of the moon when the winds permitted and a sprinkling of brilliant stars in the cold heaven. Still, radar was all that they could truly count on until the mysterious vessels got close enough for the lookouts to pick up.

"E-boats," Hardy said. He nodded to himself in confirmation. "On patrol or something; loitering about waiting for a target perhaps, but E-boats nevertheless." He leaned over the voice tube. "W/T? Send to Castle." Castle was the code name for Task Force U's Escort Command. "Ready? Possible E-boat contact. . . ." He looked up. "Where are they now, Number One?"

"A bit farther, sir. Nearly sixty miles. Course two-one-four. Speed is still twelve knots, sir."

"Possible E-boat contact," Hardy said, and then repeated the information that Land had given him. He waited while W/T read it back to him for confirmation and then said: "Yes. That's it. Send it off." He adjusted the hat on his head. "They'll want to send some aircraft out there, Number One. A big fat Short Sunderland, I'm sure. Well, fair enough. It's their show, we're just Costly Farces. I'll tell you this much, Number One. When we're through with this business, I'm going to ask out of this duck pond and get us back to sea. I'd even take convoys over the English Channel."

"Bridge? W/T."

"Still waiting, W/T," Hardy said. "What about it?"

"No, sir," W/T said. "Castle has not yet replied. It's the target, sir. They're coming about. Course two-four-two. Range fifty miles. Speed, twenty knots."

Hardy tossed Land a glance and said crisply: "Right. Well, loitering is out. Either Mr. E-boat smelled a rat and has come to investigate, or he's just fumbling about in the darkness."

"Either way," Land said, but let the comment hang; a question begging an answer.

"Yes," Hardy agreed. "W/T? Advise Castle immediately of the change in circumstances. I request permission to move against the enemy." He tapped his fingertips on the windscreen in thought. "Number One. Have Yeoman of Signals make to our Mr. Cole that we have gatecrashers. Give him the latest information and tell him to stand by."

"Right, sir."

The tapping stopped as Hardy examined the situation. Convoys to port, big, slow ships, eminently protected by anything that could mount a gun but still vulnerable to an E-boat attack. To starboard, Mr. Cole's little wooden boats of name; game vessels all right, but in Hardy's mind little more than pleasure yachts.

Continue to starboard: six boats; certainly E-boats, powerful, fast, devilish creations that could side-step *Firedancer* with ease and get deep into the convoys.

"Bridge? W/T."

"From Castle?" Hardy said, his voice sharp with irritation. He hated to wait on others to make a decision whose answer was perfectly obvious to Hardy.

"No, sir. Sorry, sir," W/T/ said.

"My aunt's pajamas, W/T, do I have to carry the mail myself?" Hardy exploded. "Did you impress upon them the urgency of the thing? Are they asleep out there?"

"It's the E-boats, sir," W/T replied calmly. "They've come completely around and their course is oh-five-three degrees." There was a pause. "Speed," W/T continued. "Forty knots."

Hardy, his anger quickly forgotten, rapidly calculated the course and speed. *They're going to intercept us*, he thought.

* * *

Reubold watched as the three Funkers scrambled to receive radio transmission, note them, and decode them. Even without the knowledge of W/T that these men possessed he could tell that something important was going on by the barrage of signals that flooded the tiny radio room.

"Report, Lerch," Reubold said. He kept his voice low and calm, knowing that it would do nothing but add to the tension in the room if he appeared concerned.

Lerch looked up at Reubold and after a moment to gather himself said: "Sir, something terrible is happening out there."

"Explain," Reubold said, his excitement building. "And be more specific than 'out there.'"

"Yes, sir," Lerch said. "I can't get all of it but the stations along the coast are all reporting some sort of activity. Air raids, parachutists, ships right in front of them. Dieppe, Le Havre, Cherbourg. The airwaves are flooded. Pas de Calais, as well."

It would be Pas de Calais, high command decided. The Allies would take the shortest route across the Channel and land at Pas de Calais. The men of Flotilla 11 had been wagering on it for some time, and the general opinion was, that for once, high command was right; the Allies would invade France at Pas de Calais. Reubold had gone to Boulogne to meet an old friend and they had traveled up to Dunkirk together to see the beaches, littered with the wreckage of what had once been the British army. On the way they had stopped at a small tavern and bought beer from a sullen proprietor before going out on a bluff overlooking the Channel. From the bluff, talking, drinking, and sharing a set of worn binoculars, they had studied the Cliffs of Dover: England.

"There's more coming in, sir," Lerch said. The message was decoded by Zickelbein and given to Lerch.

"Read it," Reubold ordered.

" 'T-29 sights several ships advancing Guernsey. Dieppe reports parachute attack. Dieppe reports enemy ships forty kilometers from port.' "

"Enough," Reubold said. He made his way quickly to the bridge, glad to be in the cool air and under the thick clouds that shimmered in the moonlight. It was claustrophobic in the W/T room, and the contradictory messages angered him.

"Kunkel," he barked, "bring us about. On zero-five-three degrees. Increase to fifty knots." He slipped the throat mike on and slipped his earphones over his cap. He pinched the small microphones against his throat. "Lerch?"

"Sir?" crackled through the earpieces.

"Signal the other boats. New course zero-five-three degrees. Speed, fifty knots. Form echelon."

"What is it?" Kunkel said.

"Madness," Reubold said in disgust. "Absolute madness. No one is sure of anything on shore. We'll go see for ourselves."

"Where are we going?"

"Pas de Calais. We might find the invasion fleet. If we're lucky."

"Shouldn't we notify Marine Gruppe West?" Kunkel said.

"And ruin a perfectly good outing?" Reubold said. He sensed Kunkel's concern. "All right, Leut-

nant. I promise that if we run across the invasion
fleet I will let them know." He turned and made
his way back along the port canvas dodgers, stopping
at the amidships doorknocker. The crew looked at
him expectantly and he smiled in return. He wanted
time to think, so he studied the other boats' positions. He could see them, or rather their wakes,
gleaming in the light provided by the capricious
moon. They kept good position and their speed
matched S-205 exactly.

Reubold noticed a young matrosenhauptgefreiter watching him.

"Spiller? Isn't it?" Reubold said.

"Yes, sir," the man said. He was bundled in his
black coverall, with the coal-shuttle helmet clamped
firmly on his head, looking like a distressed turtle.

"This is Ramsau's gun, isn't it?" Reubold said,
knowing that it was and knowing that oberbootsmannmaat Ramsau, the gun captain, was standing
next to Spiller.

"Yes, sir," Spiller said, perplexed.

"Tell me, Spiller," Reubold said. "Does Ramsau
still fuck ugly women?"

The gun crew burst into laughter. Ramsau shook
his head, wondering how officers expected him to
keep young matrosenhauptgefreiter in line if the
officers showed the oberbootsmannmaat no respect.

"I don't know, sir," Spiller said, looking around
as if he expected the other crew members to help
him.

Another wave of laughter swamped the gun and
Reubold winked at Ramsau, although he wasn't
sure if the chief petty officer could see the wink in
the darkness.

"Fregattenkapitan," Ramsau said in a weary voice. "Pardon me for saying so, but we would be better served if you were in the skull's cap."

"Indeed, Ramsau?" Reubold said, making the decision that he had come aft to consider. Pas de Calais was the shortest route, perhaps the easiest, but Reubold thought that if it were he, and he was expected to do one thing, he would, naturally, have to do the opposite. "I just came back to tell you that British and Americans are out there and we are going to hunt them." He felt the tension in the gun crew increase. They realized immediately what the implication was.

"The invasion, Fregattenkapitan?" Ramsau said.

"Yes," Reubold said, and started forward. He turned and said. "But even if it isn't, we shall make the best of it."

Chapter 28

Cole hooked the microphone back into its cradle and turned to DeLong. He had just received *Firedancer*'s message and ordered it passed on to the other boats. "You heard the man, Randy, come about and let's go find out who these folks are."

"What are you doing?" Edland said.

"*Firedancer* reports a fast boat coming this way. They're not PTs," Cole explained in a tone that said that the reason for his action should be obvious. "They're not MTBs, so that leaves just one candidate."

"I understand that, Lieutenant. *Firedancer* said that he has contacted Castle for further orders," Edland said. "Shouldn't we wait on verification?"

"You know," Cole said, "not more than five minutes ago you were all ready to take on the Kriegsmarine. Now, you've gone cautious on me. You can't have it both ways, Commander. I'll just proceed on my own initiative and let the chips fall where they may." He pointed into the darkness. "That's where the enemy is, and that's where I'm going." And then Cole added: "Sir." He picked up the microphone and depressed the TALK button. "Let the other boats know, we're going in. Pass the word to *Firedancer*."

"What?" Hardy said into the voice tube. "Going where?"

"The PT boat commander reported that he is turning toward the targets and shall investigate," W/T said.

"The impetuosity of the man," Hardy said to Land. "Going off without orders. I would have thought better of Mr. Cole. Well, he's a disappointment, I can tell you that."

"Yes, sir," Land said.

"Never catch me doing such a thing," Hardy said. "Have I ever done such a thing, Number One?"

"No, sir," Land said. Countless times, Land thought. *We've gone off on your order alone and even after we were recalled and chastised, you've been less than contrite. The two were cut from the same bolt, Hardy and Cole.* Land fully expected what came next.

"W/T? Hardy here. Send to Castle. I'm just going out for a peek. I shan't be long." He made it sound as if he were going down to the corner newsstand to pick up a paper. "Not to worry about anything." He straightened and looked at Land innocently. "Can't let the boy face whatever is out there alone, now can I?"

"Bridge? W/T, radar here. The enemy formation has just deployed into a wing formation, speed increased to fifty knots steady. Now at forty miles, same bearing."

"Right," Hardy said. "Make to Cole. 'I shall take up position to port and a bit ahead of you. Look for my signal by Aldis lamp. Enemy course, break at double X, enemy speed, double X, distance. *Firedancer.*'" He turned to Land, satisfied. We're put ourselves between the enemy and Mr. Cole and track them on radar. We'll be positioned in such a way as to keep our Aldis lamp signals from the enemy's eyes."

"That should do it, sir," Land said.

"Of course it should," Hardy said impatiently. "Unless we are sunk." He pulled the bowler from his head, scratched his scalp vigorously, and holding the hat under the soft glow of the binnacle light, examined it. "This hat has occupants, Number One."

"Sir?"

"The damned thing's infested." Hardy handed the bowler to a yeoman. "Set this thing aside until I can have it fumigated. My God," he said. "Lice at my age."

Cole cradled the microphone in his hand, switched the radio to All Boats and said: "First Division, deployment ahead. Second Division, deployment thirty degrees to starboard, into line." He watched as the boats moved smoothly into their new formation; a long line, bows on to the enemy, or where the enemy was supposed to be. "Commander," Cole said, satisfied with the maneuver, "do you believe in fate?"

"No."

"Me either. But something tells me that those guys out there are your famous flying boats."

Edland looked at him.

"They're out of Cherbourg," Cole continued, "like your boats, and they're coming in hot. Of course nobody's paying me to make guesses . . ."

"Signal from *Firedancer*, Skipper," DeLong said. He read the tiny flashes of light. " 'Zero-five-three degrees, break, sixty . . . holy shit! Sorry, sir. Sixty knots. Thirty-five miles.'"

Cole turned to Edland with a triumphant grin. "Want to see your boats again, Commander? Close up?"

Edland nodded. He was beginning to appreciate Cole. It was hard to fathom the insubordinate PT boat commander, but sandwiched between the arrogance and dislike of authority was a very capable officer. "Do you have a plan?"

Cole seemed amused. "Yeah, try to sink them without getting killed." And then he grew serious. "They'll try to outrun us, so we've got to get in as quickly as possible and break up their formation."

"They've got a large gun, mounted in the bow, from what I can determine," Edland said. "Standard armament is probably the same; twenty-millimeter and forty-millimeter guns."

"Okay," Cole said. "Any suggestions?"

"*Firedancer* again, Skipper," Delong reported. "Same course, same speed. Thirty miles out."

"Yes," Edland said. "Get in as close as you can."

"No offense, Commander," Cole said, "but that sounds like suicide to me."

"The boats are up on wings, stilts, or whatever you care to call them. That means their hulls are out of the water.

"Okay," Cole said, listening.

"Same, same, and twenty-five miles, Skipper."

"If the big guns are in the bow wells, then they fire almost parallel to the surface of the water," Edland explained.

Cole finally realized what Edland was saying. "They can't be depressed."

Edland nodded. "The only guns that you have to worry about, besides small arms fire, are the aft 40mm and the 20mm amidships. Look," he said, holding out his left hand, the palm down, the fingers slightly elevated. A make-believe E-boat. He brought his right hand alongside, slightly below the other. "Get right next to them, worry them. Force them to constantly turn away so that they can't employ their superior speed. Once they break free of contact they can outrun us. If we force them in a constant turn, they'll have to reduce speed. We have a chance."

"Skipper," DeLong said. "Fifteen miles. Our radars picked them up as well."

Cole nodded in understanding. "Herding cats." He was still far from comforted by the commander's theory.

"There's one other thing," Edland said.

"Boy, I sure hope it's good news," Cole said.

"If these boats break away long enough to employ those big guns . . ."

"It's Good Night, Ladies," Cole said.

"We've got to stick to them like glue."

Cole thought that Edland's advice made sense even if the action bordered on insanity. He asked a hopeful question. "Is this a theory or fact?"

"Does it make any difference, now?"

"I guess not," Cole said.

"*Firedancer*'s got them, Skipper," Delong said. "Visual confirmation." The Aldis lamp flashed in the darkness. "Six boats, in echelon. Sixty knots. God, that's fast."

"Okay," Cole said, confirming the information. He picked up the microphone. "All boats, all boats from Cole. These are Edland's Sea Eagles. Take it in on the step. Get in close, bulwark to bulwark. Get me? Get under their guns. Keep forcing them to turn. Don't let them put any distance between us and them." Cole turned to Edland. "I sure am going to be upset if you're wrong."

Zickelbein's voice came through Reubold's earphones. "Targets, sir. Just over twenty thousand meters ahead. Six MTBs, one destroyer."

A screening force, Reubold thought. *For what, the invasion? Or a patrol? Well, no matter, they were in the way.* "We'll go around them," he told Kunkle. "I don't want to waste my time here if the invasion is to the north. Take us around them." Hardly the thick hide that Walters spoke of. A destroyer was always something to be concerned with, but MTBs? Then a dark thought entered Reubold's thoughts, so logical he was surprised that he had not thought of it before. They will report you to the fleet and the hide will certainly grow thicker as more enemy ships are dispatched to meet the threat. Reubold grew irritated at the unexpected encounter with the MTBs. He was hoping to pass through the Channel unnoticed. He had lost the element of surprise.

Zickelbein spoke again. "Fregattenkapitan. I copied the boat's transmission. They are Americans. Torpedo boats."

Reubold was about to respond when he realized the signal flaw in his tactic. He could not go around them. The two forces would clash in minutes and if he attempted to turn away he would expose the broad beams of his boats to the Americans. And the fragile wings of his boats. Better to drive through the enemy force. But again, a flaw. He looked over the skullcap as if to confirm the obvious. The Trinities, buried deep in the gun well, could not fire over the bow and strike a target unless the enemy vessel was several thousand meters distant—which the Americans were sure to be, but only for a very short time. The relative speed of the opposing forces sent them hurtling at one another so quickly that every action had to be instantaneous. So be it; close quickly, blast through the enemy force, find and attack the invasion fleet. "Kunkle. Ignore that order, maintain course and speed."

"Sir?" Zickelbein's voice came over the earphones. "Yes?"

"Targets closing rapidly, sir. Now fourteen thousand meters."

Kunkle glanced at Reubold with a look that said everything: These Americans want to fight. Going through them will not be such an easy thing.

Reubold understood. He would have to scatter the enemy formation. He pressed the microphone to his throat. "Zickelbein, all boats that can bring guns to bear on the target. Fire at seven thousand meters and for God's sake take aim. Who knows what we'll run into once we're past these fellows." It was a chance—a random throw of the die. It would be difficult to aim the Trinities over the bow, and the targets were so small that he doubted even the doorknockers would be of much help. But then he didn't expect to sink any of the enemy boats, just discourage them. They'd been up too long on the wings, more than Waldvogel stipulated, but he needed the speed, and he would continue to need it to outrace the enemy boats. Waldvogel. Reubold smiled at the thought of the myopic genius who hovered continually between puzzlement and concern.

"Ten thousand," Zickelbein reported.

Americans this time. Smaller boats, swift lines but far too fragile for the English Channel. His first encounter with the Americans, at sea that is. He'd raced against them, years before the war, when seaplanes were long, lean aircraft with small cockpits that trapped a man as surely as if he lay in his coffin.

There was a crash and a flash of light as the doorknocker on S-205 opened fire, and an instant later a dull explosion as a Trinity fired, followed by a second, and third. The boat to his right fired its doorknocker, a long graceful stream of green tracers arching into the darkness, followed by a flash and low boom. The blast of the Trinity's discharge illuminated the bow and skullcap of the E-boat for an instant, but then darkness swallowed up the boat.

Blind men in the darkness, Reubold thought. *It will be a fight of blind men in the darkness.*

The first shell thundered over Cole's head, and without realizing it, he, DeLong, and Edland followed its progress, their heads twisting in unison. There was a tremendous explosion aft of them.

"Holy shit!" DeLong said. "Those are cruisers."

"The German guns I told you about," Edland said, moving close to Cole. The roar of the engines made it difficult to talk and everything was delivered in a near shout. "They must be using tracers as some sort of aiming device."

"Well, it's working out pretty well for them," Cole said. "That landed too close for comfort."

A round exploded to starboard followed by a round to port as the diabolical green tracers swept the water.

"They've got us straddled," Cole said. "Okay, Randy. Evasive action." He leaned over the bridge roof. "Murray?" he shouted to the gunner on the forward 20mm. "Commence firing." He turned again to DeLong. "I've told everybody that you're the best boat handler in the fucking navy. Now I want you to get us alongside one of those bastards without so much as a dented gunnel. Cover him like paint."

DeLong nodded. He wrapped his fingers around the three throttle knobs jutting out of the instrument panel and eased them to full power. It was hell on the engines, running at top speed for an extended period of time, especially engines that were several hundred miles past rebuilding—but then so was getting blown up.

Cole watched as dozens of tracer rounds split the darkness, red and green, passing one another in a merry game of hide-and-seek. The 37mm cannon on PT-155's bow began to fire, a steady chunk-chunk-chunk, and he thought he could feel the boat shake with each discharge. The forward 20mm just in front of the bridge and offset to port joined in; somehow its bark nothing more than an ineffectual bang. With each blast came an intense blaze of white light from the powder flare. He looked away from the contest in the blackness to see De-Long working frantically to keep the boat on course but away from enemy shells. His concentration was inhuman, his eyes boring into the darkness, and for a moment Cole was convinced that the young ensign saw everything clearly and that night had been replaced by full light.

Harry Lowe.

The thought struck as surely as it had been a punch in the gut. It was night, like the night that Harry was killed, and they were fighting E-boats, like the night that Harry was killed. Cole quickly turned away so that no one saw the horror that he was sure was etched on his face. *Get a grip*, he commanded himself. But a voice reminded him, in barely a whisper, that he was responsible for his men, responsible for Randy, like he was responsible for Harry. But now Harry was dead and Randy was standing in his place. The same place. And it was night. And those were E-boats.

Suddenly radio chatter from the other boats broke into Cole's thoughts. They were random bursts of excited commands and warning, the PT boats trying to maneuver into position, trying to stay out of the reach of those guns.

Cole snapped up the microphone, all other thoughts gone, and began directing the fight. "Cole to all boats. Get in. Get in fast. Don't get fancy. Close with them as soon as you can and don't let any daylight between you and them."

The water erupted nearby, shaking the boat, and Cole saw Edland sitting with his back against the day room housing, stunned. He reached out his hand and Edland took it with a wry: "Thanks."

"You're welcome," Cole said. "The navy takes care of its own."

The battle increased in intensity and Cole realized that it was every boat for itself. There was no structure to it, no definition. It was fire and flee, return and do the same thing. Try to hit the enemy boat but not those of your companions.

"Here we go!" DeLong shouted in a burst of excitement. Suddenly PT-155 whipped to port and heeled over so heavily that Cole thought she would capsize. He heard men shouting, and then a fierce barrage of blasts, and finally saw tracers flying in every direction.

He realized what had happened. DeLong had taken PT-155 directly at an E-boat, forcing the enemy vessel to change course, and as it had, DeLong had practically thrown the PT on her beam, coming completely about and alongside the E-boat.

Alongside the E-boat, and within yards of her.

Cole had prepared himself to see the hydrofoils, and in his mind knew what they looked like, but the unexpected sight of them shocked him, and even seemed to calm the racket of battle. "Jesus Christ," he whispered in awe as the E-boat grew. "That's a big son of a bitch."

"Port thirty," Hardy shouted into the voice tubes as a shell landed aft. *Firedancer* had been drawn into the battle almost immediately and into the role that Hardy had seen her playing, that of coach with an occasional foray into the midst of combat. All that had disappeared with the first blast of the E-boats' big guns. *Firedancer*'s pom-poms, 4.5-inch guns, and deck-mounted Lewis guns joined in the moment that the two forces slammed into one another.

A steady stream of glowing green tracers sped out from the darkness and ricocheted off of the hedgehog mount where A-turret had once been. Shells bounced into the air, screaming like banshees—a shrill, hideous scream that raised goose bumps on a man's skin. The sound ran its fingertips up Hardy's spine, looking for a place to enter his soul.

Somebody fired a flare, not from *Firedancer*, because, by God, Hardy would have anyone's head that had done such a thing. Then the whole scene was suddenly frozen in the ghastly yellow light—a rich tableau of destruction. He was frozen for an instant, as was everything around him. Number One at the tubes, yeoman of signals at the Aldis lamp, the chief petty officer; what-was-his-name?— at the Tannoy, awaiting orders.

The only movement that Hardy saw was below him at B-turret. It was the twisted act of a gunner kicking the 4.5-incher's breechblock, until the loader could swing it open and slide another shell into the breech. Calmly Hardy thought: I shall have to have a chat with the gunnery officer about this; it appears that the gun has jammed again.

Seconds passed, so slowly that they should have been hours and even the explosions were muffled to the sound of distant thunder, a natural sound in a wholly unnatural event.

"We've taken bricks aft," Number One called to him above the din. "Two I think. After supply party's on it."

"Take us back half a mile," Hardy returned. "I want to be clear of the Americans so that we don't fall into them. Whoever comes our way has to be the enemy. Can you see anything? I can't see a damned thing."

Number One pointed. "Two points off the starboard beam. Two boats are burning. I don't know whose." Another hit shook *Firedancer* and Hardy felt someone hit his arm with a cricket bat. He looked down to see the sleeve torn away and the arm glistening with some kind of liquid.

"Captain?" Number One said.

"Let it be, Edwin. Take us back and set us up again. By God, Jerry won't get past *Firedancer*."

Reubold pulled an MG-42 out of a deck locker and balanced it on a cutout in the armored bridge. Kunkle whipped the E-boat back and forth trying to disengage from the enemy boat, but the Americans, despite the S-boat's greater speed, hung so closely to S-205 that none of the guns could be

brought to bear. The enemy boats continually
snapped at the sides of the boats, forcing them to
turn, driving them back on their own wakes, crowding them so that the S-boats could not break free.
Reubold's boats, on the thin hydrofoils, shuddered
against each sharp turn, protesting the weight of
the boat and water. They were too fragile. Reubold
knew that he was aboard a thoroughbred who
would race until its heart burst, but she demanded
a straight, unimpeded course. And this, he could
not give her.

"Break out small arms," Reubold shouted as he
fed a belt into the machine gun and worked the
action. The American guns were chewing the hull
and superstructure of the S-boat to shreds, pumping rounds into the boat's body at point-blank
range. Reubold saw two crewmen slump over as
bits of the boat were blown away by the heavy machine guns. Red tracers whined just over his head
as he squeezed the trigger, firing into the night.

The two boats raced through the darkness, side
by side as if joined by a mutual desire to see the
other destroyed even if it cost the victor its own
life. The American boat kept pushing into S-205,
forcing it to compensate, snapping at its heels like
a despicable little terrier.

A matrose joined Reubold and was in the process
of throwing a hand grenade when a stream of bullets ripped the top of his head off. The grenade
fell over the side and the seaman's body, blood
spurting from the wound, slumped to the deck.
Reubold screamed in frustration and tipped the
muzzle of the machine gun as far over the side as

he could, depressing the trigger. He saw others take their place along the side, using pistols, rifles, and hand grenades to break the deadly grasp of the American boat.

Reubold went through one belt and began feeding another belt into the receiver when he heard a blast aft. Even in the darkness he could see oily smoke boiling from the vents of the center engine room. But worse than that, much worse, he felt the boat begin to lose headway, and for the first time in many years, he felt panic.

PT-155's starboard twin fifties roared incessantly as the aft 40mm swung as far forward as it could against its stops and fired once before a grenade disabled it. DeLong's hat had been shot off his head and a steady stream of blood, driven into a weird pattern across his forehead and right ear by the wind, gave him the look of a madman.

Cole grabbed Edland and jerked him to a single .50-caliber machine gun mounted on a pipe stand on the edge of the day room canopy. Slapping the commander's hands on the grips Cole said: "Hold this. Press this until it stops." He pointed toward the E-boat's glistening hull just feet away. "Shoot at that."

Edland depressed the triggers on the heavy .50-caliber machine gun and the night seemed to explode. The concussion of the gun threatened to jerk the weapon out of his hands and he realized that the tracer rounds were flying high over the enemy boat's hull. He depressed the muzzle until he saw chunks of enemy vessel thrown into the air. He wasn't aiming; he was trying to hold the damned thing on target.

Cole chambered a round into a Thompson submachine gun, stepped back so that he could get a better shot at the E-boat's bridge, and sprayed the enemy boat with short bursts. He felt the gun jump in his hand and he pressed the stock into his shoulder, watching sparks dance all along the superstructure.

He had no time to think of anything except bringing this monster to a halt. He saw an enemy seaman pop up, let loose a few rounds with a machine pistol, and then drop out of sight. He heard someone shout, "Grenade!" and watched as a German stick hand grenade shot far overhead. Cole took careful aim at a German sailor, fired a full burst in his chest, and saw him disappear. He heard the dull chug of the 40-millimeter and then realized that it had stopped firing. But it didn't make any difference—the sharp crack of two 20-millimeter guns shattered the darkness.

DeLong's shouts brought Cole back to the bridge.

"Skipper? Skipper!" The ensign nodded at the E-boat. "She's losing power."

Cole saw the boat begin to slow and settle. But it wasn't giving up—the two boats continued colliding against one another, racing over the water.

"Rich!" Cole shouted. He tossed the Thompson on the deck and pulled his .45 caliber automatic out of its holster. He worked the slide, glancing around. "Murray?" He shouted. "Grab some weapons and four guys. Get ready to board that son of a bitch."

"Board?" Rich said, shocked.

"Hell, man," Cole said, trembling with excitement. "We've just begun to fight."

The Mosquito shook violently and a blast of cold night air raced in through the shattered Perplex canopy.

Gierek kept glancing at the still form next to him—Jagello wasn't moving.

The starboard engine was running away, alternately speeding up and slowing down of its own volition. The instrument panel in front of Gierek was virtually destroyed so that he had no idea where he was, how much fuel he had, what his altitude was, or even what direction he was flying.

"Jagello?" he shouted above the roar of the hurricane-like winds. "Jagello? Can you hear me? Can you hear me?"

"Yes," the bomb-aimer/navigator said in a weak voice.

"Are you all right?"

The wounded man slowly lifted his head, blood pouring from a dozen wounds in black rivulets. "Can you stop this bloody plane from shaking?"

"I'm trying," Gierek said. He gripped the wheel as tightly as he could, but no matter what he did the plane didn't respond. Cables had been cut, Gierek knew, and control surfaces blown away, and she had to be leaking hydraulic fluid. The Mosquito had all of the aerodynamics of a rock. He was surprised that the aircraft was still aloft. "Are you all right?"

"No," Jagello said patiently. "I am shot. You are shaking me to death. Stop shaking the airplane."

"I'm trying."

They were alone in the sky, and the roar of the air through the canopy blew bits of the aircraft around the cockpit like a maelstrom. The starboard engine whined maniacally, in a wild attempt to wrench itself off the wing while Gierek tried to nurse the port engine.

Jagello slumped against the edge of Gierek's seat as the plane began to shudder more. Gierek wondered if the bomb bay door was open or if the wheels had dropped out of their wells. He hoped not. If they reached England, he could bring her in on her belly and they might have a chance of surviving. But if the doors were open they were dead men because they would catch the ground and flip the plane over. If the wheels were down, it meant that they were down because the hydraulics had failed and they couldn't be locked in place—they would collapse. And the aircraft would flip.

He peered through what remained of the windscreen, trying to make out anything in the darkness. He glanced at Jagello, quickly took one hand off the wheel, and shook him.

"I'm alive," Jagello said. "How are we?"

Gierek said nothing.

"Well," Jagello said weakly, "I have one thing to be thankful for."

"What?" Gierek said. His hands were starting to cramp and he worked the fingers around the form of the wheel, trying to ease the pain.

"At least you're not singing."

Chapter 29

Edland was at Cole's side.

"What are you doing here?" Cole said.

"I came to get that boat." Edland said, pulling out an automatic.

"Skipper!" Rich shouted, and fired three rounds from an M-1 over Cole's head. A German sailor screamed and fell. The other guns on the PT boat kept up a deadly torrent of fire against the E-boat's superstructure as the boat slowed and dropped heavily into the sea. The moment that DeLong cut 155's power Cole shouted: "Okay."

The six men scrambled aboard the E-boat. A German sailor aimed a pistol at Edland, but before he had a chance to fire, the commander got off two rounds.

Another German swung the amidships 20-millimeter toward Cole.

"Down!" he shouted, dropping to the deck.

The cannon fired directly over their heads as

the gunner struggled to depress it. Murray slid along the port canvas dodger, pulled the pin on a hand grenade, and shouted: "Fire in the hole!"

There was a loud bang followed by a scream, and the gun was silenced. The firing was continuous now and the German crew moved against Cole and his men. They were trapped unless they could force the enemy to fall back.

"Stay down!" someone shouted from PT-155, and suddenly the air was filled with the ragged sound of twin .50-caliber machine guns. The slugs ripped through the superstructure and housing, toppling the mast, splintering the gun shields, and chopping the deckhouse and life raft to pieces. The fire ate its way aft, catching enemy sailors as they turned to run, spewing blood and tissue over the deck.

Cole rolled over on his back and jerked a finger across his throat, signaling the gun to cease fire.

"You two, forward," Cole ordered two men. "You two, aft." He looked at Edland. "Stay with me. Randy?" he shouted to DeLong over the sounds of scattered gunfire. "See if you can raise the other boats and *Firedancer*. Find out what's going on. Have some men lay aft and prepare to take this monster in tow. Okay with you, commander?"

Edland was about to answer when a single shot rang out. Cole grabbed the side of his neck and dropped to a knee, trying to find the shooter. He saw a dark form on the deck, near the starboard side of the bridge. He raised his gun to fire when Edland moved in front of him. Cole tackled him, dropping the commander to the deck.

"Wait," Edland said. "Don't shoot. He's an officer."

"I don't care if he's Santa Claus," Cole said. "The son of a bitch tried to kill me."

He thought the shot came from the shadows of the E-boat bridge. He searched the darkness, looking for any sign of the enemy, any movement that would give him away. In frustration he fired three shots at the bridge and thought he saw someone move. He fired again and ducked as a half-dozen shots sliced the air over his head.

"Let me talk him into surrendering," Edland said.

"Let me kill him first," Cole said, sliding forward. "Then he can surrender."

"Hey, Skipper?"

Cole twisted around to see Rich hugging the deck behind him. He held up a hand grenade for Cole to see, and then tossed it. Cole caught it as it clattered across the deck. He took it firmly in his right hand, slid a finger into the pin, and glanced at Edland. "If I were you, I'd dig a hole." He pulled the pin, counted silently to three, and lobbed it into the bridge. He dropped his head and prepared himself.

There was a crash and the deck shook. Cole could smell the acrid stench of explosive and burning metal. He jumped up, fired several shots into the darkness, and rushed the bridge. Edland was at his side as they pulled a bloody officer away from his machine pistol.

Edland wrested the pistol out of the officer's hand and checked the man for a pulse. "I think he's the boat commander. He's alive, barely. We need him as a prisoner. Help me get him to his feet."

Cole rose, slipped his pistol in the holster, and joined Edland. Both men helped the officer stand and tried to steady him. The German looked from Cole to Edland. He said something in German to Edland, and then repeated it to Cole.

Cole turned to Edland: "What'd he say?"

" 'You would have made Goering a very happy man if only you killed me.' "

"It wasn't from lack of trying, Fritz," Cole said to the German.

They guided him to the gunnel and handed him over to a couple of seamen on PT-155.

"Skipper," DeLong shouted. "I'm going to pull forward and toss you a line. Tie it off."

"What's the word on the others?" Cole called back.

"One sixty-eight and one seventy-two are taking on water. I think the Krauts lost another boat. Nothing from *Firedancer*. The rest of the guys are pretty shot up."

"Okay," Cole said. "Have the other boats pick up survivors and bodies. Ask *Firedancer* if she can do the same. We'll take this monster on in. Advise Portsmouth what we've run into and the disposition of the boats." He noticed that his men had grouped the surviving Germans aft. The defeated men sat dejectedly on the deck, their hands folded over their hands. "Rich? Get forward and take that line. Tie us off."

"Hey, Skipper?" Murray said. "I think this bastard's taking on water. I mean real fast."

"We've got to get it back to England," Edland said. "We've got to save this boat."

Cole ignored Edland. "Murray? Keep an eye on it." He moved forward as the line was tied off on a bow cleat. He took a moment to look around. The E-boat's deck was a slaughterhouse. Blood, bodies, and parts of bodies littered the shattered deck. He noticed the gun set deep in the boat's gun well. It was a squat, ominous-looking weapon with three thick barrels. A tiny shudder overtook him. This had been close. He noticed DeLong circle his finger above his head, signaling that he was increasing power. Cole watched the line grow taut as the slack was taken up. The line snapped water from its surface and he felt the boat move forward slowly.

"Remarkable," Edland said, standing next to him.

Cole noticed Edland examining the guns.

"Rube Goldberg," Cole said. "But they had my attention." He pointed at the 20mm. "That's why they were so accurate. Paint the target with tracers, and boom."

"Recoilless," Edland said.

Cole looked at him. "Oh, yeah?"

"Look at the breech. That funnel. That's how they expelled the discharge gases."

"You can't argue with progress, can you?" Cole said. "I wonder how many more little surprises the Krauts have waiting for us?"

"I wonder how it's going?"

"What?"

"I said, I wonder how it's going," Edland said. "The invasion."

"Oh," Cole said, watching the progress of PT-155.

"I'd say that they have their hands full. We've done our bit. At least for now."

"Skipper," Murray called from the center engine hatch. "You'd better get down here. We got problems."

"I see something," Gierek said hopefully to Jagello. The fierce wind piercing the cockpit caused his eyes to tear, and he was so numb from fatigue that he was hallucinating. That might be land ahead; it could be England. Or maybe it was his mind creating hope where none existed. It could be a low bank of clouds sitting on the horizon. He couldn't tell. His eyes stung and his shoulders burned from fighting the wheel. His hands were blocks of wood. Worst of all, his mind was numb, he could not concentrate. He had to talk his way through every action.

"What do you see?" Jagello managed. His wound was serious; Gierek hoped that they had time to get someplace where there was a doctor. Jagello was still awake—that was good, very good. And talking. Better still. The bomb-aimer/navigator was so frugal with words that anytime he spoke was an event.

"Land," Gierek said, praying that he was not holding out false hope. "I think."

"Ours," Jagello said, "or theirs?"

The man's humor was resilient.

"England?" Gierek said, stretching the fiery ache out of his back. It had to be a question because at this moment he was not certain of anything.

The Mosquito began to tremble violently, and a wave of fear swept through Gierek. He cursed the wretched plane's capriciousness; the words, kept low so that Jagello didn't hear his frustration, helped to mask Gierek's terror. The wooden aircraft was falling apart; the stress of flight and the constant pounding of the runaway engine were shaking the airframe. It could not last much longer. They would make land; Gierek had declared that low, dark mass ahead land—but that did not mean safety. He did not know where they were, he could not see the ground, and it was just as likely that they would plow into a fence during landing as skid across a clean field.

Plow.

His family had been tied to the land, and his father had insisted that Gierek embrace that life as well, but he found no charm in dirt. Sister could make things grow, and his father, it was claimed by the other farmers, could make crops sprout from rock. He can go into the mountains, one grizzled old farmer told Gierek, and return with a full yield. Gierek followed the old man's finger to the mountain and decided that would be a poor use of the mountain's majesty. He would not be a farmer.

"It's land," Gierek confirmed to Jagello. He tried to fight back his excitement, but it felt wonderful to have one small triumph in the conflict. He sensed Jagello stirring and saw the bomb-aimer/navigator sit up, trying to keep his face out of the frigid air that blasted through the shattered windscreen.

"Home?" he said. The pathos in Jagello's voice was painful for Gierek to hear.

"Yes," he said, trying to sound confident. "Yes."

"Thank the Almighty," Jagello said. He twisted his head slowly, gazing for a moment at Gierek.

"How many Germans did we kill today, friend?"

Gierek laughed. "Plenty, Jagello. More tomorrow. More the day after." But the left engine began to shake as if to remind Gierek that they weren't safe yet. Perhaps it would not be Germans who died. Perhaps they would never see Poland or their families again. Gierek was suddenly very cold, fear shaking his body so violently that he thought his hands, wrapped tightly around the steering wheel, would be snapped off. Perhaps they would die in a foreign land and be buried beneath soil that offered no solace for them. He saw a movement out of the corner of his eyes and turned to see a thin stream of black smoke rolled around the nacelle of the left engine. Then the flames came, tiny fingers that curled from within the engine and danced along the leading edge. They grew longer, fatter. They would travel quickly within the wing, seeking a way to the fuel tanks, and there they would consume the fuel, tanks, and aircraft in one violent burst of gluttony.

Murray climbed through the shattered hatch and wiped his hands on his pants. He was soaked and his face was black with grease, and the look he gave Cole said it all.

"Skipper. I can't keep this son of a bitch afloat."

"All the pumps going?"

"Yes, sir. The starboard engine is the only one

working, but just barely. That ought to be enough
to run the pumps, but she's a goddamned sieve."

"We've got to keep this vessel afloat," Edland
said. "We've got to get it back to Portsmouth."

"What do you think, Murray?" Cole said. "Can
you keep her afloat until I can get everyone off
her?"

"Your guess is as good as mine, sir. I'll tell you
one thing; when she fills up our boats won't be
able to handle her. She's just too damned big."

"Okay. Carry on. Do you need some help back
here?"

"Nah," the seaman said. "Stew and I got it."

Cole headed to the bow with Edland at his side.

"Cole, we can't let this boat go. We've got to
make every effort to save her."

"I know." Cole steadied himself on the listing deck
and shouted to the 155 boat. "Get Mr. DeLong."
In a few moments DeLong appeared at the .40 millimeter mount. "Randy? Contact *Firedancer*. Tell her
we need her up here as soon as possible."

"What's up, Skipper?"

"Edland's prize is sinking."

"I thought she was dragging some," DeLong
confirmed.

"See if *Firedancer* can tie up to us and take part
of the weight. She's taking on water like there's no
tomorrow. Then cast off and come alongside. Take
off these prisoners." He turned to Edland. "Okay
with you, Commander?"

"Why is it that everything you say to me sounds
like an insult?"

Cole smiled and turned at a shout from 155.

"Hey, Skipper. Mr. DeLong says that British tin can is beating feet. We're going to cast off now and come up on your port side."

Cole waved a response and turned to Edland. "Get below. Into the radio room. Get everything not nailed down. I don't know why I didn't think of that sooner. Probably trying to save your damned boat."

"Rich. Come with me." The sailor joined Edland and they felt their way into the dark interior of the vessel. Edland, in the lead, was up to his knees in ice-cold water. He let out a gasp and continued forward.

"I've got a Zippo, Commander."

"No," Edland said. The light would help ease the darkness but he could smell fumes. It was probably diesel fuel but he couldn't be sure. His feet bumped into something in the water and he knew it was a body from the way it reacted. He felt its arms try to wrap themselves around his legs as if begging for help. "Forward?"

"Yeah," Rich said. "I mean yes, sir. Come to a passageway and hang a left. That's how we're set up anyway."

Edland felt along the bulkheads, his hand running over splintered timbers. She was a wreck. The water didn't seem to be getting any higher, but it was difficult to tell as the boat wallowed in the sea. He tried to see through the darkness. It was no use; he needed the light.

"All right, Rich. We'll need your lighter."

"Coming up, Commander."

He heard Rich fumble through his pockets in the darkness, the familiar heavy clunk of the lid being flipped off the lighter, one grinding strike as the wheel rotated, and then another. He tensed for the explosion.

"Must have got wet, Commander. Hang on a second."

Rich blew on the flint several times, rolled the wheel with his thumb, and light flooded the tiny compartment. Edland began to breathe again.

They were in the radio room and it was a mess. Equipment had been shot off the bulkheads, there were two dead men slumped over narrow counters, and from the looks of it a small fire had been started and then extinguished. Edland saw radios, something that was probably a radar unit, a strange device with oversized typewriter keys, piles of codebooks, and a safe mounted on the counter and secured to a bulkhead.

"Get the codebooks and all of the papers you can carry," Edland ordered. Rich began scooping piles of documents and a dozen or so books with the Kriegsmarine eagle holding a swastika stamped on it. Edland examined the safe. It was locked.

"Here you go, Commander," Rich said, handing him the Zippo.

"Think we can open this?" Edland said.

Rich looked over the safe. "Maybe we can blow it with a grenade?"

Edland thought Rich's idea was dangerous, but he looked around the interior for a place to hide from the blast, just in case. He decided that it was too risky, for them and for the boat. "Leave it," he said.

Rich, papers clutched against his chest, eyed the safe critically. "Hey, maybe it ain't locked."

Edland tried the handle in the off chance it was open. The handle didn't budge.

"Well, it was worth a try."

"Let's get topside," Edland said. The darkness and confined area seemed to close in on him.

"Okay, sir," Rich said. "I got everything. I think."

Edland picked up the typewriter; except he knew that it had to be some kind of encryption device. "Lead the way, Rich."

The two made their way back on deck. Edland noticed that it was early dawn—the darkness had begun to fade away the short time he was below. He saw more of the deck now and the surrounding waters.

There were more than a dozen bodies scattered about and blood ran freely from the still forms. Blood on the deck, he thought, and realized that as garish as the statement was, it applied to the heavily damaged E-boat. Blood ran in streams along the deck and disappeared beneath the canvas dodgers, and he found himself almost hypnotized by the scene. He turned his eyes away and saw burning boats littering the sea; funeral pyres of flames and rolling black smoke that marked the death of boats and men.

"What'd you get?" Cole asked.

"Codebooks. This," Edland said, showing Cole the machine.

"Get it over to the 155, and don't come back. You'll just be in the way."

Edland started to protest when Cole said: "Yeah, I know. It's your boat. But you're in my way. And make sure Rich gets his lighter back. Those things are worth their weight in gold."

* * *

"Yes, yes, yes, yes," Hardy grumbled as the medico wrapped a bandage around his arm. "It was perfectly all right until you started manhandling me."

"It's a deep wound, Captain. You'll need stitches when we get in."

"Supply parties reported in, sir," Land said, examining the bandaging process out of curiosity.

Hardy noticed his interest. "Shall I have the men set up a chair for you, Number One?"

"That's won't be necessary, sir," Land replied. "I won't be staying. We've twenty-two wounded, including you, sir. Two dead. Most of the damage is from shrapnel although we took two solid bricks on the starboard quarter, but well above the waterline. I'm afraid that Courtney's reported one of the shafts may be dislodged."

"Good Lord, Number One. Two bricks did that?" Hardy slapped the medico's hands away, glaring at him.

"Yes, sir. We were lucky, sir."

"Bridge, foremast," a lookout shouted down. "MTB dead ahead, three thousand yards. MTB dead ahead, three thousand yards."

"Engine Room, Bridge," Hardy said. "Down seventy-five revolutions on all engines. Helmsman, starboard twenty." He turned to Land. "Number One, you will have a party assemble on the boat deck with lines and fittings, prepared to assist Mr. Cole's boat. And you, sir," he said to the medico who was replacing items in his canvas bag. "You will gather up your lot and make ready to assist the Americans in any way you can. Yeoman of Signals? Make to the American boat: 'Where do you want

us?'" Hardy moved his arm gingerly, trying to gauge
the injury. "Well, it's liable to lay up my art for a
bit, Number One. Still, it could have been worse,
eh, Edwin?"

Land considered the quality of Hardy's work
and decided to take the high road. "We shall all
miss your art, sir."

Hardy gave him an irritated look that said that
his diplomacy was not appreciated. He leaned over
the voice tube. "Helmsman. Port ten." He watched
as *Firedancer* approached the E-boat. The American PT boat was alongside the enemy boat, taking
off prisoners.

"Engine room, back one hundred. Helmsman
starboard five. Steady on now, I don't want to ram
her." He turned to Land, the pain in his arm becoming more noticeable. "Take her in alongside
that beast, Number One. I shall go down and direct the deck crew. Besides, I want to see one of
those big bastards."

"Yes, sir," Land said. "Give my regards to Mr.
Cole."

Cole watched as *Firedancer* maneuvered alongside the E-boat. He turned aft and shouted: "Murray? How's it looking?"

"You'd better get the lead out, Skipper."

"Rich?" Cole shouted. "Get a couple of guys and
grab those lines."

Rich and two men jumped the short distance
from the PT boat to the E-boat's deck, made their
way through the carnage to the starboard side, and
waited for *Firedancer*'s crew to deploy the lines.

Cole found Edland at his side. "What are you doing here?" He saw the 155 boat pull away, its deck crowded with prisoners. "You missed your ride."

"Like you said; it's my boat."

"Prepare to receive lines, Mr. Cole," someone shouted from *Firedancer*.

Cole smiled. He recognized Hardy's voice. He was happy to have his old friend close by but he didn't think they could save the boat. She was taking too much water and although she was only half the length of the destroyer, the seawater racing into her hull would make her too heavy to tow. Or even keep afloat. He watched as three lines floated out from the destroyer and were tied off to the cleats. Three more followed and were secured as well. A swell drove *Firedancer* against the E-boat and the enemy craft groaned in protest. She was wallowing heavily.

"Mr. Cole?" Hardy shouted. "Shall we pass you a cable to feed through that gun mount forward?"

Cole glanced at the heavy gun in the gun well. She was probably well secured and could take the cable. "Okay, Captain. Rich, get up there and tie her off."

"I'll help," Edland said.

"Mr. Cole?" Hardy again. "You have yourself quite a catch, haven't you? Can you make headway?"

"No. She's dead. And she's taking on water."

The E-boat twisted slightly in the waves and rubbed her length along *Firedancer*, steel against steel sent out a piercing squeal. Cole couldn't be sure but he thought *Firedancer* was listing; she was being pulled over by the floundering E-boat.

"Are her pumps working?" Hardy shouted.

"Barely working," Cole said. "We've got one engine but no headway. I don't know how long she can last."

"Stand by, then. We'll get ours up and pump you out."

Cole felt the E-boat shift to starboard and the rumble of items breaking loose below. He knew that she couldn't be saved. She was doomed. He heard a snap like a pistol shot and saw a line whip through the air. There was another shot and a line aft parted. It whipped a cleat high over *Firedancer*'s superstructure and Cole felt the E-boat begin to settle at the stern.

Cole cupped his hands around his mouth. "*Firedancer*? Cut us loose. We're sinking." He turned fore and aft shouting: "Abandon ship."

"Skipper!" It was Rich. "Get up here."

Cole ran forward, dodging debris and bodies. He found Rich, in the gun well, trying to free Edland's hand from the mount. He jumped into the well. "Get out, Rich."

"I got . . ." Rich began.

"Get off the goddamned boat."

Edland's face was white and he bit his lip in agony. "I was trying to feed the line through the mount and the gun shifted. It caught my hand."

Cole turned on Rich who hadn't moved. "Rich, I swear to God if you don't get out, I'll kill you."

"No way, Skipper."

Cole turned his attention back to the gun, trying to figure out a way to free Edland. He saw a way, but he needed Rich's help. "Okay, Superman. Put your back under the barrel." He turned to Edland. "We're going to lift and if we don't tear your arm off, pull it out."

The E-boat's stern slid to port as her bow nosed against *Firedancer*'s hull. Edland cried out in pain and looked at Cole. His eyes said everything: Hurry. She was sinking.

Cole joined Rich, bent down, and slid his back under the thick gun barrels. "On three. One, two . . ."

The E-boat began to shudder as more water rushed into her dead body.

"Three." Cole and Rich pressed backs against the barrels. "Push," Cole shouted, straining to bring all of his strength against the immobile piece. He felt water lapping at his ankles and knew they had only seconds.

"I'm out," Edland called.

Rich and Cole pushed away from the mount and scrambled out of the well, joining Edland. Cole dove over the side, and as he did he felt the deck of the E-boat slide away. When he came to the surface he located Rich and Edland and swam over to them. *Firedancer* had lowered a boat and it was quickly pulling toward them.

Cole spat out a mouthful of water. "We lost your boat."

Edland nodded weakly.

Cole turned to Rich. "And the next goddamned time that I give you an order, you'd better damn well carry it out."

Rich's teeth chattered uncontrollably as he fought to keep his head above the choppy water. "Okay, Skipper. But could you at least wait until I get into some dry skivvies before you chew me out?"

Chapter 30

Gierek couldn't wake Jagello. He shouted at the bomb-aimer/navigator above the roar of the wind, and pried his numb hand off the steering wheel long enough to awkwardly punch Jagello's shoulder, but the man had not moved. He wanted him to wake up, to be alive, to see home.

The sun had finally emerged and burned away most of the gray clouds, and had even managed in some places to reward Gierek with a glimpse of blue sky. It was a miracle, a sign; it was God saying that there is hope, and it is now given to you and that battered wooden craft with no instruments and a wild engine, so that you can come home. Not to your village, or even to bask in the power of the mountains that teetered on the edge of the sky—or Poland. Ahead was the base.

"Wake up!" Gierek shouted. "Jagello? We're here. Home. I can see it. We're home." Suddenly a single green flare wobbled into the sky from the control tower, the wind pushing gently on the trail of smoke that said two things: the green flare meant that you are cleared to land on any strip, and the wind is light out of the northwest.

He had no radio, he couldn't cut the engines and feather the props; he wasn't even sure the damned airplane wouldn't shatter into a thousand pieces the minute it touched down. He knew the fire and medical crews would be out and ready to come to his aid, but he also knew—although his mind did not linger on the thought—that sometimes they fought valiantly but hopelessly until the flames could finally be subdued, and blackened, twisted bodies removed from the wreckage.

The starboard engine began to race again, much faster this time as if excited that salvation was near. Gierek was afraid it would explode; he had known this to happen. The wing would be severed from the aircraft and she would spiral into the ground leaving nothing more than a twisted mass.

He had one chance to land. He could not coax her back into the air after a pass nor could he be certain that she would not explode. One chance.

Everything happened quickly. He chose his landing strip, reducing power and landing speed, but maintaining enough to prevent the aircraft from stalling. He saw that the grass strip was peppered by pools of shimmering water, the remnants of earlier rains, and he tried to guide the Mosquito away from them. The ground was coming up and shapes on either side flew by. The aircraft resisted, shaking with fright as it neared the earth, trying to snatch control away from Gierek.

Thoughts raced through his mind at a fantastic

pace—faces, events, scenes—but everything was
secondary to his struggle to get the aircraft to the
ground. He suddenly remembered the undercarriage and wondered if the wheels and bomb bay
doors were down, but he just as quickly dismissed
the notion. He could have bailed out over the Channel with a one-in-ten chance of being rescued, but
Jagello would have had no chance to bail out, and
even if he had, he would have not survived in the
water.

Gierek chose the aircraft and his friend.

The aircraft hit. Gierek screamed and thought
at first that the Mosquito had exploded, but then
realized that they had collided with the ground
and were skidding across the soggy grass. The damp
earth had helped—cushioning the impact. But the
wet grass was slick and the aircraft was in no hurry
to stop. Gierek felt the tail twist to the right and
then heard a blast as something broke free. Both
engines chewed themselves to bits because their
propellers had been running when they hit. Now
the props could not turn and the shafts raced
within the hubs, screeching in distress. Parts of the
engine peppered the body of the Mosquito, slam-
ming into the cloth-covered wood frame—angrily
punching holes through the flimsy skin.

Gierek tasted blood in his mouth and realized
that he had bitten his tongue. He tried to clamp
his mouth shut. It was impossible; the plane was
shuddering so much that he couldn't keep his
hands on the wheel—there was no need to do so
anyway—or from being slammed about in his harness.

The Mosquito continued to slip to the right,

until Gierek discovered that he was looking back at the control tower and base, and racing behind him, like a scene from some sort of American comedy, was a phalanx of vehicles.

He was frozen. His brain refused to comprehend what he saw. He decided that there was nothing he could do but ride this ridiculous ride and watch a random collection of frustrated vehicles chase him. He had become part of the seat, so fixed from fear and weariness that he could not, or would not, move.

The vehicles grew closer and he knew that the aircraft was slowing down, but now he became more frightened than he had ever been because he caught the heady stench of aviation petrol. The tanks were pierced and he saw the thin, iridescent trail of fuel that shimmered in the soft light of the young sun. All this, simply to burn alive in front of your chums.

The Mosquito jerked once, heavily, and then again, but not as much this time. Everything was silent and then the silence was replaced by the woeful moan of a siren and the harsh sounds of engines.

Gierek's eyes were focused straight ahead, and through smashed Perplex he saw rough shapes. They moved about the aircraft, like demons dancing around a fire, and then he heard the sound of things being smashed and he felt a dozen hands on him and men shouting. The hands roamed over his shoulders, head, ribs, and he felt a hard blow to his chest as a fist was driven into the three-point harness release.

And then he was floating and above him was blue sky filled with gentle white clouds that moved with grace. He realized that he was suspended in air by strong arms and he felt relief. Suddenly he was blinded by the soft sun and thought, ridiculously, that he was being held up in some outlandish ceremony of survival. He found himself lowered until a sheet of canvas caressed his back. *A stretcher. They do that for the dead and dying as well as the living, don't they?*

Men were still shouting and he heard the powerful hiss of foam being sprayed over his aircraft. A dozen faces appeared above him and examined him with a curiosity that he found disturbing. He recognized the kind face of the flight surgeon, who began carefully cutting away his flying togs and at the same time asking him where he was injured.

Finally Gierek was able to say. "I am not injured," although he felt the way he had when he ran his automobile into a ditch—everything hurt. He was too weak to answer any of the surgeon's questions, but he managed one of his own. "How is Jagello?"

The flight surgeon's hands expertly probed Gierek's ribs, head, arms, and legs. "A bit banged up, I'm afraid," the flight surgeon said. He drew a syringe full of clear liquid, flicked the vial twice with his fingertip, and then added: "He'll be back at it in a month or two. I shouldn't worry about him. You'll be fine as well, I imagine. Set of bruises. Broken ribs."

Gierek tried to manage a nod, but failed. Instead his eyes drift to his left as he felt the sting of the needle and fixed on the Black Prince. The animal sat placidly, unconcerned with the mayhem around him, his pink tongue lolling out of the corner of his mouth, watching Gierek. The dog seemed to Gierek astoundingly wise, but the thought vanished as he felt a bandage being roughly bound around his head.

Gierek began to puzzle through the presence of the dog a short distance away, but because of the drugs and the adrenaline, his mind refused to cooperate in the process. A haze appeared and moved like a fog over his vision, and as it did, the dog stood and moved to him until it was at his side.

Gierek could smell the grease and oil that permeated the animal's coat, and he thought that the dog remained standing for that reason—to establish his presence. Then the dog dropped to the ground, pushing his body heavily against Gierek's. The pilot felt the dog's warmth and watched as the animal carefully laid its head down on its paws, closed its eyes, and took up station next to him. As Gierek slid into unconsciousness, his hand sought out the filthy, thick fur, and he intertwined his fingers in the oily thatch. As full darkness claimed him, Gierek's mind relaxed to the rhythm of the Black Prince's breathing.

Chapter 31

PT-155, her deck cleared of prisoners transferred to *Firedancer* on the open sea, slid peacefully
into her berth at Wayside Dock. She was battered,
bits of her torn away by the gunfire of the E-boat,
and there were streaks of charring as rounds burned
across the wood. Her crew was worn out; the deep-
seated fatigue that excises the excitement of battle
so completely that all that remains is a collection
of random images. They had fought and failed to
save Mr. Edland's boat. That was what they had
taken to calling the vessel that had thwarted their
attempts to capture—Mr. Edland's boat. It was gone
now, deep in the waters of the English Channel,
along with the remnants of two PT boats that had
burned down to the waterline and then slid below
the surface.

The 155 boat brought back three of the dead—
American dead. Still forms under dark gray blan-
kets with the initials USN stenciled on them. It was

always difficult to travel with the dead, although they never asked anything of you. They were content to lie neatly arranged on the Day Room canopy, bothering no one. Their voyages were over. Their presence, though, was a different matter. They represented the unspoken guilt of the survivors—guilt mixed with relief that they had not died. The guilt was heavier, as if the survivors shared a responsibility with the dead, and for the dead. And that by living they had somehow betrayed the dead. That was the nature of war.

"How's the hand?" Cole asked Edland as the commander rolled his fingers back and forth.

"In one piece," Edland said. "Thanks for saving me back there."

Cole shrugged. "The navy takes care of its own."

"That's what I hear," Edland said. "But thanks anyway."

DeLong brought the boat alongside the dock expertly, barely causing the canvas bumpers to sway as she moved in. Several crewmen jumped to the dock and tied her off as DeLong signaled to disengage the engines. He stepped away from the wheel and stood motionless for a moment before searching the pockets of his jacket for cigarettes. Cole saw the action and tossed him a crumpled pack.

"Now what?" Edland said.

"We gas up, re-arm, and go back out," Cole said matter-of-factly. "There's an invasion on, you know. Why? Want to go along?"

A thin smile crept across Edland's face. He'd finally had his fill of PT boats. "No. Not this time. I'd better get up to London and report."

"Sorry about your boat," Cole said, catching the pack that DeLong threw back to him. "It would have looked swell mounted on the wall."

"We got some important stuff. Codebooks. The decoding machine. That's something."

"Yeah," Cole said, stepping off the boat and onto the dock. Edland followed him. "So long, Commander."

Edland nodded, looking at Cole. "Take care of yourself, Lieutenant."

Edland headed up the dock, passing a British naval officer who looked familiar. Then he realized it was the man he'd met at the briefing in London; the one who knew Cole. A seaman second class, standing next to a jeep on the wharf snapped to attention.

"Commander Edland, sir?" he asked.

Edland nodded.

"They want you back up in London, tout de suite. They sent me to pick you up."

"What's going on?" Edland asked.

"Got me, sir," the seaman said, sliding behind the steering wheel and pressing the starter. "Something big, I guess. Nobody tells me nothing."

"Okay," Edland said, suddenly weary. He looked back to see the naval officer talking to Cole, and then he looked at the other PT boats coming in. They looked as weary as he felt, he decided, and thought of something he had once heard. Where do we find such men? He felt, for a moment, something very unexpected. It was pride. Honor. Emotions that he gave no consideration to because he always held them suspect. They could not

be quantified and there was no empirical evidence
to support them, but here they were, nevertheless.
Where do we find such men?

"Ready to go, Commander?" the seaman asked,
shifting into first.

Edland nodded and settled back in the seat.

"Hello, Jordan," Dickie Moore said as he approached Cole.

"Hi," Cole said. "Take over a minute, will you,
Randy?"

"Rough, was it?" Dickie said, looking over the
boat.

"Pretty rough," Cole said. "I lost some men. What
brought you here? I thought you'd be up in London with the big brains."

Dickie shook his head and managed a troubled
smile. Cole saw him preparing himself. Finally,
Dickie took a quick breath and blurted: "She's dead,
Jordan."

It took a moment before Cole could repeat the
words to himself, but they still made no sense. He
looked at Dickie, his tired mind trying to shift
through the meaning. "What?"

"Rebecca's dead, Jordan," Dickie said. His voice
caught as he looked at Cole with sheer helplessness.

Cole stood motionless. Everything from his last
visit rushed at him. Rebecca on the settee, William
the butler, her mother, Rebecca slipping the bookmark between the pages of the book, the comb,
mirror, brush, bottles . . . a box, some kind of box,
the coverlet on the settee. There were plants all

around them; he could remember the scent and he thought that the broad leaves of some must have been heavily waxed because they shone so. He recalled her mother's cool voice, and the slow, fluid motion of Rebecca drawing her feet back so that he could sit down.

Dickie was talking again, the words taking some form, becoming distinct now.

But the words meant nothing; they were as unreal as his friend's presence. Slowly Cole felt his body weaken and his hands turn very cold, as if he had shaken hands with death and seen its horrible face for the first time.

"That's not true," he said stupidly, and then grew numb as a thousand questions rushed at him. "No. That's not true." He knew death. He'd seen it in war. This was not war and Rebecca could not be dead. There was no reason for it.

"Her heart," Dickie said. His voice was strained. "Her mother told me. When she was a girl. She was quite ill."

Cole felt anger well up in him. "It's a lie," he snapped. "You're a goddamned liar."

There was silence between them before Dickie tried again. "No," Dickie said. "You must be reasonable about this, Jordan. Rebecca's dead. Her heart gave out. She's gone. Don't make me say it again. I loved her, too, as well you know. Like a sister. She was a decent person."

Cole's legs gave way and he half-stumbled to the PT's gunnel and slumped against it. "That can't be," he said in a whisper. "It can't be." These things don't happen. Men die in battle. He'd seen the death of civilians during the Blitz, but not a single person, not Rebecca. Not someone who meant so much to him. The only words that could have come to him, came. *It's not fair. Not her. Not Rebecca. It's not fair.*

"She loved you, Jordan. Very much. She wanted to live. It wasn't possible. More death in this god-forsaken world. Hers . . ." Dickie began but then stopped in defeat. "I'll never understand it."

Jordan looked up, tears rolling down his cheek. "What am I going to do?" he said. "I can't take this." He stood, looking about as if for answers. "Dickie? What am I going to do?" He walked away. *What will I do?* he asked again. He pushed the tears out of his eyes with the heels of his palms. Given and then taken, he thought, but nothing in those words was meant to comfort him or explain the death of a woman he was truly beginning to love. There was no rationale behind it. All Jordan Cole had was a sense of loss, a sure knowledge of abandonment, and the certainty of survival; he would have to bury, again, all human emotion. He returned to his friend.

"She didn't tell me," he said, his voice cracking. "Why didn't she say something?"

"She pretended. She pretended that she was getting better. She probably convinced herself. She had me convinced." Dickie shook his head and then looked up, as if he were about to curse God. "This bloody awful life."

"When is the funeral?"

"Three days."

Cole nodded. "I probably can't . . . I mean I won't be able . . ."

"I know, old friend," Dickie said. "I'll pass on

your sentiments to the family," he added quickly as he watched Cole struggle to find words.

"Would you tell her mother," Cole said. "Tell her that I loved Rebecca. Tell her . . ." He shrugged; there was nothing more he could say.

"I'll supply the message. Don't worry about that."

"Okay," Cole whispered.

DeLong appeared behind Dickie Moore. "We got the word, Skipper. We've got to hustle." He noticed Cole's face. "You okay, Skip?"

Cole cleared his throat. "Yeah. Yeah." He took a deep breath. "What is it, Randy?"

"They need us right back out there, Skipper."

"Okay," Cole said, taking another breath. "Okay. Tell the guys to saddle up. I'll be right with you." Cole waited for DeLong to leave before turning to Dickie. He wanted to find the right words; he wanted to say something that would make everything all right, that would wipe away the pain. But he could think of nothing. Finally, he managed a troubled smile.

"You know, Dickie. . . ." He felt as if he had been abandoned. "I never got to tell her how much that she meant to me."

"Jordan," Dickie said softly. "She knew. She loved you. She'd want you to carry on. Sometimes . . . sometimes there aren't any words."

"Yeah," Cole said. "Yeah. I guess you're right. Sometimes all you can do is put one foot in front of the other and keep on."

Dickie nodded.

Cole straightened. "Time to shove off." He swung aboard the PT boat and looked down at Dickie. "There wasn't enough time, Dickie."

"There never is, my friend," Dickie said. "God bless you."

Cole turned and spun his finger in the air. "Crank her up, Randy."

Dickie watched as the crew cast off lines and the boat slowly backed away from the dock. He saw Cole make his way to the cockpit and watched as he took up station to one side, away from everyone. He would make himself alone, Dickie knew. He would seal himself up inside and never emerge again. He was a child, Dickie realized, as Rebecca said he was. He had never dared let himself grow emotionally for fear of being hurt. Once deeply hurt by someone he would only come slowly to trust again. The pain was too great, otherwise. A fragile man, Dickie reckoned, who found it safer to live in a cold world than seek the warmth of human companionship.

The PT boat moved slowly into the harbor and, joined by several others, headed out into the Channel. Dickie waited until they were nearly out of sight and then turned and walked back to his car.

Waldvogel nodded slowly as he listened to Oberleutnant zur zee Waymann. The young man's account was delivered slowly, a calm detailed explanation of what had happened in the Channel. It seemed totally out of place in the pandemonium that had broken out in the hospital. Orderlies and nurses rushed about, trying to gather up those patients that were ambulatory, stuffing records in boxes, carefully packing the medicines that were left. Men were shouting orders down corridors that had once been avenues of faint whispers. It was offensive to Waldvogel, this lack of order and organization.

The Allies added to it with the constant bombardment of heavy artillery and the deep rumble of exploding bombs.

Waldvogel's bandage had been removed, and now all that remained of his injury was a jagged line of stitches along his skull and an occasional headache.

"We tried to get past them," Waymann continued. "The boats performed beautifully, but we lost Fregattenkapitan Reubold."

"Lost?" Waldvogel said.

"Captured," Waymann said. "Or dead. I don't know. I'm sorry. I would have told you before but I couldn't get away. There was simply too much going on, you understand. The invasion."

"The others? The other boats?"

"We lost two, then. One was strafed and sunk on the way back. In the past three weeks," Waymann continued—his face was drawn and his sunken eyes were those of a man who had seen far too much—"we lost three in combat. All of them are gone."

"Oh," Waldvogel said. "Then it's over."

Waymann shook his head. "They want you back in Germany. You and me. I received a dispatch this morning. They're sending some of us out. A few of us."

"But why?" Waldvogel said.

"Your boats, I think," Waymann said. "They're important to the war effort. You're important, Korvettenkapitan. You must return to Germany."

Waldvogel watched as a nurse rushed by, carrying a bundle of uniforms, crying. It was collapsing—the city would fall soon as the beaches fell, and the heights and villages beyond them.

"It's only a matter of time," Treinies had cried as the fighting neared the city and the crash of the cannons grew louder. "The Fuehrer won't abandon us. Don't you see that? Can't you understand? It's only a matter of time until he sends reenforcements and we push those Jews back into the sea." He said it as if he intended to pick up a rifle and lead the assault—as if he were merely waiting on the phalanx of storm troopers that he knew would arrive soon. "Only a matter of time," the surgeon insisted, but it was a desperate cry. Waldvogel realized that Treinies was a prophet.

It was only a matter of time before Cherbourg fell, before France was carried away in the Allied onslaught, before they arrived at the steps of Berlin demanding entry.

He had seen it in the sky—thousands of bombers that flew overhead, uncontested by German fighters. He had heard about the invasion fleet: thousands of ships that disgorged hundreds of thousands of men and then returned with more.

I am a scientist, Waldvogel told himself when the shock of the invasion and the panic that surrounded him had worn off. *I gather facts and analyze them and from that information, present my conclusion. It is indeed only a matter of time.*

"We are to go down to Lorient," Waymann said. "Winter has a U-boat waiting to take us to Germany. We don't have much time, Korvettenkapitan."

"Yes," Waldvogel said, broken from his thoughts. "Of course." He hesitated a moment and then said: "Tell me, young man, were they fine boats? Were they as wonderful as I had hoped?"

Waymann looked shocked and then gave the question some thought. After a moment he smiled. "Korvettenkapitan. They were such wonderful boats."

Topper heard first, at the pub of course. Because any news worth knowing found a home at the pub. Then he rushed home to tell Beatrice, who did her best to hide her delight and barely had time to snatch her hat and coat while Topper ushered her hurriedly out the door.

"You go on now, Bea. I'll see to everything here," he had said.

Beatrice hurried down the street, hopped on the Ellsworth Street tram, and silently begged it to go faster. It was crowded with riders—seamen, men and women, mothers with crying children, old men who were as patient as Job—knowing that the tram would arrive where it was intended to arrive in a timely manner.

She tried to keep her mind busy by studying the passengers, pretending they had come for a sitting and she was going to paint their portraits. She examined eyes, noses, chins, and the way that hair curled around ears, eyebrows bristled, eyebrows curved gracefully, nostrils flared as their owners breathed. She studied everything. How coats hung off bony shoulders, how fabric fell over breasts, how pleats formed in slacks and dresses, and all the time the tram seemed to be getting slower and slower.

Beatrice felt that she would scream with frustration until she saw the gates of the naval yard, and then her heart raced.

Before the tram came to a complete stop she was on the ground and running, trying to shoulder her way past others moving through the gates. Two bored sailors stood, one on either side of the gate, watching with amusement as the throng made its way into the yard.

It was unseemly, Beatrice thought, all of this pushing and shoving, and much more so because she had every reason to be there and they didn't. Then she realized with shame that the others were just like her; their loved ones were coming back from war. She forced herself to a casual walk, trying to catch her breath. Around her she heard people talking and laughing. It was celebration—homecoming. She caught bits of conversations. Bill will be so proud of little Andy. Do you think he'll recognize me, Floe? Well, first I'm going to buy the boy a pint because he's earned it.

She stopped when she saw *Firedancer* and had to catch her breath. The boat was blackened in spots, and pieces of metal hung away from her superstructure. There was more rust covering her and Beatrice couldn't be sure but she thought *Firedancer* was listing. She was a terrible sight, all right, all bruised and battered. And if ever there was a ship that looked worn out, it was *Firedancer*.

She saw men filing down the gangplank and stood patiently, knowing that it would be best if she kept her emotions in check. She watched with

envy as women and men held each other closely
and men scooped up children and held them
close. There was a swirl of humanity on the dock,
sailors and civilians, all in a common ritual of sailors
coming home once more. She looked for Hardy,
stepping first to one side and then the other, her
hands clasped in front of her, fingers so tightly intertwined that she realized they hurt.

Beatrice saw him at last. Captain George Hardy,
moving slowly through the crowd, stopping to remark on a child, being introduced to a wife, tip-
ping his hat to an elderly lady. She saw that he had
his arm in a sling and for a moment was overwhelmed by panic, but that quickly subsided. She
would take no notice of it, she decided; George
wouldn't approve.

Finally he broke free and as he moved toward
her she removed her hat and carefully patted her
hair into place.

"Hello, old girl," he said when he got to her. His
voice was caring and surprisingly soft.

"Hello, George," she said, her mouth dry with
anticipation. "You've hurt your arm," she added,
forgetting her earlier vow.

He glanced at it. "Not much of a hurt. More an
inconvenience, I'd say," he looked back to her and
smiled. "Nothing to worry about, my dear."

Beatrice looked past him. "Your poor ship.
Firedancer looks as if she's had a hard time of it."

Hardy followed her gaze. "That she has. We tan-
gled with some E-boats and she took a few bricks
all right. We lost a couple of the chaps. We were
lucky though—we could have lost more."

"Are you home for a bit, then?" Beatrice said.

"Yes," Hardy said. "She needs tending to before we go out again, so she'll go to the yard man for a spot of fixing up."

"Perhaps you'll need that as well," Beatrice said, gently touching his arm.

"Old girl," Hardy said, locking his good arm into her and turning her around, "I was thinking the very same thing."

They walked away, arm in arm, as *Firedancer* watched them go. The crowd that had gathered around her gangplank began to dissipate until all that remained were the few personnel of the duty crew. *Firedancer* was silent, still, resting quietly alongside her quay, waiting until she was led to dry dock—until the yard gang boarded her and began repairing the battle damage.

She had gone out and had done what was expected of her in service to the King, but more important, she had returned the men who sailed aboard her to their families. She was no longer young, and there were faster, bigger, stronger vessels, that, when moored next to her, made her look shabby. But she was a fighter and would go where she was sent, and at the end of each encounter she would do what she had always done in the past—come home.

THE CODE NAME SERIES BY
WILLIAM W. JOHNSTONE

More Thrilling Suspense From Your Favorite Thriller Authors